CW00458422

The Gimmel Ring

KAREN HOWARD

Copyright © 2014 Karen Howard

All rights reserved.

ISBN: 1495263274
ISBN 13: 9781495263279

About the Author

Karen Howard grew up near the Malvern Hills in Worcestershire and later in the historic market town of Devizes, Wiltshire. With a degree in environmental science and a PhD in environmental chemistry, she has followed a career in science and travelled extensively. She lives in Shropshire with her husband and border collie.

You can find more information about *The Gimmel Ring*, including a glossary of the more unusual terms used in the book, at www.thegimmelring.com and https://www.facebook.com/thegimmelring

Acknowledgments

I owe a great deal to Manfred Evans and Eileen Evans for their invaluable comments on early versions and for their constant encouragement and belief in me throughout the long process of creating this novel. Much gratitude goes to Emma-Jayne Covington-Cross who deciphered my disorderly script and typed large segments of it. I am also extremely grateful to the mid-version readers, Adrian Watts, Becky Baker, Heather Keeling, Nancy (Beattie) Barr, Mallen Baker, Merren Jones and Tim Jarvis, who gave me such helpful, positive and constructive feedback. I am indebted to my talented and tenacious editor, Sally Sutton and particularly wish to thank her for her patience with my *tha*s and *thee*s! Huge thanks also to Trish Williams for the wonderful cover illustration.

Finally, there is one person without whom I simply could not have completed this novel: for days, months and years of support; for cheerfully maintaining the house and tending the garden while I secreted myself away to scribble; for his understanding and acceptance during many holidays when my head was in my notebooks and my mind deep inside the world of my own making; I thank my wonderful husband, Andy.

This book is dedicated to him.

Contents

Prologue

November

A mantle of mist lay heavy over the quiet little village in the dark of the night, hovering above the glistening grass. If there had been a street light it would have looked like a watery orb, a far off underwater shimmer through the myriad miniscule water droplets. But there were no street lights in Brockby; instead a cosy glow emanated from the windows of the old sandstone cottages huddled around the green, the light diffused and divided by wooden latticework.

The Triumph Stag entered from the narrow lane to the south and screamed around the green, parting the silence in invisible waves before slewing to a halt outside a small double-fronted cottage encased in the thick denuded stems of an old wisteria. A blonde couple rapidly emerged into the damp blackness. The girl turned quickly to the man with a worried expression. She did not say anything but her eyes pleaded silently for reassurance. The man squeezed both her hands and bent down a little to kiss her forehead. She turned and ran up the short stone flagged path to the front door. It was locked.

'Jennifer!' she called up at a first floor window, dimly lit from inside, curtains neglected to be closed. 'Jennifer, are you there?' No answer. '*Jenny,* ' she shouted, 'Are you there, are you alright?' No answer. 'She's got to be inside, ' she cried desperately to the man. 'Her car's here and the light's on in her bedroom.'

'Light's been on day and night fer two days, ' a passing elderly woman walking her dog called to them suddenly through the gloom. 'We thought it wor a bit strange. I wor goin' t' call on her t'morrow, see if she wor alright like.'

The woman's last words were lost as the couple sped around to the back of the house. The stable door to the kitchen was also locked. The man shoved a hand into the pocket of his winter fleece jacket and retrieved a small Maglite, which he quickly shone around. The narrow beam picked out a woodpile stacked neatly against the back wall. He thrust the torch into his partner's hand and ran over to the stack where the oak and hawthorn logs scattered and crashed about him as he searched urgently for a long heavy one.

'Oh God, please hurry, ' the girl said under her breath.

'This should do.' He launched the dense piece of wood several times at the place where the two halves of the back stable door met until the bolt gave way. Without a word, he stepped back to let the girl through, then followed her as she raced up the stairs. They found Jennifer lying fully clothed on her side on the bed. One hand was clutching a sheaf of papers, the other was on her stomach. Her long mahogany curls obscured her face.

'Jenny!' the girl screamed again and rushed forward, hastily brushing the tendrils from her friend's face, which was ashen and still, the once cherry lips slightly parted as if uttering a faint cry, like a clockwork toy whose mechanism has come to a halt mid-action.

'Oh God... oh my God!' she looked up in horror at her partner. He didn't give her time to say any more, but stepped forward and gently prised her away, his hands on the top of her arms.

'I know what to do, ' he said quietly but firmly. He looked in Jennifer's mouth and felt around inside with his fingers then rolled her gently onto her back. Placing two fingers under her jaw, he lifted it, tilting her head back with his other hand. 'Sarah, ring for an ambulance.'

She was already doing so. 'Jesus! There's no bloody signal on this.' She threw down her mobile and rushed downstairs to the house phone.

He listened for signs of breathing. He could detect none. He felt for a pulse in her neck. Her body was silent. He started CPR with thirty chest compressions and proceeded to give two big breaths.

Sarah reappeared. 'They're on their way. They're sending a helicopter' she said breathlessly. 'Let me help you.'

'OK, you take over the ventilation. Take a couple of deep breaths and try to stay calm. Thirty compressions, two rescue breaths, OK?' She nodded. 'Right, pinch her nose and breathe deeply and strongly, but keep it steady and keep her head back.'

They worked silently, side by side, their two spiky blonde heads bowed over Jennifer's mute body. Time stood still. Seconds were interminable; minutes limitless, infinite. Sarah was in a daze, a no-man's land between reality and nightmare, and the two were becoming one.

The man checked for a pulse after every ten of Sarah's breaths. Jennifer's quiescence seemed to fill the room. He fought against it, urging her to respond. Sarah was doing the same.

'Hang on Jenny! For God's sake hang on. Don't let go, *please* don't let go!'

The helicopter arrived in a frenzy of light, gingerly settling on the edge of the village green, avoiding the trees in the middle. Sarah left her station briefly and flung open the window, oscillating the torch beam and shouting to the paramedics. Suddenly there was another flurry of activity. An arm was around Sarah's shoulder, moving her away from her friend, and her partner was talking to the medics as they rapidly tore Jennifer's clothes away from her chest and placed the electrodes of the defibrillator onto her skin.

'Stand back.' One shock and more CPR. Another shock, CPR, a third shock. Then Sarah thought she heard: 'We have a faint pulse.'

Sarah's heart jumped into orbit. She clenched her hands tightly together, her nails digging into her palms. *Please* let her survive, *please* let her be OK. 'Breathe, Jenny, breathe!' she cried. With every sinew of her body, every element of her mind, every last atom of strength that remained, she urged her best friend to respond. She found herself desperately trying to project the energy necessary to elicit a reaction into the body that lay before her, and it felt like a long, silent scream.

'She's breathing, but it's very shallow, ' said a voice.

Sarah heard something said in low tones about possible brain damage as the oxygen mask went on. Suddenly Jennifer was whisked out to the waiting helicopter, and the papers she was still clutching went with her. All was silent again.

Sarah turned her tear-stained face toward the only person left in the room. 'Where?' she said.

'York Central.'

'Let's go.'

November 1762

The funeral procession moved slowly up the grassy hill towards the burial ground. Villagers, most in their Sunday dress, some more fortunate souls in silk or satin which had been dyed black for the occasion, led the solemn crowd. There followed the lower and upper servants, respectfully in mourning livery of grey or black as befitted their status, and the pall-bearers, their cold hands covered with identical black chamois gloves. A group of professionals, lawyers, merchants, physicians and clergymen and the presiding parson preceded the hearse, which was pulled by six beautiful black horses decked in black velvet caparisons and harnesses trimmed with silver. Black plumes rose from between their ears and rosettes adorned their foreheads. The hearse carried a tabard embroidered with the Fernleigh coat of arms, and on the oak coffin lay a single red rose from the Fernleigh hothouse.

Seven young women wearing identical black bombazine gowns trimmed with crepe – a show of unity to the watching world – trod in the wake of the coffin with increasingly faltering steps. Black silk hoods covered their heads, obscuring their faces, the thin mantle of privacy providing a brief respite from staring faces but affording no comfort. They proffered support to one another as each, at one time or another, stumbled upon the little-used, uneven stony path, blinded by curtains of tears, their eyes stinging in the cold air and with the senselessness of it all. The eldest tended solely to a gentleman of greater years than they, who, though dignified in his stature, was clearly distraught and bewildered.

His wife, too weak to walk but determined to be present, followed in a stately carriage pulled by four horses. She was accompanied by three men in suits of warm black velvet.

Three dozen or so carriages followed, bearing other distinguished mourners. Two empty carriages, sent by their absent owners as a mark of respect, brought up the rear.

The cruel November wind, insensitive, icy and razor sharp, heartlessly whipped the faces of the grief-stricken mourners. For all the stately ritual, the grief was absolute. A blanket of intense sorrow lay over the entire ensemble. This was a wretched day. So acutely did the family feel their loss, it signified to them the very end of joy, of happiness, of love itself.

One

April.

*A*s he turns from the window, Jennifer's eyes begin to bring his lithe, muscular body into focus. He is around six feet tall with ink-black hair which falls in loose curls around his shoulders. The light from the luminous full moon shining through the casement illuminates him from behind and to one side, lending a sheen to the myriad of fine hairs on his forearms, buttocks and thighs, a silvery stratum which imparts an ethereal quality to his form. He is moving silently across the room towards her, sinews stretching and relaxing, tendons taut and supple. His ice-blue eyes are fixed steadily on hers as he bends over her and gently kisses her on her parted lips. She is tilting her head back slightly waiting for his next kiss, closing her eyes briefly in anticipation, but it never comes. Instead she feels his warm, sweet breath on her left hand. He is taking her soft, slender fingers into his mouth one by one. She flexes her arms and hands in response. Holding her gaze with his, he is tracing the outline of her body with one finger, softly, deliciously, from the tip of her outstretched fingers, over the smooth skin on the inside of her arm and slowly down the side of her silky body to her toes, sending tremors down her spine. He is taking each of her toes into his mouth, making her gasp with sudden delight. Working his way over her tender inner thighs, interspersing soft kisses with gentle nibbles; she feels the whole of her body tense and her hips arch upwards, silently crying out for more. Finally, his tongue induces such spasms of ecstasy that she cries out in pleasure.

Jennifer awoke with a blinding headache, and it was minutes before she fully figured out where she was. Coming to full realisation of the previous night's events, she looked around in panic. Where the hell was he? Oh my God, *who* was he? She heard a noise at the bedroom door and instinctively jumped out of bed to open it – but it was not him. Her cat Smokey purred past her, delighted to be given the opportunity of an early cuddle, and settled herself on the bed on the warm patch that Jennifer had just vacated.

As her mind began sliding slowly into reality, she felt a mixture of relief and disappointment.

'Hello my lovely, I bet you're pleased with yourself, ' she smiled, picking Smokey up and giving her a big hug.

The beautiful long-haired black and white cat gave a little chirrup, a noise that was peculiar to her and signified contentment. Jennifer wandered around the little cottage in the oversized T-shirt that she slept in with Smokey in her arms, trying to put together the events of the night before. Of course there were no signs of the striking man who had shared her bed. No clothes, no empty wine glasses, no rose laid romantically on her little bedside table. Although she felt remarkably silly for doing so, she checked, just to be sure. The front and back doors were locked from the inside and the keys to the mortice lock hung on the hook in the larder, where she had put them as usual before going to bed.

She shrugged. It was obviously a dream. But it was so vivid! She struggled to remember his name… but she couldn't. Had he even mentioned it?

She went back into her bedroom and glanced at the pillow that lay beside her own. It was dented, but she could easily have rolled over during the night, as she often did when she was waiting for sleep that wouldn't come. As she moved around the room, Jennifer felt a familiar slight flow from between her legs. The flow seemed like more than hers alone. This was impossible! She felt a sudden flood of anxiety originating in her stomach and rushing upwards in a wave of heat, causing her forehead to tingle. She sat down on the side of the bed and rested her head in her hands, elbows on knees. She seemed to be losing her grip on reality. For a moment she asked herself: *Could I really have slept with someone and not remembered any of the past night's events other than the actual act?* Such a loss of control was a most frightening thought.

She took a few deep breaths, exhaling slowly. No – she took control again – it was just a particularly vivid dream. She glanced at the clock nestling in its little dent on the crooked oak beam mantelpiece. Six thirty a.m. Time to get on with the day.

Having showered, dressed and applied the usual concessionary eyeliner, looking at herself in the bathroom mirror she absent-mindedly traced the outline of her breasts with one hand, reconstructing his gentle touch. *You look tired today,* she thought, which was unsurprising in view of the headache and the rude awakening. *You need some sunshine.* The mirror spoke to her of a slim girl with long mahogany-brown hair which fell in loose curls around full, firm breasts and halfway down her back; of a girl who used to turn heads in the street, whose beautiful green cat eyes and full generous mouth would smile in acknowledgment of the compliment; of a girl whose waist was the envy of all the girls at the office. But that wasn't her. Not the real her, inside. Inside she was grey, without spark, joyless, an aching cavern starting to manifest itself in the shadows under her eyes, seeping through her skin, turning her inside out.

She summoned up some energy.

'You've got to make the effort, ' she said firmly out loud to her reflection. 'Stop hiding behind these walls.' She quickly turned from the mirror before her reflection could come up with another excuse.

Smokey was meowing, reminding Jennifer that she was hungry and needed feeding – now!

'There you are, my darling.'

Jennifer stooped to place the food on the stone-flagged kitchen floor. The two-bedroomed sandstone cottage was around three hundred years old and stood at one end of the small village of Brockby in North Yorkshire. Its cottages, gathered prettily around a large village green centrally speckled with cherry trees, were mainly privately owned now, although some still belonged to the Fernleigh Estate and were rented out. Jennifer hadn't been there long, having moved to this rural idyll from her city flat only four months previously. She had fallen in love with her cottage the moment she saw it. The minute she'd walked into the cosy living room with its stone inglenook fireplace and singular low, blackened beamed ceiling she'd felt curiously at home, as if she'd always been there. Some houses are like that, she'd thought at the time. Some houses have a soul and speak to you.

She was slowly refurbishing the place, to suit her tastes and because it needed it, but making sure that she kept the decor in character with the beamed ceilings and sandstone walls.

She was twenty-eight and worked as a buyer for a successful international lingerie company whose headquarters were based in the nearby city of York. She often travelled to Paris and Milan, which took up much of her time. She didn't mind: since her long-term relationship had ended very distressingly a year and a half ago Jennifer had sunk into desolation, and when at home had become something of a recluse. All her friends were happily settled in relationships, most with children now, and didn't seem to have time for socialising. Or was it that she felt left out now that the popular topics of conversation were, 'Justin cut another tooth today!'; 'Tabather said "Daddy" for the first time!' (it was actually 'Ahhhheh', but Mummy and Daddy were convinced it was 'Daddy'); or the strange and complex evolution of baby poo. Jennifer figured that what she didn't have couldn't hurt her. She had convinced herself that she didn't really want kids anyway. The thought of all that pain giving birth terrified her.

She occasionally had phone calls or visits from a well-meaning colleague who would try to drag her out to one of the night-clubs on Micklegate in York, but usually she managed to find an excuse; 'I'm fine. Honestly, Barbara. I've tons of work to do and a heavy schedule tomorrow. You go with John – I'm sure you don't want me around playing gooseberry all evening, ' she would plead. Invariably when this happened and she stayed at home she'd feel relieved at having escaped from the club music (which wasn't really her cup of tea), half-inebriated guys with wandering hands just itching for a pull, and people feeling sorry for her when she deliberately sat on her own, praying that the evening would come to an end soon. However, having made the decision to remain at home she'd inevitably begin to feel sorry for herself for being alone with no-one to share the evening with: no romantic candlelit dinners for two on a Friday night, no-one even to talk to about simple everyday things, to share the day's events. Finally she'd remind herself what a bloody awful time she'd had in the last couple of years of her relationship with Jim and curl up in front of the fire with Smokey, whom she adored and who at these times, she decided, gave her a lot more love and loyalty than she'd had from any man.

Jennifer did have one particularly close friend, with whom she'd been at school. They had kept in touch ever since, and although each had grown in different ways there remained a very strong bond between them. They still approached the important aspects of life in the same ways and shared the same essential beliefs. Sarah was Jennifer's best friend, and the only person, she felt, who really understood her. However, Oxfordshire is a long way from North Yorkshire, and they both had such busy jobs that it was months since they'd seen one another. Although they often spoke on the phone, Sarah hadn't yet managed to visit Jennifer in her new home.

Jennifer returned home that evening from work after another hectic and very long day, her head swimming with details of the forthcoming collection. She placed her bags of groceries on the kitchen floor with a sigh and was greeted enthusiastically by an exuberant Smokey, her mouth full of feathers.

'Oh Smokey, what have you done, you naughty girl? Bloody hell! Another mess to clear up. I suppose you've left bits of bird all over the lounge again?'

Smokey looked up at her — much too pleased with herself to note her mistress's exasperated tone — and wound herself around Jennifer's legs, rubbing her head against them contentedly.

By the time she'd cleared up the whirlwind of feathers in the sitting room, fed the cat — although she didn't deserve it — put the shopping away and made herself a cup of coffee, Jennifer felt exhausted. As she stood at the sink rinsing the teaspoon with which she had stirred her drink, she lowered her head, resting both hands on the bottom of the washing up bowl in the hot water. The warmth drew out suppressed emotion like pus from a wound. Her shoulders began to shake and tears poured down her cheeks. Her mouth was open, but no sound emerged. There was at first too much despair to be given a voice. But eventually she allowed it to leave her body. Her sobs came from deep within and she shrank into the gaping hole left inside by their emergence. Her undulating wail was low and fragmented by short, sharp intakes of breath. She was at once crying out for some sort of divine help, for her lover, and because she was so desperately lonely.

When eventually the tears were no more she washed and dried her face and turned to her cat, who, worried by this strange noise and sensing something not quite right with her owner, had come to sit at her mistress's feet.

Jennifer knelt down and kissed the top of her cat's warm head.

'Beautiful girl' she sniffed. The cat's smiling eyes seemed to kindle an ember within her exhausted heart. 'I'm too bloody tired to do any more work tonight, so you and I are having an evening by the fire watching the telly.'

She threw open the fridge and pulled out a few of her favourite things for supper to cheer herself up. Some garlic-oil dressed salad from the night before, pitta bread, olives, a nice piece of mature brie and a large pot of taramasalata.

'What a mixture! Still, never mind - I'm too tired to cook. We'll just binge on this, eh, Smokey my love?'

She didn't feel silly talking to the cat – she didn't think about it most of the time. It was only when she had company that she realised, through copious teasing remarks, that she sounded like an eccentric old woman. At these times she pictured her future self as a completely batty sixty-something-year-old spinster with dozens of cats, the kind of character that children would taunt and intolerant neighbours would shun. But when there wasn't anyone else around, which was most of the time, she would chat away to Smokey as if she comprehended every word. Theirs was a comforting symbiosis. Smokey would sometimes chirrup or meow a reply, although most of the time she simply purred like a steam train. On this occasion she meowed obediently.

The phone rang about half an hour later, pulling her away from a depressing documentary about childless couples. Why she was watching it, goodness only knew – she didn't. However her last reserves of energy had abandoned her and she seemed to have become bonded to the sofa, too tired even to change the channel, her mind floating above the intrusive sounds emerging from the television. On a subconscious level the programme reminded her that she wasn't the only one with problems, although perhaps that was an entirely selfish interpretation.

It was Sarah on the line.

'Hello Jenny, eh up, howst tha doing?' her friend said in her best Yorkshire accent, which wasn't that good but which always made Jennifer laugh. 'Thought I'd give you a ring to see how you're coping with the wilds of north Yorkshire!'

Relief. A reprieve.

'Hi Sarah! I'm so glad you rang! I've had a bloody awful day, and I was just thinking about you and how it seems like ages since we've seen each other.'

'I know, it must be nearly five months. It's ridiculous!' Sarah accorded. 'I haven't even seen your new home yet. I feel neglected, ' she added teasingly.

'You and me both! How about you coming up for a weekend soon. Can you manage any days this month?'

'Well, next weekend I'm off to visit my parents, but I think the following weekend would be OK, ' Sarah replied, a little concerned.

She knew immediately from Jennifer's tone that she was trying really hard to be cheerful, so guessed that her attempt at stoicism had failed again. To the less perceptive observer, Jennifer's depression seemed to come and go. However, Sarah knew her friend better than anyone except perhaps Jennifer's parents, Pam and Jack. They had been the ones that Jennifer had first turned to after the split with Jim. But Sarah had always been there for Jennifer. She knew that her friend's melancholy did not phase in and out, but rather – and worryingly consistently – lay beneath her everyday countenance. Jennifer seemed to be able to veneer a cheerful disposition over her true temperament, its thickness dependent on the depth of the unhappy underlay and the merit of the occasion. This provided her inner self with a cushion against attack in case her defences were breached and the depression leached out and engulfed her.

'Jen … are you are alright? You sound a bit tired. What have you been up to lately?'

Jennifer told Sarah about her day, her busy spring schedule and the cat's greeting present. Sarah listened and threw in comments with just the right combination of empathy and benevolence.

'I'm fine really, I'm just feeling a bit lonely at the moment, ' Jennifer eventually acknowledged, making light of it. 'Hey! We haven't been out shopping for a while. If you can make it, why don't we go into York or Newcastle for the day and have a nice meal somewhere. Then maybe a good long walk on the Sunday to take off all the extra pounds we'll have gained on the Saturday!' Jennifer tried to sound positive.

Sarah laughed. 'OK, you're on, ' she said. 'That sounds great! I'll pencil it in my diary.'

She tried not to sound so concerned for her friend's sake, as Jennifer was obviously putting a brave face on and Sarah didn't want to discourage her while she was on her own. They talked some more about everything and nothing, enjoying each other's company through the telephone wire until one of them thought of the bill.

'See you then Jenny, lots of love and virtual hugs! Oh, Jenny?' Sarah paused. 'One more thing. Are you still taking those natural sleeping tablets?' she ventured carefully.

She didn't like the thought of Jennifer taking anything that hadn't been prescribed by a doctor, particularly considering her recent state of mind. Not that she thought Jennifer unstable enough to do anything silly, but who knew what side-effects they could have? By all accounts they didn't even come from a health food shop. God knows what could be in them. Her scientific mind had rung warning bells in her head when Jennifer had first told her that she had bought them.

Jennifer sighed to herself and began to turn the pen that lay next to the telephone pad around in her fingers. She really didn't want a lecture today about the rights and wrongs of taking local remedies for sleepless nights, although she knew her friend was always genuinely concerned about her when she bent her ear about this. Should she tell the truth? She decided she should be honest.

'Well, only occasionally, ' she said, a little too hesitantly, 'but don't worry, I've been sleeping a lot better lately anyway and I'm sure I can cope without them really. It's just comforting to know they're there if I need them. Hey, don't worry! See you in a fortnight.'

Famous last words.

Necessity, excitement, regret, a delicate, ever-changing balance; a variable fusion. At what point did regret tip the balance, influencing her subsequent behaviour? Or necessity? Or excitement for that matter? Doubt and caution may have been in the mix, but in inferior proportions to the rest, that much was clear. It had begun: Jennifer had triggered the circumstances, the events, that were to change everything; and she was unaware of it.

April 1762

*E*mily stepped from the house and crossed the small stone-flagged courtyard. Unlatching the iron catch, she passed through, securing the little black iron gate between its matching railings behind her. Rounding the corner of the narrow lane, she made her way carefully over the wet cobbles of Precentors Court towards the Minster. The magnificence of that great building never ceased to inspire awe and incredulity within her. The entrance to Precentors Court brought her directly to the western facade, which was all arches and exquisitely carved cream-coloured stone. A pair of dark oak doors divided by a pillar sat sternly but comfortably embedded in arches of decreasing proportions, drawing the onlooker towards them, beckoning the passer-by. Above the twin doors, also set into the concentric stonework, was a perfectly round, prettily segmented window and above the whole, a wonderful composite stained glass window of huge proportions gazed down upon the place beneath where Emily was standing. To the right and left of the central twin doors, further oak doors of similar design and proportions were set into the seats of two glorious bell towers, their arches and intricate carvings, lancet windows and pointed spires reaching up towards the heavens like a pair of outstretched arms thrust high into the sky, fingers extended to the tips, celebrating God in all His glory.

Emily crossed Minster Yard and passed in front of the seemingly infinitely smaller church of St Michael-the-Belfry and into High Petergate. Her mistress had instructed her to pay a visit to a milliner located on Fossgate, where she was to supervise the making up of an order that Lady Charlotte had sent ahead. She was also to collect a pair of gloves from a proprietor in Glover Lane and to seek out a particular lacemaker of some repute who, her ladyship had heard, resided somewhere on Langton Lane.

The afternoon was bright after a heavy shower of rain. Light grey clouds scudded north-eastwards underneath the light white sky. The eaves of buildings dripped raindrops, collected and channelled between umber roof tiles or trickled over thick brown thatch. Emily set off along Petergate towards Colliergate. She was familiar with this area of York, having accompanied her mistress to their York residence on many occasions and having been sent on errands about the city. She loved the vibrancy and colour of the city; the rows of neat, smart houses each nurturing a family, servants, folk with lives very different to her own, with their own stories to tell and secrets to keep. She loved the glass-fronted shops with their colourful displays of everything imaginable: watches and clocks, fabrics and furniture, pots and pans, fruit and vegetables, grains and flour, teas and coffee, sugar and spices, breads and cakes. Ironmongers, stationers, haberdashers; the goods available were seemingly endless, if you had the money.

Emily was treading carefully, picking up her feet to avoid horse dung and potholes full of filthy water in equal measure, taking care over wet flagstones and cobbles. She was also proceeding slowly because she had plenty of time to complete her errands, and since this was the case she was thoroughly enjoying gazing through the shop windows and taking in the sights, sounds and smells surrounding her.

Halfway down Petergate she discovered a hosier and bought herself a new pair of woollen stockings. She had three pairs, two of which had been mended frequently but were fast becoming threadbare and would not last out the month. After counting the coins in her purse she chose another three pairs, one for her mother and one for each of her sisters. No doubt they could do with new stockings, for theirs suffered harder wear than hers. She was looking forward to seeing them in a few weeks on May Day, when she would have some hours to spend as she wished and could visit the farm.

As Emily reached the top of Colliergate the street became more crowded. A commotion was taking place before her. Two carts, each facing the other, had overturned in the narrow street. Nearest to Emily, a piebald mare was being helped to stand by three men. The brown colt harnessed to the other cart was jumping around nervously, held somewhat ineffectively by a young lad while an older man, presumably the driver, was swinging heavy sacks back onto the righted cart. A few of the sacks had split open and brown flour spilled out across the cobbles, and a variety of goods from the nearby grocer's cart had distributed themselves in disarray across a wide area. Some kindly folk were picking items up and bringing them back, while several young urchins darted about seizing stoneware jars sealed with beeswax, regardless of their contents. Whether coffee or cocoa, tea or turmeric, sage or sugar, it mattered not. A buyer could always be found for the right price, provided they did not get caught – and the risk was worth it.

The grocer was shouting and cursing at the driver of the flour cart and the urchins in turn, shaking his fists at them, while he and the other two men righted his cart and began to retrieve the spilled goods.

'Stop thief! Stop thief!'

His cries followed the young lads as they fled the scene, each carrying as much as they could run with. Several men stepped forward and tried to apprehend the youthful robbers, grabbing at the rags on their backs or holding out a foot perchance to trip one up; however the boys were too quick, and darted through Coney Garth into the market beyond and disappeared into the crowd amongst stalls and benches, vendors and purchasers.

Several jars had cracked and one leaked treacle over the cobbles. The slow tide of heavy black liquid oozed forth, incorporating dung and dirt, leaves, straw and flour in its wake, rendering the way impossible.

The two drivers were still arguing over who had caused the unfortunate accident. Each would lose money over this. Each had important customers waiting. Each would have to make repairs to his cart. Each had lost valuable goods.

Emily turned from the scene. One of the youths had passed close to her – close enough for her to see the desperation in his pale blue eyes, his grimy skin drawn tight over his bones, clothes in tatters. He had no shoes. She had made no attempt to stop him – he would easily have knocked her over in any case. She knew that it was wrong to steal, but she also knew what it felt like to be hungry if she probed her memory deeply enough. Secretly she wished the urchins luck and continued on her way. That is to say on a changed course, for Colliergate was blocked and she had to choose an alternative route. This was a little disconcerting, as she now had to pass through the Shambles, a narrow lane between many old timber buildings, some of which nearly came together at the third storey so that it might be possible for a man at each opposing casement to lean out and shake hands with the other. These, interspersed with tall brick buildings, their shop fronts jutting out into the lane, made for difficult passage, particularly if you were to avoid the putrid mix of muck and blood, rotted vegetables and dirty water which ran down the centre of the way.

Emily gathered her skirt a little and tried to avoid the worst of it. Keeping her parcel close and her wits about her to guard against pickpockets, she hurried down the street past pawnbrokers and pie shops, a purveyor of painted wooden toys and an ironmonger. The stench of blood and entrails filled her nostrils as she passed three butchers in a row, the benches outside their front windows bearing all manner of animal parts, some freshly butchered and bloody, others looking slightly rank. A small handcart half full of innards stood by one door, waiting to be pushed down to the river.

Emily tried to hold her breath as she walked quickly passed the foul-smelling mess and was glad to finally reach Pavement, a much wider and more respectable street along which stood two churches, a number of fine merchant's houses and a market. She turned left, crossing in front of the old church of St Crux towards Whip-Ma-Whop-Ma-Gate.

As she walked, her thoughts, triggered by the recent event in the street, took her back to a time in her childhood when her dear father's wheat and barley crops had failed, blighted by the constant rain that summer. That was a time of intermittent hunger, at least for a short while. Her father and mother had worked hard with what little they had, nurturing their stock, replanting wisely and making the most of the food they had stored, sometimes going without in order that Emily and her younger siblings would have something to fill their bellies. She had a vague memory of Lord Fernleigh; indeed it was the first time she had seen him, standing in the parlour whilst a man unloaded a sack of grain from his lordship's carriage and her father stood with hat in hand, working his hands over the brim, turning the thing round and round. Her Pa had looked uncomfortable, but Lord Fernleigh had sounded insistent about something and the sack came in and was deposited in the larder. After that they had received several visits from Lady Fernleigh, who always looked gracious and delicate and who, it seemed to Emily, always floated into the house bearing a basket of food, spoke with her mother for a while and floated out again on a current of serenity.

It was that winter that her mother had first miscarried. But her father was a good farmer, prudent and perceptive. His shrewdness and hard work had ensured that the family was never hungry after that time. Indeed, they had all worked hard, as young as they were, she and her two sisters Georgina and Prudence, and her little brother for that matter when he came along and was old enough. For as much as siblings are bound to argue, theirs was a close family and each of the children had a strong sense of belonging, so that each derived satisfaction at one time or another from contributing to the well-being of their family and the success of the farm. That's not to say there weren't squabbles; but when Lady Fernleigh had expressed a wish to employ Emily as a maidservant, living and working at Fernleigh Hall, Emily had been torn. It was of course an honour to be asked, to be thought reliable and trustworthy, as her mother, Mary, had explained to her. Yet she was nervous about leaving her family and going to live in the big house. She knew she would miss them very badly. Her mother had agreed to the request, despite the fact that she was nursing a newborn at the time. *It must have been hard on her*, Emily reflected. However, she would have been certain that her eldest daughter would be well cared for, sure of having clothes on her back and shoes on her feet and indeed well-fed, and only a mile or so away.

Emily crossed the street and headed down Fossgate towards the little bridge. The milliner was located in a small whitewashed premises with an oversized wooden lattice window displaying a colourful variety of hats and bonnets. Emily gazed at the display for several minutes before entering. Silks of green, apricot, mushroom, lavender, primrose, rust and black bowed and bobbed about their stands in the draft emanating from the ill-fitting door, showing off their trimmings and feathers, ruches and pleats, ribbons and bows.

Inside it was a veritable Aladdin's cave. The silk hats and bonnets were accompanied by linen and woollen caps, quilted children's bonnets, folding calashes and exquisitely embroidered lace bonnets for infants. Emily herself was wearing her best apricot satin hat, delicately pleated around the brim with ruched cream ribbon in two concentric circles about the crown, and was right glad of it, standing as she was amongst this finery. Not that she wasn't used to running this kind of errand for her mistress of course. However, the knowledge that she was respectably and indeed well dressed for walking about the city gave her a degree of confidence that she would have otherwise lacked. She knew she looked reasonably pretty in apricot, the muted shade of the hat complementing the few strong red curls given leave to show themselves beneath it. The bonnet and its matching gown were recent acquisitions from Anne Fernleigh, apparently a design or tint that the young lady had grown tired of. Emily was pleased to receive them, and was lucky enough to hold not a small collection of gifted garments nowadays. She tried to pass on what she could, within the bounds of appropriateness and sanction, to her mother and sisters.

The order having been duly checked and the packing suitably supervised, Emily turned her attention to the lacemaker. She enquired of the proprietor at the milliner's where she might find Mistress Clegg of Langton Lane.

'Indeed I'm not rightly sure of the whereabouts of Langton Lane, ' she admitted in the hope of receiving some assistance.

'Don't you worry tha'self, Miss… er?'

'Popple, Emily Popple.'

'Miss Popple. 'Tis not far, but thee wor right to ask, for its tucked away down a snickelway and out o' sight t' those that don't know its situation. An' thee'll be sure to enter from Stonegate and not Grape Lane!'

The woman spoke in tones of one trying to improve herself but with some way yet to go, and inclined her head towards Emily, raising her eyebrows in a polite but stern warning.

'That's not t' place for a respectable young lady such as yerself.'

Emily waited for further instructions. After a moment of silence, the woman smiled at her through yellow teeth, putting a hand to her neck.

'Oh, ah'm a foolish woman. Dear me. Excuse my silliness for ah've not told you what to look for.' Her purple bonnet bobbed to and fro. 'Proceed to the top of Fossgate, ' she said slowly, as if this would ease Emily's understanding and commitment to memory of the route.

'Turn to tha left and walk along Pavement past t' Golden Fleece inn up to t' market cross. Then thee turns right and proceeds through t' market an' along lane until you reach St Helens Square an' entrance to Stonegate. Find the little red printer's devil in Stonegate. You can't miss it, close by t' Star Inn. There lies t' snicket to t' lodgings where you'll find old Mistress Clegg.'

Emily thanked the milliner and proceeded on her way, following the instructions. She passed through a large and busy market where every item imaginable seemed to be for purchase and she had a difficult time of it making her way through. There were numerous lanes and passageways to the right and left; however at length she came upon Stonegate. The street was similar in some respects to the Shambles, although wider and significantly cleaner. She was familiar with this area, although not the inns, with which the milliner appeared to have a customary association.

On reaching the old inn she looked about her for any devilish signs and recognised the printing works where she had once delivered an order for her mistress. There, below the carved wooden lintel between the ground floor and the first floor above, squatting on a wooden furl, was a little red devil, hands on knees, staring down on the passers-by.

Emily turned right into the narrow brick passageway that led underneath the buildings on either side to a small yard in which stood a run-down timber building in the shape of the letter L, the point at which its two halves joined furthest away from her. A set of wooden steps ran upwards and leftwards from the middle to a covered balcony on the first floor, under which was a large dark oak door.

Emily had no clue where the lacemaker should be found, so hesitantly knocked at the door. A fair-haired woman in a grubby apron opened the door, wiping her hands on an equally grubby rag. She peered at Emily for a moment.

'What's tha want?'

'I've come to see Mistress Clegg. I'm told she resides here.'

'Upstairs, ' the woman nodded briefly and closed the door.

Emily proceeded up the steps and through a door at the top. She found herself in a dark, narrow corridor off which there appeared to be two rooms. She knocked at both, but received no reply. Beyond the second door the corridor took a right turn and widened out. She was in some kind of gallery with windows to the left. To the right, three horn windows allowed light into a large chamber below on the ground floor, though she could not make anything out distinctly. At the end of the gallery an elderly woman sat spinning wool. A younger woman, judging by her garb, sat facing her with her back to Emily, carding a fleece.

Emily approached and asked them where Mistress Clegg could be found and the old woman, saying nothing, nodded to her left and continued spinning. At the very end of the corridor, past a set of stairs on her right, was another door. Emily knocked, and the tones of an indistinct voice from within came to her. She took this as an invitation to enter, opened the door and stepped in.

The room was sizeable and flooded with light from a window fashioned partly into the slope of the eaves. In the corner nearest her were a small truckle bed and an old armchair. This seemed to be the only concession to comfort, as the remainder of the space was filled with all manner of articles and tools designed for sewing. A spinning wheel, reels of silks and cottons and even silver and gold thread, thimbles, tweezers, scissors and needles lay in designated pockets and drawers of a candle stand case which stood on top of a large, open lockable chest, presumably frequently in use. A number of skeins of cotton and silk lay on the floor against a wall. Pin cushions, boxes of pins, two craquettes of differing shapes, a sharp stiletto, rolls of ribbon and a large open bobbin case filled with piles of bobbins variously carved of wood and ivory were stacked precariously on a table.

A middle-aged woman dressed in grey with a white cap was at a large worktable underneath the window.

'Mistress Clegg?'

She looked up from the intricate pattern of pins and thread fastened to her lace pillow and nodded.

'My apologies for disturbing you.'

Silence.

'I… that is my mistress, Lady Fernleigh, was given your name by an acquaintance of hers.'

'Oh aye?'

'Yes… you come highly recommended.'

'Oh aye? By who?'

'Oh, please forgive my rudeness. By Lady Snaith. She said you could be found hereabouts, in Langton Lane. I must say you're a little difficult to locate.' Emily smiled shyly.

At the mention of Lady Snaith the woman's face relaxed and she smiled a toothy grin and arose from the table.

'Oh, why didn't tha say. Ah keep m'sel to m'sel. Never know who's about these days like. But ah've me select customers. Those that appreciates quality 'andiwork when they sees it.'

Mistress Clegg edged around her worktable and came towards Emily, pushing aside the many pieces of exquisite finished lace hanging from a wooden rack attached to the ceiling by a pulley.

'See 'ere, this un's fer Miss Susan Snaith. T'aint finished yet though!'

The woman gestured behind Emily to a wickerwork mannequin wearing a beautiful apricot-pink lace-patterned silk contouche, the bodice of which was all silk and silver thread lace, reflecting the silver thread in the weave of the skirt. Layers of delicate lace at the sleeves and hem matched the bodice.

Emily gasped involuntarily. 'It's beautiful! Quite beautiful.'

She had tried making a piece of linen-thread lace using her mother's lace pillow when she was about nine or ten, but had not the patience for it, nor the eye. She grinned.

'You have a marvellous talent, Mistress Clegg. My mistress would be very pleased to see some of your work, if you will call upon her.

'Aye, 'd be pleased to, ' she beamed.

They talked for a while longer. The lacemaker seemed delighted to be complimented on her work, as any artisan would on their creation. At length, Emily left by the nearest set of stairs, which brought her level with the entrance to a large hall. She recognised the three horn windows high up on one side. A fire was lit in the centre of the room with a kettle and large cooking pot suspended above it. To one side was a spit with a plucked chicken on it, waiting to be roasted. The grubby fair-haired woman that Emily had seen earlier was bending over, stirring something in the pot and shooing away a small dog that was sniffing at the uncooked chicken. The woman straightened up, clutching her lower back. She looked miserable. Emily turned, lest she be caught staring. She found her own way out and hurried back through the snicket and up to the top of Stonegate where it joined High Petergate.

She found herself thanking the Lord for her favourable position. She smiled to herself; it was a good job that she did not have to live by her needle skills, for she would have starved long ago. She remembered when she was first at Fernleigh Hall and been taken under the kind wing of Mrs Cumley. The plump, convivial cook had enquired after her sewing skills. Emily had sheepishly admitted that she was no good whatsoever with a needle. However she had asserted that she was a mighty fine cook, having been taught by her mother, who was the best cook ever. Mrs Cumley had raised her eyebrows and smiled.

'Is that so?' she'd laughed. 'Well tha better start be 'elping me wi' t' dough for t' bread.'

She might have been a laundry maid; however, Mrs Cumley was under instructions to keep her close by to begin with. So she became a kitchen maid, and besides advancing her cooking skills Mrs Cumley had encouraged the improvement of her basic reading and writing. After a time she had become a housemaid and came into frequent contact with Lady Fernleigh when she was eventually assigned to some of the family rooms. Lady Fernleigh seemed well-disposed towards her, perhaps because she was so eager to learn and so capable a young girl. Over the next few years Emily had continually been encouraged to improve herself. She had even been allowed the freedom of the extensive library. She had eventually become Charlotte Fernleigh's personal lady's maid. Emily smiled to herself; she was indeed fortunate.

She collected the gloves for her ladyship from a proprietor in Petergate and made her way back to the Fernleigh residence with news of Mistress Clegg and a sample of her lovely lace. Although she was excited to be in the city — she would be accompanying her mistress to the theatre the next evening — she missed Will and was looking forward to seeing him again, however briefly. The sight of him, a nod, a smile, the briefest of touches, hidden from others, an acknowledgement of what lay between them, was enough to send thrills through her body, to make the tiny fine hairs on her arms stand up and set her heart racing. A few more days in York and then she would see him.

Two

*W*illiam threw open the doors and surveyed the gardens below. He could never tire of this sight, particularly on a splendid day such as this. A small area of formal garden lay immediately beyond the sweeping stone steps, divided into three rectangular sections, each dissected lengthways and in cross section by stone paths. Each of the oblong sections was delineated by box hedging and contained small shrubs and roses. The central path led to a scalloped-edged fishpond with a fountain in its midst. The whole gave way to a softer, more gentle landscape of a series of lawns dotted with clumped and single specimen trees. Beyond this lay a lake, surrounded on the western and southern sides by large areas of woodland where yew, beech, birch, alder, larch, elm and chestnut stood proudly together. The lawns and trees were interspersed with winding paths imitating a meandering river and its tributaries flowing towards the lake, whose calm waters glinted in the strong afternoon sunlight. A series of cascades had been cleverly created where water from the small river feeding the lake entered from the west. At the other end of the lake, on its eastern side, stood a castellated stone deer lodge, its gothic windows overlooking the lake on one side and the deer park on the other.

William stepped outside, turning to close the double doors behind him. Glancing at his pocket watch, he hurried down the steps and walked quickly towards the fountain, his boots crunching the gravel beneath. A voice close by startled him.

'Dear William, might I take the air with you awhile? 'Tis such a fine day, do you not think?' Anne looked up from her roses.

'Dearest sister, you quite startled me! As usual, you see, I was lost in contemplation.'

Anne stood up and laughed. 'William, you are always found to be in your own thoughts these days. What do you say, may I accompany you?' She placed her rose basket on the path in anticipation of a positive response.

William panicked inwardly. He must not disclose the true intent of his outing at any cost, even to his sister.

'Darling Anne, ' he smiled, 'I would not presume to bore you. I am to discover the state of completion of the tree-planting in the east woods. Father has instructed me thus and wishes for a full report at dinner. Besides, ' he said, thinking quickly, 'I hear Mr Calder is coming to take tea with Mama today.'

'Indeed?' Anne tried to conceal her interest in this matter, though a hand went unbidden to her neckline and the other sought out a stray brown curl brushing against the side of her cheek, which she deftly hooked back under her cap. 'Well then, I must not be so impolite as to be absent from the tea party. Forgive me, William – I shall take these roses in to M'ma.'

With that, she gathered her basket and hurried back up the path towards the house.

William laughed, partly with amusement at his sister's poor attempt at remaining detached and concealing her interest in Mr Calder, and mostly with relief. He continued on his way towards the lake.

They met in an area of densely-planted woodland on the eastern side of the lake. William helped Emily into a small rowing boat, then reached for the cloth sack concealed under his coat and placed it in the boat. It was but a short distance to the largest of the islands, although Emily gripped the sides of the vessel the whole stretch. They alighted at a small wooden jetty, boarded on one side for safety by a rough fence constructed of strong coppiced boughs. William held Emily's arm for support and bade her tread carefully as the jetty was slippery. She placed her delicate black laced shoes cautiously one before the other on the algae-covered boughs as if her life depended on it, for she could not swim. The path from the jetty led to a small clearing in which stood the most perfect rustic tea house. Pentagonal in shape, three sides faced into the clearing while the other two bordered the woodland and were without windows. The thatched roof rose on all sides to a point in the middle and overhung the walls by a foot or so all the way around, supported by thick wooden poles.

Her aquatic ordeal now rewarded and therefore largely forgotten, Emily ran toward the cottage.

'I remember, I remember!' she cried. She spun around to face William, who was in pursuit and was grinning at her. 'My father brought us here once when I was a child' she said. 'When he worked on the Estate, before he rented the farm from M'Lord.'

William nodded, his blue eyes twinkling 'I remember, we sat upon the jetty trying to catch fish!'

'I caught two, ' Emily said proudly.

'Did you now, you clever girl?' Suddenly William bent down, swung one arm under the back of Emily's knees, picked her up and carried her towards the door of the cottage. Emily shrieked with delight and then pretended to scold him, ambivalently drumming his chest with her right hand whilst her left hand held him tightly around his neck. Protocol prevailed.

'Unhand me, sir, ' she laughed. 'It is not seeming for a lady to be treated in such a way! Though the Lord knows I am no lady, ' she added with a sigh.

'To me you are as fine as any noble lady in Yorkshire, ' he said seriously, looking into her verdant eyes.

'Only in Yorkshire?' she teased.

'Well then, in the whole of England!' said he, as he set her down upon the wooden floor inside the cottage. Sunlight streamed in through the open door and the adjacent lead-latticed window.

'Will no-one find us here?' Emily asked a little worriedly, as she stood upon a low wooden bench to look out upon the sun-filled glade and the comforting screen of the woodland beyond.

'No-one, ' he replied confidently; although inwardly he was not completely certain of this he did not wish to alarm her, and thought it well worth taking the risk this day.

'How can you be certain of that?' she ventured, her brow temporarily furrowed around the question.

'M'ma, Mary and Anne are entertaining Mr March and Mr Calder this afternoon and have requested that Rebecca and Elizabeth join them, Father is occupied in his study, and many of the labourers have been given leave to make their May Day celebrations. If you recollect, there is to be a feast this evening and dancing in Brockby.'

'Oh, I nearly forgot! I left my basket in the boat. Mrs Cumley was very kind to give me some May Day cakes from the kitchen to take home to my family. There are enough to go round and more besides. And I have other vittles in the basket which I fear may spoil if left in the sunshine too long.'

William went back to the boat to retrieve the basket. On his return they sat together on the grassy floor of the clearing amidst burgeoning bluebells and the fading hyacinths, planted in abundance around the tea house by the head gardener for the benefit of its occasional occupants. Each ate one of the delicious pork, apple and pear pies, although Emily would not part with the mushroom pickle or the almond pudding, which she insisted were for her Mam. William had also brought a contribution to the picnic; thick slices of venison pie and a small jar of strawberry pickle, which he too had procured from Mrs Cumley's kitchen. She, being a kindly sort and having known him from an infant, did not mind his frequent visits to her domain, putting it down to his voracious appetite, which indeed he did have. As a child he would steal into the great larder to which was attached the cold store and look upon the shelves in wonder. He recalled a time after a recent kill. A side of beef and half a salted pig hung from the great hooks in the ceiling, and the pig lard rested in pots on the stone shelf next to large rounds of cheese. All manner of meat pies, tarts, puddings and pastries sat upon the upper shelves, and in one corner stood rows of neatly placed pickle jars - cucumbers, beans, beetroot and turnip, tongue and walnut. Great wooden boxes of apples and pears lay about the stone floor accompanied by turnips and potatoes covered in straw, and strings of onions kept company with the beef. It was truly an awe-inspiring sight to a young boy.

After consuming their delightful fare he read to her, as was customary when they managed to steal a few hours together. Such was his desire to assimilate every modicum of knowledge or considered opinion of the natural world around them and the order of things, his preferred reading encompassed the papers of most of the philosophes, together with those volumes of Diderot's Encyclopaedia which his family had managed to procure despite the current prohibition in France on its printing and sale. Emily was as intelligent as she was keen to learn, despite her lack of formal education. Together they had enjoyed Newton, Kepler and Galileo on the wondrous skies above them and the principals of motion and planetary orbit, Pope on the science of human nature and Voltaire and Montesquieu on the laws governing ethics, economics, politics and religion. Emily did not always understand the text at first, but William took great pains to explain and interpret the written words, enabling her comprehension of the subject and provoking discussion.

Today William read from Voltaire's *Philosophical Letters.* 'An Englishman, as a free man, goes to Heaven by whatever road he pleases.' Emily closed her eyes and listened. She neither questioned the existence of God nor had supposed how others might view the Church; however, she understood that there was a contemporary feeling of condemnation of religious intolerance and a concurrent scrutiny of the Bible among certain of the educated.

Once he had finished reading they sat for a while in the afternoon sunshine, she with her back against a large oak tree and he with his head resting in her lap. As he lay there with his eyes closed she contemplated him, one hand laid carelessly on his shoulder, her long fingers gently stroking the top of his arm through his shirt. His shoulder-length dark curls were tied back with a black ribbon. His finely-shaped face was turned away from her, and although they were at this very moment closed, he possessed a pair of ice-blue eyes the like of which she had never seen before. She noted that his garb today reflected his rebellious nature: there was not a gold thread in sight. He had removed his plain brown frock coat, which now hung from a tree, for greater comfort, and was simply dressed in leather breeches and a cotton shirt overlain by a white quilted waistcoat. The only concession to his status was his boots, which sported gold and silver buckles.

She loved him passionately, more with each passing year, it seemed, and had done so since they were children. They were of similar years: she nineteen, he twenty-one. She recalled how they had occasionally been allowed to play together when she was four or five and her father worked on Lord Fernleigh's lands. William had been fascinated with the farm animals and was sometimes allowed to help with their husbandry. His father thought it sensible that his only son grew up to be familiar with certain aspects of running the estate, as he himself took a great interest in these matters. Emily smiled to herself when she thought of how his lordship was affectionately known as 'Farmer Fernleigh' by her people because he took a great deal of interest in the running of his farmlands rather than leaving it all to his agent. She had also realised that this term was used a little more scornfully amongst some of Lord Fernleigh's acquaintances, as she had recently overheard Mr Chesterfield and Lord Fox remark upon it. *Almost as damnable as that confounded Farmer George. Disgraceful, the man should devote a great deal more time to the election, in my humble opinion,* one of them had remarked disloyally, likening Thomas Fernleigh to the King.

Lambing time was a particularly busy period, as was the harvesting of the wheat and barley. When she was a little girl at home, at harvest time Emily was expected to help her mother, Mary, preparing vittles for the faggers and their wives, and earlier in the year she would be helping with the lambs. Ofttimes William would also help with the lambs. She remembered how he would chase her with a newly-cut lamb's tail and she would shriek. At harvest, when the corn was neatly stacked they would play amongst the great straw towers, then follow the harvest home. A merry feast of fine food and cider was consumed in thanksgiving for the good crop safely brought in and afterwards there was dancing till the early hours. Little William was also allowed to experience this festival, and on more than one occasion had taken Emily by the hand to dance a jig, much to the entertainment of the older folk, who looked upon it as something endearing at the time. Emily wondered what they would think now. In truth, she knew.

By the time she was thirteen her father was a tenant farmer, having rented, for a small yearly sum, a parcel of land from Lord Fernleigh near to the estate cottage in which they had been allowed to continue to live. It was at about this time that she had gone to work in the big house. Their chance meetings became more frequent after that.

Emily gently stroked William's dark hair. His soft curls felt warm, having absorbed some of the heat of the afternoon sun. Emily smiled to herself as her mind conjured up the image of her Pa's black collie lying in the sun like a lizard on a lunchtime break, its fur almost hot to the touch.

She was full of happiness. She felt the good Lord had given her a blessed lot in life and that she was very fortunate. She was devoted to her ladyship and to her Mam and Pa. Yet certain thoughts always clouded her happy world; she was betraying the people she loved most. Every single day she felt guilt for the love she bore Will and for the manifestation of that love. Although she had seen only nineteen summers and was hardly wise in these matters, she knew that a love such as they had was wrong in the eyes of polite society and could not lead to a happy conclusion. But the love itself was overpowering, all-consuming, and she could not fight it, did not wish to fight it even if she could. It seemed that she lived each day imprisoned in her guilt and a great, great fear of being discovered and the inevitable ruin and shame that would follow — shame that would fall upon her and upon her family. She would undoubtedly lose her position and become a burden to her family, or worse still, perhaps be driven out by them in order to preserve their integrity. Ironically, the only thing that made this bearable was being with Will. If she ever lost him or he ceased to love her, she felt, she would not be able to go on living.

William stirred. He reached up for Emily and pulled her down towards him, kissing her lightly on her forehead, then on each cheek and finally on her mouth. He glanced up towards the sun, in its aura of bleached sky, which was moving slowly down beyond the trees behind them.

'The hour is approaching when my family expect me. I must not be tardy, ' she whispered.

'Sweet Emily, how can I let you go? You have kissed me, consequently I must keep you here beside me forever on this island, ' William teased, his arms lightly around her back.

'Dear Will, please do not entreat me to stay here with you. I am weak and would do as you bid. All I wish is to live here forever with you, ' she half-teased. She jumped up from him, spilling his arms from about her, and laughed, 'But my dear mother would be without her May Day cakes!'

She darted behind the oak as he sprang up to catch hold of her again, and he chased her around its sturdy trunk, catching her by the arm.

'Emily, sweetheart, let me show my love for you, ' he whispered earnestly.

'I know your declarations, Will, ' she smiled brightly, 'but the hour is late and we should be undone if we were to be seen leaving here.' There was a mixture of concern and reluctance in her response. 'Anyway, ' she said, adding another reason to support the first, if rather tame and unconvincing, 'cannot you see that I am wearing my finest gown in your honour and do not wish to spoil it?'

William looked at the gown. He thought the dress was infinitely better suited to Emily than to Amelia.

'It is indeed a fine gown and suits you well, ' he said, trying to placate her, 'although I know you wear it not for me but in honour of this May Day visit to your family, ' he teased.

Emily conceded that this was true. She had worn the new gown proudly this festival day, yet her excitement at wearing it was tripled because she knew Will would see her in it and she would be alone with him.

'You would break a poor maid's heart with your unkind words, ' she teased back, pretending to be upset. 'Is it not enough for you that we are alone together this afternoon?'

William pulled her towards him.

'It is enough for me that you do me the kindness of allowing me to keep company with you, ' he said softly, with mock seriousness. Then: 'Almost!' His voice deepened and acquired a slightly hoarse undertone and his breath began to come more quickly. 'Emily, my beautiful sweetheart. I have a longing for you that refuses to be satisfied by your company and mere words. Indeed your very presence excites and intensifies it. I beg you to let me show you how much I love you. We have time.'

Emily looked radiant in her light green silk sack and petticoat edged with silk lace and lightly embroidered in silver thread. The shimmering green contrasted perfectly with her long red hair, now drawn back from her face, ringlets falling about her neck. Perhaps a little provocatively, she had removed her silk handkerchief in the heat of the afternoon, placing it carefully in her basket lest it should spoil. She recognised his urgency and felt it too. She wanted him as badly as he desired her, and her sense turned quickly to sensibility. She turned her face up towards his and the yearning aching through her body was written clearly in her expression.

William placed his left arm around Emily's waist and his right hand on her bare chest, pressing her against his arm rather than the tree supporting it. He moved his fingers slowly beneath the delicate lace of her stomacher; cupping her right breast and bringing its nipple upward out into the light, whereupon he bent to take the bud in his mouth. At this Emily parted her lips, drawing in a quick deep breath. She felt wicked for a moment only before her passion for this man enveloped her and she allowed herself to succumb to it.

Still with his left arm around her waist, William drew up her gown and let his fingers explore the soft skin of her thighs underneath her shift. He parted her legs to better explore the very core of her.

29

Emily gasped at this invasion. As William entered her, she could think only of his touch and the heady perfume of the hyacinths.

Mary Popple was preparing herself for the bedchamber, her husband now abed and sleeping heavily, his nose rattling loudly as was usually the case after a night of excess such as that evening's. She placed her cap carefully on top of the large oak chest to the right of the casement window and proceeded to remove her cotton apron, which she hung by its straps from a hook on the door. As she discarded her gown and petticoat in favour of a quilted linen nightgown, her thoughts were of the splendid night they had enjoyed celebrating May Day. Her dear Emily had come to help with the feast, for which she was grateful, for not only did she love to keep company with her precious eldest daughter but preparing dishes for the party was hard work. Still, there'd been plenty of willing hands; Beth's, Joanne's and the other bairns' and those of Mistresses Jones, Acomb and Farthing from nearby farms. Folks had all brought something. What a sight had greeted people as they sat down to eat at the long wooden tables on the green! Carved hams and baked fowls, meat pasties and baked potatoes, stewed beet and onions and of course the May Day cakes that Emily had fetched, to which she had added her own.

Beer and cider flowed and there was elderberry wine for the ladies, though Mary was sure she'd seen more than one young lass quaffing beer. And afterwards, out came the fiddles and the bairns danced around the maypole until they fell to the ground, exhausted. But that didn't last for long, and up they'd jump and go round again. Even she herself had been persuaded to dance a jig or two.

Only one cloud had impaired Mary's horizon of contentment. Towards the end of the feasting, before the dancing began, she had noticed a large ominous figure sitting on his horse in the distance in the middle of the road into the village. He'd been watching the proceedings for a few minutes when one of the menfolk had invited him to drink a tankard of beer. The sound of his booming guffaw sickened her and made the fine hairs on her forearms stand to attention. There was not a scrap of doubt in her mind that he was up to no good. He had spoken to Acomb's eldest girl, a pretty thing, barely fifteen, and made her laugh. Mary had immediately called her over to help clear some dishes into the dairy, and he had looked straight at her, almost through her, with utter disdain, then had slowly formed his ugly features into an evil grin before turning his back on her and gulping down the remainder of his ale at once. Mary watched as he remounted and cantered off in the direction of the big house.

As she brushed her long red-brown curls in the flickering candlelight her memory transported her, an unwilling traveller, to an earlier time – an unhappy time.

She was picking early blackberries from the long hedgerow that ran between pasture and woodland in the north-western corner of his lordship's estate. John Fernleigh, accompanied by his wife, had been staying with his brother for a short while, and on this day was out riding alone. He had spied Mary from a ridge overlooking the woodland and cantered down to take a closer look. The day was warm, and she had taken off her cap. Her tresses were fighting their captor ribbons and one long silken curl had come loose, reflecting the low-angled late afternoon light. She had spied a lone rider silhouetted against the sun and thought nothing of it. The sun had washed the pasture between them a light yellow, though with her back to the sun the land before her was a brilliant green. Further away, fields of slain corn glowed golden.

All at once they were about her like a storm whipped up from nowhere. Horse flank shining with sweat, black boots, creaking leather, flared nostrils spluttering foam, hoof on stone. He laughed as she flung her basket down, spilling its contents, and crouched upon the track, her hands instinctively to her head, fearing she would be mortally trampled.

He dismounted.

'And what, pray, do you think you are about?' he uttered intimidatingly, prodding her back with his riding whip.

Left to its own devices, his mount moved a little further away and put its head down to the lush grass.

Mary lowered her arms slowly. 'Simply picking a few blackberries sir, ' she replied quietly, 'fer a pie or two.'

'Are they your blackberries?' said he.

'No sir, they grow wild.' She hung her head low in a servile stance, for she knew better than to look him in the eye.

'I did not ask you for a lesson on how they grow, you impudent girl. My question was to whom do they belong? The answer to which, as you know very well, is Lord Fernleigh, my brother. You have stolen from my brother and I have apprehended you in the very act. Thieves are scum and must be punished as such.'

He exuded menace from every putrid pore. Mary was panic-stricken. Her heart stumbled and lurched ahead of itself. She was fully aware that this was not about the picking of berries but had a far more sinister basis, although she found herself trying to explain that His lordship had given leave to his workers and their families to avail themselves of whatever plants grew wild on his lands.

It did not suit John Fernleigh to listen. He had designs on the girl.

'Must be punished, ' he stated in a matter of fact fashion. 'I shall spare you from His lordship and see to it myself, and you will consider yourself disciplined.'

He grabbed Mary by the wrist and pulled her through a small gap in the hedgerow and into the wood beyond. Mary screamed out in terror, trying to pull away from him. He shouted at her to be quiet and struck her such a blow to the right side of her face that she was knocked to the ground and hit her head on a low, moss-covered tree stump. Dazed and bleeding from a corner of her mouth and the back of her head, she was dragged five yards further to a clearing in the brambles.

As she felt the weight of him upon her she managed to breath a final plea.

''Ave mercy on me, 'tis but a month till my wedding!'

Then the breath was pushed from her lungs until there was barely enough to keep her alive and she could speak no more. The pain was akin to someone taking a poker and burying it deep within her, and the shame a hundredfold greater than the pain.

He left her in the woodland. She lay sobbing for some time, her arms clasped about her knees, which she had drawn up against her. Her shift was stained with the inconceivable mix of her blood and his expulsion, and she felt the stain grow until it poisoned her veins and choked her heart. This was certain to be God's punishment for the sin she had committed not long before. How quick the path to debasement and ruin. How could she ever again face her dearest Daniel, engaged to be married but a month hence? And what of her family? Who would have her now? That bastard had laid claim to her for no other reason than that it was his will, and now her life was over.

'Oh Lord, *tis my fault, tis my fault,* ' she sobbed. 'I am undone. Lord, *forgive me!*'

Her linsey gown and petticoat were torn but had protected her limbs from the bramble barbs, that still clung to the material. Her face, though, was scratched and had begun to swell on the right side. Her head throbbed from its wounds, which were nothing to those she felt below. She buried her face in her arms once more, begging the feelings to wash over and away from her. She felt nauseous with pain and the realisation of what had passed. He had taken his horse whip to her, used her like a whore and then like a boy.

Suddenly it was upon her – she lifted her head and spewed violently.

After a while longer she managed to stand, and shakily picked her way towards the edge of the wood, eventually pulling herself free of the brambles. Her basket lay on its side, its berries given up. In a brief moment of futile defiance she righted it and, kneeling beside it, returned those berries which the horse had not trampled into the ground. She slowly stood again, leaning on the handle of the basket for support as she rose. All at once she was seized with an uncontrollable urge to cleanse herself. Summoning every last ounce of willpower, not knowing quite how she made it, she dragged herself down to the river. The flow, swollen with late spring rain, cut its way purposefully through the valley bottom, forming a wide pool in the meadow where the land was flat.

Mary stumbled into the shallow water at the edge and eased herself onto her knees in the cold mud. She had to rid herself of him. She cupped one hand between her legs over and over to remove his seed. The water stung and made her gasp, and her skirts caught in the flow and she nearly overbalanced. She couldn't swim, and in that moment did not care whether she drowned. One thought only kept her from throwing herself to the mercy of the river. *Daniel.* Though she did not know how she could face him, she longed for his strong arms around her, his quiet low voice telling her he loved her and comforting her in her shame.

It was enough to make her choose life. She pulled herself out of the water and onto the bank. With a supreme effort, she stood up, turned her back on the river and wood and slowly made for home.

Mary turned her tear-stained face from the window and slid silently under the bedcovers next to her husband. She stroked his hair lightly so as not to disturb him. 'Tha's a good man, my 'usband, ' she whispered. 'What would ever 'ave become of me without thee? I owe my life to thee.'

May

The evenings and weekend before Sarah's arrival were spent decorating the tiny second bedroom, a task that Jennifer had been meaning to take on since she had moved in. The weather had turned warm for early May and sunlight streamed in through the half-open wooden-latticed window creating a pretty dappled effect on the strong, polished oak floorboards as Jennifer stood in the doorway surveying her work, redundant brush still in hand.

'Yes, although I say it myself... that looks pretty good, ' she told the cat proudly, nodding, her critical eyes darting over the paintwork.

She had chosen a light mint green for the walls which complemented the white ceiling and contrasted perfectly with the rich-coloured wood. Sanding the floor had been hard work and had taken the best part of three evenings, but it was worth it. The boards had turned out to be in excellent shape and now gleamed appreciation through their varnish. Jennifer was just inspecting the oak beam for any signs of woodworm when Smokey gave a chirrup and jumped after a tardy cherry blossom which had blown in through the window. She landed on the neglected upturned lid of the paint pot and proceeded rapidly towards Jennifer, across the dust sheet on which the painting materials were carefully placed and onto the unprotected middle portion of the floor, leaving a trail of little green footprints behind her.

'Oh Smokey, no! Don't move!' Jennifer admonished, scooping the cat up and rushing to the bathroom for a wet cloth to clean the floor and her paws. 'You've never any respect for this home, have you?'

She couldn't be really cross with her cat – she shouldn't have left the paint tin open – but she was annoyed with herself. However, the emulsion came off the polished wood easily, so no harm done. *Anyway,* she thought, *that's that job done now and it will have to be the last one for a good while.* She had a busy time at work ahead. She turned to Smokey.

'So no more opportunities for you to be creative all over the floorboards!' she pretended to scold.

As was, unfortunately, fast becoming the norm, her satisfaction was short-lived, being slowly drowned by angst sourced from her subconscious whilst sleeping. That night she tossed and turned, her head full of Jim with girls dressed in her spring collection. Sleep came in short bursts intercepted by fitful wakefulness. By 2 a.m. she had decided to take a couple of sleeping tablets.

A thick layer of guilt coated the tumult of other emotions swirling around in her head. She tried in vain to justify her decision. It's not as if she was addicted to the tablets. Damn it, she could do what she liked. She just wanted some sleep! God, how she *needed* sleep! She'd take just enough to dull her busy mind. She wasn't dependent on them – she just had a busy day tomorrow, that was all. But the guilt had formed a hard crust and stubbornly remained, trapping her other feelings, overwhelming her reason. Having broken the habit, she really did *not* want to go back to that soul-destroying routine of taking tablets, sleeping heavily at night and feeling subdued in the morning because she had a headache or had overslept, her brain furred and unable to focus, as cotton wool in the ear impairs the audible range. By lunchtime she would have sunk into depression again as thoughts of her broken relationship with Jim broke free and surfaced through her subconscious. She would then promise herself that she'd get through the next night without any help, to break the debilitating sequence. Then at night she'd lie awake again for hours, her mind involuntarily sifting through past events, stirring up unwelcome emotions. Finally she'd give up and resort to the magic bottle again, simultaneously completing and initiating the cycle.

Despite the serious drawbacks, the tablets *had* given her what she really needed at the time – wonderful, comforting deep sleep. Her work was demanding and she could simply not afford to try to participate in meetings feeling like death warmed up.

Jennifer had stumbled on them by accident. She was in the health food shop in the nearby market town of Malton, looking for a natural solution for sleeplessness. Something based on lavender perhaps. That was supposed to work. She hadn't been able to find anything, so had enquired at the counter. An elderly lady next to her had taken her arm, telling her about a local remedy that her husband had been taking.

''E swears by them now' she had croaked. 'Mrs Beakes is mi name, luv.'

'Do they work like lavender oil then, you know, the aromatherapy stuff?'

'Ah dunna know about no aromatheerpy what-you-ma-call-it. But ah tell thee now, it's changed 'is life, it 'as. Ah'll tell thee that for nowt.'

'Quite a few folks 'ave tried that y' know, ' the lady behind the counter interjected. 'It's made locally, ' as if that made all the difference.

'Why don't you sell it in here then?' asked Jennifer.

'Oh, couldn't do that. 'Er that makes it don't do it for commercial like. She makes it for her family like, and those folks that know 'er. It's an old recipe. Tried and tested like. Nothing to worry about.'

Jennifer wasn't so sure, but she assumed, perhaps a little naively, that the health food shop assistant should know something about her trade. While common sense screamed at her not to be so foolish, desperation to get something quickly and an illogical fear of conventional sleeping tablets prevailed. So she agreed to let the old lady show her to the source of this fascinating remedy and purchased a bottle of capsules, only after having been recommended to the supplier by Mrs Beakes, of course.

Jennifer now reached for the bottle, hidden from view and temptation at the back of the spare-room wardrobe cupboard. She swallowed two capsules and stumbled back to bed, already feeling their effects. Within minutes she was asleep.

The lagoon is bordered on three sides. Pink and grey rocks jumble and tumble gently towards the rippling waters. Up away from the sea, here and there the rocks are capped by compact dark green bushes with thorns as sharp as needles. A crown of bright green stubbly pine trees top the three islands forming the lagoon, their dark brown cones nesting in the swaying branches.

The breeze drops, the pines cease their chatter, the waters become still. For a brief moment the silence is complete. Then all at once it is broken by a symphony of cicadas, little groups in each tree being brought in and faded out by an invisible conductor.

The turquoise waters fade to deep blue as the rippled white sand below gives way to sculptured rock. There are no clouds. The powerful, pulsating sun illuminates the heavens. The warm rays refracting through the clear water create a Raku effect on the sands beneath. Hundreds of fish swim comfortably in shoals in the dancing light.

The breeze has evaporated. The exposed rocks shimmer in the heat and the surface of the water becomes a sheet of silver-blue crystal. Jennifer cuts effortlessly through the transparent film and enters the watery world. A shoal of slender young garfish part instantaneously in front of her and regroup behind as she passes, their long silver bodies flashing in the iridescent light.

Jennifer's beautiful body glides slowly and smoothly across the bottom of the lagoon. Over the sky-blue fans of a cluster of peacock worms; over the tiny tracks made by an industrious little hermit crab, dragging its snail shell home; over the cleverly concealed flounder, only its small black eyes giving it away as they look out from under a cloak of sand. A myriad of fish appear around her as Jennifer nears the rocky margin. Turquoise and purple striped rainbow wrasse browse on algae amongst small brown and cream striped combers and yellow and brown bogues. Bright red cardinal fish dart in and out of the rocks while tiny damselfish seem to hover and then disappear in a flash of vivid blue.

Jennifer's heart is singing as she becomes an honorary guest, if only briefly, in this phenomenally beautiful world. She runs a hand gently over the soft, furry seaweed which carpets the rock surfaces like a green, brown and purple patchwork quilt. As she does so, thousands of tiny filaments sway back and forth in the current. She is transfixed. Breathing seems easy and she doesn't need to return to the surface, it just... happens, somehow.

A little rock goby tries its luck at one of her fingers, which still lie amongst the fronds. Jennifer cups her hand and the goby scurries over the fingers in search of more fruitful quarry. Yet more beautiful colours catch her eye. It feels to Jennifer like discovering a mosaic floor in a Roman villa lost for centuries, or a new star, so struck is she by the perfection and splendour surrounding her. She dives further towards the clusters of fragile urchin skeletons.

Colonies of tiny creatures form exquisite fan-like structures around them. Like curtains of old magnolia Victorian lace, they graciously wave their delicate fronds. The urchin shells form an artist's pallet of soft hues; pink, purple, green, lilac and white. Jennifer picks them up, one after the other, turning them over and over, feeling their texture and marvelling at the colours and patterns. She places each back where she found it and swims nearer to a crack between two rocks in time to see the tip of a grey suckered tentacle poised to catch its prey unawares before it is withdrawn into the shadows. She feels another surge of delight: an octopus! What a privilege! What a wonderful watery world!

Suddenly she feels a hand on her arm. She spins around in the water. It is him, the same blue eyes and dark hair, this time pulled back into a ponytail tied with a thin black ribbon. She immediately senses that he too is part of this magic. He belongs here, with her, in this paradise. At that moment she longs to throw her arms around him, to surround him with her singing heart. He swims for the surface and she follows. They burst through the water into the sunshine and he catches her in his arms and presses his lips to hers. She feels his urgency and her senses explode like the hundreds of tiny air bubbles trapped on her skin as she rolls over in the water.

'Race you,' he says quietly with a glint in his eye. And he is off, not needing to wait for an answer. He swims with strong, powerful strokes towards a small stretch of sand between the rocks on the other side of the lagoon. Jennifer races after him, laughing as she does so, watching his back muscles flex as he cuts through the water. She follows him into the shallows, putting her feet down onto the warm sands beneath. Suddenly he dives under the surface and comes up behind her. She laughs and continues wading towards the beach. Walking behind her he places his right arm across her chest above her breasts and gently squeezes the top of her left arm with his other hand. 'My sweetheart,' he whispers, kissing her neck. 'I knew you'd come.' They walk onto the beach together, the warm, dry sand trickling luxuriously between their toes. She looks up into his beautifully chiselled face and down over his glistening naked body, his muscular chest, the black hair that grows between his nipples, his hard stomach, the sensuous line of hair growing downwards from his belly, tempting her gaze still further. He lifts her chin and takes her delicate face in his strong hands, softly kissing her forehead, her nose and finally her lips. 'I love you, more than you could ever know,' he whispers softly. She is overcome with exhilaration! She looks into his eyes and smiles a wide, uncomplicated smile. She is so happy! She takes him by the hand and together they lie upon the white sand. They lie for a while simply basking in the sunshine, drinking each other in, touching, stroking, exploring.

Finally, he runs one hand gently up the inside of her thighs, pressing and stroking between her legs whilst the other hand explores her breasts. His fingers enter her and are bathed in her warmth. They lie foetally on their sides, he clasping her in front of him. He enters her warm body from behind, caressing each breast with light, gentle squeezes. He pulls her tightly against him as he moves slowly in and out of her. His fingers explore the nucleus of her sensations with rhythmic strokes as he quickens his pace. She feels gorgeous shivers running from deep inside her to her toes as his fingers press more firmly and his thrusts grow stronger and deeper. Her juices flow freely as her excitement grows. She starts to moan with pleasure. Then he stops.

'Don't stop, ' she whispers.

He begins to move gently inside her and stops again. His fingers stroke her lightly for a few seconds and cease. He is prolonging the magic, for her and for himself.

The intense tingling within her subsides a little and her body cries out for him. He moves slowly again, reaching deep inside her, his fingers starting their own caresses. She feels her whole body begin to give itself to the exquisite sensations beginning deep inside her. He stops again and pulls out of her. She is so close!

She closes her hand over his and squeezes it tightly. 'I love you' she cries. He thrusts into her once more, making her explode in an orgy of sensations, giving her his life force. She contracts again and again. Shivers run down her legs and a warm glow spreads over her belly, her fingers and toes tingle and her head feels light and dizzy. She has never had such an orgasm!

'Don't ever let me go, ' she murmurs as she turns to face him, and he gathers her to him, stroking her long hair and enveloping her slender body in his strong arms.

'Jenny, my Jenny, ' he whispers her name over and over.

Jennifer awoke, feeling confused and disappointed when she realised that it had all been another dream. It was even more vivid than the last. *Why couldn't she meet someone like this in real life?* She was shocked at the intense sexuality of her thoughts. Sex had never been quite like that with Jim. She experienced a delightful mixture of extreme contentment and well-being and just a little wickedness. *But it wasn't real, was it? Just a dream.* Jennifer shook her head and tried to shrug it off.

Reluctantly, she swung her legs out of bed. She shivered as she went to the bathroom, suddenly realising that she wasn't wearing the tee-shirt that she normally slept in. *That's odd, I'm sure I put it on last night.* It was still too cold in the cottage to sleep naked as she preferred to do during the summer. She looked for the night-shirt and found it in a crumpled heap by the bedroom door.

She shrugged again, trying to dismiss thoughts of the night before, but her mind continued to play tricks on her. For a while she continued to immerse herself in the fantasy overspill, that margin between dreaming and rational thought; to think about the erotic stranger in real terms. Completely illogically, a little defiance started to creep in. Why the bloody hell shouldn't she have him? She deserved him. She'd waited long enough for someone like him to come along and release the pent-up desires she hadn't even realised existed before now. She wanted him badly. She wanted his touch and the smell of him on her body. She wanted his gentle strong arms about her. She wanted to feel safe, and above all to be loved.

The sound of ringing shook her from her thoughts. It was Sarah.

'Hi Jenny! Thought I'd surprise you. I've got a day off work so I'll be down early.'

'Oh... that's great, Sarah! When will you be arriving then?'

Jennifer felt so relieved. She loved having Sarah to stay. She always made her laugh, and that was just what she needed right now. Defiance gave way to excitement.

'Well I thought I'd start in about half an hour, so I can be with you by lunchtime – is that OK? We could have lunch in town and then you could give me a key and I can let myself into the cottage, if I recognise it! Or can you get the afternoon off?'

'Yes, I may be able to. Hang on a minute, I'll just look at my diary.'

Jennifer paused, grabbing her diary from the telephone table and quickly flicking through the pages to today's date, praying that there would be a big empty space on the page. 'Yes... yes, I'm certain I can, ' Jennifer replied. 'Oh God, I'd better do some shopping – there's not a bean to eat in the house. Hey, I'm glad you phoned! I really didn't feel like going into work today and I've a lot of time owing to me anyway. Did you get my directions?'

'Yes. It seems pretty straightforward, but if I get lost I'll ring you on my mobile. I liked the picture of the cottage you drew on the map! Looks like you need builders in. The roof's lopsided!'

'You cheeky bugger! See you later then!'

Jennifer was relieved that she had an excuse not to have to face the office today. She felt oddly excited and relaxed at the same time. She couldn't contemplate working; she didn't think she would be able to concentrate for a minute. Even though she told herself last night was just a dream, she had a very peculiar feeling about it all. She rang in. They were good about her snap decision to take time off, as she usually worked such hard, long days. They trusted her judgement implicitly when it came to running her department and organising her workload. In return, she had proved that their confidence in her was well-founded. Hooray – she had the day off!

She quickly busied herself with tidying the cottage, feeding Smokey and getting some food in from the local shops. Then she had a shower and pampered herself a little, drying her thick shining hair slowly and carefully, nurturing each of her long curls. She chose *Sensura* black silk pantics and matching bra, covering all with bright green and purple leggings and a black figure-hugging vest-top set off with a purple hip-belt. She expertly chose her make-up to compliment her clothes and took care to apply it lightly, highlighting her well-developed cheekbones and exaggerating her beautiful wide eyes. She surprised herself – she was actually enjoying making the most of herself for once.

As Jennifer readied herself, her thoughts turned again to her fantasy man and the tricks began again. What if he was really out there somewhere? She must look her best. What if she met him in the street in the stark light of day? She would have to face him with confidence, to attract him. She looked at herself sideways. Was she putting on a little weight on her tummy? She pulled herself in, a movement which accentuated her breasts. She ran her hands lightly over them. He loved her breasts.

'Jesus! What am I thinking?' she suddenly said aloud. Drifting between reality and fantasy was bewildering. Her imagination was taking over, and this loss of control was a bit weird. She had to get a grip. Her mood quickly turned yet again, this time to self-reproach.

'You stupid woman, ' she muttered to herself, 'pull yourself together. *He's* not real – go out and find yourself a real man.'

Her thoughts turned to Jim. They'd had such a good loving relationship in the early years. She had worshipped him, and he her, before it went sour. She did miss him. Her sadness materialised as a sigh and her eyes involuntarily filled with tears. *How come you're so organised and cool-headed at work,* she thought, *and such a bloody mess at home.* Once she stepped through the door in the evening she seemed to simultaneously step onto an emotional roller coaster. It was so hard to keep her feelings and thoughts under control. It was as if someone had injected her with a syringe full of extra hormones that raced around her body causing havoc. She was a mess. She turned quickly from the mirror and walked out of the room.

Sarah arrived full of smiles and parcels.

'Sarah! It's so good to see you! What have you brought with you?' laughed Jennifer as they hugged.

'Hey Jenny, you look great! What you done with yourself?' replied Sarah, squeezing Jennifer's hand.

They walked through to the kitchen and Sarah put the parcels down on the oak table.

Jennifer dismissed the compliment. 'Oh, I thought I'd brighten myself up. I seemed to be letting myself go a bit!'

Sarah nodded her head in agreement and shot her friend a kindly look. She said cautiously 'Hmm – I didn't like to tell you, but there's been quite a change in you over these past months. I know that it's because of you and Jim splitting up, but you were doing *so* well. I thought you were really beginning to get over him.'

Jennifer sighed.

'Yes I am… I mean at least I thought I was. But I just couldn't be bothered, you know? I thought I was finished with men for good, and I suppose I got into a bit of a state and just didn't feel like making the effort.'

'Oh Jen, ' said Sarah slowly, giving her best friend another big hug, 'you look *really* good today.' She thought she noticed a slight change in her friend's face, yet she knew Jennifer would be making a special effort to disguise her sorrows. 'So, c'mon, tell me, what's new?'

They unpacked the goodies Sarah had brought. Some Bavarian blue cheese, wild mushroom and garlic pâté, crusty rolls, slices of turkey and ham pie, a jar of cranberry sauce, a bottle of St Emilion Larmande and a fine tawny port.

'Just a few things for lunch!' Sarah laughed. 'I thought I'd treat us and bugger our waistlines! So come on, get munching and tell me what you've been up to.'

Jennifer made a green salad and they sat and chatted over a wonderful lunch, catching up on all the news in between glasses of claret and fits of giggles. Sarah told Jennifer about her new job. She had worked as a water quality scientist for the Environment Agency, analysing water samples for organic pollutants. Just recently she had started a new job, a big promotion to an oil spill consultant with an international firm based in the UK.

'It's really interesting work, Jenny. It takes me all over the country to meetings and conferences, and we've got some work coming up in the States.'

'It sounds very different from the routine job you had before, ' said Jennifer. 'You weren't really that happy then, were you?'

'God yeah, it's really exciting. Obviously we cover emergency situations, you know, ascertaining the source of the spill, how much has been spilled, what type of oil it is, whether it's likely to dissipate or evaporate quickly and what the toxicity implications are for the environment, ' Sarah replied enthusiastically, her hands moving as if a choreographed accompaniment to the resonance of her voice. 'And then of course there's the clean-up side of things. But also – in fact most of the time – we advise clients on preventative measures.'

She went on to explain vigorously exactly what her duties were. Jennifer thought Sarah was lucky to feel so passionately about her job. She had always been interested in the environment, and to get a job which involved protecting it had been one of her main aims. Since they were at school together they had followed quite different paths, Jennifer taking a marketing and business studies course after her English and history A levels and becoming a buyer and Sarah going on to a degree in chemistry, eventually to work in the water industry.

Sarah chatted away, telling Jennifer what she'd been doing and the latest about her man, Rob. Sarah was quite the opposite to Jennifer in her looks. She had a petite frame, being only five foot two, with short blonde hair which was perfectly cut after a spiky fashion and framed her rounded face. She was pretty, with hazel eyes and lots of freckles, especially around her little, slightly upturned nose. Although she was small she was plucky, and her colleagues teased her at work, calling her the 'little tiger', so she'd had some dark lowlights put in her hair for effect! She hadn't had it easy all her life, and had worked hard at college to get a good degree, just as she'd worked hard at her first few jobs before landing this one solely on the basis of her past effort and accumulated expertise. She was happy in her work, but until recently had lacked a long-term relationship. She'd had quite a few lovers in the past but none of them quite matched what she was looking for until she met Rob eighteen months ago. He was a classically good-looking, blonde-haired blue-eyed man. He looked like the archetypal all-American boy that you saw on the TV in second-rate movies. And she fell for him – hook, line and sinker!

Jennifer had only met him a few times as he seemed to be busy on the majority of occasions that she and Sarah got together. Privately she thought he was arrogant and a little too keen on his work for her liking. But even if she didn't like him she supported Sarah in her choice, if that was what her friend wanted. Jennifer always supported Sarah whatever she decided to do, however extreme or dull. And she knew Sarah would respond in the same way. Of course that didn't mean they didn't discuss things and offer each other opinions or advice. However, the persuasion and discouragement were always gentle.

Sarah continued to sing Rob's praises, perhaps a little too enthusiastically. Jennifer knew her friend well and thought there might be a tiny element of Sarah trying to convince herself of what a superb catch he was, but she didn't say anything. Best to leave it for the time being and hope, for her sake, that things between them were OK.

Eventually Sarah said, 'Come on now Jenny, I've been chatting away nineteen to the dozen here, and you haven't told me what you've been up to! Have you got a new man in mind? You certainly shouldn't have much trouble finding one looking like that!'

'Well, not exactly, ' Jennifer hesitated, not sure if she should tell Sarah about her vivid recurring dreams and the dark-haired man that she repeatedly seemed to conjure up. The whole thing sounded so stupid.

'Oh, come on, tell me – I know there's something to tell by the look in your eyes, ' Sarah encouraged.

'No, it's nothing … I mean, there's nothing to tell, ' Jennifer shrugged.

'Jen, love, if you want to talk about something you know you can say anything to me.'

'Well then, OK, but you mustn't laugh.' In her heart of hearts Jennifer knew Sarah wouldn't laugh, but she still felt silly. The dreams were so real to her, but it wouldn't seem like that to anyone else. And she was worried that she was going a little crazy. Best talk about it.

Jennifer told Sarah everything in great detail, from the moment her fantasy man first entered her bedroom a couple of weeks ago to this morning when she woke up feeling disappointed again. She told how her feeling for this imaginary character had got a little out of hand and how, immediately after the dreams, her thoughts were confused between her real and imaginary worlds. Sarah listened patiently and sympathetically without speaking, her heart sinking.

Finally she said, 'Look Jenny, you've really got to be logical about all this. You know he's a figment of your imagination and you're letting him take over your thoughts because you're lonely. It's natural to be a bit confused when you first wake up after a particularly vivid dream. Lots of people experience that. I understand you doing it, but don't try to hang on to the dreams; that's not going to do you any good at all. You mustn't mind me saying this – but you must try and be a bit more sociable in your free time, you've got to live in the real world. I know you travel all over the place with work, but that's not the same as making opportunities socially. Hey, you're often in some beautiful romantic places – Paris, Milan. You must meet some interesting people?'

'Yeah, but that's work, and what's the point in trying to meet someone in another country? We'd hardly see each other. I know I seem to go away a lot, but the majority of the time I'm back here, and I love my country life. I need someone here at home.'

Jennifer was beginning to feel a little vulnerable. She'd been persuaded to open up and now her fantasy had diminished by the act of sharing it.

'Well, you could try going out with the girls from the office occasionally, or join a club or something, meet some new people, anything! Just don't sit in this cottage night after night on your own. There's a danger you'll be sinking into a rut you won't be able to get out of if you let things go on as they are, ' Sarah said gently, taking Jennifer's hands in her own. 'You look as though you've started to feel a little more lively already, which is great. Only don't do it for *him,* for some imaginary creature – do it for *yourself.* You've got *so* much going for you, you're a great person to be around. Let other people see you as you used to be - as you really are! - and I guarantee they'll love you as much as I do.' She gave Jennifer's arm a squeeze.

Jennifer fought the wave of self-pity that abruptly washed over her. She bit her lip as she looked at Sarah with tears in her eyes.

'I know you're right, ' she whispered, 'but sometimes it's so hard to make myself do things and so easy to just not bother. I know Jim was a bastard at the end, but I loved him so much, you know. I still do.'

'I know. I do understand.'

An image flashed into Sarah's mind of the devastated look on Jennifer's face as she had walked through the door when first she'd gone to her after Jim had left. It was an expression of absolute incomprehension and complete and utter devastation. The memory of that look still brought tears to her eyes and she became choked up. She had been so helpless to do anything except comfort her friend by just being with her, and had felt Jennifer's hurt so keenly herself.

They hugged each other tightly, gently rocking back and forth until Jennifer's tears had subsided.

'Hey, Jen, c'mon. Life's not that bad, you know,' Sarah said finally, leaning back and gently gripping Jennifer's arms, giving her the tiniest of shakes as if to encourage her good humour, to dislodge some positivity from its hiding place in her friend's psyche. 'Look, why don't we clear the lunch things away and you can show me around. The sun's shining and I want to see your village and this wonderful countryside you've been on about! And tomorrow let's go for a good long walk,' she added, 'I really could do with some sunshine and exercise. We can take a picnic. What do you say?'

'OK, you're on.' Jennifer laid a hand on Sarah's arm and gave it a squeeze. 'Thank you,' she nodded, smiling sheepishly. 'I guess I've been a bit blinkered, haven't I?' She raised her eyebrows. 'But I'm going to be all right,' she added in a confident tone, trying to convince herself as much as Sarah. She felt ten times better now that her friend was here to show her the way. Perhaps Sarah could lead her through the mess that seemed to be her life.

That afternoon they went for a walk around the village and out into the surrounding countryside. They followed the little path past the last cottage, over a wooden stile and round a large field newly planted with potatoes. The hawthorn hedge on their right supported an early burgeoning dog rose, and blackberry rambled over it in several places further along, its new bright-green leaves revealing its position. They bore right at the end of the field and crossed a makeshift bridge of two wooden planks over a small stream into a meadow. The cows looked up inquisitively from their grazing as the two girls passed. Some walked towards them, stopping short a few yards away, curious but afraid to go any closer. Others joined them, jostling and pushing from the back but still keeping their distance, as if to say *You go! — No, you go*. They had beautiful faces. Sarah and Jennifer, sitting for some time at the west side of the meadow, had fun naming them according to their markings and characters. There had to be Daisy and Ermintrude of course. Then there were Nosey, Spot, Blob, Eager-beaver, Snuffles, Stamp, Amble and Windy.

Across the meadow they joined a narrow track which led through an area of mixed woodland. Patches of pine, and fir lay between large deciduous arrays. The ground beneath was carpeted with bluebells and the whole bathed in dappled sunlight. Where there were gaps in the trees bright green ferns held sway, their newer fronds tightly curled at the ends. Here and there the path became narrow, almost non-existent, and they had to beat a way through the encroaching brambles with sticks. Mostly the path was wide and easy, curving gently upwards around the hillside, leading between occasional glades of fresh green grass encouraged by larger breaks in the canopy. Where conifers bordered the path it was soft underfoot, carpeted by old needles. Here in the very thick of the wood the air was still and the only sound was the occasional crunching of feet on a fallen twig. Through the distant trees a roe deer, startled by the intrusion, turned tail and disappeared. For a split second Jennifer saw its white tail and then it was gone. As the girls walked steadily towards the other side of the wood the trees began to sigh and creak in the gathering breeze. They murmured and rustled, each whispering to the next, their branches swaying demonstratively.

They emerged into full sunlight once again and turned north. The breeze had picked up and now fluttered around their faces as they climbed the hill along the edge of the wood. To the south-west, green pasture sloped away down the hill to the farm in the valley bottom. The red-pantiled stone buildings were surrounded on two sides by trees and on the other two sides, white dots of grazing sheep punctuated the landscape. A track wound its way northwards from the farmhouse through the trees to a narrow lane that crawled up the hill on which they stood and ran along the top, leading eventually down the hillside on the other side of the wood towards Jennifer's village.

'What a gorgeous place to live!' Sarah exclaimed.

They soon reached the top lane, and Jennifer kept her eyes on Sarah's face as they did so. Sarah gasped. Not because of the strengthening breeze, which hit them full in the face as they walked over the brow of the hill; it was the sheer beauty of what now lay before them in the gently undulating plains below. A patchwork of greens, rich red-browns and bright yellows met their eyes. Pastures and fields of young wheat and barley were interspersed with newly-ploughed land, and winter oilseed rape, deeply in flower, lay in swathes among the rest. The patchwork was neatly intersected with old hedgerows dotted with oaks and hazels. In the far distance the land rose steeply again. Sarah could just make out the ridge in the hazy sunshine.

'That's the edge of the North York moors, ' Jennifer pointed.

'Oh Jenny, it's absolutely the most beautiful area!'

They spent a long time admiring the landscape. Jennifer pointed out all the hamlets, farms and smallholdings and the network of little lanes that connected them like tiny blood vessels, bringing vital supplies to the area.

They watched a bright yellow sprayer moving slowly and purposefully up and down the tram lines of a field of young cereal, its long arms outstretched. A red tractor armed with a reversible plough chugged up a ribbon of tarmac that wound away from them in the distance. The distant whine of an electric saw and the occasional creaking of timber reached their ears. The whole scene was somehow comforting, as if confirming that the working nature of this landscape was synchronous with its beauty.

'Jenny, you're so lucky living here.'

'I know — it's pretty special, isn't it? I've never lived in such an incredible place.'

'Well, you said it was a lovely area, but until you see it you really can't appreciate the beauty. It seems to be both wild and tranquil at the same time. I can't easily explain it.'

'I know exactly what you mean. Sometimes I come up here and sit for hours, just looking. I feel absolutely at home here; it's strange. I come up here and I really feel part of things, part of... of *life,* like I really belong. It's so... so peaceful.' Jennifer's voice broke slightly as she wiped away an escaped tear. 'I just want to share it with someone, ' she whispered sadly.

Late May 1762

$\mathcal{W}$illiam walked back up towards the house from the lake, then hesitated and turned southwards away from the house again. He was faced with the most terrible dilemma. He had a decision to make, perhaps the most important of his life, and he could not defer it any longer. He changed direction and headed towards the deer lodge. As he rounded the corner of the building he came across old Robert Butler, who worked in the stables. He was looking after two horses that were tethered to the high wooden fence which ran around the boundary of the enclosed deer park. William knew that the horses, one a Lipizzan grey stallion belonging to his father and the other a roan mare, did not particularly need tending, but that his father would have given Robert this undemanding task to make him feel useful. Robert must be three score and ten if he was a day, William thought. He had always seemed ancient to William, who had known him since childhood.

'Good afternoon, Robert, ' William called as he approached the man. 'How are you?'

'Oh, i' fahn fettle, fahn fettle, thankin' you sir, Master William, ' Robert replied, making to doff his hat before remembering that he wasn't wearing one so wiped his hands on his buckskin breeches, feeling slightly embarrassed.

William noted that Robert was wearing an old maroon waistcoat and dark brown fustian frock rather than the formal dark blue and grey livery colours now in use. His initial guess had been correct, then.

'Whose is the roan mare?' William asked.

'This mare, she belongs t' Colonel Napier.'

'Ahh, thank you Robert. Look, I don't expect Father will mind – I'm going to borrow his horse for a short while. Will you please inform him of this when he comes back? I shall return him to the stables presently. I know he will not be averse to riding the short distance to the house with Colonel Napier.' William knew that James Napier would, as a matter of course, let Lord Fernleigh ride his mount and walk beside him.

'Aye, as tha says, Master William.'

James was married to Charlotte, the second eldest of William's five older sisters, and had recently returned for a brief period from Portugal, where he had been fighting under the command of Burgoyne since the war with Spain had broken out in January. Previously he had been in the West Indian Islands and had played an important part in the capture of Guadeloupe. They had a house in Richmond bordering the Yorkshire Dales, and this was where they resided whenever James was back in England. William believed James to be an amiable sort of chap. Good-hearted, sensible and decent, he suited Charlotte, who was strong-willed but also kind and honest and very dear to William's heart. Indeed, Charlotte was very much like her mother, who had named her second eldest daughter in her own honour. James accorded Charlotte much freedom to engage in activities which took her interest in a way that allowed her to believe she was in control. In reality, they had a remarkably democratic arrangement. Charlotte respected James mightily and would obey him without question if the situation warranted it. In short, they had a progressive relationship. William envied them this and their enduring happiness. He knew that if James was visiting, Charlotte would be too, and he looked forward to seeing her. The love he bore for his sister Charlotte, indeed for all his sisters, did not make his decision any the easier.

William mounted the stallion and rode on before turning west beyond the woodland surrounding the lake, towards the sun, which was still bright in the sky. He passed through three small fields running beside the trees, picking his way carefully between groups of ewes with their lambs. How he loved this time of year! A time of fast-growing lambs, of days growing longer and warmer, of spring flowers and the promise of summer. He laughed as a group of plucky young lambs raced into the corner of the field and up onto a dung heap, vying with one another for the top spot, kicking their little legs out and nodding their heads in playful butts. Another fat lamb lay quietly upon its mother's back, its sibling at her side, both looking inquisitively toward the bodies leaping and jumping around the dung.

William encouraged his horse to gather pace and they trotted along the margin of two further fields in which oats and barley had been sown. On reaching the road running though the western side of the estate, he turned north. William shook his head at the poor state of the road. Although winter had passed not more than two months hence, April had afforded plentiful rain and the road was filled with mud. A narrow hollow-way barely more than a carriage's width, the track was flanked by an elevated causeway, here and there covered with flags but for the most part with smaller stones. William made a mental note to talk again to his father about this. It was the main route southwards from the estate and the surrounding farmland, and was frequently used to carry butter and corn from the estate to York quay and thence along the river Ouse to Hull for passage to London. Wool was also carried along this route to York for conveyance to Leeds by means of the Aire & Calder Navigation. Often carriage goods had to be taken on single packhorses as the roads were so bad. Thomas Fernleigh had recently become involved in the establishment of a local turnpike trust with several other landowners and merchants in the area. They planned to improve this important route by much drainage and laying of stones to enable packhorse carriages to use this route with greater ease and hence speed. Presently the road was full of holes and still little better than a ditch. William wondered when the next meeting of the trust would take place. He would attend with his father, who wished him to be intelligent of all matters of importance regarding the running of the estate. This greatly pleased William, for he embraced his duties with much enthusiasm. Like his father, he loved this land and the ability, through the partnership of man and beast with the miracle of God's nature, to produce and harvest a wondrous variety of crops and animals for the eating and materials to furnish the cloth trade. William took his responsibilities towards the Fernleigh estate very seriously. This land was in his blood. It was unthinkable that he could exist anywhere else; yet in spite of this, he might have to. A shiver ran through him involuntarily, despite the sunshine on his back.

William and the stallion trotted on, turning to look at the entrance to Brockby, whose neat cottages, prettily gathered around a common patch, stood to attention facing his father's house on the distant hilltop behind him. William thought they looked like soldiers, forged into shape by the same expert stonemasons who had laid the innumerable stones of his formidable family home. Together with seven other such villages constructed gradually and purposefully around the few existing dwellings for the tenant farmers and estate workers and their families, each assemblage formed a distinct unit belonging to a proud regiment.

Thomas Fernleigh firmly believed in tenant farming. He knew that many folk worked harder and with more diligence at their own tasks on their own lands, particularly when their livelihoods depended on it. A proportion of the Fernleigh lands were contracted out to tenants on a yearly basis, though seldom were any such arrangements revoked. William smiled as he thought of how his father's agent, Mr Bottesford, a punctilious man, though given to being irascible and at times downright peevish, had recently thrown his hands up in frustration at the news that Thomas had commissioned yet another group of dwellings to be built and more land to be enclosed to entrust to common folk rather than pressing it into service for the estate at the expense of the villagers, as was fast becoming the norm. Thomas had held his ground, insisting upon it.

William rode north for a short while. He was aiming for the western end of the ridge that rose up beyond the village. He could have taken a shorter route through the village, but that would mean riding across some areas of the enclosed land that surrounded the cottages on all but the east side. William was respectful of the agreement his father had made over the enclosure of lands some seven years ago, and did not wish to trespass. Spurred on by the parliamentary enclosure process, which was beginning to happen elsewhere, Thomas had reached an agreement with the commoners, including his tenant farmers, for each to enclose a small piece of common land proportionate to the size of his farm. This meant that his tenants each had land they could call their own in addition to the land they rented and managed for the estate. William proudly knew his father to be a noble, upright and kind man, sensible of the needs of the less fortunate, and loved him greatly for this and for encouraging his children to do likewise. He had thought to provide his tenants and the small local farmers with the means to fence their new allotments, for this was an expensive business, and in practice some of the poor were disadvantaged by the small compensation of land in return for the common rights they had once had. Nevertheless, Thomas Fernleigh looked after his tenants and they respected him mightily.

As he neared the forest-covered ridge, William again bore west. As he entered the trees he let his thoughts rest finally on the purpose of this excursion. His mount picked its way between elm, hazel, oak, sycamore, birch and ash and the occasional prickly hawthorn. The evening sun fell through the canopy, sprinkling the forest floor with shafts of warm light. Wild garlic held court in the dells and bluebells flourished everywhere. This was William's favourite place, and he often came here to enjoy quiet contemplation. This time it was different. This time he had to decide his future. It was a terrible thing he had to face, and this was the most comforting place to do it. As the undergrowth grew thicker he dismounted and led his horse upward to the top of the ridge. As he followed the narrow path fashioned by feet much smaller than his own, the trees whispered her name. Emily, Emileee... The sound was carried away in the breeze and echoed through the trees, akin to her laughter being picked up and whisked away when he had brought her up here secretly many months past.

William reached the top of the ridge and emerged from the forest into the warm glow of the setting sun on his left. Pasture on which sheep grazed lay immediately before him, stretching down the north side of the ridge. He allowed the stallion to graze on the lush new grass while he sat himself down on the cusp of the hill under a lone rowan tree seemed to be making a bid for freedom from the gossiping forest behind. Many of his father's beef cattle were grouped in fields lying between areas of dense woodland below. What used to be mainly pasture was now mixed with much arable land. Barley and oats grew side by side with peas, beans and turnips, and on the lands further north towards the rising moors, clover had been sown to improve the soil and further support the expansion of their livestock. His father had even begun to grow small crops of potatoes, eager to experiment with any crop. As William watched workers in the fields below casting what he guessed would be pea or bean seed, he thought of his Emily.

He loved her with a passion. He thought of how he had never really been without her. She had always been there, a part of his childhood and adolescence, and now a vital part of his adult life. He could not begin to envisage even a day, not to mention a lifetime, without her. Her beauty seemed to shine from deep within. She was indeed beautiful. William closed his eyes to better conjure up her delicate features. High cheekbones, a long, straight nose and deep green eyes, and the whole framed perfectly by curls of deep red, tumbling down her back when she allowed them to or else gathered back under her lace cap. One stray curl was always to be found. William laughed to himself; like her spirit, he thought, it could not be structured or imprisoned. There was a delicateness about her; a gentleness and grace that did not seem entirely fitted to her place. She also had an iron will and a determination that any could be proud of. Her fine looks were tempered by the ruddiness of country life. William thought of how she would pretend to scold him when he interrupted her as she was going about her duties, then laugh and steal a look at him over her shoulder. How her laugh would echo through the adjacent corridors and cause others to smile. How that little frown appeared on her forehead when she was trying to concentrate on a poem or text – be it Pope, Collins or Gray, Shakespeare or Voltaire – she wanted to read them all. She was always striving to improve herself, perhaps to make herself more worthy of his affections or perhaps, as William hoped, for her own self-esteem. He sensed she felt a great need to hasten her education in any way possible in order to try to narrow the distance between them in that respect. He did not mind in the least. He loved her in spite of her station, and sometimes because of it. William loved her even more fiercely for her temperament, for her compassion towards others, which was given freely and equally to all – her family, those she worked with and lived amongst, the less fortunate and those above her status. For her undeviating loyalty to her family, to her employers and to him, William thought her as fine as any high-born lady, though he knew others would not share his view – and therein lay the serious dilemma. Her love for him shone as bright as any star when she allowed it to reveal itself. How could he cause that light to cease shining? If he abandoned her the light in his own life would surely also be extinguished.

William's contemplation turned to his mother. He knew that in her eyes it would be unthinkable for him to engage in a serious liaison with her own maidservant, or any maidservant for that matter. It would never be allowed. He would never be able to marry Emily with his Mama's or indeed his father's blessing. To marry her without his parents' consent would be the only alternative course of action. This was also unthinkable. William believed that the shock of this terrifying betrayal might seriously harm his dear mother, such was her delicate and refined temperament. He loved her with almost as great a strength of feeling as that which he felt for Emily, albeit in a vastly different manner.

For the second time William closed his eyes, the better to concentrate. He could hear his mother's gentle laughter tinkling across the valley. She was elegant and slim and for the most part given to a quiet disposition. Like her husband, Charlotte refused to be simply a lady of leisure, preferring to be closely involved in running the vast household. Her time was therefore more often than not occupied in other than drinking tea and holding polite conversation. Moreover, she could not abide gossip. Not that she did not care for entertaining; the fact of the matter was that she was unceasingly involved in planning dinner parties for dear friends, her daughter's suitors or her husband's Whig compatriots. Her dinner parties and evening entertainments were of great repute and much talked about. Consequently she was often to be found in the study planning the evening's repast with great interest in all the latest French dishes, taking great pains to obtain recipes and uncommon ingredients, or conferring with the head housekeeper about the chosen menu. However, French dishes were only served for certain dinner guests, for some preferred 'solid English fare, not that damnable French mess', as her husband liked to declare. Charlotte also took an interest in the gardens, particularly the rose garden, in which she loved to walk. Early morning turns among the dew-laden delicate blooms were a pure delight to her. She always enjoyed this time of solitude before the busy day ahead. William respected his mother's 'quiet time'; however, he did like to walk with her in the gardens later in the day. He treasured the time they spent together in this way.

Charlotte adored her only son. As was in her nature, in all things she was equal and sought to give each of her eight children a comparable degree of affection. She adored all of her children, but could not desist from devoting just a little more attention to William. Though busy, she always had time for him and would involve him in any task she occupied herself with that she thought fitting for her son. Together with the master gardener they would discuss aspects of garden design and planting schemes and personally choose the prettiest, most fragrant flowers to be placed in closest proximity to the house. She gained great pleasure from improving her knowledge of matters botanical, and wished to share this with her children. Will had shown a particular interest in these activities, which greatly pleased Charlotte. She was also devoted to the proper education of her children. Of course she left such matters in the capable hands of their excellent tutors; nevertheless, she would often sit with them, encouraging each to read aloud to the others or to discuss suitable topics of a social or political nature. Both Thomas and Charlotte encouraged this. Charlotte was accomplished on the harpsichord, and she passed this skill on to her son, preferring to make time not only to practice herself but also to nurture his talent. This was another way she found time to devote to him. She had always rightly presumed that he would continue the management of their great estate someday, although she also had political aspirations for him, possibly progressing further than his father who was an enthusiastic Whig supporter both idealistically and financially, enjoying and investing in county election battles. She felt William would make a successful Member of Parliament, as he was progressive in his thinking and sensitive to the commercial and social changes taking place in agriculture and industry, and to the needs of the local workforce of the lower classes. Besides, York was a major political, social and commercial centre, and this was a propitious time for a Whig to be entering the political world as the King's health, and thus perhaps his power and his grip on parliament, seemed to be weakening. Will was now twenty-one, Charlotte thought, and it was high time for him to be considering joining the Cavendishes, the Walpoles, the Yorkes and the Duke of Newcastle in the House of Commons to campaign for measures as his conscience guided him. Charlotte thus envisaged this future for her son and assumed that he would marry into one of the great Whig houses, thereby eventually increasing his estates as his father had done before him. She already had someone in mind for him.

William buried his face in his hands and – uncharacteristically – allowed his grief a little freedom. He returned his parents' adoration. He could not bear to hurt them in any way or to so grossly disappoint them, or indeed to lose the affection of his sisters, particularly Anne, Amelia and Charlotte, who he greatly respected and loved dearly. And what of his inheritance, his means of income, of status, of family name, of honour? These magnificent lands before him would be seized from his grasp. William concentrated his thoughts, desperately seeking a solution. He could not face the future without Emily. The situation seemed utterly hopeless.

As if to capture the last modicum of inspiration, William scrambled to his feet, threw his hands in the air and focused his eyes northwards towards the moorlands beyond his father's lands in inexorable determination.

'Lord, help me!' he cried. 'Liberate me from my dilemma, my misery, my misfortune. How should I resolve this? Is there yet a solution, a deliverance? For I am determined to have my way *and* to pacify those I love so dearly.'

For a moment or two there was nothing. Then, as sure as a bolt of lightning will reach its earthly target, a thought struck him. The thought gathered form and became an idea. It could just about work if he engaged the assistance of his Uncle John. Oh please God, may it work!

William had decided what to do. He quickly mounted his father's horse and rode for home in the fading sunlight and lengthening shadows.

Three

*J*ennifer and Sarah had spent a great weekend together, walking, sightseeing, talking and laughing – lots of laughing. For the moment Jennifer felt like her old self again, a little more content with life, that after all wasn't as bad as it might be when persuaded to view it from an alternative angle. She was sad when Sarah had to leave, but had resolved to get out and about more, to try and meet new people. Sarah promised to come and visit again as soon as she could.

'Rob's away such a lot, ' she said frustratedly, 'but he loves his job and he earns good money. We live very well. Anyway, you must come down for a weekend soon. And…' Sarah held both of Jennifer's uppers arms and shook them slightly as she spoke. Her tone was serious. 'Please don't go taking any more of those sleeping pills. You're OK now, really you are. You've got such a lot going for you and you're strong, you *can* cope.'

Jennifer promised to visit as soon as she'd managed the next three trips to Paris, which would leave her with a few clear weeks in the UK.

The next few weeks she worked hard in the office, at her buyers' meetings in Paris and at home in the evenings. She stoically persuaded herself that the right man would come along in his own time and that she wasn't going to mope around looking for him.

She had other, far more important things to do. She threw herself into her work. The weather was fine, so when she wasn't working at home she was in the garden, creating splashes of colour everywhere and keeping down the weeds. Delicate aquilegia, blue lupins and foxgloves swayed elegantly between tall columns of sweet peas, while multi-coloured antirrhinum and slender montbretia leaves were emerging under a beautifully fragrant philadelphus, a shrubby mallow, a magnificent purple rhododendron and a pale-pink and dark-leaved viburnum. The whole colourful swathe was edged with trailing lobelia and white alyssum. An area for wild poppies and cornflower was set aside, and Jennifer created a rockery with a little pond in front of it. Some of the goldfish she gave new homes to didn't last long, however. Smokey delighted in sitting beside the pool, patiently waiting until one swam too near the surface, and then she'd scoop it out and play with it on the lawn for a while before bringing it proudly to her mistress. The clever fish, of course, stayed hidden in the weed.

Jennifer also went for many walks, exploring the network of local footpaths and along the colourful wild-flower-strewn lanes around the village. The rape flowers had ripened and waned in the warm, lengthening daylight and the hedgerow flowers were in full bloom.

All this kept Jennifer very busy, and a few weeks had passed before she found herself one Friday evening with nothing to do: no reports to write, no housework to do and the garden looking a picture. She couldn't go for an evening stroll, as gentle summer rain patted the windows in a persistent way which seemed to indicate that there would be no let-up for hours. Having worked so hard for the past weeks, Jennifer's mind was restless. She wandered around the cottage, picking things up and putting them down again, and in and out of the porch looking up at the sky to see if the rain had stopped. She played with the cat and pottered around the house again. Eventually she settled with a book about the history of smuggling and the origins of old superstitions, but she couldn't concentrate and her thoughts drifted back to the days when she and Jim had been wildly happy.

He had been so young and handsome when they met. A tall, brown-eyed sandy-haired guy with perfect bone structure, very good-looking. They'd met at college in Exeter when she was doing her degree. He was studying engineering. She smiled as she remembered their first date. They'd gone to a night club on the weekly student night. She'd been thrilled to be asked by this man she'd admired from the moment she laid eyes on him. He, struck by her beauty and charm, was also eager to impress. They hadn't talked much that first evening but sat in a corner, tasting each other between sips of beer. It was a whirlwind romance. They saw each other almost every night after that, each day finding new things in common: music, politics, art, a love of the countryside, of life, of each other. Within a few weeks they were inseparable. Jennifer laughed when she thought of how he'd tried to impress her with his guitar playing, sending her tapes of himself playing famous guitar riffs. She was so naïve; she'd actually believed the strains of the Scorpions to be him playing, and when she finally demanded a demo he'd turned out to be hopeless! Smiling, she hugged herself thinking about the time he'd left little notes saying 'I love you!' hidden all over her room, in every pot, underneath every book on her desk, in every cupboard, even in her tooth mug. That was the first time she'd really known the strength of his feelings, and she still remembered the overpowering warmth that had spread through her body as she read the notes, the feeling of absolute joy it brought her.

And what about the time he'd had that fishing competition with a flatmate for the double room in the apartment they shared? Jim had won by the skin of his teeth when he'd caught the same crab twice and Pete had only caught a bra! She remembered how she and a friend had gone down to the quayside armed with dozens of egg sandwiches for their long night ahead, only to find them in the pub! Still, they'd ended up with the double room. Heck, they'd needed it! They had used their spare time very effectively, making love at all times of the day and night. The first night they'd spent together they'd made love five or six times, so strong was their passion and need for each other.

Jennifer remembered those early years with such fondness. She remembered the time Jim, in a drunken stupor, had nearly been arrested for climbing a lamppost on the way home from the pub, to shout to all the world how he loved her. She thought of the night he'd arrived back late at the little terrace house they'd shared with a bedraggled bunch of flowers. A lovely thought, but they'd still had soil around the roots from where they had been unceremoniously yanked out of someone's garden – he'd been well-oiled that night too. And all those hours in bed having play fights under the duvet, trying to suppress fits of giggles when her flatmate came home unexpectedly in the afternoon and played the 1812 Overture at top volume in the room next to where they were trying to make love. It had put them off, but not for long!

Jennifer went out into the kitchen and made herself a cup of coffee, returning to curl up on the sofa with her hands around the mug for comfort. She thought of all the walks they had been on together. Weather and studies permitting, they had tried to get out at least once a week, usually at the weekend. They had walked all over Dartmoor, clambering up every high tor, making their way over boulders along every rushing Dartmoor stream, exploring the landscape, studying the wildlife and sharing apples with the ponies, although you weren't meant to. And the south Devon coast was so wild and untamed in places – the places they liked best. They loved to sit and watch the sea crashing against jagged rocks, the spent waves rushing and bubbling like boiling water back to re-form and join their companions, gathering for the next attack. On calmer summer days they would run over the warm sand and plunge into the sea, each splashing and screaming at the other in shock and delight. The coldness would take their breath away, but the eventual tingling of their bodies as they played in the clear, chilly waters and the immense feeling of well-being that followed as the warm breeze dried their goose-pimpled skin was well worth it.

They had eventually found a secret secluded place. To reach it you had to walk a couple of miles from the nearest main coastal path over rich pasture, where early in the morning in late summer you could find plenty of juicy field mushrooms to take home for breakfast, and then scramble down a narrow winding cliff path, battling with brambles and nettles as you went. The reward was a little rocky bay with a tiny pebble beach, interspersed with wide flat rocks jutting out into clear turquoise waters. In one place the rocks drew round in a circular fashion to enclose a deep, still pool joined only to the sea by a narrow ribbon of water which swelled and fell with the rising and ebbing tide. Jennifer recalled how they'd lain together on a warm rock after swimming naked in the pool, their bodies intertwined, making love slowly and deliberately, making every minute last forever, soaking up the fading warmth of the setting summer sun. It was *their* place. Afterwards they'd gone in for a final dip and then realised that they hadn't brought their towels, so they'd dried themselves off with their underwear before going to their favourite pub to finish off the day nicely with a pint. Jennifer remembered sitting on the harbour wall outside the Ship Inn in Noss Mayo watching the little boats bobbing about in the creek, giggling into her pint because she had no panties on and the wall felt cold through her short skirt.

Those first passionate months turned into years. Years of loving, of telling each other they'd be together for always. Years of laughter and doing crazy things. Years of hopes for the future, of sharing all of life's ups and downs. Years of memories.

He'd had to move away to Manchester to work when he'd graduated. Manchester was so far away, but they saw each other every other weekend to begin with, even though they didn't have a lot of money to play with. At this time Jennifer had a steady job working for a shipping company as a junior marketing assistant. It wasn't particularly stimulating, but it was a start. She knew she'd look for something better once she had a couple of years' experience under her belt. The pennies were tight, so they began to see each other less frequently, but she told herself that it would only be for a while. To begin with the times they were together were magical, intense. They vowed they'd always stay together; she'd find work in Manchester and they'd settle down.

But after a while he began to make excuses not to come down to see her so often, and she couldn't afford to increase the frequency of her visits up north.

As she cuddled Smokey, Jennifer began to remember her doubts, her fears and jealousies. Jealousy. She couldn't help herself. She recognised now that it had been one of her big problems, even when they had been together all the time. She would see him laughing with another girl, perhaps from his degree course, and a wave of immense jealously would flow over her. Was it that she was so afraid of losing him? She knew it was stupid – he'd never given her any cause for suspicion. But he was so good-looking, and other girls inevitably found him attractive and flirted with him. She would go up to them and claim him as her own by linking her arm with his. It got particularly bad sometimes when they were out partying at one of the many nightclubs. She'd go to the bar and come back to find him dancing away in a group of friends from his course. There was always a good mix of male and female, but somehow she didn't see the guys, only the girls who were laughing and joking with him. So instead of joining in she'd make a point of sitting out, glaring at them until he noticed she hadn't come back from the bar and come over to pull her up onto the floor. Perhaps it was that she felt inferior to them somehow, as if she wasn't quite as good as them. Of course there was no reason she should feel this way; after all, they were all doing degree courses. Perhaps she felt that Jim's dancing with other women would in some way jeopardise her relationship with him. She didn't really know; she only knew that afterwards she always felt she'd behaved like a spoilt child, but couldn't seem to stop it. He meant so much to her. She couldn't bear to lose him, or even to share him.

He had made an excuse not to come down once more. Why the hell did he let her down again and again? He'd raise her hopes with a letter or a phone call declaring his love and promising they'd be together for a weekend soon, then change his mind at the last minute. It was always work. Sometimes she'd go up to Manchester to see him, up to that little flat at the top of a big Victorian house which he shared with several others. They were always girls, and she'd get jealous when she saw how familiar they all were with each other. She'd behave awkwardly and he'd get annoyed and frustrated with her and she'd get upset. It never did either of them any good. He stopped remembering their anniversary, the night when they had first made love. Jennifer tried to talk to him about it, but even after all they'd shared he somehow couldn't talk to her. Perhaps it was *because* of all they'd been to one another. He never used to be like this. Now he clammed up when confronted with the kind of remarks designed to draw his feelings out. So then she shut it all out, pretended things were OK and almost convinced herself that they were.

After two and a half years of commuting they had reached the superficial stage. Everything was fine on the surface, but she was building a wall around herself, hardening her exterior to protect the vulnerable soul within. He perhaps mistook it for rejection, all the while struggling with his own feelings which he could no longer show her. Once she wrote a brave letter, telling him she understood that he needed space to grow, time to think. She loved him incredibly and hoped that they would eventually be able to come together, to grow together again. Perhaps they should give each other a little space for a few months. It had taken enormous courage to write those words. She had struggled with her love for him, wanting to cling to him and understand him at the same time, but loving him meant understanding him and recognising his needs, didn't it? So she'd posted the letter. He'd replied simply, 'I agree.'

Their relationship never really recovered after that. Each time they saw one another it was strained. Trying to laugh, to talk, even to make love. The spark had gone. Still she tried to shut it from her mind, to pretend it wasn't happening. She had not known it at the time, but by then he had someone new.

When the final letter from him came — *Christ, he did it by letter* — it read '...I cannot find the feeling inside me to spend the rest of my life with you. I am falling out of love with you.' She was numbed to the bone, to the very soul. It seemed, at that moment, that the very reason for living was gone.

Jennifer, still curled up on the sofa with Smokey, fought back the tears, trying to forget the sour ending to their affair. She still felt so raw inside. She knew the only way to even start to recover was to push all thoughts of him, of what had happened, into her subconscious. But it was so difficult. She had opened the window just a tiny fraction into that place where she kept him and now the memories came flooding back, rushing through the open gap into her conscious mind, pushing aside all other thoughts, desperate to be given form again.

Jennifer's reflections returned to another time when she had been curled up on a different sofa with Smokey alone with her thoughts, trying desperately to make sense of what had just happened, to cope with it, to find a reason for going on. So many emotions: hurt, dismay, bewilderment, bitterness, anger, frustration, disbelief. Pain and hope struggled against one another. Above all, she felt completely empty, as if he had reached inside her and removed her very core. She ached with emptiness as if she would collapse in on herself. She truly believed that she would.

What was the point of it all? What was the point of struggling for years to build a life together, a future – even to dream of a future together? What was the point of love? A love like theirs was not meant to be transient, was not superficial but deep, committed, true, exhilarating, wonderful, all-encompassing and lasting. What was the point of love but to carry you through whatever life has to throw at you? Love should be stronger than anything. It should be the safety net, the support, the one thing that can be relied upon in times of distress. What was the point of anything when a love so strong could be thrown away for an easier solution, for a new young love which had fulfilled a particular need but which she believed related to a situation in Jim's life that was undoubtedly fleeting. He had since moved to a new post in Brighton and was with yet another woman. Jennifer knew that love wasn't easy; no-one had ever said it was. Love related to a lifetime of memories, hopes, plans, sharing, good times, bad times, dreams, pain and ecstasy. They had been loving for nearly six years – they could have had sixty together, a lifetime of loving. What was the pain of being apart for a couple of years compared to being together for a lifetime? What was the point in throwing this love away? Would Jim go on throwing love away every few years and trying to start again until he found someone who happened to be in the right place at the right time? Jennifer didn't believe there was an inexhaustible supply of 'right' people with whom you could build your life. She did believe that in a relationship good times followed bad, but she wasn't given the chance to prove to Jim that the right love, the true love – their love – should be respected for what it was and used to bind them together through the difficulties. It was as if they were at the bottom of a huge chasm with their love the only rope that could pull them out into the light once more. But he had had another, shorter rope to cling to. Jennifer knew that it would not lead him out, but he had chosen it, and he had left her in the darkness forever.

Jennifer began sobbing uncontrollably. Smokey looked up at her with a worried expression. She didn't understand, but she instinctively knew something was wrong. When at last her tears had subsided, she wiped her face with the back of her hand and looked at her.

'Oh Smokey, ' she said softly as she drew her cat nearer to her and buried her fingers in her long silky fur. 'Come here and give me a cuddle. Your mum needs a big hug right now. Come up and keep me company.' She gathered her soft, warm cat in her arms and went upstairs to bed.

Jennifer looked at the clock for the fourth time. It was 3 a.m. and she hadn't been able to get any sleep. The bright moon cut through the still night, throwing a sharp beam between a gap in the curtains that fell obliquely across the room, painting the furniture in ghostly shades. Jennifer's mind was still full of troubled thoughts, and try as she might she could not lock them away again. She'd been up for a drink of hot chocolate and had tried reading for a while. She felt she badly needed a release, but the mood wasn't right. Sometimes it helped her to get to sleep, but tonight she couldn't summon up the interest. After another half-hour she decided to take the pills. Just this once... one last time.

She went to the cupboard where she kept the bottle and then downstairs to the kitchen. She placed it on the table in front of her. *Oh God, I really shouldn't be doing this.* She felt so mixed up; her mind was in turmoil. What if it really was dangerous? After all, they weren't from the doctor. But they were supposed to be 'herbal', made from 'natural ingredients', whatever they were, and that was good for you, wasn't it? What if there *were* side effects? There might be long-term effects no-one knew about. No – that woman probably had half the village taking them by now, and Jennifer herself had taken them before with no ill effects, hadn't she? She was still in one piece, wasn't she? She left them on the table while she went to pour herself a drink, then stopped. Better not take alcohol as well. She made herself a weak cup of tea and sat down in the living room. *Damn these guilty feelings.* She thought about Sarah and felt even worse.

Oh bollocks to this, it's my bloody life! In a moment of pure defiance, she took the usual two capsules.

She is walking down a winding narrow lane, a thin ribbon of grey stone between the bright green foliage which liberally blankets the old stone walls beneath, hidden long ago from the sunlight. Wispy clouds hang here and there in an otherwise clear blue sky. There is the faintest hint of a breeze. Jennifer passes swathes of white cow parsley intermingled with the bright green leaves of sorrel and dock. Delicate red campions in full bloom sprinkle the lush hedgerow and here and there a hairy borage is to be found sporting its bright blue clusters. Bush vetch clamber through the other vegetation, their pinnate leaves like tiny ladders reaching towards delicate tendrils which curl and twist, cunningly holding tight.

The lightness in Jennifer's step echoes the lightness in her heart. She hums as she goes, occasionally brushing her hands through the flowers and turning to look back towards the rise of the road. She is full of expectation. Walking backwards for a few steps and gazing up the lane she is listening hard, thinking she has heard something. But it is only the shadow of a breeze, momentarily catching in the trees of a nearby woodland. She continues on her way.

The day is warm and she is wearing only a light silk shirt with her jeans. She feels the sun on her back and neck, comforting and caressing her skin. At last she hears the sounds she has been waiting for. The clip of metal on stone, the creaking of leather, the snorting of nostrils filled with the perfumed air. She smells a familiar scent of musty sweat, the essence of horse. Suddenly they are around her, prancing excitedly, circling, surrounding her, and she spins around and around in delight! She takes his outstretched arm with her right hand, placing her right foot in the abandoned stirrup and swings herself into the saddle behind him. She flings her arms around his waist and he gives her hands a squeeze. They turn left through a gateway and canter over rolling fields towards the woodland. She shrieks with joy and her rapture is carried in their wake to float above the pastures behind them, like an invisible mist.

At last they come to rest in a dappled glade by the edge of a wide stream. The water rushes excitedly between large, lichen-covered granite boulders, forming impatient eddies in quieter pools. Gnarled oaks line the banks, leaning towards each other over the water, their outstretched leafy branches protectively interwoven.

They alight and he leads his mare to the water for a well-deserved drink. Jennifer settles down on the mossy bank, leaning against a sturdy tree trunk, and studies him. The black of his denim jeans mirrors his hair, and his curls are again caught back with a black ribbon. His loose, coarsely-woven collarless shirt, tied roughly with thin cords at the neck, is part open, revealing little black curls of hair. He has the most beautiful finely-sculptured cheekbones complimented by a perfect straight nose, and there is just a hint of stubble. He turns to her and the smile he throws at her lights up his face. His blue eyes twinkle mischievously as he walks towards her.

He offers his hand and she takes it. He plants a gentle kiss on the back of hers before pulling her to her feet. She is surprised as she expects him to sit down beside her. He puts his hands on her shoulders and kisses her on the lips. His kisses grow stronger. Still engaging her lips, he slowly unbuttons her silk shirt and slips his hands around her waist inside the soft material. Jennifer's heart is beating wildly, so loudly she is afraid it can be heard for miles around. She is helpless, captivated. She is consumed by him. Her feet feel as if they are rooted to the spot on which they rest, whilst her body trembles wildly. He slips the silk off her shoulders and it floats to the ground. She kisses his head as he bends to kiss her breasts. The touch of his hands on her breasts, of his lips on her nipples, causes waves of arousal to wash through her. She feels light-headed, urgently *craving more and more of him. He is helping her out of her jeans and panties, removing his own clothes. He stretches the fingers of his right hand apart and places it flat against her chest. He runs it over her skin, in between her breasts, his fingers lightly brushing over her erect nipples, over her flat stomach, and rests it between her legs, cupping her gently in his palm. She gasps and tilts her head back slightly to abandon herself to him. He kisses her hard on the lips, but instead of entering her with his fingers as she anticipates, he removes his palm and grabs both her hands with his own, stepping backwards towards the river as he does so.*

Jennifer opens her eyes in surprise, but does as he silently bids. At once he is laughing and they are walking alongside the river, hand in hand. He leads her to a place where the babbling waters have quietened to a murmur, to a deep clear pool surrounded by rock. He is looking at her expectantly, and she nods her approval. They plunge into the icy water screaming in delightful shock. As they play, splashing each other, gasping as each new drop of water touches their quivering skin, they laugh and gasp alternately. The laughter lines around his eyes gather together as he grins at her and she throws herself upon him, tipping him off balance and dipping him underneath the surface. He splutters as he emerges, shaking his head to remove the water from his face. He is now lunging for her, catching her around the waist. 'Jenny,' he laughs, 'Jenny, I love you so much!' She kisses him quickly and they scramble out of the pool onto the bank. They are running back towards the glade, their bodies tingling, trembling, half with cold and half with excitement.

He is laying her down upon a bed of moss, and his touch again triggers waves of arousal in her. He takes her hand and places it around his rapidly-growing erection. He is hard and strong. Jennifer runs her fingers over the beautiful shaft, feeling him pulsating, quivering beneath her fingertips. She is aching for him. She takes him in her mouth, and her tongue induces quivers of ecstasy which radiate through his body, causing him to moan with the sensuousness of her touch. She is astride him now and they are one. Their love for one another is infinite and their simultaneous climax seals the bond between them.

They are lying entwined on the mossy bank in the afterglow. Jennifer feels complete. Waves of emotion are sweeping over her and a tear is starting to trickle down her cheek. 'You make me feel so alive, so happy!' she whispers. 'This is how I used to feel. This is how I want to feel. You complete me. I need you.'

'You can have me any time you want, you know that,' he says quietly. 'All you have to do is call for me. I can be anything you want.' He takes the ribbon from his pony tail and presses it into the palm of her right hand.

Just call for me… Just call for me… The words rang constantly in her head, which seemed to be frantically spinning. God, she felt terrible. Jennifer opened her eyes. The room was in semi-darkness, but she could make out the stone fireplace by the glint of light shining through a chink in the heavy drawn curtains onto the narrow brass surround of the black abandoned grate. She was in the living room. She lay quietly for a while trying to focus on something – anything – that wasn't moving. The spinning persisted, inducing nausea. Presently she managed to roll awkwardly off the sofa and stumbled across the carpet, falling against the far door, still feeling extremely dizzy. She felt for the light switch. Something soft brushed against her legs.

'Meooooow.' Smokey was desperate for something to eat. She meowed again and again as Jennifer sat down on the floor by the door to the kitchen, trying to get herself together, her chin supported and steadied in her cupped hands to prevent her head from drooping under its own incredible weight. She looked up at the wall clock. It was half past five.

'Hey Smokey, come here my love. What's the matter?' Jennifer mumbled through a blinding headache. Speaking was an effort and the words came out cracked, as if forced through broken eggshells. 'Anyone would think you were starving. I only fed you a few hours ago.' She tried briefly to cuddle the cat, who struggled from her arms and raced into the kitchen. Jennifer tried to follow and found that her legs were very weak. Eventually she managed to make it into the adjacent room by holding onto the furniture.

What the hell is the matter with me? she questioned. She was frightened. 'This is crazy,' she croaked, although she couldn't discern whether she had actually spoken out loud. *I must have dropped off for an hour or so. It must be those bloody pills.* As she filled the kettle for a reviving cup of coffee she glanced at the kitchen clock. It had a digital display giving the time, date and day. It read Sunday.

What? That can't be right! Her heart began to beat even faster and she was confused.

'Hang on a minute, ' she snapped uncharacteristically at Smokey, who was purring around her legs. 'Just wait a minute, will you?'

She walked slowly back into the living room and checked the date on the television handset. It was June the third. Sunday. Jennifer went cold. She'd been out for over twenty-four hours. No wonder the cat was starving and she felt so awful. How could she have been so stupid! She returned to the kitchen, sat down at the sturdy table with a cup of strong coffee, drank it as quickly as its temperature would allow and poured herself another. Then she fed Smokey a double portion to make up for the missed meals. She didn't feel much like eating anything herself; however, the nausea had subsided and she forced herself to make a piece of lightly buttered toast which she took into the living room along with her second cup of coffee.

Having imbibed the warm, comforting liquid and eaten the toast she began to feel a little stronger. She allowed her mind to wander over the events of the last twenty-four hours – not that she could remember anything except the dream. It was all so incredibly real. Surely she couldn't have imagined such a place? She was *sure* she'd been there. She was convinced that she could still feel his touch. He made her feel so wonderful inside. It felt as if he was still with her. How could that possibly be just a dream?

In truth she wanted to be back in her fantasy, and so it was comforting to think on it. He still had a grip on her and it was easier to float back towards him than to struggle free. She lay down on the sofa and tried to think what exactly it was that she sensed with him. He made her feel wanted, loved, beautiful. Above all, he made her feel *free*. Wild and free. He broke the chains of depression that bound her. He lifted her from under the great weight of loneliness and bitterness that had become her life. That was it! He *lifted* her. Her spirit was free when she was with him. Only with him did she have the confidence to be her true self. With him, she felt she could do anything, be anyone. He believed in her, and that gave her the confidence to believe in herself.

She lay there for some time, letting her mind float and lead her where it wanted to go, but after a while tentacles of the existing world began creeping into her thoughts, invading her privacy, curling themselves around her dreams and smothering them. The euphoria subsided. At last Jennifer began to realise what a dangerous thing she had done – she had been unconscious for twenty-four hours. This brought her down to earth pretty damn quickly. *You bloody fool*, she said crossly to herself. *For Christ's sake get a grip on reality.* She had finally really frightened herself.

She decided that she would give Sarah a ring later that morning, but in the meantime she still felt very weak. So she curled up in bed with the cat, who by this time had eaten her fill and forgiven her neglectful mistress. Jennifer dosed off to sleep, dreaming of nothing more than cuddling Smokey.

She woke at about 11.30, feeling much better but still a little weak. She felt really hungry now, so after a refreshing shower she busied herself with making bacon and eggs with warm crusty rolls, steaming coffee and some fresh orange juice.

As she beat two large duck eggs together with black pepper, garlic salt, chives, a little cream and lots of butter – a delicious recipe she'd inherited from her grandmother – Jennifer listened to the Sunday news on the radio and desperately tried to keep her body and mind together and in the present. As she sat down to her hearty breakfast she thought about what she was going to do at work the following week and made a mental plan of the major meetings she still had to arrange before the end of the summer. Jennifer decided to record a carefully-timed plan of work for the next few months and display it in a prominent place to remind her of her duties in the real world and keep her psyche firmly grounded. So why not start right now?

She jumped up from her plate to fetch a large piece of paper from her office upstairs. Between mouthfuls of the scrumptious meal Jennifer slowly drew up the chart.

When she'd finished and was satisfied with the result, she turned to Smokey. 'There, I'm going to keep to this and you're going to help by giving me lots of cuddles when I need them.'

She laughed, scooping up her cat and giving her a big hug. Smokey chirruped in her singular way.

Later that day Jennifer was giving the cottage a good clean and tidy when she found Smokey playing with something between two of the cushions on the sofa. 'Come here my love! What have you put down there, you silly old thing?' she laughed.

The cat continued to play, darting both her front paws between the cushions then rolling onto her back, still grasping at something. Jennifer put her hand down into the gap and pulled out something long and black.

It was the thin silk ribbon that he had taken from his hair and given to her.

She sat for a full ten minutes gazing at the ribbon. All manner of thoughts were somersaulting through her mind. She tried to dismiss them. An object couldn't just materialise from a dream – it had to belong to someone. She never wore ribbons and didn't possess any. Maybe it was Sarah's? No, that was silly. Sarah had short hair, and Jennifer had never seen her wear ribbons in her hair or anywhere else for that matter. However, to be quite sure she made a mental note to ask Sarah when they next spoke. Perhaps it had been dropped by someone else visiting the house. She thought this unlikely. She'd lived such a solitary life for the past few months that almost no-one had visited the house, not even local tradesmen. Her letterbox was at the front gate; the refuse collectors only needed to walk a little way down the side path to collect the bin, and the coal had only been delivered once so far, not long after she had moved into the cottage. As far as she knew none of these people had actually called at the cottage, and she had seen none wearing ribbons – in fact she was sure that one or two of the tradesmen would be highly affronted if they knew she had even contemplated them sporting such an item! She tried another idea for size: perhaps Smokey had picked it up from somewhere and brought it in? Yet it looked remarkably clean, not as though it had been outside in the dirt.

Jennifer picked up the ribbon, climbed the stairs and placed it carefully in the top right-hand drawer of her dressing table. As she held it she felt a curious tide of adrenaline which surged through her body, causing her heart to respond excitedly with accentuated energy. For some reason she felt thrilled. She was shaking. She returned to the living room and sat quietly for a few moments, taking deep breaths, trying for calm. The buzz in her body gradually subsided.

She caught sight of the work chart she had drawn up earlier and tried to shrug the whole incident off. *There's got to be a logical explanation for all of this,* she thought. Over the next days and weeks Jennifer fought hard to keep her grip on reality, or at least on what she thought was reality. The events of the next few months were to change all that.

⌒

At first Rob had offered Sarah an exhilarating lifestyle, with the worthy bonus of commitment and financial security. They ate in expensive restaurants; they enjoyed expensive skiing trips; they experienced white-water rafting in New Zealand, canoeing on the Amazon and mountain walking in Nepal. For a long while she was the envy of many girls at their respective workplaces. The attention was not something she had craved or even thought about. However she found herself experiencing a real thrill whenever they attended functions; walking into a room with her arm linked in his, sensing that they were being watched and commented upon by others. They did indeed make a striking couple. The time that she spent with him was incredibly exciting, and such a contrast to her everyday hardworking and dedicated professional life. They had so much fun together. He was such an amazing catch — she was so lucky! Or so she thought at the time. His sophisticated charm had curled itself around her, flattering and pampering, enveloping her in its allure, captivating her in its magnetic energy and lifting her gently off her feet so that she felt swept along by him, almost entranced. After a few months, when he'd asked her to live with him, she hadn't hesitated.

Rob worked long hours as an assistant director in a small but successful firm of insurance brokers in Oxford. He was clever and assiduous. His ambition was to become a director as quickly as possible and expand the company extensively within Europe. His family were wealthy, and consequently he had always enjoyed the best of everything their money could buy; private education, trips abroad with his parents from an early age, fine dining, membership of exclusive sport and health clubs, a social life fashioned around other such privileged families and, once he had reached the impetuous age of seventeen, a series of sports cars which he had variously written off in one reckless accident or another. There was always another car.

He and Sarah had agreed upon a large modern detached house on a quiet exclusive estate on the outskirts of the city. However, only a few months after they had set up home together she began to realise that she was seeing less and less of him as he spent more and more time at the office. When she gently complained about this he usually gave her a conciliatory hug while pointing out that everything he was doing – all his hard work – was for her, for them both. Security for the future – she wanted that, didn't she? Mollified, she would have to shrug her shoulders and abandon her quarrel with him. After all, she had become accustomed to a highly comfortable lifestyle and didn't particularly want to give that up.

As the months passed and their exciting exploits grew infrequent she grew significantly disheartened and had to try hard to convince herself that he really did love her. She longed for the raw excitement that had been the keystone of their relationship at its inception. And she yearned for those essential moments that sustain the love of two people through the daily round: that first long, luxurious morning kiss, the gentle touch of a hand on her cheek, his breath on her hair as they hugged, that certain smile, his arms around her waist as she tried to prepare the dinner; holding hands in the street.

On the increasingly rare occasions when they were able to spend quality time together, such as on a weekend away in Paris

or Amsterdam, he was extremely romantic, albeit in rather a tra-
ditional way. In an old-fashioned manner he would shower her
with flowers and gifts: *A rose for my lovely lady*; *Wear this ring for me,
darling, for eternity*; *Krug Grande Cuvée Brut Champagne, s'il vous plait!*
Under these circumstances she obviously couldn't resist him –
indeed why should she? He overwhelmed her so that she forgot
their mounting differences and the long hours she spent on her
own. Each time she would be swept off her feet again and made to
feel extremely special. She would fling her arms around him and
swear he was the one and only man she'd ever want and need and
that she would love him forever. She would almost forget to notice that he no longer actually spoke those three tiny but weighty
words – *I love you.*

However, once home his mood would change and he would disappear into his study. 'I just want to catch up on a few things, I'll be
down in a minute, ' he would invariably say, and she wouldn't see him
for the rest of the evening. Later she might gently try to persuade him
to stop working. 'Rob, darling, come and relax for a while. You've
been working for ages. You must be tired *after the weekend*, ' she would
raise her eyebrows provocatively, 'come and keep me company downstairs. There's a good film on.'

However, her persuasion would not remove him from his study.
'Sarah, ' he would reply in a firm tone, ignoring her pleas, 'now
come on, don't spoil a lovely weekend. You know how hard I have to
work to make these weekends possible. Please stop nagging. Go and
watch the film, I'll be down later.' She would inevitably end up going to bed alone, feeling slightly guilty about the amount of money
he had lavished upon her – which he was always sure to inform her
of – while knowing that the increasingly mundane ritual of their
daily lives had begun again.

Eventually the periods between sharing any kind of excitement or romance grew longer and longer and the time they spent
alone together shrank almost into oblivion. In a little over eighteen
months they had practically become two people simply living in the
same house.

'Okay Rob, see you later then.' Sarah closed the front door behind her and jumped into her Triumph Stag, a legacy from her favourite uncle which she greatly treasured, not least because it reminded her of him.

She was off to the gym for one of her twice-weekly sessions. Rob played in a squash league at his club, but Sarah wasn't up to his standard so they didn't play together. She worked out at a local health club which had a luxurious spa with a swimming pool, two saunas at different temperatures, a steam room, a jacuzzi and a sun shower. She found a lucky space in front of the entrance, parked the car and ran up the steps into the club.

'Hi Jo!'

A tall girl with short brown hair, clothed in a green tracksuit and sporting a bright multi-coloured sweatband, looked up from behind the reception desk.

'Hi there, Sarah! Had a good weekend?'

'So-so. Nothing exciting. Hey, I'm going for a swim after the gym tonight and I'm going to finish off in the sun shower. I'm really treating myself this evening!'

'Well! You're really pushing the boat out tonight, ' laughed Jo, giving Jennifer some tokens. 'Why don't you try out our massage some time if you want to really treat yourself?'

'Maybe I will, maybe I will, ' Sarah smiled thoughtfully. To her, a massage conjured up memories of a small hot room with dark wallpaper, incense burning in one corner and a sizeable woman with arms of steel chopping merry hell out of her legs and back, or else a bright clinical room containing a number of hard benches, lots of white towels and a team of stringent Swedish women acting equally roughly. She'd had only two massages and this, unfortunately, was the sum of her experience. She preferred to be the one to give her body hell!

She slipped into a pair of black Lycra leggings and a turquoise leotard, checked herself in the mirror — you never knew who might be in there — and entered the gym. It comprised two rooms on slightly different levels joined by a short wide flight of steps. In one room were the weights and in the other, the aerobic exercising machines. She headed for the step machine, briefly checking her weight first. She was aiming for about twenty minutes on one piece of equipment, but right now she usually split the time equally between the steps and the running machine. After a couple of minutes she increased the pace, treading her way steadily up though the floors: twenty, thirty, fifty, eighty – she was aiming for a hundred to start this session off with. Stepping done and target achieved, she went through to the weights room, did a few stretching exercises and began with the pull-over to exercise her upper back and shoulders. After forty repetitions she moved on to the bench press and did forty sit-ups with the board hooked over the third rung up from the floor so that her legs were higher than her head. That really got her stomach muscles working!

She rested briefly, looking around her at her fellow gym-goers. There were a couple of girls in one corner who were plastered in makeup and hadn't worked up a sweat in case it looked uncool. They seemed to be making eyes at an Italian-looking guy with chest hair exuding from under his tiny white vest. A small gold coin dangled on a chain around his neck and he was flexing his muscles, pretending not to notice the girls. He really fancies himself, thought Sarah. On the other side of the room was a weedy guy with slightly protruding teeth whose legs looked like a couple of pieces of string hanging from his shorts. To give him his due, he was pretty fit. Sarah always had to decrease the number of weights by eight or nine if she followed him on the equipment. And there in the other corner was the man who seemed to sweat copiously just by looking at the weights and whose unfortunate aroma trailed him like the tendons of a Portuguese man o' war, catching others in its wake. Sarah shuddered involuntarily.

The scene wasn't all bad, though. She was looking out for a couple of the instructors who managed to match their fine-toned muscular bodies with beautiful faces. They weren't always around, but she'd seen them a few times. They were both tall and tanned. One had blonde curly hair and a pair of verdant eyes twinkling beneath his long fringe. The other wore his dark brown hair short and well-cut, which perfectly complimented his piercing blue eyes. She liked the look of them both, but had not yet managed to strike up a conversation with either beyond the usual pleasantries.

She had rested for a minute or two and so went back into the second room to use the running machine. Having relatively short legs she couldn't run particularly far in ten minutes; however the exercise was good, and it helped her to maintain toned leg muscles. She started off at a steady ten kilometres per hour. Once into a steady pace, Sarah examined herself in the mirrored wall in front of her. She had a flat stomach and well-developed but firm breasts which softened her solid shoulders and chest. As she jogged her breasts swayed slightly from side to side under her figure-hugging leotard, which was high-cut, creating the helpful appearance of longer legs. She figured she needed all the help she could get in that department. She liked the way her breasts moved. She had large nipples which stood out in all weathers. They were standing to attention now, caressed by the slight movement of the Lycra over them.

Someone else had noticed the way that her breasts moved and came over for a closer look. He stopped short, deciding to wait until she'd finished running before trying to start a conversation. You can't talk to someone whilst every breath is being whisked away with the effort of keeping the pace going. Hmm, she was a lovely little thing. He'd noticed her here before, but his duty roster hadn't often coincided with her sessions. Anyhow, he was certainly enjoying the sight of her now. Many of the girls came to the gym dressed to pull, but when you talked to them they didn't seem to have much imagination or charisma. Sure, they were attractive, but they weren't really interested in the fitness programmes they asked him to set them. They would flutter their eyelashes and giggle and pretend fascination; however, more often than not they were trying to outdo one another. It was like being handed it on a plate. He'd taken advantage of this a few times, he had to admit, but had soon been bored; they were all the same. But this girl was different. She seriously put a hell of a lot of effort into each exercise and looked great on it, and you couldn't shovel the makeup off her face! Great breasts too! Were those nipples for real? He felt the familiar warm sensation between his legs as he started to throb involuntarily. It was a good job he was wearing a tracksuit today instead of his Lycra cycling shorts.

She slowed the running track down to a halt and bent over to get her breath and steady her legs.

'Hi! You did well there, better than last time, ' he guessed.

She turned round to face the voice. It belonged to the gorgeous guy with the green eyes.

'Hi, ' she grinned. 'Not bad today. Seven out of ten, could do better.'

'No, I think you're doing really well, I've noticed you in the weights room; you have a good technique and you've not been coming here that long, have you?'

'A few months, ' Sarah replied.

'Well, keep up the good work, ' he said, and turned away to deal with someone in the other room.

Sarah's eyes followed him. She felt half excited, half disappointed. Was that it? Still, he'd spoken to her first, so that was something. She came down to earth again when she thought about meeting Rob for a drink after her session. She looked at her watch; it was time for the swim. As she was fairly tired she eased herself gently into the near-empty pool and swam a few slow easy lengths. First one stroke, then another. She was lucky tonight: there weren't many people around. A few more lengths to relax her muscles and she would be off to the sun shower for fifteen minutes. She looked forward to its warm rays caressing her skin and soothing her muscles.

As she glided through the water he watched her from the coach's balcony. His eyes never left her as she pulled herself out of the pool and walked its length towards the changing rooms.

Her atmosphere of calm relaxation changed as she sipped her beer.

'Don't look at me like that, darling. Come on now, be reasonable. This trip is important both to me and to the company.'

She continued sipping in silence, glaring over the top of her pint glass at him.

'Sarah, for once in your life stop being so bloody selfish!' He slammed his hand down on the table. People stared.

'For Christ's sake keep your voice down, ' she hissed. This was their local and it mattered how they behaved in public. She was not to be made to look a fool or embarrassed in front of anyone. Her anger and frustration were rising; this was the time to depart and settle the argument at home. He always won in the end, but she was being pushed further and further each time. When would she snap? She put down her beer.

'I think we should go home, ' she said quietly. They went out to the car in silence, both slamming their doors as they got in. He drove the seven-minute journey home, both of them going over things in their minds – things they wanted to say, things they thought but knew they could not say. As they entered the house, he first, he turned round to face her.

'You think you're so damn smart, you try and earn the money to pay this mortgage and keep us in this lifestyle. Functions, dinners, drinks parties. What the hell do you expect from me? It takes more than a few hours looking at some goddamn water sample report to bring home what I do.'

Incensed, Sarah tried to interrupt.

'And don't interrupt. I haven't finished. That's another thing you do so well, darling, ' he said sarcastically, 'you never bloody listen to me. Too busy with what *you* have to say – well you can fucking listen now 'cause I've had it up to here with you this time.'

Sarah clenched her fists until her nails dug into her palms. He'd gone completely over the top as usual.

'I have to make this trip because it's vital for our links with the continent and our plans to expand depend on it. What the hell is so unreasonable about that? You know my work often takes me away for a few days. So what is your fucking problem?'

Sarah was angry; really angry. Who the hell did he think he was, talking to her like that, demeaning her job and the part she played in their relationship?

'You think all I care about is the fucking money, ' she cried. 'You've got such a bloody high opinion of yourself, haven't you? And just because I don't earn as much as you, don't think I don't work bloody hard because I do. And my job is important to me too, but it doesn't take over my life completely to the exclusion of everything else. Oh, you love your trips away, don't you? How many is it this month already – four, five? What's so bloody important that they can't send someone else for a change – or is it that you volunteer every time? Any particular reason for that, is there?'

'Oh, I see now, ' he shouted as he walked towards her. 'Are you accusing me of having it off with someone else? Are you... are you?' His face was two inches from hers. Angry beads of sweat appeared on his forehead. 'My God, you don't even trust me any more.'

'Well you must be giving it to someone 'cause I sure as hell don't get it any more. All you ever give me is money.' She turned away from him and he caught her arm.

'You ungrateful bitch, ' he said, 'I work my ass off for us both and you throw it back in my face.'

He let go of her arm, turned around and walked out of the room. Sarah heard the front door slam. She hadn't meant it to go this way. She hadn't meant to accuse him of sleeping with someone else, but she was bitter at him for so many things and the words had just come out wrong. She didn't want his damn money. She wanted him. The old him. Him the way he used to be with her. But she was damned if she was going to tell him that after he'd talked to her like he had. No, let him stew for a while. When they'd both calmed down they could discuss things again calmly and she could tell him how she really felt.

However, he didn't come back that Friday night. She wasn't worried. *He's sulking with one of his mates*, she thought. When he didn't appear all the next day she phoned his office. *No-one there, so he's not working. I'm not ringing around his friends*, she thought defiantly. When he didn't appear all night and wasn't around on the Sunday morning either Sarah began to worry and phoned his boss.

'Hello, Oxford treble three, five, one, seven, ' said a smooth female voice.

'Oh hello, Mary, its Sarah here. Look, I don't suppose Rob has been round to see James this weekend?'

'No, I don't think so, Sarah. Is everything okay?'

Sarah hesitated. 'Yes, I just wanted to check when his meeting in Switzerland was, only I've been away.'

'Hold on one moment, I'll just check with James.'

Sarah waited. She could picture Mary on a Sunday morning, her hair neatly fixed in a French pleat, dressed smartly for church in a lightweight summer suit or skirt and silk blouse. Always calm, always organised; a well-managed large house and garden, children grown up and at college. The perfect wife of a successful insurance broker! Sarah looked down at her crumpled T-shirt and leggings. Would she ever make anyone a perfect wife? Would she ever want to?

'Hello, Sarah? Yes Rob and Susan left early Saturday morning for Geneva. They're due back on Thursday.'

Sarah thanked Mary and put the phone down. Susan was Rob's secretary. Well, she shared her with the other assistant director. *Though not in the biblical sense*, thought Sarah grimly. Did Susan go on all Rob's trips abroad? She was quite pretty; medium height – tall enough to look slender but not aggressively lofty – with a delicate face which was framed by shoulder-length dark brown hair with a reddish tinge that was straight and neatly cut. She always looked as if she'd just come out of the hairdressers. She was young and unattached. *It's easy to be impressed by the boss*, *just like I was*, Sarah mused, *especially when he looks like Rob*. She wondered why they had gone to Geneva on a Saturday. Her mind started to work overtime as sticky tendrils of suspicion grew around her thoughts, shading them its own dark hue.

July

Sarah came to stay in July. She and Rob had decided to give themselves time to think about their relationship by having a short break from one another. He had denied any improper behaviour, stating simply that they'd had some extra meetings to fit in. Sarah wasn't sure whether she could believe him. So it was agreed that she would visit Jennifer for a couple of weeks. She didn't know what Rob was going to do – whether he was intending to take any time off or to continue working. He seemed keen to carry on at work. In any case, he'd promised to ring her.

The girls had planned to spend some days exploring the North York Moors and the Yorkshire Dales and some days relaxing around the cottage and garden, reading the papers, drinking wine, eating nice meals and generally having an easy time. They loved one another's company and talked a great deal, Jennifer about her work, her life at the cottage, her past life with Jim, her hopes for the future, her dreams and the recent events with the sleeping tablets, and Sarah about her problems with Rob, her fears, her work and her encounters at the gym. Each listened carefully to the other, giving support and encouragement. Each tried to cleanse bad feelings and to build upon positive thoughts.

They had enjoyed exploring further afield. They had covered a wide area from Settle to Hawes, Ingleton to Pately Bridge, driven through most of the Dales and across the moors from Hutton-le-Hole to Whitby. On the longer journeys Sarah had driven them in her Stag, which was a real treat for Jennifer. They had followed countless narrow winding roads which turned this way and that, up and down, weaving their way along the sides of the Dales and every now and then crossing the rivers running through the valley bottoms before traversing the hillsides.

Sarah decided that she liked Swaledale best of all, its fertile wide valley bottom at the Richmond end becoming narrower and narrower, the hillsides becoming increasingly steep. Dry stone walls segmented the pastureland, which was dotted regularly with stone barns and liberally sprinkled with sheep. As they drove the length of the dale, little villages with wonderful names like Crackpot, Oxnop and Muker appeared every now and then along the sides of the river Swale. They drove over beck and bridge, alongside plantation and enclosure and past countless farms – Barney Beck, Scabba-Wath Bridge, Doll Gill Plantation, Friar Intake, Turnip House, Nettlebed,

Duckingdub Bridge and Doctor Wood. They even passed a Bleak House. It was truly delightful.

They moved slowly through the countryside with the soft top of the Stag pulled back so that they could fully appreciate the wonderful scenery, stopping to explore clusters of stone cottages and little shops or to picnic by a river where the road came suddenly upon it, sharing their sandwiches and fruit with the sheep and birds. But on the way home along the major roads Sarah would put on some loud up-beat music from her eclectic collection – Pearl Jam, Lenny Kravitz, Tom Petty, Muse, Kings of Leon, the White Stripes – whatever suited their mood, and they would sing at the tops of their voices, the wind whisking away the words to be lost forever amongst the Yorkshire hills.

After a few days Sarah had made some decisions. With Jennifer's help and encouragement she had examined her life and questioned what made her happy and when she was most unhappy, what caused her stress and when she felt content. Away from Rob, she realised how much she valued being able to make her own decisions. She was surprised at the extent of liberation that she felt. She began to realise that he regarded her as merely as an extension of himself – a fashion accessory when it suited. And she had become just that. Only her work made her independent of him. Being with Jennifer and having had time to step outside her life for a while, she now felt calm and strangely satisfied. Things in her life would have to change.

It was the Thursday of the second week.

'Hey Sarah, do you fancy going to have a look round the Fernleigh Estate today? It's only up the road, and the grounds are pretty amazing.'

'Yes, why not? It seems as though we've been to half of Yorkshire already! It'll be good to see something a little closer to home today.'

'Well, I didn't think you ought to go without seeing it, especially as this cottage was once part of the estate. I've been round the grounds before but I haven't been in the house yet. Some of the houses in the village still belong to the Fernleigh family.'

'Eh up! Do we have to doff our caps on t' way in?' Sarah joked. 'I'd better practice my curtsey. Pleasure to meet you, M'Lady.'

'Yeah, yeah. This one doesn't belong to the estate now you know. But I'll tell you what – one of the terraced cottages at the far end of the village is still rented by an old lady, I think she's in her late nineties, who worked as a chambermaid up at the house in the 1920s and '30s. She still pays the same rent as she paid when she worked there. Something to do with the Rent Act, I think.'

'That's amazing!' Sarah laughed. 'Does she still pay in groats?'

They entered the grounds through the large sandstone southern gateway. Beyond them lay a straight road rising slightly to the top of the low hill on which Fernleigh house stood. To their left was a large lake with several small floating islands in the centre and one larger island on the western side. Waxwings and warblers nested among the dense trees and shrubs which clung to the surface of the islands and each was encircled by reeds, from which reed bunting and marsh harrier darted and returned, and the occasional heron could be seen. On the shimmering water little chains of swans, moorhens and grebes cautiously paraded their young.

The house itself was very grand. Built, unusually for the period, in the Baroque style, it consisted of two large rectangular one-storey wings joined by a narrower three-storey centre, six bays wide, of local stone. The two main facades of the house faced north and south, and each was decorated with a series of pilasters between the central Venetian-style window and the surrounding arched windows. A series of stable buildings lay adjacent to the east wing, and the west wing had been extended to encompass a further kitchen block and courtyard. A pair of sweeping flights of steps, magnificently edged with a stone balustrade, curved convexly from a central doorway in the south facade to the formal gardens below, beyond which lay a softer landscape, leading the eye down to the lake.

The girls entered through this central doorway to find themselves in an immense hall reaching up through all three floors to a beautifully-decorated ceiling. Balconies ran along all sides on the first and second storeys and a huge staircase bordered by wrought-iron balustrades swept towards the ground floor, seemingly landing at their feet.

They paid the fee and Jennifer found herself buying a brochure. Probably a waste of money, she thought as she handed over a ten-pound note.

They caught up with a guided tour in the music room and surreptitiously joined its ranks for a while, straining to hear what Mrs Twinset-and-pearls was saying.

'... and married her in 1731, being his only son-in-law, thereby inheriting the estate in 1736 when her father died, ' she recited in a monotone. 'Her father had already commissioned the construction of this grand new house in his northern estate in 1713, engaging the services of one Captain Vanburgh to make the designs' – here she nodded at her audience knowingly as if all should realise the significance of employing this particular architect, as indeed most of them did. 'The building took eleven years to complete.' The guide went on to recite the order in which various parts of the house had been built and the associated costs.

Why doesn't she make it more interesting? Jennifer wondered. There was so much life she could probably bring to a telling of the history of a place like this. She and Sarah caught one another's eyes and tried not to giggle. Jennifer turned her attention to a blue-and-white-striped upholstered cabriole armchair. The brochure attributed the chair to Chippendale.

'... and the rococo ceiling, in pale blue and white, was redecorated in 1759 and dates from that time.' The guide drew breath and continued quickly. 'Moving over to the doorway...' Jennifer lost interest and instead moved over to the splendid walnut harpsichord placed by one of the windows. The inscription above the two-stage keyboards read *Thomas Hitchcock, Londini, Fecit.* The blurb in the brochure mentioned the date as *ca 1725* and that keyboards such as this were a speciality of the Hitchcock family. Jennifer longed to place her fingers on the keys. Although she did not have a piano at the moment, she'd had lessons as a teenager and had tried to keep her standard up at college, using the practice rooms occasionally when music students happened to be scarce. It would have been too embarrassing to have been heard by someone talented! Jennifer felt an odd sense of familiarity standing in the corner by this wonderful instrument. She could imagine sitting here on this stool in an elegant gown, tinkling on the keys, and afterwards a group of handsome acquaintances, equally well-dressed, politely acknowledging her talent with dainty applause.

Jennifer and Sarah slipped away from the tour, preferring now to make their own way. They wandered through the public rooms in silent reverence, admiring their splendid grandeur. Both felt they were somehow reaching back into history, as if they could simply touch a doorway or a tapestry and become a part of the living history of the place. But, strangely, Jennifer also now began to feel a strong sense of intrusion, as if for some odd reason she shouldn't be walking through these grand rooms.

She left Sarah admiring a table top made from pieces of mosaic from Pompeii and hurried into the next room. It was then that it happened.

He looked at her through ice-blue eyes. He was standing slightly sideways with one foot placed on a footstool and wearing a powdered dress wig. Its mane of curls rose high on his forehead and tumbled to above his ears, the remainder being tied back with a black ribbon. A richly-flowered satin waistcoat fell over plain breeches, its skirt descending to mid-thigh. His coat, a heavy brocade embroidered in gold, was equally splendid. Its skirt, falling open over his raised leg, was the same length as the waistcoat. His shoe buckles seemed to glisten, setting off the rest and matching the glint in his eyes. It was unmistakably *him*. HIM! The man that persisted in appearing in her dreams. The man her imagination had conjured up — *hadn't it?*

Jennifer stared back, transfixed, her heart racing. It seemed as if he was looking straight at her — *her*, and no-one else. As if this glorious portrait had been painted for no other reason but this moment. The room she was standing in melted away, along with the people in it; she was transported to the room in the painting.

'*A pretty likeness, do you not think, Miss?*'

'*Aye sir, the subject does greatly benefit your canvas. 'Tis an agreeable reflection!*'

Another voice, this time strangely familiar: '*On your way, Miss, be-fore I am quite overcome with immodesty!*'

A hand on Jennifer's shoulder made her jump, breaking her from her thoughts. She whipped around. It was Sarah.

'Jeez, Sarah! You made me jump!'

'Jennifer, what's wrong? You look as if you've seen a ghost. Are you OK?'

Jennifer hesitated. 'Oh, er... yes, yes I'm fine... I think. Look, do you mind if I meet you outside? I'm feeling a bit dizzy in here. It's probably the heat; this room's quite stuffy.'

'Yeah, sure. Do you want me to come with you? You look pretty pale.'

'No, it's alright. I'll be fine. I just need some fresh air. You finish looking round, and I'll meet you outside by that statue of the boar, you know – on the lawn opposite the tea room.'

'Well, if you're sure you'll be OK. I won't be long.' Sarah kissed Jennifer on the cheek and walked off into the next room.

Jennifer took another look at the painting. She moved closer and peered at the plate beneath. *William Fernleigh, by Sir Joshua Reynolds (1723-92), thought to have been painted 1762.* In a daze, she read the accompanying information before finding her way out of the house. On reaching the little wooden seat overlooking a magnificent stone statue of a boar held on high by a tall pedestal she burst into tears and then immediately felt silly. She didn't understand why she felt like this, but she was experiencing a mixture of shock, excitement and incomprehension. The one thing she felt certain of was that the man in the portrait and the man who came to her in her dreams were one and the same.

'How *can* you know this?' she said out loud. 'This is just stupid!' she chided herself.

Just then, Sarah appeared with two ice creams. 'Here you go – thought this might buck you up a bit, ' she laughed as she handed one of the cornets to Jennifer. 'You feeling better now? You've got the colour back in your cheeks!'

'Yes thanks, ' Jennifer lied. 'Mmm, this is nice – banana, my favourite!' She tried for a smile but the shock seemed to have pulled at her features, which were fixed in a look of incredulity. 'Look Sarah, I've just got to tell you something. Promise you won't laugh at me?'

She told Sarah what she'd seen and how she felt. Sarah listened patiently, her scientific mind quietly and logically analysing Jennifer's words, operating in the background and computing possible explanations.

'D'you think you could have seen the picture before somewhere, and then perhaps your memory's been triggered in your sleep?' Sarah asked softly and tactfully.

Jennifer screwed up her nose a little, her head to one side in the pose of someone conveying on-going memory-sifting. 'I suppose it's possible – in the paper, perhaps.' After some moments more she shook her head. 'Y' know, I *honestly* don't think I've seen that portrait before.'

'Well, how about another painting of him?' Sarah continued to probe thoughtfully. 'If he was one of the Fernleighs there must be other portraits hanging around somewhere. Have you ever been to the house before, even as a child?' Sarah indelicately licked the fingers of her right hand, over which the ice cream had melted.

'No, never, ' Jennifer replied, this time with surety. 'In fact none have ever been displayed before. I read the information in the brochure – look here. It's a bit odd actually, ' she continued, thumbing quickly through the pages of the glossy guide that was balanced on her knees to find the relevant page while trying not to cover it with rapidly liquefying ice cream. 'It says that the portrait of William Fernleigh was recently discovered concealed under the floorboards in one of the family bedrooms.' Jennifer pointed to the article. 'Once they cleaned it up and authenticated the artist's mark they put it on display. That was only four months ago. No other portraits of him are known to exist!'

As Sarah bent her head to read the text the late afternoon sunshine illuminated the tips of her mousse-fashioned hair, giving her the appearance from above of an albino hedgehog. There was no picture accompanying the piece, which was no doubt a deliberate endeavour to bring inquisitive visitors to Fernleigh Hall to view the painting for themselves.

'Well...' Sarah curled her lips inwards in thought, willing some perfectly sensible explanation to come to mind, but nothing else came to her. Eventually she said slowly, 'If you've never seen this picture before, and there aren't any others known to be in existence, and you're sure he looks exactly like the man in your recurring dreams... well then, I suppose...' She gave up and shook her head. 'I don't know — what does it mean? A huge coincidence?' This was an unsatisfactory conclusion to Sarah's thought processes, but more realistic than trying to read something that did not exist into the scenario.

Jennifer found herself feigning agreement. 'Yeah, I guess so. What other explanation is there?' She was not at all convinced.

'I honestly don't know, but if you say you've been dreaming about *this* man then I believe you. I'm sure we could easily find out whether any pictures of this fella William have been released to the public since the painting was discovered. That wouldn't be difficult. And if so, we could put your mind at rest, ' Sarah concluded. 'Look, how about we go home, get the dinner in the oven, then go for a drink at that nice pub, you know, in the next village, ' Sarah said brightly, changing the subject. 'The Farmers Arms? And we can talk more about it there.'

'Yeah! That sounds like a good idea. Come on, last one back to the car buys the first round, ' Jennifer responded positively, trying to shake off the likeness in the portrait and the sensuous images in her mind of herself and this dark stranger together.

Sitting in the pretty pub garden, bathed in the still-warm late evening sunshine, the afternoon's events seemed to have less significance for Jennifer. She concluded that she must have seen a local newspaper article about the discovery of the painting and completely forgotten about it. All the same, she decided that she would investigate a little.

The two women spent the next couple of days relaxing in the hot July sunshine, reading, talking and sunbathing, savouring each other's company before Sarah had to return home. However, their time together and recent events had permanently etched their mark on both women, albeit in different ways.

Jennifer could not forget that face — the beautiful features of William Fernleigh, whose piercing blue eyes had stared out at her from the canvas as though they could see into her very soul. She had to find out more about him. She was even contemplating trying to conjure him up, willing herself to dream about him.

The powder had been ignited; the shot, fired from fate's pistol, was already speeding down the barrel, the impact and ensuing consequences inevitable.

July 1762

'*H*appy birthday, Will.'

'Charlotte!' William turned around in surprise. 'I did not know that you and James were able to come today. Mama did not tell me. Now I suspect that it was on purpose. You look a picture. Come here and give your favourite brother a kiss!'

'My only brother, ' laughed Charlotte, 'though I believe if I had another you would most certainly be the favourite.'

'Such flattery. Would that I were flattered in the same manner. Alas, I am only the husband!'

'James, welcome, ' William said warmly. 'How are you?'

'Soon to return to Portugal, I'm afraid, though between you and me I think it will not be long before the Spanish are defeated. Havana has been captured and Choiseul will come running like a dog with his tail between his legs.'

'Who is Choiseul, and why does he have a tail?' asked a small voice.

'Elizabeth! Hello, come and give your uncle a kiss.' The child ran to hug her sister and uncle in turn.

'So you want to hear about the man with a tail between his legs, do you?'

'James, remember she is only thirteen, ' whispered Charlotte, 'she knows little of these matters.' James winked at his wife and turned to Elizabeth.

'Choiseul is the French foreign minister, ' he explained. 'He negotiated a treaty last year which protects all the Bourbon family territories in Spain, Italy and France.'

'What does that mean?' asked Elizabeth.

'Well it means that King Carlos of Spain and Louis of France formed an alliance, which is why Spain declared war on us earlier this year. And that is why, my little peach, I go to Portugal to save it from the Spanish!' He made two pretend cuts and a lunge with an invisible sword. 'One, two, three.'

'The tail, ' William whispered.

'Oh yes, I had quite forgotten. Have you ever seen a frightened dog, Elizabeth?'

'I saw two dogs fighting near the stables, ' she replied.

'Well, did the loser have his tail between his legs?'

She nodded.

'That's your answer then, ' said James. 'Now we had better go and find your mother.'

'Oh, Mama!' Elizabeth clasped her hands across her mouth, abashed. 'I was sent to tell you that Mama is in the orange house and wishes to see you on your arrival.'

'Until dinner then.' William bowed and kissed Charlotte's hand.

'And then you shall have my gift, ' Charlotte laughed, and went off in search of her mother.

As he dressed for dinner, Will's thoughts were of Emily. This was his birthday and he had not yet managed to speak with her alone. He must see her tonight. He had something of great importance to say to her. James had earlier confirmed the rumours he had heard and he was greatly pleased to hear the good news. With the Spanish defeated, Choiseul would have to come to terms with Bute, and that meant peace between England and France, which was vital for the success of William's plan. He knew that at this moment Emily would be attending his mother. He must try and whisper a few words to her before dinner.

His mother had organised a splendid dinner in his honour this evening. They were celebrating his birthday, but also the grand opening of the new dining room, the redesign and refurbishment of which had been completed in the last few days. This task had occupied his mother for a considerable time and she was very proud of what had been accomplished and could not wait to show it off. There would be many important guests attending: politicians, lawyers, physicians and other noblemen – even the Bishop of York had been invited. This evening would be special in many ways.

Emily rolled a strand of her mistress's soft brown hair expertly through the fingers of her left hand, following the movement with the rose-engraved silver-backed comb in her right hand. Charlotte's hair was beautifully shiny and smelled wonderfully of orange and cinnamon, having had the fortnightly wash with soap earlier in the day and been treated with scented vinegar to counteract the effects of the soap. She had long hair to the middle of her back and only a few grey hairs, so there was no need to employ hairpieces or, thankfully, to use powder to cover the grey or blend wig with hair. Charlotte much preferred to realise her hairstyles naturally and show off her natural beauty. Indeed, for a woman of two-score years she was beautiful. Emily looked at her mistress in the large oval mirror before them. Will had Charlotte's eyes and well-defined bone structure.

'How would you like your hair styled today, my lady?' Emily asked Charlotte's reflection.

'I fancy your pompadour a little too formal for tonight Emily. I think I should like something a touch more extravagant. After all, tonight is special, ' Charlotte sighed happily. 'I have been so looking forward to this evening! What do you think? Shall we have the Hängelöckchen?'

'I think that would be most appropriate, ma'am, ' Emily beamed. She loved working with her mistress's hair, and the more complicated the style the better. 'Perhaps a few more ribbons than usual? I ordered an extra length of yellow silk ribbon to match the primrose contouche you will be wearing this evening, ' Emily suggested.

'What a clever girl you are. That will be perfect!' Charlotte responded enthusiastically.

Emily set to work dividing Charlotte's hair into a front portion and several portions on each side, then placed and fastened a padded roll across the top of her head so that a roll of hair at the front was expertly caught and raised above her mistress's forehead. She then began rolling each side portion around her left index finger, tying it back and fastening it neatly to the middle of the pad until she had four gathered rolls on each side.

Emily hummed to herself quietly as she worked, occasionally stopping and bending her head this way and that for a better view of her handiwork, to catch a stray wisp of hair or to ensure perfect symmetry. Engaged in her own thoughts, she was unaware that Charlotte was gazing at her intently. Her mistress's voice broke her rhythm.

'My dear Emily, how expertly you work, ' she said appreciatively.

Emily looked up and smiled. 'Thank you, M'Lady.'

As Emily returned to her task and her thoughts of Will, Charlotte continued. 'You know, my dear, how important you are to me.'

Emily blushed and looked up, a little startled.

'Ever since you came to us you have worked hard and striven to please. And please you certainly have, and you must know it, ' Charlotte stated.

Emily nodded slightly and thanked her again. 'You are very kind, my lady. Some would not convey their satisfaction at a job well done, but you always do and for that alone I am ever grateful. Although there is *so* much more that I am grateful for, ' Emily added, her voice low and serious.

Charlotte smiled kindly and, in an unguarded moment, divulged her deeper thoughts. 'I suppose I consider you more than a lady's maid. I value your companionship.' She paused. 'Were it not for protocol, I could regard you as my companion.'

Emily lowered her eyes and tried to continue rolling the middle portions of Charlotte's hair around small woollen pads in an arbitrary fashion at the back of her head. Her eyes started to fill with tears but she fought them back.

'I am so honoured that you would think of me so, ' she managed to whisper hoarsely.

Detecting the break in Emily's voice, Charlotte spun around, sending one of the woollen rolls under the dressing table. Emily bent to pick it up, taking the chance to quickly wipe her eyes lest a stray tear should escape. The emotions boiling within her vied with each other to be given release as steam from a kettle left on the stove for too long. She truly loved her ladyship, and to be spoken to thus was a tremendous compliment. She did not know what she had done to deserve it. She felt it an honour to be allowed to spend so much time in Charlotte's company, let alone to be considered a kind of companion. Emily knew that the status of her birth would keep her a lady's maid and she would never expect anything else, *should* never expect more – but what of her and Will? How would this play out?

As Emily straightened up, Charlotte laid a hand on her arm. 'Do not upset yourself on account of my words, ' she responded gently.

'Thank you, M'Lady. But I am not... upset exactly... just... so... well, so *pleased*, ' Emily returned carefully, guarding those thoughts that could not be revealed, at least not for now. 'Though I am sure I really do not know that I deserve such high praise.'

'We talk a great deal, ' Charlotte retorted, 'and you read very well. Indeed your reading is extraordinarily soothing.'

Charlotte leant forward slightly towards the mirror, as if to share a confidence. 'Forgive me – and you must not breathe a word of this – but you surpass my daughters on that score! Anne is so impatient and gallops ahead of her words; Elizabeth does well for her age, but has not the inclination – she'd rather be outside playing with the dogs if truth be told, and Rebecca... well, Rebecca asks so many questions that we barely get through a passage uninterrupted!' Charlotte laughed.

Emily laughed too, an image coming into her mind of Rebecca questioning the motives of Hamlet and getting frustrated at Romeo's impatience to be with his beloved – *Why couldn't he have waited a little longer? Could not he have sensed the blood moving in her veins!*

'If my reading is to your liking, ma'am, it is you who have taught me and to you that I entirely owe this compliment, ' Emily replied quietly.

'Forgive me. I have embarrassed you.' Charlotte smiled, returning her gaze to the mirror once more. 'Let us return our thoughts to the process in hand. How comes it?'

'I am just about to make the curls at your neck, my lady, and then have only the top to do.'

Emily curled the long strands at either side of Charlotte's neck with the curling irons and finished off the rolls above her forehead. She had incorporated several small silk roses and strands of yellow ribbon into the design, and the whole endeavour now looked very pretty indeed. She took a silver-backed hand mirror from the dressing table and showed her mistress the back. Charlotte clasped her hands together in delight and uttered a small gasp.

'There, you see! So clever! Now to the paint!'

Emily opened two small lidded caskets which nestled in their designated placeholders in Charlotte's toilet set. One contained red carmine and one the white powder she had ground from pre-prepared pellets earlier that day. With a small silver spoon she expertly mixed portions of the two in a third container to give a light rosy blend and set to work with a soft brush on Charlotte's cheeks, forehead, nose and chin. Then she added a touch more red to the mix and highlighted her lady's cheekbones, blending and smoothing into the paler colour beneath. Charlotte chose a dark red lip pomade and the visage was complete.

'I really do not know what I should do without you!' Charlotte exclaimed, admiring Emily's handiwork.

As she crossed the room to retrieve Charlotte's stays Emily's stomach churned with anxiety and guilt lay heavy upon her chest. She fastened the stays over her mistress's shift and tied the pockets and parries around her waist. Then followed two thin linen underpetticoats and the two halves of the primrose damask silk jupe. As she dressed her beloved mistress, displaying an air of complete serenity and concentration, inside Emily's anxiety was silently devouring her. She was in an impossible situation. How could she betray her mistress, who had encouraged her to do well, played a part in teaching her to read, allowed her access to the family library and given her the much sought-after position of lady's maid – and who now regarded her as almost a *companion*? On the other hand, if she and Will were to have any future together at all, how could they possibly stay at Fernleigh Hall? Emily knew that she could not live without Will – the thought was devastating, appalling. But she could not bring herself to betray her mistress. The situation was hopeless.

One of the pins she was using to fasten the stomacher to the front of Charlotte's stays hit the boning and broke, stabbing Emily's finger. Her thoughts returned to the task in hand with a jolt and she subsequently took care to keep them there lest she drove a pin in too deeply and hit flesh.

Charlotte was humming to herself as Emily worked, turning slightly this way and that so that her maid could complete the dress. At last, when the primrose robe and satin shoes had been added, Charlotte stood in front of a long gold-framed mirror. The gold-embroidered yellow gown perfectly complemented her colouring and she looked a picture.

'You look perfectly beautiful, ' Emily pronounced, forgetting herself for a moment.

Charlotte raised one eyebrow the tiniest of fractions and smiled. 'Thank you, Emily, ' she responded with the exact amount of gravity appropriate to such a compliment.

William finished dressing, walked down the first-floor landing to his mothers' dressing room and knocked on the door. Emily opened the door and her heart leapt when she saw it was Will. Just the sight of him was enough to consume her anxiety for a moment, to drown it in delight.

He had just enough time to whisper to her, 'Emily my dearest love, may I come to you tonight in your room?'

Emily glanced around her before whispering back. 'I look forward to it, I should be sorry not to be able to celebrate your being even older than I!' she teased.

'Tonight then. There is something of great importance we must discuss.' He quickly kissed her forehead before entering the dressing room.

'Oh Will, ' said his mother, 'you must decide which of these necklaces I am to wear, for I simply cannot make up my mind.'

Flushed and excited, Emily left the room, closing the door behind her, and continued her duties, leaving her lover and his mother to their discourse.

At dinner William sat between his mother, at the head of the table, and his sister Anne, facing his sister Amelia, Colonel Napier and Mr Calder. There was much praise of the new décor.

'I believe Robert Adam was employed to bring about this wondrous transformation, ' remarked Mr Calder between mouthfuls of woodcock, himself an aspiring architect.

'The Palladian proportions have been quite changed. The replacement of those two far windows in the bow with niches is, in my humble opinion, exquisite.'

'See how each urn and its niche complement one another, ' responded Anne excitedly. 'Papa had the Etruscan copies commissioned for that very purpose.'

Mr Calder, do you not think that the sideboard is an agreeable companion to the bow?' asked Charlotte. The semi-circular piece, also designed by Adam, was laden with dishes for the table and fitted perfectly into the bay. Its attendant green and white urns on pedestals at either end reflected the Wedgwood style, the shade of green exactly matching that of the walls and the background colour of the ceiling.

'Ah, the sideboard, ' said Calder, waving his fork around with exuberance, 'remarkable in its reciprocal nature. However, I believe the finest work to be on the ceiling. The stucco motifs are very grand. I must confess to noticing the carpet as I entered the room. Ceiling and carpet mirror one another, as I suspected they might.'

'Indeed, ' said Colonel Napier, rapidly devouring a large piece of beef, 'Most gratifying. May I enquire who painted the ceiling vesicas?'

'Ah, that was Zucchi's wife, Angelica. Are they not beautiful landscapes?' remarked William, tucking into a tasty portion of peacock pie.

'The paintings behind you and on the wall to your left are by Zucchi himself, ' observed Charlotte.

William enjoyed the delicious fare as much as the conversation. There were tasty dishes of mutton, beef and veal and a great variety of birds: mallard, plover, partridge and quail, to name but a few. Despite his fathers' current distrust and dislike of all things French, there were ragouts aplenty. Even Thomas was enjoying the asparagus, and William thought the cucumber and onion ragout particularly delightful. As was the company: Mr Calder was a most interesting man and clearly appreciative of Anne. William guessed there was some kind of understanding between them. At twenty-three years of age Anne was ready to marry, although William suspected that his parents were waiting to see what Mr Calder made of himself. It was true enough that he was from a good and very reputable family; however, a man must prove his own worth.

'You seem well-informed in matters of architecture sir, ' Colonel Napier observed, wiping his mouth liberally on his napkin, having finished a plateful of scallops in oyster liquor.

'You are most kind, ' Calder replied, 'I do have aspirations in that direction.'

'Mr Calder is too modest' Anne interrupted 'He is apprenticed to Mr John Wood, who resides in Bath.'

'Is this so?' enquired Amelia 'Such an elegant city. My husband Mr Chatham and I have visited friends there on many occasions. Mr Wood is responsible for much handsome building.'

'Madam, I believe you may be referring to Mr Wood the elder, who sadly passed away several years ago; however Mr Wood the younger is blessed with his father's talent and continues his work.' Mr Calder spoke so as not to offend.

'Indeed? I had not that appreciation. However, may I say that I believe Bath to be much improved by the recent building of the Circus. I assume that to be the responsibility of Mr Wood the younger?'

'Quite so, Mrs Chatham, and I am fortunate enough to have some small part in it.'

William caught Anne's eye and winked at her. Try as she might she could not contain her admiration for the man. She blushed immediately and turned from William's perceptive gaze only to meet her mother's. William turned his attention back to the conversation. Mr Calder was again praising the talents of Robert Adam, 'He is esteemed in the highest circles.'

'Was he not recently appointed architect to the King?' queried William.

'That, in my humble opinion, is the one deed we have Lord Bute to thank for. Dreadful man. Still he appreciated Adam's genius, even if he cannot be relied upon in other matters!'

'I cannot agree more, Mr Calder' remarked Colonel Napier. 'Bute is a perfidious man, obsessed by power. It was Pitt's shrewdness that secured the capture of Havana and Bute's lack of insight which prevented us from mounting a pre-emptive attack on the Spanish. With Newcastle's recent resignation we have only Bute to negotiate peace for us. I admit he does not have my absolute trust. It is said by some that he is in the pocket of the French.'

'Do you not pray for peace, Colonel Napier?' interjected Charlotte, turning her attention back to the conversation, having nodded to the house steward to bring in the second remove.

'I pray, madam, for peace and justice, ' he said with all seriousness, 'and for the maintenance of our Newfoundland fishing rights, ' he added lightly.

'Sir?'

'As Pitt once remarked, "Cod is Britain's gold", Madam.'

'Spoken as a true strategist sir. The preservation of such a great fishing fleet not only provides fish for the table, but more importantly, I suspect, is a continuing source of recruits for the navy, ' William teased.

'Such discernment in one of so tender an age, ' James teased back. 'You will make a fine politician!'

Following the remove, an impressive boar's head constructed of sponge cake and the dessert course – a delicious syllabub, plum pudding, cherry and damson tarts and potted cheese, the rinse water was presented in finger bowls, followed by more wine as soon as the assembly was ready. The ladies then retired, taking their glasses with them. William and the other gentlemen were left to express themselves more freely. The talk was of Newcastle's resignation over the abandonment of Prussia, of Peter of Russia's recent military alliance with Prussia and of Bute's refusal to renew the subsidy treaty with Russia so as not to finance an alliance designed to prolong the war and enable Russia to attack Denmark. Prussia and the Austro-Russian coalition were no longer at war, England was succeeding against the French in the West Indies as they had done in Canada some two years since and Martinique had already been captured, with the other islands now falling rapidly. The defence of Portugal and the defeat of the Spanish now remained, and most believed an end to be in sight. There was much distrust of Bute's handling of the peace settlements in a manner that maximised Britain's territorial advantage, for much vital trade and commercial power depended on it.

William was relieved and excited by predictions of a settlement with France in the near future, perhaps even this year. He believed that his future with Emily, his happiness and his very life may depend upon it.

He could not wait to see Emily, to talk with her, to tell her of his plans and to hold her in his arms. However, he knew he must be patient; for the remainder of the evening he must hold onto his feelings and keep his countenance. He knew this would be difficult, even though he had had much practice. Yet tonight was special.

An evening of coffee and cake, cards and conversation with the ladies ensued, followed by music and dancing. William received most thoughtful gifts from his family. He particularly preferred a delightful snuffbox from his sister Charlotte made from Sheffield silver, a set of exquisite mother-of-pearl buttons from Elizabeth and, most precious of all, from his parents the most recently-published volume of Diderot's *Encyclopaedia* and a copy of Voltaire's *Candide*. How he would enjoy sharing these texts with Emily.

Much later, the evening of entertainment drew to a close, the guests departed or retired and William's family went to their beds. The night was now theirs.

William tiptoed across the bed-chamber in his stockinged feet, holding aloft a candle. He had removed his day clothes and was wearing his bedgown underneath. He placed one finger to his lips as he moved silently around the end of the small wooden bed, knowing exactly where to place his feet in the shadows. Emily watched him, her heart racing. He sat on the edge of her bed, placing the candle on a nearby table, and proceeded to take off his garters and stockings.

'Sweet Emily, come let me hold you, ' William whispered, his voice slightly throaty. He gathered her to him and held her tight, stroking her hair. I love you, sweetheart, and I *will* prove my devotion to you.'

'Beloved Will, ' she whispered in return, 'come place your head on my breast. I love you so very dearly. Come, lie here with me.'

'My dearest Emily, how I have longed for your sweet words today, every hour that you were not in my presence, every minute that you were when propriety forbade me to speak with you.' He interspersed his words with soft kisses. 'You do know that my intentions are truly honourable. Please believe that above all else I love you with my very soul. You know that I wish our liaison one day to be blessed by marriage.'

'Oh how I wish that could be so, but I really fear it is impossible!'' Emily cried, her emotions momentarily 'winning' over her efforts to keep to a cautious whisper.

William pressed his finger to her lips. 'Shhh, come now, do not torment yourself with such thoughts. *I will make it so.* Will you not do me the honour of bestowing your trust upon me?' He took her hand in his and kissed it lightly.

She nodded at him through watery eyes and pressed his hand to her breast.

William left it there for a moment, then took both her hands in his.

'Emily' he said seriously in a low voice, 'we cannot continue like this. I cannot live in such a manner. I wish you to be my wife, to be at my side always, whatever may befall us.'

Emily made to speak, but William continued 'Hear me out, please, my love. If you will have me, I mean to marry you in secret; a clandestine coupling, north of the English border, ' he squeezed her hands, 'and then to France, my beloved! There we shall reside for some considerable time. I am able to converse in French and you will master the language in no time at all, I am sure of it. You have grace and beauty, you have the comprehension for *les philosophes*. You are discerning, perceptive, you have ample wit! Refinement in the nuances of etiquette, the subtleties of social conduct is but a minute step away, an *étape miniature!*'

William had jumped up and was now pacing about the room in the shadows. Emily's startled face, half illuminated by the shaft of moonlight that stole through the small panes of the narrow window, reminded him of where he was and that he must keep his voice to a whisper so as not to be heard from without. He threw himself unceremoniously back upon the bed in excitement.

'What do you say? *Will you marry me?* Come and live with me in France, and I *promise* you that in time it will be possible to present you back here as my French wife.'

Emily felt a myriad of emotions sweep over her in an instant. Shock, delight, trepidation, rapture, foreboding, astonishment, disbelief, but above all a profound love for this man. She was overwhelmed and sat in stunned silence, trying to make sense of what Will had just said whilst attempting to sort her emotions into something that made sense to her. William sat with her in silence, holding her hands in his, gently stroking the delicate skin on their backs with his thumbs, sensing that she needed time to take it all in.

Eventually she spoke softly and deliberately, in low tones.

'My dearest Will, we have known each other a long time and you know how very much I love you. I am deeply... honoured... and a little astounded by your serious proposal of marriage. To think that you would even consider me for that role, to be by your side through all the years of our lives, is... *incredible*. I...' she paused searching for the right words, 'I fear I'm not worthy of you. I am no lady, I have no land or property, I have no allowance, I have no proper education. Yet

I will not betray the honesty between us by dismissing this as mad-
ness, an impossible scheme. If you say that you love me and wish for
us to be married then I believe you and I trust you implicitly. This is
more than I ever could have dreamed of! I will gladly be your wife and
follow you wherever you may go and be by your side always! Yet I am
afraid that I may disgrace you, that I will not be able to become the
lady that you speak of. People will *surely* see me for who I am, I cannot
believe that they would mistake me for a high-born French lady.' Her
voice had sunk to a murmur, 'And what of your father, ' she added
softly, 'and mine?'

William put his arm around her shoulders as a means of reassurance, 'I plan to engage the assistance of my uncle, my father's brother,
in that respect, ' replied William. His brow became furrowed as he
contemplated his plan. 'He has a most unconventional nature, which
leads me to believe that he may help us. Perhaps he may be able to
persuade Papa. Besides my uncle, I do not intend to disclose my intentions to anyone excepting your parents and mine. We must honour
them and do right by them in this. To behave in any other manner
would be to discredit them and ourselves.'

Emily did not know what to think. What she had seen of William's
uncle she did not like. He was certainly unconventional, and not in
the nicest sense of the word. However, it was not for her to speak
against him. William knew him better than she. And William had far
more confidence in her than she had in herself. Could she do it? Could
she really become so different on the outside, create a shell so necessarily refined? In truth she did not know. Yet she trusted her lover and
above all wanted to be with him.

William kissed Emily gently on her forehead. 'Sweetheart, there
is no need to be afraid. I will be by your side to support you in all
this, to help you, to teach you, to love you. I believe in you absolutely. Besides, it is the only way for us to be together. Let not your
disquiet over this matter spoil your mood. For you have given your
consent, and we are to be married!' He swept her up in his arms and
kissed her full on the lips. Emily flung her arms around his neck and
held him so tightly she felt she would extinguish all breath from his

body. Yet she could not let go. She would be his wife – she could not believe it!

'Will you take this, ' he said finally 'as a mark of my constancy and intention to marry you? I know you cannot yet wear it openly, however would you wear it when we are alone and keep it about your person at other times?' In William's hand was a beautiful gold gimmel ring. Three rings in one, designed to be worn by the intended couple and a witness, to be brought together on the day of the ceremony.

Emily gasped. It was exquisite. Even in the diffuse pale moonlight it exuded a soft, rich golden glow.

'See here, the inscription, ' bade William, looking into her eyes and then at the ring, smiling gently, enjoying her delight.

'Oh Will! It is the most beautiful thing I have ever seen! I will wear it with honour. I shall treasure it with the greatest pride.' Emily's joy spilled over as tears on her cheeks as she held out her left hand and he, deftly separating the three loops, placed one upon her fourth finger.

'And I shall do the same, ' he smiled as she reciprocated.

'Who shall wear the third ring? Who shall be our witness, Will?'

'We shall see in the fullness of time, ' said he. 'For now it shall be our secret.'

'Our secret, ' she echoed, softly, contentedly. She lay down upon her side, one hand supporting her head, and contemplated him in her blissfulness, her long curls falling tantalisingly around her bare shoulders.

He too felt elated, and waves of intense desire began to wash through him. He slowly moved his hand inside her cotton shift, which fell open exposing her small high breasts. He gently moved the material aside, uncovering each breast in turn, and tilted his head back momentarily to look at them, finally revealed in all their glory in the flickering candlelight.

'Throw your head back, my love, ' he said softly, 'that I might better savour your beauty, for you are the most wondrous creature I have ever seen.'

Emily lay down, arching her back slightly and tilting her head so that the wooden beams above her bed came into view. This very act made her rosy nipples point upwards also, rising and falling with the quickening pace of her breathing. William surveyed the wondrous sight before him.

'I shall forever think on you like this, ' he whispered, as he cupped each breast and placed his lips around each nipple in turn.

His right hand now moved to the hem of her shift and he slowly pulled up the material to her waist. He gently parted her legs and entered her, moving himself deeper with every thrust, until at last their passions were satisfied.

Later, as the lovers were lying peacefully entwined, a young girl in the attic room next to Emily's chamber moved quietly away from the dividing wall where she had been crouched, listening.

Rachel moved to the window and looked out into the clear night. The moon deflected its brilliant illumination over her world. An owl swayed suddenly over the stable block and re-emerged with a struggling mouse in its talons. Nothing could hide on a bright night such as this. The girl smiled a slow malevolent smile. *Nothing can be hidden from me*, she said to herself. *Ah'm clever, ah am. T' impudence of believing Master Will wor interested in 'er, that horrid girl Emily. Aye, she had airs and graces above 'er station, so she did. Readin' an writin.' Why wor she treated different from t' other maids? Huh, thought she wor special. An 'er laugh, you could 'ear t' laugh way down corridor. Huh, conversin' with Mrs Cumley like she gave the orders. Mrs Cumley don't treat me like that. Ah'm as good as Emily. Why, ah do t' work of a score of Emilys and more besides. Huh, what did that girl do? Prattle around ladyship, 'elp 'er t' dress. That worn't difficult wor it? An' clothes she wor given t' wear, silks, brocades even, of fine quality, some not even been wore that many times by mistresses. True enough, ah've been given a dress or two in t' past two years since working in kitchens. But that girl, she'd 'ad plenty more. Always out an' about with 'er ladyship. Tryin' to talk like they did. She should know 'er place. 'An' it worn't only 'er that 'ad noticed. Why, Daisy 'ad mentioned it only t' other day, and she worn't only one neither. An' now hobnobbing with Master Will! Well! Mrs Cumley won't be so pleased when she 'ears about this. Mebbe ah'll be favoured more fer it.*

'Ahm a good girl ah am, ah know my place in t' order of things, ' she whispered to the owl.

Rachel hadn't exactly been able to hear the topic of William and Emily's conversation. However, she had recognised William's voice and had noticed them whispering once before. Now she knew for sure, and knowledge was power. Emily had given herself to him! She would be damned for such immoral behaviour. Rachel believed that she would be neglecting her duty if she didn't inform Mrs Cumley. God would damn Emily for what she had done. Salvation lay in the path of self-restraint and remorse. Perhaps Emily's soul might still be saved if she were cast out and made to repent of her sin. Rachel must tell of what she had seen and heard. She was doing this for Emily's own sake. Emily should be thanking her.

Thomas was sleeping fitfully, and his quilted cotton nightcap and matching bedgown were plastered to his body with sweat. His mind was full of past events which every now and then came back to torment him.

'E's takin' mah lass, 'e's took mah lass, I tell thee!... Ah'mreet sorry like... y'know... t' ave t' come t' you...' ' ... Good Lord 'elp me. How d'ah say this?...

Calm down man. Would you not sit, and speak slowly? Don't be afraid — you know I am a fair man. Don't be afraid... don't be afraid...

S'cuse mah jabberin', but she be taken... Mary, mah own fair lass, she be taken and undone, she is... undone!...'Gainst 'er will t'was... she be shamed... 'gainst 'er will!... 'gainst 'er will ...

'Who Daniel, who?!... Who?'

Thomas turned heavily in his sleep, flinging an arm out, hand clenched tightly.

Oh no... Dear Lord... What of Constance... does she know?... Good God, John, this could kill her! Have you no conscience, have you no shame?... Shame... Constance... John... Mary... this could kill her... kill her...

Please Mah Lord, don't let tha brother touch 'er again. We want no trouble. She's a good lass is Mary...'

... Is the wedding going ahead, Daniel?

With respect, Mah Lord, ah love 'er an ah'll do reet by 'er, so ah will. T' bairn'll be mahn, could be mahn, an' we won't say owt... not 'avin' er shamed... not 'avin' er shamed... will you 'elp me? 'Elp me!...

... John... Brother! I can see this is not the first; why do you look so surprised at my disapproval? Think of your wife, Brother, think of Constance, even if you do not consider that poor unfortunate girl whom you have deeply wronged...

... I consider her as I would consider a juicy peach from your orangery, Sir, to be plucked and devoured when ripe. In my opinion they are there for the taking... Constance? She knows nothing of my affairs... This is not the first... will not be the last!... Not the last...

'Not the last, ' murmured Thomas repeatedly, his head thrashing from side to side.

'Dearest, ' Charlotte was gently shaking his arm in an attempt to wake him from his distress. 'Dearest, wake yourself. 'Tis only a dream.' She knew only too well what he was dreaming about.

Eventually Thomas's consciousness was dragged into the present, seemingly unwilling, as though leaving behind issues unresolved. When he had regained his composure he was able to face his wife and spoke more calmly.

'My dear, ' he said, despondently, staring up at the canopy of their bed, the pale early morning light throwing shadows around the room. 'Why does the past still torment me so? Did I not do right? Am I to blame for my brother's wrongdoings? I live in fear that one day Constance may learn that her devoted husband is a miscreant and a rake. It greatly saddens me that he is my own flesh and blood.'

'Ssh, there, my dear, ' Charlotte held his head against her breast and cradled him in her arms like a child.

'Would that I could dismiss him from our lives, yet I must tolerate him for the sake of Constance.'

'You have done nothing wrong, ' retorted Charlotte tenderly. 'You did right by Daniel and Mary Popple, you challenged John about the matter, and see how Emily has blossomed and flourished in our care.'

Thomas reluctantly nodded in agreement.

'She knows nothing of her genesis, ' Charlotte continued, 'and Constance lives in blissful ignorance. They are both content, and so you should be. Remember there is no-one else knows anything of these events. You are a just and honest man, and I am proud to call you husband.'

'Dearest Charlotte, once more I bow to your sagacity. You are a constant comfort to me. I will try again to put these unfortunate thoughts to rest.'

Each time Thomas almost let Charlotte convince him; indeed he had almost convinced himself. Almost.

Some twenty years before, one of his long-standing and loyal estate workers, Daniel Popple, had come fearfully to explain that his wife-to-be had been taken advantage of by John Fernleigh, Thomas's brother, and he feared that she might be with child. Daniel adored his betrothed, Mary, and was understanding of her plight when many would have abandoned her. A brave man and fiercely faithful to his convictions, Daniel had approached Thomas and asked that he be kind of heart and ensure that John Fernleigh did not go near his wife again. Knowing his brother's countenance and Daniel's trustworthiness, Thomas had gone into a rage and subsequently tested the allegation. When prompted, John, an outspoken, cold-hearted and callous man, had boasted how he had plucked a pretty young lass a few weeks before her wedding, confirming Daniel's accusation.

Highly distressed, Thomas had at once resolved to behave in a correct and just manner and to do the right thing by the child. He had given Daniel a small sum of money to pay for the upbringing of the child. At the time Thomas had resolved to keep the secret and support the child indirectly, part of his decision founded on his desire to protect his delicate sister-in-law, whom he loved dearly. Thomas and Charlotte believed that the shock of her husband John, publically a very attentive man, being unfaithful to her and the circumstances of his betrayal could kill her. By protecting the child he was both protecting his sister-in-law and allowing his dedicated servants to keep their good name. It was the only reasonable course of action. Since that day Thomas had always been angered by the fact that his brother's behaviour had gone unpunished, and that he was powerless to prevent the same unhappy events from being repeated.

But something else tormented him and would never leave him in peace.

Four

*J*ennifer had had a hectic couple of weeks since Sarah had left. She was putting the final touches to the winter collection and had been to Milan for a series of meetings. She'd attended several business dinners with smart-suited, smooth-talking Italians eager to please her, yet had always returned to her hotel room on her own. They were used to her now; in fact it had become a bit of a challenge. Who would score? Would any of them? Some were married; of course these were the men who were most confident, safe behind their shield of marital bliss.

'Ah Jennifer, you would be mine if I had not my beautiful wife.'

Jennifer would laugh, 'Ah Franco, if I were only twenty years older! Besides, I am spoken for.'

'What is this "spoken for"?'

'My heart is already given to another.'

'Can you not love two people at the same time?'

'Of course, but you cannot be faithful to more than one.'

She had always pretended to be attached. She knew she shouldn't have to, but it was her choice. It made things easier. It was not a total lie, just a partial fabrication of the truth. Her heart *was* 'spoken for', although it was occupied by two lovers. She was trying to let go of one and the chains of love that bound her to him had become rusted by her tears and were gradually breaking in places, releasing her slowly. So cold had he been towards her, it was as if their love had been plunged into liquid nitrogen, rendering their relationship brittle and impossible to handle without destroying it. Another love had begun to creep in, an ephemeral love for someone which was not of this world. The first love seemed to be fading very gradually – or was it being driven out? She didn't know. She did not understand. Why did she keep the black ribbon? She liked handling it, stroking it, winding it around her wrist. She liked to have it with her. It made her feel… safe. She had even taken it to Milan in her briefcase. It represented all she wanted; her hopes, her desires, her lost lust for life. It gave her dreams substance. She could not comprehend what seemed to be happening to her, yet she knew that the ribbon, wherever it had come from, represented something very special.

Sarah was on her way home from London, where she had attended an important weekend meeting at the Royal Park Hotel. Researchers at Bradford University had recently developed a synthetic hydrogel which could hold huge amounts of water. There was talk of spraying a liquid form of the gel onto oil spillages on water and land to soak up the oil. It was reputed that the gel would then thicken and could be rolled up like a carpet, taking the offending oil with it, and could be reused after the oil had been extracted. The formula was yet to be patented, but everyone could see that this would have a major impact on environmental clean-up techniques.

Sitting on the crowded train full of tourists returning from London on this hot late-July Sunday, Sarah was full of enthusiasm. She felt very positive about her future with the company. The work was fulfilling, and she believed she was doing something worthwhile. She reasoned that since that she took a lot from this precious earth she should give something back. She was also optimistic about her relationship with Rob. Since her return from her holiday with Jennifer they had both made an effort with one another. They had taken turns to cook for each other, something they hardly ever used to do. The last couple of weekends they had put work completely aside and spent time together visiting a couple of country houses and new art exhibitions at the Ashmolean Museum and Modern Art Oxford. They had even squeezed in a punting trip down the Thames one sunny evening, with a champagne picnic on the bank. Things were definitely looking up.

Sarah started to hum happily, much to the annoyance of the grey-haired suited man next to her. He shot her an accusing look, tutted a few times and screened himself off behind the pages of his broadsheet. He got off at Reading and was replaced by a young mother with her toddler. There was nowhere for the little boy to sit, so he ran up and down the aisle, chocolate ice cream in hand, grinning at the more receptive passengers and occasionally poking his tongue out at those who stared blankly back at him. His frustrated mother, a woman with apparently no control over him whatsoever, was constantly getting up and down to drag him back to the vicinity of her seat. For once Sarah didn't mind the incessant interruption of her thoughts. Soon ice cream in hand turned to ice cream in hand, around mouth, on chin, t-shirt and shoes. Dark brown sticky fingers went everywhere. Sarah smiled. Amazingly she didn't even mind the fingerprints on her briefcase when the chocolate-ridden child crawled underneath the table. She was happy today, and all was right with the world. She was just fantasising about what she was going to do to Rob when she got home when she felt a sharp pain in her right calf. The toddler had just stabbed her with a pencil.

OK, that's it! Enough was enough. She smiled sweetly at the mother and said through her teeth, 'Look, why don't you let him sit on my seat out of harm's way. I'm getting off soon anyway and I could do with some fresh air'. The exasperated mother nodded gratefully. Sarah moved into the corridor at the end of the carriage. The train cantered through the sunny Oxfordshire countryside to the comforting rhythm of wheels on track. Sarah let her thoughts turn again to Rob. He'd been working this weekend too, but had suggested they get a takeaway and a good bottle of wine and spend a relaxing Sunday evening together. He'd even gone so far as to hint at a lie-in on Monday morning, which was pretty unheard of. 'Excellent idea, ' Sarah had murmured in his ear as she kissed him before leaving for the station early on Saturday morning. 'I'll really look forward to that. Have a good weekend, love, and try not to work too hard'.

Now she was nearly home she felt a little excited, which surprised her. The way she felt today was like the feeling you have at the beginning of a relationship. It seemed a long time since she'd experienced the rise of heart. Perhaps it shouldn't come as such a surprise – they were both trying hard to be sensitive to each other and to please one another, weren't they? Wasn't that a little like starting again? Sarah put the analysis to one side and concentrated on her plans for the evening. As the meeting had finished a couple of hours early they'd have more time together. She planned to jump in the shower as soon as she got home and then dress herself in the new black silk and lace camisole she'd managed to buy during Saturday's lunch break. The high cut flattered her, making her legs look longer than they were, and was tantalisingly revealing. She fancied they'd jump into bed and have passionate sex, oh for at least an hour, until they'd worked up an appetite for dinner and wine! Or maybe Rob would join her in the shower. The few times they'd made love under sensuous jets of warm water, soaping each other provocatively, had been wonderful. The changing rhythm of the train broke her fantasising. They were slowing down for Oxford. Yippee!

Sarah jumped into the Stag and drove the fifteen-minute journey home. The trip was easier on a Sunday. As she made to turn into the driveway she saw another car parked behind Rob's BMW, so she parked outside in the road. She recognised the Astra as Susan's. A wave of disappointment swept over her. *They're still working*, she tutted to herself. Then she carefully put the disappointment to one side; she wasn't going to let it spoil her mood today. *Oh well, they can't have much more to do, and I am early. Now I'm here they'll wrap up, Susan will go home and I'll pull Rob into the shower.*

'Hi, I'm back, ' she called cheerfully towards the study door from the staircase as she walked upstairs to change her shoes and dump her suitcase. She opened the bedroom door and gasped. The scene that greeted her made her reel back in horror. Rob was lying on his back on their bed, his wrists secured to the wrought iron headboard by a couple of silk scarves. He was naked. Susan was astride him in a similarly naked state. Their shocked faces stared back in horror at her, then for a second at each other. That horrendous moment seemed infinite. Sarah took a couple of steps back in dismay, immediately feeling faint. There followed an almost overpowering urge to run, to get out of the house, away from this unbearable scene, away from the two of them. Then her adrenaline kicked in. In a split second she was angry — angrier than she had ever been in her life. How could he betray her? How could he do this in their home, *their bed*? Sarah was incensed.

She took a step into the room.

'You fucking bastard!'

Susan had dismounted and was frantically trying to cover herself, to claw back some modicum of self-respect. But the duvet was on the floor on the other side of the bed and her clothes were out of reach.

Sarah noticed that Susan's blouse was on a hanger over the wardrobe door and the rest of her garments were placed carefully over the back of a chair by the window, *neatly folded*. A thought struck her; this was not the action of a woman in the throes of passion making love with a man for the first time and overcome with abandon. This was part of a premeditated routine. My God, how long had this affair been going on? *How many times?* Sarah was incensed. How could they do this to her? In her house, *in her bed?*

She turned her eyes towards them. 'For Christ's sake untie me, ' Rob was saying.

'Leave him, ' Sarah hissed. 'Put these on, you bitch.' She threw Susan's panties in her general direction. Susan hurriedly retrieved them from the carpet and covered her immodesty.

'Sarah, I'm so...' she faltered.

'Shut up, you little cow, do you think I want to hear your pathetic excuses?'

'Sarah, darling. Look, this isn't what it seems, I mean, it is, well, you know. But it was just... sex. It didn't mean anything, I promise!' Rob protested.

Susan shot him a hurt look.

'Look, for God's sake untie me and we can sort this out like three reasonable adults.'

'*My God!*' Sarah screamed, '*You're fucking pathetic!* This is just like you. Even when you've been caught red-handed you come out with the tritest, most meaningless cliché of all time. "It didn't mean anything," she mimicked. 'And then expect me to be reasonable. God, do you really think I'm that stupid? I mean exactly what d' you think of me? OK, don't answer that, it's perfectly obvious from the way you've behaved with her. You've both betrayed me. How could you do that?' Sarah turned to Susan: 'And I thought you were a friend, ' she said disdainfully.

She turned back to Rob, who was struggling with the scarves, becoming increasingly angry but getting nowhere.

'I should hope it did mean something, Rob, because it better be worth losing me and the house or you're really fucked!'

'Sarah, *please*. Honey, don't be so *dramatic*, ' Rob responded, emphasising the last word with the implication that he thought Sarah was making a fuss about nothing. 'I love you and you love me, remember. I don't want to lose what we have, and I don't think you do either. I can explain all this. He gave a nervous little laugh. 'We'll laugh about this in a few days, believe me.'

If this was meant to have a calming effect, it made things even worse.

'*Shut up, shut up!*' Sarah was beside herself, white with rage, and her hands shaking. She grabbed one of Susan's nylons from the chair and stuffed it into Rob's mouth. Susan was heading for her blouse, but Sarah got there first and ripped it off the hanger.

'You're such a hot chick, Susan, ' she cried. 'You know you really should learn to cool off a bit!'.

By now Susan was in a state of complete shock. Ordinarily so cool-headed and efficient, she was completely out of her depth. Dumbfounded out of sheer embarrassment, she was afraid Sarah might even hit her.

Sarah snatched Susan's garments off the chair and Susan began to cry. Sarah was still too angry to break down. She marched over to the open window and flung the clothes out. They landed with a slap on the roof of the Astra.

'Now get out of my house!'

Susan grabbed her handbag from underneath the chair and rushed downstairs. She recovered the garments from the roof of the car and dived inside. Sarah could see her struggling for a moment with the blouse before the car screamed out of the drive and she was gone.

Rob was livid. He'd wrestled with the scarves so much he'd succeeded in tightening the knots even further. Sarah removed the stocking from his mouth.

'Oh you think that's clever, do you! Christ Almighty, I could have choked, ' he spluttered. 'For God's sake, Sarah, it's not her fault. If you want someone to blame, blame me, OK? Look, just bloody untie me, will you! We need to talk and we can't do that like this.'

Sarah looked at him. His beautiful blonde hair was bedraggled and sweaty. His deep blue eyes were staring wildly and starting to look a little bloodshot. She noticed that when the corners of the his mouth were turned down when he was angry or sullen, as they were now, it made the whole of his face look mean and nasty. She realised that over the past year or so she'd seen that look more times than she cared to remember. It occurred to her that he was like his dick: once strong and glorious and beautiful, now limp and pathetic, washed-up, expended, finished. They were finished. He wasn't the man she'd fallen in love with.

She suddenly felt very tired and tears started to flow as she threw a few essentials into a sports bag.

'I guess you've done us both a favour, ' she said sadly. 'There's really nothing left of what we had, is there?' She took a pair of scissors from the bathroom cupboard and cut him loose. He sat on the bed rubbing his wrists, looking defeated.

'I don't want to know how long it's been going on, ' Sarah continued, 'it's obviously been a while. I guess neither of us are getting what we need from each other any more.'

'Look, honey, don't just walk out now. Where are you going to go? We need to talk. I mean, what will you do?'

'Rob,' Sarah stared at the floor, shaking her head, 'I just... I don't want to talk about this now,' she said slowly. A tear that had reached the bottom of her cheek let go and dropped to the floor. She wiped the others away with her hands.

'I need to get my head straight. I'll call you when I'm ready. Right now I don't even want to look at you!'

She picked up her bag and the suitcase, which was standing unopened by the bedroom door, and left the house.

⌒

Late July 1762

They were in the kitchen preparing food for the evening meal. A fire burned fiercely in the range, excited by drips of fat from a sizzling leg of lamb and one of pork turning slowly over the heat on the smoke-jack spit, which was automatically driven by a fan in the chimney. A pot of prune sauce simmered gently on the hotplate.

Rachel placed two roast chickens in the large oak food press against the back wall and turned to her next task of chopping apples and onions for the baked hare. With every cut of the knife she thought of Emily. The kitchen was unusually quiet: Daisy had been sent to gather sage and lemon thyme and Jeremiah to pick two fresh lemons from the orangery, Martha had been dispatched to the chicken house for eggs and the scullery maid was out fetching wood for the fire. She did not know where the others were, only that they could be back at any time. Rachel looked across the kitchen at Mrs Cumley. Her large frame, plump as the plucked birds placed neatly on trays behind her, was bent in concentration over the hare she was deftly skinning. Three others, their guts and skins removed, lay shining on the board, waiting to be chopped and soaked in milk. Now was Rachel's chance. She must speak now or burst.

'Mrs Cumley, I 'ave need t' speak with you,' she ventured.

'Ssh girl, canst tha see ah'm busy? If these dishes do not go in t' oven soon, they'll not be ready an' cold for supper.'

'But 't is an urgent matter!' the girl protested.

'Reet now, only urgent matter ah'm concerned about is these 'ere hares, an' if these apples are not ready in two minutes thee'll 'ave more t' think about besides; now hurry thasel' an' stop chatterin.'

Rachel could see that she was going to have to come right out with it, and quickly, before the others got back. She wasn't afraid, she told herself. She was doing it for Emily's sake, to save her soul. But in truth she was a little nervous. The girls respected the head cook and knew her to be fair, but she was strict and demanded a high standard of work. If you worked well she treated you right, and if you didn't – well, there was trouble.

'But 'tis Emily!' she blurted out. 'She's in big trouble, so she is, an' right now only I can save 'er, see? So I have to tell tha then so tha can save 'er.'

On hearing Emily's name Mrs Cumley sighed. She put down her knife, wiped her hands on her voluminous blue-checked linen apron and went to the stove to taste the prune sauce. It could do with a little more ginger. Her happy proportions reflected her generous nature. She knew one or two of the girls were envious of Emily's rise to her present status and of the privileges which came with that position, but these girls must know their place in the scheme of things. She would not dream of questioning her ladyship's decisions, and neither should they. She liked to think that she ran the kitchen like a captain runs a tidy ship. Her girls were hardworking most of the time and she wanted to keep it that way. So she recognised the value of keeping the peace whilst maintaining order.

She turned her rosy cheeks to Rachel and said gently but firmly, 'Come now, Rachel, do not distress tha'self; what is t' matter wi' thee? Explain thasen girl.'

'Ah'm reet afraid for Emily, so I ah am, 'er soul's surely damned unless she do repent. 'Er and Master William, y' see.'

'What nonsense tha speaks! Why on earth d' tha conjure up such fantastical tales?'

'But 'tis true, I swear it! I 'eard two o' them t'gether only night before last. Master William in 'er room, an' they be laughing and sighing and carryin' on as only man and wife do. God's own truth.'

'Hold tha' tongue, tha silly lass! Ah won't listen to this nonsense another minute. Talk like that does no-one any good.' Mrs Cumley moved towards Rachel and shook her by the shoulders. 'This imagination'll do thee no good, does tha 'ear me? Emily's a good lass and ah'll 'ear no word spoken 'ginst 'er. Does tha understand?'

She let go of Rachel, who smoothed down the sleeves of her dress, straightened her cap and began to cry.

Mrs Cumley put an arm around her shoulders, 'Look Rachel, ' she said gently. 'Tha's a good 'ardworkin lass, an' good work comes rewarded in time, tha'll see.'

But Rachel imagined she could take advantage of the cook's kindheartedness and continued with her accusations. 'I do work 'ard, Mrs Cumley, I really do, an' I don't see half the vails that she does. She's takin' advantage of 'er position, so she is. She wor in another new gown t' other day and what do I get? A bit o' dripping t' sell. You ask Mr Arbuth if I don't work 'ard an' deserve a bit more reward. I tell tha, Emily's heading straight for 'ell the way she's carryin' on.'

Mrs Cumley's temper was rising and her patience was being seriously eroded by this silly girl's allegations and whining. The slightly veiled suggestion that she might go to the house steward about this, bypassing the clerk of the kitchen and even the housekeeper and certainly undermining her own authority, was enough to make her boil over.

'Ah'll remind thee, lass, that thy present vails fairly double thy wages! Tha'st a secure position here but idle gossipin' an' spreadin' wicked rumours is most certain t' be punished. Tha'll not find another employer s' kind. So clear thy 'ead of envious thoughts an' silly stories, or I'll be speakin' to Mr Fry an' tha'll end up losin' this position. Allreet?'

Rachel wiped her face with the corner of her linen apron and nodded. She'd purposefully not wanted to bring the matter to the attention of the clerk of the kitchen, as Mr Fry was not known for his empathy and was given to watching the girls closely in case they took a bit too much fat off the meat or melted a fraction more butter than was necessary, robbing the trimmings, so she thought she'd aim higher up the chain of command. However, Mrs Cumley had the final word on the matter.

'An if I 'ear another word on this, tha'll be back in laundry, so tha will! Now what about these 'ere onions?'

Rachel didn't say another word. She looked down at her faded lilac linen bedgown and green petticoat, protected as always by the checked linen apron. She'd only had one new dress in the past eight months, she reflected, though she was due for another and Mrs Cumley had promised her a yard or two of linsey-woolsey for a new petticoat.

Mrs Cumley received her castings as a generous fabric allowance and was given to selling on any spare fabric for half its worth. This spring Martha had purchased some printed cotton at only a shilling a yard.

Rachel continued to seethe quietly. Emily was given at least four morning gowns a year and her petticoats were generally silk, not linsey or cotton. When was *she* to be given a silk petticoat? She'd worked hard in the laundry and then the kitchen for some five years. She deserved more! Why, she could be a lady-in-waiting as easy as spitting.

However Rachel knew better than to talk to Mrs Cumley again about this, or to any of the other girls, but she resolved not to let the matter rest. She would go and talk to Mrs Preedy, the housekeeper, on the quiet. She would be sure to do something about it.

⌒

August

Jennifer was having a dinner party. For the first time since she'd moved into the cottage she had plucked up the courage to invite some of her colleagues into her haven. Antonio was over from Milan for a series of meetings. Of all her Italian colleagues,

Jennifer liked him best. He was gentle and sensitive, unlike most of his colleagues, and very happily married. His wife had recently had their second child, so was unable to accompany him on this business visit, which unfortunately straddled a weekend. Bad timing, but it couldn't be helped. Sensura's spring marketing strategy needed to be finalised. Jennifer had been entertained by Antonio and his gracious wife at their home on several occasions and felt that it was about time she reciprocated. Besides, she didn't like the thought of him spending the entire weekend mooching around York on his own, missing his family. She'd also invited David, her boss, his wife, Jane, and three of her marketing team: Julia, Tim and Steve. She had asked Sarah if she would like to come up for the weekend but she was busy flat-hunting, having not found anything remotely suitable. Jennifer was concerned but not overly worried about her. They'd had a long talk the Sunday before last when Sarah rang her from the hotel in which she'd settled herself. They'd spoken every night since then.

Sarah had cried a lot at first, then over the following few weeks her manner had gradually changed from hurt through quiet resignation to fatalist. This morning she had been telling Jennifer that what was meant to be was meant to be. Rob had probably done both of them a favour. Everything life threw at you was really a learning experience, and although you probably couldn't see it at the time, when you looked back you would almost certainly be able to see the reasons for life's major events. How else would we be able to grow? Sarah was now sure there was a reason for her relationship with Rob failing, and that there was something better waiting for her.

Jennifer thought Sarah's approach eminently sensible and agreed with her fatalistic views, although she was a little annoyed at how quickly Sarah had come to this conclusion. She didn't expect her to behave in the same way or to go through exactly the same emotions as she had done, yet a small part of her thought that Sarah couldn't have been as deeply in love with Rob as she had been with Jim, or she wouldn't have recovered so quickly. Then she felt immediately guilty for being so judgemental.

She remembered a particularly useful piece of advice that Sarah had once given her: *Find something good in every day, Jennifer. Take each day as it comes and be thankful for something every single day, no matter how small. Just find something to be grateful for.* She had done this, and it *had* helped to pull her through the worst months after Jim had left her. One day it might be a successful meeting, making her working day more bearable, another day it might only be a tractor in front of her on the way to work pulling off to one side of the road to allow her to pass. They were usually little things that didn't matter one bit in the grand scheme of things, but the very act of being grateful for them kept her mood positive that little bit longer, which was so worth it.

Sarah was taking a leaf out of her own book, analysing her life as she had once analysed Jennifer's. This didn't mean she wasn't upset; she did miss Rob (though God only knows why, she asked herself) and she still felt hurt and betrayed, but she knew she had to put it behind her as best she could. Jennifer had offered to help her find a flat the previous weekend but Sarah had said that she had to sort out practicalities with Rob, and this was better tackled sooner than later. They had since agreed to put the house on the market, and as soon as she had found a suitable unfurnished flat to rent she would collect the rest of her things. It was all very clinical, and somehow less painful than Sarah had expected.

So Sarah wasn't able to join Jennifer this weekend and there were only seven for dinner. *Seven, my God!* Jennifer hadn't cooked for this many for years! Anyway, she wasn't going to let that worry her. She had carefully planned the menu and bought all the ingredients. They were having asparagus with orange vinaigrette as an hors d'oeuvre, followed by roast leg of lamb stuffed with thyme and apricot accompanied by roasted Mediterranean vegetables, roast baby potatoes in garlic and fresh green beans. The dessert was to be her pièce de resistance. She had thought of making a simple tarte au citron with homemade ice-cream, but in the end had plumped for a boozy choco-late orange fondue with fresh fruit. Fresh strawberries, slices of pas-sion fruit and orange segments would be skewered and dipped in the mouth-watering rich chocolate and cointreau sauce. Jennifer was hoping that a fondue would encourage a more intimate, relaxing atmosphere. She wanted to create an easy-going ambience, mainly to keep herself calm because she was nervous. She told herself that this was silly — she worked with these people, for goodness' sake. She saw most of them every day, so what was she worried about? She supposed it was partly because as they'd not been to the cottage before they'd be curious to see how she lived, which rather put her life on show, and she wanted to give them a good impression. She wanted them to love her cottage and her lifestyle as much as she did. Why that was so important to her she really didn't know. She was also nervous because this was the first time she'd given a dinner party like this on her own. She had no support, no-one to help with food preparation and clearing or to share the responsibility if something went wrong. No-one to rescue the conversation if it lapsed or veered too dangerously towards an unsuitable topic. She was cook, kitchen maid and bottle-washer, and the burden of being hostess was hers alone.

The telephone jolted her from her thoughts. She rinsed her hands under cold water and dashed to the phone, drying them on her apron as she went. It was Jane.

'Hello Jennifer, it's Jane. Just ringing to check what time you'd like us to arrive, ' Jane's calm tones made Jennifer feel strangely reassured, at least for a moment.

'Oh hello, Jane, seven forty-five for eight would be great.'

'Is there anything we can bring, apart from booze I mean?'

'No thanks Jane, just yourselves.'

'Sure? Like any help with anything?'

'No thanks. Thanks for the offer though — everything is under control, I think, ' Jennifer laughed nervously.

'Okay then, ' Jane replied warmly, 'see you at quarter to eight. We're looking forward to it!'

'Me too. Bye.'

Jennifer walked back into the kitchen and looked around. *Everything's under control — huh!* The vegetables needed preparing, the orange vinaigrette was only half-finished and the lamb wasn't in the oven yet. Only the chocolate sauce was ready! That figured! She'd been dipping her finger in it each time she passed the bowl for the last half hour! Now a thin crust was beginning to form as the chocolate cooled, so she'd better stop messing with it. Jennifer looked at the clock; it was four thirty. Better get a move on. The lamb would have to go in at six thirty to be ready for eight. Jennifer went back to the pestle and mortar and finished crushing the garlic and thyme. She added some olive oil and lemon juice and mixed in some dried apricots. Then she stuffed the mixture into the lamb and put some on top. OK, meat ready – what next?

In the ensuing hour or so, potatoes were scrubbed, fruit washed, orange grated, beans peeled and asparagus snapped. Then the table was laid in the dining room. Out came the best, in fact the only, white linen tablecloth. She polished the wine glasses and each piece of cutlery with a tea towel as she placed it. She only had six of everything, so had to provide extras from the kitchen dresser which didn't match the set. *C'est la vie.* She arranged cheeses and red and white grapes on an impressively large stoneware dish with a domed lid, and set this on the oak sideboard along with side plates, the wine and the fruits for dessert.

The late afternoon sun was shining in through the windows, filtered at the edges by green tendrils of clematis and wisteria leaves. Flowering over some months before, they were still expanding furiously as if to capture and incorporate the last full month of summer sun, and their leaves caressed and softened the cottage windows comfortingly.

Jennifer checked the room. The warm diffused orange light bathed the ensemble. The plain wineglasses glinted like crystal. The room looked cosy and inviting. She placed candles in individual stoneware holders on the windowsill for later and was just about to close the door on the room when she suddenly remembered. *Bugger!* She only had four dining-room chairs. They'd had a couple of others, but Jim had taken those. What to do? Okay, she had a garden chair she could use, but that still left two to find. Who could she bear asking? She rang Jane.

'Hi Jane, it's Jennifer. Look, this is really embarrassing, but is there any chance you and David could bring two dining room chairs with you?'

'Absolutely no problem, ' Jane replied. Her tone was kind and generous, so Jennifer felt easier about asking.

'If it's okay with you, shall we come ten minutes early so we can bring them in before the others arrive?'

'Jane... you are a star. That would be perfect. Thank you so much!'

Jennifer put down the phone. She was glad she'd asked Jane and not one of the others. Jane seemed to understand. Jennifer didn't know her particularly well, having only met her briefly a few times at formal company functions, but she'd warmed to her on their first meeting and again just now. She was looking forward to seeing her again; perhaps they would get to know one another a little better.

Right... chair problems solved; lamb was in the oven and beginning to smell wonderful; remaining dishes prepared for cooking when their time came; the house was sparkling. Was there really nothing left to do? Jennifer looked at the kitchen clock for the hundredth time. Five past seven. Another minor panic – what about her?! She hadn't showered or anything. She jumped through the shower, barely showing her body the water. Washing quickly wasn't a problem, but her long thick curls usually took ages to dry. That done, she chose an elegant, low-cut burnt-flame-patterned silk dress which hung easily on her slender frame and perfectly fitted her curves. The material caught the light as she moved, bringing the flames to life and making them dance to her step. She applied the minimum of make-up, carefully accentuating her wide green eyes, and had just finished putting on her lipstick when the first knock at the door resounded. A glance at her watch confirmed that Jane and David were spot on time. She ran downstairs and opened the door.

'Hi Jane, hi David, come on in. Let me help you with that.' She took a chair from Jane and led them into the lounge.

'Here, let me have that. Make yourselves at home. I'll just hang your stole up, Jane. Wow, that's a beautiful dress!'

Jane's shimmering peacock-blue sleeveless dress complimented her slender tall frame and long neck. The low-cut rounded neckline fell about her shoulders and her long black hair was neatly twisted into a French pleat. She looked exquisitely elegant.

'Where do you want these?' David shouted after Jennifer as she hurried out of the room.

'Oh, ' said Jennifer, reappearing just as quickly, 'the dining room's through here.' She went to retrieve one of the chairs.

'No – you lead, we'll carry, ' said David.

They followed her into the dining room and deposited the chairs.

'Only five pounds an hour for the two of them, ' David teased.

'Excellent rates, ' replied Jennifer, 'thank you so much! I'd have had to saw the legs off the table and we'd have been eating Japanese-style otherwise! Now, what can I get you to drink?'

'Oh, here's a couple to add to the collection.' Jane handed Jennifer two bottles of wine.

'Chilean Carménère, very nice! Thank you.'

Jane looked at the groups of bottles on the sideboard and chose a gin and tonic.

'How about you, David?'

'D'you know what I'd really like? I just fancy a glass of champagne.' Jennifer's face dropped 'Oh, I'm sorry...' she started.

David winked as Jane nudged him in the ribs. 'A beer would be great, ' he smiled.

'Theakston, Black Sheep or John Smith's? Sleeve or handle? You look like a handle man.'

'Now you're talking. Got to keep my grip in shape. Black Sheep, please.'

'He's cultivating a couple of handles of his own, ' Jane laughed, pinching David around the waist.

'Steady woman, I'm keeping those for later, ' he replied, catching her hand and giving it a squeeze.

Jane laid a hand on Jennifer's arm.

'Jennifer, I think this is the most beautiful cottage.' she said. 'I love these windows. The whole place has a kind of...' she paused, searching for exactly the right words '...of warm glow about it, a special feeling.'

It was strange, but once again Jane's calm tones soothed Jennifer's nervousness. She felt reassured, and delighted in Jane's words.

'It's lovely that you should say that, because that's exactly how I felt when I first walked into the place!' she agreed. 'I can't explain it, but I just felt at home here and I knew I had to buy it.'

'Jane senses these things, ' David observed. 'She likes touching old things and imagining the past. You know I had to drag her kicking and screaming out of the Elizabethan Coffee House in Petergate.' He turned to Jane '...Or was that because you wanted seconds of banoffee pie?' he grinned.

'You old cynic, ' Jane retorted. 'It's a good job I like touching old things!' She poked him in the ribs.

'Hey, far be it from me to remind you that you're nearer to retirement than I am!'

Jennifer left her guests in the lounge admiring her Russell Flint while she went to check the lamb. The limited edition was the prize of her modest and mixed collection of artwork, which included a couple of Mackenzie Thorpes, some bronze sculptures of women by a local artist and assorted paintings of cats. The meat was just about perfect. She had begun to hope that the others would not be late when the front door knocker sounded again. Julia and Tim had brought Antonio with them, and Steve had arrived at the same time. Several more bottles were added to the growing collection, and Antonio presented Jennifer with some Amaretto biscuits from home and a beautiful bouquet of coral roses.

The asparagus had been much appreciated, and everyone seemed to be savouring the succulent lamb. Wine and conversation were flowing freely, and the various tones of Nina Simone, Seth Lakeman and John Lee Hooker accompanied them. Finally Jennifer felt relaxed. She looked happily around the table at her guests. They were a mixed bunch. Everything about David was stylishly comfortable: his tan slacks and buff silk-weave jumper perfectly complemented his sandy hair and freckled complexion and were worn for comfort, in the style he preferred when away from the office. He was fifty-three and had an easy-going nature which he had perfected for social occasions, particularly when mixing with his underlings, although you always knew his boundaries and would never dare to cross them for fear of losing his respect. He and Steve were expounding the merits of English beer to Antonio, who was defending Italian wines. Antonio and David went back a long way, and their close relationship was well-grounded through many years of teasing one another.

Antonio's eyes flashed as he articulated passionately. His impeccable Armani-suited exterior cloaked an excitable yet gentle and sensitive nature. He was romantic to the core, and Jennifer thought his accent was to die for. He talked passionately, it seemed, about everything, throwing himself into debates, participating in conversations with his whole body. However his fervour rose to an altogether higher degree when he spoke, with great tenderness, of his wife Marlette and their two daughters.

Steve, on the other hand, though not the youngest of the group at thirty-one, could easily be mistaken for such. He was one of those guys about whom people say, 'I'm sure he meant well', or 'He wouldn't have meant to offend'. He wasn't insensitive on purpose or malicious in any way, and he really didn't mean to be thoughtless. He was the proverbial joker in the organisation. Jennifer believed that every well-rounded social group should have one, and probably did, although he was not here for that purpose. Jennifer liked him immensely – well, the majority of the time, when he wasn't winding her up early in the morning with incessant quips. Actually he'd do anything for her, and for most people. He had a heart of gold, and also a stomach for beer which had provided him with the stature to match his jolly nature. Jennifer guessed that underneath the humour he was a bit lonely.

Julia, a pretty, well-travelled twenty-six-year-old with practical but stylish short sporty blonde hair to match her personality, was the youngest of the group. She and Tim seemed to be getting on very well. Jennifer wondered whether 'getting it on' might not be a more appropriate term. They seemed to have similar outdoor interests and had been comparing Munroe-bagging, skiing tips and white-water rafting in the Himalayas. Jennifer privately named them the Scramble Twins. They couldn't have dressed more similarly if they'd been colour-matched and made over on *Richard and Judy*. Both were wearing only the best 'this-year's-colours après-scrambling-up-a-mountain' gear. They looked like a pair of action dolls.

Tim was one of those slightly annoying people you envied just a little for being good at everything he tried his hand at – except marriage, by all accounts – but whom you also admired. He was extremely capable and was Jennifer's right-hand man at the office. He was statuesque and well-spoken and had a high degree of literary acumen. Although one sensed that he was fully aware of his many qualities he was not in the least boastful, banging his drum in a far more subtle manner., Jennifer was the more experienced professionally, yet socially she felt slightly clumsy in his presence. She recalled him admiring the host's Baldwin Grand, clearly a new acquisition, at a sophisticated function in Milan and complementing him on his excellent rendition of the *Moonlight Sonata*, which even to the untrained ear was a little shaky, before surprising the assembled guests with perfect performances of 'Maple Leaf Rag' and an excerpt from Rachmaninov's third piano concerto. Extraordinary.

They were onto the dessert and various noises characteristic of approval resounded around the cosy candlelit room as succulent pieces of fruit were eagerly coated in the warm boozy chocolate and popped into appreciating mouths. Ironically the conversation had turned to ritualistic consumption.

'There is a tribe in Papua New Guinea, the Mae Enga, where pigs play a significant role in their existence.' Julia was saying. 'The pig is more highly revered than the women.'

'Ah, my long-lost kin, ' interrupted Steve, 'that wouldn't be hard, considering most of the women I know.' Eyebrows were raised. 'Present company excepted, of course.'

'Pigs are their greatest symbol of wealth and their main source of protein, but their pigs are only sacrificed for the most important occasions, ' Julia continued, waving a chocolate-covered fork, trying to ignore Steve, 'and ceremonies have to be spaced far enough apart to optimise the pig population.'

'The converse is true in our household, ' David interjected. 'I only sacrifice Jane once a week, but boy does she get plenty of pork!'

Jane raised her eyebrows again and countered woefully, 'A little beefcake would be nice from time to time!'

'And before you mention it, ' Jennifer raised her palm toward Antonio, 'don't say anything about suckling pigs, Antonio. I don't eat babies of any kind!'

'Ah, then I will not compliment you on the delicious young lamb we 'ave just eaten.'

They all grimaced. Tim brought the conversation back to tribal practices. 'There's a tribe in South America that drinks the bones of their dead in a soup. It's believed that in this way they can assimilate the wisdom of those that have died and that their spirits will live on.'

'I've read that the Tahitians really celebrate when someone dies because they believe in reincarnation and that the spirit has begun an exciting journey towards the next life, ' Jennifer added.

'You don't believe in all that, do you, Jennifer?' Steve asked dubiously, forcing his eyebrows together above his nose.

'I don't really know. I'd kind of like to, ' Jennifer shrugged. 'It seems comforting, in a way.'

'To know that this isn't our only chance, ' Jane accorded.

'Only chance to what, exactly?' enquired Antonio, running his right index finger around the base of his wine glass in deep contemplation.

'To get it right, ' Jane responded thoughtfully.

'Ah, but we 'ave to. At least as far as I am concerned. We 'ave only one earthly life to make the most of what God has given us.'

'And then what, Antonio?' Tim joined in.

Antonio raised his right hand, making it into a fist, and gave a thumbs-up sign. 'Then my friend, it's either up or...' he reversed the sign, pointing towards the floor. 'Though I'm not sure which would be more fun!' he chuckled.

'So where is heaven exactly? Cause I'd like to choose an angel, you know, for when the time comes, ' Steve teased, 'perhaps one of Charlie's'.

'You old cynic!' Jennifer laughed as she poured some more Carménère and handed a bottle of Muscat-Beaumes-de-Venise to Tim, ' – and you're showing your age, ' she added.

'Ha, ha. I used to have a poster of them on my wall as a kid, ' retorted Steve. 'Pretty nice poster!'

'What do you believe, then? Jennifer asked, as David was busy explaining Charlie's Angels to Antonio.

'Me, I believe when you're dead that's it. In a box. End of story, ' Steve declared with some finality.

'Oh no!'

'That's awful!'

'Depressing, ' Jane, Jennifer and Tim responded en masse.

'That would be terrible, ' Jane continued, 'if there was nothing at all. What would be the point?'

'The point of what?' Steve countered, enjoying the attention now that he seemed to be in the minority. 'Of life? Don't get me wrong, ' he went on, 'I mean, I believe in good and evil, but we're all just biological organisms when it comes down to it. Flesh and blood. Carbon, hydrogen and nitrogen, ' he paused for a reaction, 'with a few other elements thrown in, of course. Why should there be anything else?'

'I agree with you about the flesh and blood bit, ' Julia decided carefully, 'but how do our brains work, I mean, our memories? That's pretty amazing, isn't it?'

'Don't look at me, I'm not a bloody neurologist!' Steve helped himself to another beer.

'Have you read the Bloxham tapes, ' David pitched in, 'about people being regressed to former lives? Published in the 1960s? And there have been similar accounts in the literature since then. Some amazing stories.'

'Do you believe everything you read, David? 'Ow do you know there is any truth at all in these writings?' teased Antonio, his face giving nothing away, knowing full well that David did believe in reincarnation, as they had had many a discussion about their divergent religious beliefs over the years. He winked at David.

'What kind of stories, David?' asked Jennifer.

David leaned forward, pleased to be given the chance to talk to someone new about his favourite topic. 'Well, for example, there was a guy named Graham Huxtable who was regressed by Bloxham to a former life as a gunner on an eighteenth-century British frigate. He used all sorts of obscure nautical terminology under hypnosis. And there are other examples of people who have spoken not only in another language which they claim not to have any knowledge of, but in an archaic form of that language.'

'What my friend does not mention,' interrupted Antonio gently, 'is that there are also plenty of unsubstantiated cases and examples where people 'ave spoken inaccurately about 'istorical facts. That Murphy woman, for example – what's 'er name?'

'Oh, I read about her somewhere,' Tim said, 'wasn't she the one, Virginia someone from Colorado, I think, claimed to have become this Murphy woman under hypnosis in the 1950s? Supposed to have lived in nineteenth-century Ireland. Lots of details, but no-one could find any proof of a Bridey Murphy ever having existed, and it turns out that this Virginia woman had lived near to an Irish woman in her childhood and might have picked up all the details from her.'

'Cryptomnesia.' Antonio declared happily.

'Crypto what?' said Julia.

'Cryptomnesia. I was tryin' 'ard to think of the English term. It's where the subconscious memories that are stored away up 'ere,' he tapped his head, 'come out under 'ypnosis, but they can include all sorts of information. Things that you've read, seen in films, conversations 'eard and forgotten for a very long time'.

'Yes but why does it have to be one or the other, Antonio? Black or white, no grey?' David retorted.

Jane helped her husband out. 'For example, there was the case of someone who claimed to have lived in the time of Ramses the Third. One of the cases against this was that a true ancient Egyptian couldn't have known the pharaoh by a number because the numbering of the pharaohs was first brought in by Victorian Egyptologists. But perhaps it's possible that real experiences can also be overlain by subconscious thoughts from the present life? I mean, this person could have been recounting the time when they lived and maybe other thoughts or pieces of information could have popped in as well.'

'The Buddhists and Hindus believe in reincarnation. And the Egyptians, ' Julia piped up.

'Well, the Egyptians preserved their dead so that their bodies would join their souls in the next world, so more a belief in resurrection I think. Though Chinese Taoism and Jainism join the other two in having roots in reincarnation. Even Plato spoke of it, ' Tim corrected her gently.

Julia threw him an admiring glance that only he and Jennifer caught.

'Hmm. Not altogether convinced, ' Steve pronounced. 'But if anyone can get rid of my obsession for curries under hypnosis, I and my ever-expanding waistline would be very grateful!'

'David's had hypnosis, ' Jane announced, 'and it worked for him.'

'Hey David, I didn't realise you had an obsession with curries too!' Steve chuckled.

David smiled. 'Well there you go!' he said, uncharacteristically self-consciously.

'Oh go on, tell us, ' Jennifer nudged David's arm with her own; the others waited expectantly.

'Well, ' he said slowly and paused for effect, 'I was afraid of flying. Really terrified. Couldn't go within ten miles of an airport.'

'But you fly all over the place, almost every fortnight!' Julia said incredulously.

'Exactly. I do now, ' David returned. 'Once I began to go to meetings abroad I tried everything going. I was on beta-blockers every time I flew, which wasn't that often in the early days, but it was the only way I could get on the plane. It was awful. I was having nightmares days before I was due to go. And as the responsibility increased and the meetings in Milan and Paris became more frequent I found myself in the unenviable position of having to make a decision about my future with Sensura. Jane and I talked about it and decided that the career I wanted would involve flying sooner or later, whoever I worked for, and that our lives would be much poorer if we were restricted from flying anywhere, so I decided to give hypnosis a go as the last resort. It took nine sessions, and I've never looked back!'

Later, while the others were relaxing in the lounge with coffee, port or Lagavulin, Jane helped Jennifer with the dishes. When the dishwasher was full Jennifer began stacking the remaining pans and serving dishes on the work surface by the sink.

Jane poured herself a coffee and Jennifer another glass of Muscat.

'Here, you relax – I'll give these a quick wash. It won't take long.'

She had the tone of one who had firmly made up her mind and wasn't going to be swayed by any amount of protestation, so Jennifer didn't argue. She was enjoying the opportunity of chatting to Jane alone, getting to know her little by little. She had decided she liked her immensely. She emanated a warmth and kindness of spirit and she was generous and supportive of her husband, laughing at all his anecdotes, however corny, even though she must have heard them on countless occasions. Jennifer conceded that Jane's tranquil nature must stand her in good stead for her challenging post as head secretary in the languages department at York University, where she was constantly approached by students to deal with problems on a scale from utterly irrelevant and extremely irritating to highly important and seriously concerning, the majority falling, thankfully, somewhere in the middle. Median but never mundane.

Jennifer wanted to be more like her. As she sipped her wine and listened to Jane talking about her life at the university she watched a trickle of soapsuds moving slowly across the upturned bottom of a large earthenware dish that Jane had placed on the training board. Tiny groups of close-knit bubbles floating on miniscule aqueous rivulets followed each other gravitationally towards the edge of the platter. Some forked out independently on their own, choosing an alternative route neither significantly quicker nor slower, better or worse – just different. The bubbles dripped off the rim onto either the wooden drainer or, where the dish slightly overhung the work surface, the kitchen floor. The bubbles on the draining board collected happily together in the grooves and ran back into the washing-up bowl to be recycled, while those that hit the floor were abruptly dispersed or trodden on, their eventual fate preordained by the path chosen at the earthenware stage.

Like life, Jennifer reflected, one's fate at any juncture determined by preceding decisions about which road to tread, which dreams to follow. Like the soapsud analogy, all paths were not equal; some turned out to be worse than others although there was often no way of knowing how one would fare on a particular route when standing at the crossroads, or indeed where it would eventually lead. How incredibly hard to make a considered judgment about your ultimate fate. Perhaps, she mused, that was the point.

Jennifer picked up a tea towel and dried the dish, defiantly wiping away all traces of soap and water as if somehow to obliterate fate from her life. The gesture was futile and pointless, and she knew it.

' You look pensive, Jennifer.' Jane was looking at her quizzically.

'I was thinking about what David said about his hypnosis. I was wondering, well… I was thinking perhaps… it might work for me.'

'There's no reason why it shouldn't, ' Jane replied softly, sensing that Jennifer needed to talk.

Jane hoped that Jennifer would open up rather than feeling awkward and embarrassed, holding her thoughts tightly within, facing them alone.

'As long as you're receptive and you find the right hypnotist. You can tackle anything with someone you trust'.

Jennifer confided in Jane about Jim and how she desperately wanted to get her life back into shape and her emotions under control, or at least under better control than they were at the moment. Jane smiled and remarked that she didn't think any woman was ever firmly in control of those little devils, but at the same time she was sympathetic about the cause of Jennifer's despair. She'd been there herself, albeit a long time ago. She told Jennifer she thought it was definitely worth a try but that she needed to find at a reputable hypnotist.

'The guy David went to see is in London, and anyway he's retired now. I'm afraid I don't know of anyone locally. Oh, wait a
minute... ' she tapped her head several times with a slender index finger '... if I had half a brain, I'd be dangerous; at least two
memory cells would be better than the one I've got! I do know of
someone. She has an excellent reputation – well, she did have –
and I'm pretty sure she's still fairly local. About four and a half years
ago the West Yorkshire police were looking for a young woman missing from an abandoned car somewhere towards the upper end of
Wharfedale. The weather was bitterly cold and after almost a week of
searching in blizzard conditions they called off the search. It was all in
the papers. The woman's family was in a terrible state.' Jane paused
to take a sip of coffee.

Jennifer was listening intently. 'Go on, ' she prompted.

'Well, apparently two hours after the search was abandoned a
lady phoned the police and told them where they would find the girl.
She said they'd have to get to her quickly as she was fading fast. I
don't think they believed her at first, thought she was a crank caller.
Anyway, to cut a long story short they found the girl, just where this
lady had predicted, curled up in the remains of a derelict barn, barely
alive.'

'Was she okay?' Jennifer interrupted, 'I mean, did she live? How
did that woman know where she was? How did the girl come to be
there anyway? The woman wasn't involved, was she?'

David popped his head around the kitchen door, steadying himself
on the door frame with one hand.

'Anything I can do for you girls?'

'No thanks, we're nearly done. We'll join you in a minute, ' they
chorused. His head and hand disappeared.

'I think her car had broken down and she'd gone for help and got
lost, ' continued Jane. 'I read that this hypnotist has spiritual powers,
and although she doesn't work as a medium she does receive strong
images about things. From what I remember she described the girl
and the location to the police, and from the description they were

able to find her. My recollection is that the girl lost a couple of toes from frostbite.'

'What was the name of the hypnotist?' Jennifer asked eagerly.

'Christina someone. I'm sure her surname began with a P, or maybe it was a B; sorry, I'm not sure, but I expect you could track her down. The police used her more than once after that and she had a very good reputation for successful hypnotherapy. She was high profile for a while. She used to live in Richmond, but I think she's since moved to escape the media attention. Still somewhere pretty local though, I believe.'

'Thank you, Jane, ' Jennifer touched Jane's arm. 'Thanks for listening to my pathetic problems... and for helping. I really do appreciate it.'

Jane put a hand over Jennifer's where it lay on her arm.

'No problem is pathetic if it's a problem. Sure, people deal with aspects of life differently. What are problems for some aren't for others. If something in your life is a source of distress and pain, that's not pathetic. But it doesn't mean that you can't overcome it either. The human spirit is amazingly strong. Come on, ' she nodded toward the door, 'I'd better go and rescue that husband of mine from too much spirit!'

After her guests had departed and the echoes of their laughter had diminished to nothing the house relaxed in silence. Jennifer lay in her bed in the dark, listening to the stillness. As sometimes happens after happy hours spent with friends, on finding herself alone again the intensity of the loneliness was exaggerated by the previous cheerfulness and companionship. Jennifer suddenly felt a little morose. She resolved to track down this woman, to shed the bitterness that shrouded her like a mantle and to rid herself of the hurt which seemed to have seeped into her veins and infected every part of her body. She reached for the bottle of tablets, which had somehow found their way into her bedside cabinet. She was unsure exactly when she had decided to put them there or why, for that matter; however, her judgment was temporarily adrift in the alcohol-hazed sea that was her mind at that moment and she was intent upon another fix of her secret lover. She knew just how to conjure him up. This evening she had drunk far too much to consider or even care about the consequences of mixing the tablets with alcohol. They were simply a means to an end, and she wanted to go there – was desperate to go there. She shook two pills into her cupped hand and swallowed them with the remains of her Lagavulin.

Five

William cantered across the meadow after his Uncle John. The early morning dew still hung in myriads of tiny droplets on the grasses which swirled around the fetlocks of his mount as they passed through. Here, where the sheep had not shorn the grass, tiny white rosettes of shepherd's purse swayed on slender stems between delicate blue flax and cranesbill, and groups of pale pink orchids, their petals lined with crimson, hosted the occasional late-flowering bee orchid in their midst. Towards the edges of the longer grass and in the short grass where the sheep reigned supreme, violet and yellow heartsease fluttered in the light morning breeze.

William's heart was pounding, racing ahead of the muted rhythm of his brown mare's hooves upon the lush carpet beneath. This outing was undertaken neither with the intention of indulging his pleasure nor purely to keep company with his uncle as he took his exercise, but had another, far more serious purpose. How would he begin? How could he possibly explain the depth of his feelings for Emily? He decided that he could not even attempt this. He would account for as much as he could and no more than was necessary to convince his uncle of the sincerity of his intentions. How would his uncle receive his admission? Would he help by mediating between William and his parents, or would he be compromised by such an impertinent request? Could he be trusted to keep such an important secret? William thought he could, and believed that if the scheme could possibly be realised his uncle would help him. If it was not, John would speak his mind, as he was wont to do. Either way he would have an answer.

John had alighted under a great oak and was leading his grey mare to drink at a small beck which ran through the lowest dint of the meadow. William knew he must seize his opportunity. He dismounted and joined his uncle.

'Sir... Uncle... may I speak with you? It is a matter of a most delicate nature and of the greatest importance.'

His uncle looked up, red-faced from the exertion of the canter; he was not a fit man by any stretch of the imagination.

'Well my boy, I should say by the look on your face you mean to share a confidence. If I'm not mistaken there is a lady involved, ' he replied, poking William lightly in the ribs with his whip.

'You are very perceptive, sir, but I fear you may not... what I mean to say... I fear your ... displeasure... once you are fully apprised of my... er... circumstances.' William twisted and turned his mount's reins between his fingers.

'Ah! Now I begin to see. Let me see... a young lady has set her cap at you and you cannot return her affections.'

'No, that is not it.'

'You wish to declare your intentions to a young lady and you seek my assistance with the letter?'

'No sir, that is not it either. The theme of what I am trying to impart is infinitely more delicate than those you have mentioned.'

'Ah – I smell intimacy, ' his uncle replied matter-of-factly.

'Well, yes, that is so. You see... '

'A boy must sow his oats, ' his uncle interrupted assertively, 'but he must not let that come between himself and the semblance of propriety. Whoever she is, send her away; pay her if you must, but be aware that she can never lay the blame at your feet, for her shame will guarantee her silence.'

'Uncle, please! What you speak of is abhorrent to me! I speak not of blame but of love. I entreat you to hear me out. Then you shall pronounce your verdict.'

'Love, eh? Love and intimacy. The intrigue grows stronger. Pray continue, ' John returned loudly, half smiling to himself.

Though he should have been cautioned by his uncle's initial reaction, so desperate was he to engage his uncle's abetment and release the burden of his guilty secret to another that William did not glean any warning from the nature of his uncle's speech. He told John everything, taking great pains to praise Emily's intelligence and wit; her sensitivity and humility. William spoke of her sense of propriety and the fact that she had bettered herself and indeed continued to do so, and of how the pace of her betterment was quickening daily so that he had no doubt of her ultimate capabilities. He emphasised that he did not wish to hurt his dear mother and father, nor any of his sisters. Nor did he intend in any way to bring them shame, so sure was he that Emily could eventually pass as his French wife and appear perfect in all respects.

When at last William had ceased his confession there was a silence between them for some moments.

At first John had been about to say how ridiculous this circumstance was and that William should put the matter behind him. He also doubted very much that she could pass for a high-ranking member of society, as the cover would have to be complex indeed to fool a circle of people that lived on rumour and scandal and where one is always bound to encounter someone who knows the family of which one speaks. Will should get rid of this hussy and make sure she did not talk. But slowly the realisation of two things came upon him and he saw how he could turn this most unfortunate situation to his advantage. It was his comprehension of Emily's possible parentage, that he himself could be her father, that sparked the feeling of gleeful revenge in his belly. How exquisite to finally get the better of his elder brother – a brother who had always taken the moral high ground; a brother who thought himself more worthy than John; a brother who had inherited their father's estate. Since he had been old enough to understand the convention of inheritance, John had lived with a feeling of crushing injustice and he had hated Thomas from that time on. How delightful, then, that the focus of Thomas' only son's affections should be no other than John's own bastard child, the identity of whom Thomas had taken such pains to protect and who would consequently always remain tethered by the lowly status of her birth. No-one would *ever* say of her, *Her father is a gentleman,* although, ironically, Thomas had long made it clear that he thought his brother undeserving of that title.

The second factor to influence his decision lay in the vulnerability of Emily's position. Like her mother, it seemed she was a headstrong lass. John liked no better situation than exerting his power over women, and this was a perfect opportunity for a little compulsion.

He did not dislike his nephew. He thought him amiable enough; however, William was too like his father for John to feel any great affection for him. Besides, he could still assist William and Emily in their passage to France and simultaneously obtain his revenge on his brother.

He turned to William and said in sincere tones, 'Your testimony has touched a place at my very core. I do not pretend to understand your torment, having been in no similar situation myself, yet I sense your grief. If you are certain of your passions, as I believe you are, I will do what I can to aid your passage to France and to smooth an audience with your father. As fortune would have it, I have a contact in the Limousin area, a very rural backwater, who I believe may be able to make you an offer of accommodation. There you may suffer from lack of society to your heart's content! Do not fear — you may yet have your heart's aspiration *and* your inheritance!'

William could not quite believe what he was hearing. This was all he had hoped for! His uncle was at once an ally and a confidant, someone to whom he could now turn for assistance with the practicalities of executing his bold scheme.

He turned to his uncle. 'Sir, I am overwhelmed by your understanding and your kindness. I am forever in the greatest debt to you. If I could in any small way even begin to repay your benevolence I should be the happiest man alive! Please ask of me what you will.'

'All I would ask of you is that you remain calm and sensible of the gravity of your predicament, ' replied his uncle, thoroughly enjoying himself. 'You would do well to remember that I have not promised a fortuitous outcome, only a degree of positive intervention. I cannot be held responsible for the ultimate reaction of your mother and father to this proposal. However, for your own sake, and yours alone, ' he affirmed, 'I concur that this plan of yours is worthy of our endeavours.'

As they rode for home there was no other thought in William's head than his impatience to reveal the outcome of this discourse to his lover. For the present his mind was devoid of caution and full of excitement. Finally he and his dear Emily would be together – it was actually possible! By the very act of sharing the secret, the nature of his relationship with her seemed to have changed from almost illusory to phenomenally real in a moment. He wanted her now more than ever before; to make her his wife and keep the love of his family was all that he desired of life, and as God was his witness, he would have his way.

That afternoon, William found his mother in the drawing room. He was hoping that she might be attended by Emily, as he had sought his lover unsuccessfully.

'Ah, William, ' Charlotte looked up from her book, 'I had hoped I might see you before dinner.'

William walked over to his mother, struck a casual pose on the window seat next to her chair and kissed her hand.

'Mama, ' he acknowledged. Then, looking at the text in her lap, he raised his eyebrows. '*Emile*. What would Papa say?' he teased.

'It may surprise you to know that your Papa and I share many opinions. Indeed there are many commonalities between us and therefore much equality according to Rousseau, ' she riposted, inclining her head, her eyebrows raised in answer to his, though she spoke the last slightly disdainfully. She continued, 'Though you were not fed at my breast, you were not swaddled either.'

'Mama, please!'

Having challenged her son's sensibilities in the presence of his mother, Charlotte playfully persisted, enjoying her upper hand. 'And you cannot deny that your education has been only part book learning, that you have had much interaction with your wonderful surroundings and have been taught much in the way of agriculture and the running of the estate. There your Papa and I also agree with Rousseau.'

William grinned at his mother, sensing a chink through which he could dart a counter-argument. 'One can hardly call that a *trade,* Mama. However, you would agree, would you not, that our lands and the folk that benefit from them flourish under the careful, knowledgeable and sympathetic management of my father. Hardly an example of *degeneration in the hands of man.*' Without waiting for a response William continued, confident of winning the debate, 'And I'm not entirely sure that Papa's belief in constitutional monarchism would go so far as to support the *denaturing of man*, or indeed the concept of *general will.*'

'As neither do I, young man, ' Charlotte interrupted, raising her chin to her son, 'and before you begin on the differences in the moral relations of men and women, neither do we believe that women are made specially to please men! However, it is as well to be advised of publications of controversy so that one can converse intelligently in society... do you not agree?'

William conceded with a wide smile, bending down to give his mother a kiss on the cheek.

Her face was gracefully illuminated by his show of affection. She changed the topic. 'I am to leave tomorrow for York, where I shall reside for some days. Do I understand you to be accompanying your father to Northallerton?'

'Indeed, Mama, we plan to attend the cattle fair in search of fine black oxen. There are always a good many more beasts of excellent shape and breeding at Northallerton than at any other market hereabouts, ' he replied enthusiastically.

Charlotte smiled. Will was so like his father.

'So then, ' William continued, 'may I ask what your plans are? Will you be at cards or perhaps the theatre? His thoughts now were not of cards or the theatre but of his dear Emily. He *must* find her, he *must* see her this night and tell her of this morning's events before she was gone to York with his mother, as she would undoubtedly be instructed to do.

'There is a performance of Romeo and Juliet that I am mindful to attend. And I shall of course be entertaining the Snaiths.'

Charlotte looked into her son's face for any sign of curiosity. With her husband and son safely ensconced some twenty miles from their residence in York she had invited Miss Susan Snaith and her mother and sisters to join them. The Snaiths owned land near the port of Selby, twenty or so miles south of York. Their vast fortune was founded on merchant business; they had been a family of merchants for some five generations past, although the current Lord Snaith engaged mainly in politics now. Besides being of immense fortune and a Whig, Lord Snaith had three daughters and no sons. Miss Susan was their eldest, and although given to irascibility she was well-mannered and pleasant enough. Charlotte believed that her fine features more than compensated for her occasional sourness, and was of the opinion that her acidity would be tempered by marriage to an appropriate man. The right man, of course, was Will. He would bring out the best in Miss Susan. Charlotte was sure that she had already witnessed the beginnings of such a transformation at the Snaiths' last Christmas ball.

Charlotte looked again at her son. He did not seem to be paying due attention to their discourse but was staring at the oak and rosewood long-case clock which stood against the opposite wall. In her enthusiasm for matchmaking Charlotte mistook this as a sign that the very mention of Miss Susan's name brought her son into deep contemplation.

'Of course Anne, Rebecca and Elizabeth will be accompanying me, ' Charlotte continued. 'Rebecca especially enjoys the company of Miss Susan's younger sisters, they being of similar age. And although Anne has a full three years on Susan, they seem to do very well together. Besides, Mr Calder has some business in York, and I have no doubt that he will call upon Anne while we are there. I have it in my mind to invite the Snaiths to stay here for a week or two next month to coincide with our summer ball.'

'I did not know that you and Lady Snaith were on such close terms, ' replied William, finally managing to focus on his mother again, this time with some effort.

'She is amiable enough, but it is Miss Susan with whom I particularly would like to make better acquaintance, ' replied Charlotte, patting her sons' hand.

'Why on earth..?' The focus of the present conversation finally began to dawn upon William. 'Mama, ' he warned, 'Mama, with respect...'

'You cannot disagree; she would be a most excellent match, ' his mother interrupted, raising her shoulders, 'and so convenient, their estates but forty miles or so from ours!'

'Mama, please!'

'Come now, Will. She has a pretty face, do you not think?' Charlottes eyes glinted. She knew her son well, and she knew how to bring him round. Her determination grew with every counter from him.

'Her visage is pleasing, that I cannot deny.'

'And she is intelligent, witty?'

'She has a reputation for a quick temper, Ma'am.'

'Nonsense. Have you seen evidence of this, Will? In my opinion she is a sweet girl. I did not think you one to heed gossip, ' Charlotte rejoined.

'She has been the essence of politeness in my company. That is all I can say, ' William replied flatly.

'As I recall, she has a quick wit and light feet — did you not dance four dances with her at the Snaiths' Christmas Ball?'

William was growing frustrated. 'I do not remember. If I danced with her it was out of respect for our hosts and for no other reason. Mama, when I marry it will be for love.' William descended to his knees and took both his mother's hands in his own. 'I cannot comprehend a union without love. It is as impossible to me as day without a night to follow, or the setting of the sun for the last time. Marrying without love would indeed be as perpetual darkness to me. Is not a person's happiness the most wonderful of God's gifts?'

Charlotte looked into her son's beautiful blue eyes and, for the first time, saw something she did not recognise and could not put a name to. It was as if torment and passion were somehow intermingled. She found herself agreeing with him, though caution chose the words she spoke.

'Happiness and love can grow strong from the most unlikely of roots if nurtured with care, yet a minimum of tenderness is required as sustenance until the bloom, ' she said softly. 'For my part, I should never force you to marry against your will. However you must allow me to exercise my judgment in presenting suitable candidates. My role is merely as a facilitator of opportunity.'

William rose from his knees. 'I respectfully acknowledge your erudition in these matters, ' he returned, 'yet my heart will have a say. If I presented to you a person of high intelligence and wit, sensitive and kind-hearted, sensible and strong, who strove every day to improve upon those attributes – I am theorising of course – would you agree to the match?'

Charlottes eyes followed William as he paced about the room. 'Is she agreeable, this hypothetical creature?'

'Oh yes, she has the face of an angel.'

'And what of her fortune?'

William spoke cautiously. His mother's belief in the education and improvement of women did not transcend tradition and proper social practice.

'Ah, that I cannot say, for my dreams have not instructed me thus.'

'Well then, ' laughed Charlotte, 'if you can find such a lady as your fantasy dictates you will be most fortunate indeed, and I would be honoured to meet her. Although you would be well advised to imagine also a large estate and a father with similar political tendencies to those of your own Papa in order to gain his consent, ' she added.

William left her to her schemes and went in search of Emily once more. Judging by his mother's mood for matchmaking, it was imperative that he meet with his lover to discuss the progress of his own designs. Above all he wanted to hold her, to stroke her hair and allay her fears, to look into her beautiful eyes and reassure her again of his unswerving love and of his intentions. An urgency was about him now. The time to approach his parents would soon be upon him. He must act before his Mama became too deeply enveloped in matching him with Miss Snaith, else she would be near impossible to move on the matter. He feared his Papa's reaction the most. In dealing with this, his reliance upon his uncle would be heavy indeed. William was of course aware that his father and uncle did not always see eye to eye; however his desperate situation blinded him to the true nature of their relationship, and instead he chose to believe in the strength of kindred blood.

Thomas was pacing about the drawing room, turning every now and then to look at his wife and shake his head. Charlotte sat quietly continuing her embroidery, a picture of serenity. She had become a practiced expert at projecting one emotion whilst inwardly controlling another. It was the best way of dealing with her husband at times such as this. Inside she was furious that he should dictate to her how she should treat her maidservants – even more so because she knew he was right, although of course she would never admit it. She had been speaking of her imminent visit to York, mentioning her plan to request that Emily accompany her, as her waiting maid, to the theatre. Thomas had strongly objected, Emily being but a lady's maid and not a lady-in-waiting. He had pointed out that Charlotte would have all the company she needed in their two daughters, who were to accompany her to their home in York, and Lady Snaith and her brood.

Charlotte had defended her decision with the justifications that although Emily was not a lady-in-waiting, her manners were such that she could be infinitely trusted to represent her in polite society, and that she would benefit from attending the planned performance of Romeo and Juliette, having read it to Charlotte a number of times.

'I do not doubt that Emily would greatly enjoy the performance, ' Thomas said frustratedly, his eyebrows brought together in the frown he directed towards his wife. 'My objection is seated in principal and protocol. You favour her significantly above the other servants, far more than her position deserves. She is often dressed above her status. You allow her to accompany you when you visit your charity school. And now you want her with you at the theatre, not simply to hold your seat but throughout the performance! It is unnecessary. You are elevating her. She will not thank you when the other girls become too jealous. Think on that!'

An image popped into Charlotte's mind of Emily helping her to teach some of the poorest children in the parish to read at the little school established by their vicar, which she patronised; of Emily patiently listening to a shy lad only a couple of years younger than her, turning the pages of the Bible and mouthing the words as he spluttered his way through a few simple paragraphs. She had shown just the right combination of encouragement and respect to avoid causing him embarrassment and to help him to enjoy the words. She smiled inwardly, and at her husband.

'I confess I do think of her as more than a lady's maid sometimes. I cannot deny it. Sometimes I forget myself a little with her. She is so... improved.'

'Yes, and you have played no small part in that, my dear, ' Thomas returned matter-of-factly, 'but there are limits. You will end up elevating her above her family status and no good can come of that, I can assure you, ' he continued firmly, his features set in worry and frustration clear in his voice.

'But I feel strangely... drawn towards her. Almost like... a... companion.' Charlotte defended hesitantly. 'Perhaps it's because she might be, you know, she could... be ... John's...'

'Yes, yes – and she could equally be Daniel Popple's child!' Thomas interrupted angrily.

A shadow crossed his face momentarily and he turned towards the window away from his wife. His skin prickled and his heart beat furiously for some moments before subsiding into its usual rhythm. When he had regained his composure he turned again to her.

'We have spent all these years ensuring that the possibilities of her parentage have never been divulged, ' he said forcefully. 'And for good reason. And I will *not* have this repeatedly raised, nor risk any suspicion brought about by your favoured treatment of her. Think of Constance – she would never survive the shame, having so delicate a nature.'

Charlotte chose her words carefully. 'My dear Thomas, I would never risk hurting Constance, please believe me! I shall do as you ask, and will be more guarded in my treatment of Emily in front of the other servants... in the future.'

'Thank you, my dear.' Thomas patted his wife's hand and made for the door. 'If circumstances were... different... well, you know...' he muttered as he headed down the corridor towards his study.

Charlotte sighed and turned towards the window. Emily would be accompanying her to the theatre in York – that was already decided upon and she was not about to change her mind. However, she would have to behave in a more appropriate manner towards her maid at home and in company. It was true, she did feel great affection for the girl. She sighed again – in her eyes the matter had been exaggerated beyond its appropriate proportions. *Ah well, no matter.* She turned her thoughts back to the Snaiths and Miss Susan, and to a much more important topic: her son's future happiness.

Much later that evening, when the last of his family were in their beds, William set out for Emily's room. He had, at last, located her directly before dinner. She had been in his mother's dressing room laying gowns and some of Charlotte's personal items in a trunk in preparation for its conveyance to York. The family kept wardrobes at their York residence however there was always some fluctuation of personal and favoured clothes and belongings. Emily was to accompany her mistress to York and therefore would not see Will for a few days. She was longing to be in his arms, and the thought of being away from him increased the potency of that longing tenfold.

As he entered her room, closing the door quietly behind him, Emily ran to him from the small window seat where she had been sitting waiting, watching the night. She had been musing about how endless were the stars and how immense the sky. That was how she felt about Will. There were not words to describe the love she bore him. She flung her arms around his neck and he lifted her and carried her to her bed. They lay facing one another, speaking in low tones, the gravity of their voices signifying the great secret between them. As she listened to Will telling of his uncle's support Emily felt both excited and terrified. Her dreams were becoming a reality. The very fact of Will's uncle's encouragement lent much-needed weight to her lover's convictions and hence to her belief in a future with him. Her terror arose from a fear of the consequence of divulging their intentions to her ladyship. Beyond that she could not think for the moment. She pictured a multitude of reactions: shock, disappointment, betrayal and rage combined to produce an effect of volcanic proportions. She hoped desperately that her loyalty and years of devoted service to her beloved mistress and the kindness and encouragement she had received in return would count for something, and at least temper the eruption.

'Tell me again how we shall live, ' she murmured, trying to erase the dark thoughts from her mind and replace them with images of a happy married life in rural France, and ultimately England.

William smiled and squeezed her hand. 'We shall journey via Paris to Orléans and thence to the town of Limoges, where we shall first reside for a few days as guests of Monsieur and Madame Beauenne. His work as a physician in the town leaves him little time to visit his cottage, which is some seven or eight miles from Limoges near Verneuil-sur-Vienne and is surrounded by woodland, ' he said reassuringly. 'It is completely safe, and my uncle says that the good doctor is very likely to agree to us living there for a modest yearly fee. I believe there is a staff of three, which would be perfectly adequate for our needs whilst you continue with your education.'

He squeezed Emily's hand again, then gently stroked the curls framing her face with the back of his fingers. 'There we shall have our peace; there in a tranquil forest glade we shall keep company with the deer, and you shall become a French nobleman's daughter.'

'Oh Will, can it be possible?' whispered Emily. 'Is it really to be so?'

'On my life, ' he replied.

'What will happen if your parents do not consent, ' she returned, 'to us... to me? What will become of me then?'

'Do not distress yourself so, my love. I will stand by you. Whatever happens, I shall be by your side. I cannot lose you. To live without you would be to live in hell.' He took her face in his hands. 'Emily, I will *not* abandon you. You *must* believe this.'

'I believe you, Will.' Her words were no more than a whisper, for she felt choked. 'Your words calm my heart and bring me strength. I know I can face anything if I face it with you. I shall do my very best to deserve the faith you have placed in me, to make a respectable French wife! Whatever happens, know that I love you beyond words.'

They made love slowly and with great tenderness. Every movement deliberate, every action designed to afford the greatest pleasure, extending every moment, knowing that this would be the last time they would be together before the coming storm. When at last their passions had subsided they lay entwined throughout the night until the stars began to fade into their canvas and the birds began their celebration of a new day.

Late August

Jennifer and Sarah were flying through the Grand Canyon at sunrise. In fact they were sitting in the dark in a cinema on the outskirts of York in front of a huge IMAX screen, but they could almost believe that they were in Colorado. They were lost in an autumn tapestry of sandstone columns and cliffs, ravines and gullies, outcrops and fissures. As the sun slowly rose the craggy shadows shortened, and a glorious mist of yellows, oranges, burnt reds and terracottas surrounded and enveloped them. Through the wonders of technology they could actually feel the changes in temperature as the heat rose up from the canyon floor as the De Havilland Twin Otter descended and rose, sweeping in and out of the many tributaries, returning to follow the magnificent Colorado River as it snaked and tumbled effortlessly along the stupendous path it had chosen and carved out over hundreds of thousands of years. The bedding patterns of the rock formations twisted and turned about one another as the eastern sun licked at their columns and protuberances, climbing higher and higher, drenching yet more of the seemingly bottomless ravine in its glow.

Both girls had come here to lose themselves for a while. Sarah felt lightheaded one moment, and the next as though her stomach were rising up through her diaphragm and falling again as their virtual vehicle dived and soared that glorious autumn morning, her body now mirroring her recent emotions. For the past month, various thoughts of her new admirer and her former lover pierced her conscious mind in a disorganised and uncontrolled fashion, vying with one another for her affections and her consideration. Her stomach had turned somersaults and her head was filled with relief, dismay, hurt and excitement, guilt and anticipation in turn and all at once in disarray. However this morning she was flying through the most breath-taking scenery she had ever laid eyes on, and she was completely lost in it.

Jennifer, too, had forgotten herself. She was an insignificant dot in an incredible, almost limitless landscape. Their virtual vessel climbed and began a slow left turn, circling over the north rim of the canyon to come about and head west and back the way it had come. While autumn reigned in most of the Grand Canyon National Park, a few miles from the edge of the ravine the rim hosted an extended summer fuelled by the sun's energy which had heated the sandstone gorge like an oven. A mile below the rim the blue river shimmered in the heat. The experience made Jennifer feel very small. For a while she had forgotten her troubles, abandoned her real life and exchanged her second virtual world for another. She was an insignificant being in an immense universe, and her worries were inconsequential in nature's grand scheme. She had made a decision and had to follow it and see it through. And she had to do it alone; she could only do it alone. She could not speak about it, even to Sarah. It was as though she were about to embark upon a journey, and she had no thought or care for the fateful consequences of her decision. It was do or die. That she might *actually* die in the process did not even enter her mind.

Late August 1762

*E*mily looked around her at the audience in the pit and the gentry in the other boxes. Her mistress and her daughters and the Snaiths were in the Fernleigh box to her left. Sent to keep their seats at four thirty, she had moved two boxes away upon their arrival and was sitting with Lady Snaith's waiting maid, Martha, a gentlewoman and the daughter of a clergyman. Martha was engrossed in the performance, forgetting herself occasionally, laughing heartily at the short farce that was concluding the evening's series of performances. Emily was trying to attain as deep a sense of engrossment in the play – ironically entitled *Wedding Day* – as Martha's, but all attempts had failed. She could not concentrate. Romeo and Juliet was her favourite Shakespeare play; she had read it many times and even seen it once before – however, this evening her thoughts had been only of Will and what was soon to come to pass. Even through the tragic climax when Romeo entered the sloping proscenium that was the crypt to find his dear, cold Juliet, when she could almost reach out and touch the players on the forestage so close to the audience were they – even then, at the height of the play's emotional dialogue, she could think only of their impending responsibilities.

During the intervening musical interlude – the playbill listed it as '*Dancing by Mr and Mrs Saunders*' – Emily studied the theatre and its occupants, hoping that concentrating her mind on something a good deal more interesting than the cavorting figures before the footlights would engage her attention sufficiently to distract her from her fearful contemplations. The row of tallow candles floating in their water-filled vessels flickered before their reflectors, which were occasionally turned to dim or accentuate the yellow light. Large round candelabras hung in pairs from the high painted ceiling, which was fashioned after a blue-green sky sporting fluffy white clouds. Their light and that of the pairs of candles hung in a similar fashion around the walls below the gallery illuminated the auditorium, which had recently been given its annual redecoration to remove and replace the previous year's build-up of tallow grease and candle soot.

On a previous occasion when Emily had accompanied her mistress's party, she remembered, the decor had been blue. This year, like the ceiling, the walls and columns of the gallery and boxes were painted a light blue-green, their darker green panels adorned in the classical style and edged in coral and white. Emily thought what a pretty picture the whole made and momentarily lost herself in a dream of a room of her own decorated in such a fashion.

Last year, from her position with the two-shilling audience in the pit, Emily had been able to clearly see the Fernleigh coat of arms, the gleaming red lion standing out from the white shield. This time she had been elevated to a position among the gentry. Now, as she fought in vain to focus on the farcical events being played out before her, she felt butterflies in her stomach and hummingbirds in her head as she thought of Will. As the end of the entertainment drew to a close, the night encroached on day, and with that the following day came ever closer. Tomorrow they would be returning home. In a few days she would see Will and together they would face the consequences of their actions and of their love.

Now with every thought emotion washed through her, a complicated mixture of glee, passion, excitement, trepidation, apprehension and pure fear. Each emotional wave seemed to flush her body of nourishment, draining her energy, and she felt quite faint. She was drowning in him. She had to get some fresh air. The atmosphere in the auditorium hung heavy with tobacco and candle wax, the fine perfumes of the gentry and the potent scents of the one-shilling folk in the gallery above. The farce was ending. Soon she was at her lady's side and out in the night where their carriage awaited.

Much later, in her room, she opened the casement, drank in the cool air and lay in the stillness waiting for dawn and for her fate to be decided.

Six

September

*J*ennifer made the discovery in September. Of course she couldn't know it, but it was to have extreme consequences and would change her life forever.

Christina Peters was not at all as she had imagined. In the process of tracking her down she had developed a strong feeling that this was the right thing to do – the right path to take, the next inevitable step. But as she arrived, unannounced, in the little village just outside Thirsk, Jennifer began to feel extremely nervous. She hadn't been able to get hold of a telephone number for this woman and had had difficulty finding her current address. It was only by a lot of asking around in the area of her last registered practice that Jennifer had finally traced Mrs Peters to this quiet rural backwater. She walked slowly up to the white door of the semi-detached cottage, pulled the wrought iron cat's-head knocker back and let it fall against the door with a sharp crack.

A short, slim elderly lady eventually answered the door, wiping the soil off her hands onto her trousers. The smears joined those from many previous soil-laden wipes.

'Yes? Can I help you?' the lady asked, matter-of-factly.

Not exotic at all, she had a plain face and short straight grey hair cut in a practical style. Jennifer suddenly felt very small and was momentarily lost for words. But she noticed that the woman's eyes looked kind and there seemed to be a hint of twinkle in them. This gave her just enough confidence to speak.

'I'm sorry to bother you, but are you Christina Peters?'

The lady gave the slightest hint of a sigh. 'Yes, ' she said.

'I'm sorry, ' Jennifer repeated 'I didn't mean to disturb you. I found you through the UK Hypnotherapy Association. I mean to say... you weren't on their register now but... I found an old record of where you used to practice... and... well...' Jennifer's voice faded and came to a halt.

The lady gave another little sigh, though smiled briefly at Jennifer. 'I'm retired now, you know. Well, as retired as I can be.'

'Oh... so... you don't practice hypnotherapy any longer?' This seemed rather a pointless question.

'No – not for a living, though...' the woman paused and reconsidered. 'I'm retired now, you see.'

Jennifer was suddenly flooded with disappointment and she burst out crying. She just stood there on the doorstep, head hung in embarrassment, with tears streaming down her face. Her legs didn't seem to want to move.

After a few moments Christina Peters stepped towards her, put one arm around her shoulders and guided her into the house. 'Come on, ' she said brightly, 'I'll put the kettle on. Come in and sit down.'

She sat Jennifer down in a sitting room at the back of the house and disappeared into the kitchen to make a pot of tea. Jennifer heard the kettle starting to hiss. Christina appeared with a small box of tissues and put them down on the wooden coffee table beside Jennifer's armchair and returned to the kitchen. Jennifer dried her eyes and blew her nose. She felt a strong sense of embarrassment and of being a nuisance, but the intense need to talk to this woman kept her there. It was as if she would find answers to what she was looking for here in this little room, though quite what she was looking for she really didn't know. As she listened to the chinking of china from the kitchen she began to look around. The sun was streaming in through a big bay window through which she could see a long garden. Beyond a small stone-flagged patio was a large vegetable plot, and there seemed to be lawns and flowerbeds beyond. The room itself was cosy and reflected an earlier age, although there was no single style to it. A slightly saggy sofa dressed in floral material accompanied the two armchairs, their arms worn and frayed with age. One wall was almost entirely covered in bookshelves; books of all shapes and sizes, standing and piled in all manners, jostled each other for space. On the mantelpiece above a small black wood-burning stove there was a series of photographs in small frames featuring people of various ages. One man in particular was represented a number of times, from a young chap to an elderly man. Jennifer guessed he was or had been the lady's husband.

'My husband Brian, God bless his soul.' Christina had reappeared with a tray of tea things which joined the tissues on the coffee table. She nodded towards the last photo that Jenifer had been looking at. 'Been gone now for two and a half years and I still miss him as if he was with me yesterday. Still, he talks to me and asks if I'm alright, which is a comfort, ' she said straightforwardly. 'Now then, my dear – goodness me, I don't even know your name! Let's have a cup of tea and then we can talk. What *is* your name, flower?'

They chatted over steaming cups of tea and homemade shortbread biscuits. Jennifer found herself telling this stranger about where she lived, about her job, where she had grown up and even about aspects of her childhood she thought she had forgotten. Throughout their conversation, Christina gently asked her questions and encouraged responses so that Jennifer gradually became more and more relaxed.

'You must have been persistent to find me, ' Christina said at length, leaning back in her armchair. 'I moved here with my husband about three years ago to escape the spotlight after the Wharfedale incident – I expect you know about that.' She didn't wait for an answer. 'For a while I kept my practice in Richmond, but then when my Brian died I realised that I needed to stop and regroup. Now I only see a few of my longstanding regulars... and the occasional lost soul.'

Jennifer gave an involuntary shiver. As Christina looked into her eyes she felt as though this woman, this total stranger, was seeing into the very core of her mind, almost reading her thoughts – although her thoughts were confused like the broken strands of a spider's web dangling and shifting in a gentle breeze, becoming more and more entangled as they brushed against each other.

'You have lost someone dear to you, but that isn't entirely why you're here. You need help to control something, but you're not sure whether you want to control it.' Christina paused. 'Do you?'

Jennifer was taken aback. 'I... I don't really know. I don't really know where to start.'

'At the beginning dear – start there. The rest will come.' Christina smiled and softly patted Jennifer's arm. Her manner was so matter-of-fact that Jennifer felt almost normal conversing with her, as if it were the most natural thing in the world to bare her soul to someone she'd only known for thirty minutes.

Jennifer took a deep breath. 'I guess it starts with Jim and me – well, really with the end of Jim and me, ' she replied slowly. Over the next hour or so she told Christina everything, from her relationship with Jim and their break-up to her feelings of rejection and depression, her sense of desperation, her vivid dreams and her feelings for the man who had taken over her thoughts in her sleeping and waking hours, and finally to the moment when she saw his portrait hanging in a drawing room at Fernleigh House. Throughout, Christina prompted gently now and then, nudging Jennifer along. Coming to the end of her narrative Jennifer suddenly felt desperate again. Little waves of panic rose from her stomach and seemed to be choking her. She forced the words out: 'You have to believe me! I *am certain* I never saw a picture of him before that moment! So how did he get into my dreams? How is that possible? Am I going crazy?!'

'If you say you haven't seen him before or known of his existence then I believe you, ' Christina said calmly. 'We can explore this and I can help you with your depression. I can help you to get your life back together.' she ended quietly but firmly. 'Are you willing to undergo hypnotherapy? It's a bit of a silly question since you sought me out, but I have to ask.'

'Yes… yes of course… anything.' Jennifer wiped the corners of her eyes with a tissue plucked from the box beside her.

'OK; well then…' Christina got up and moved across the room to a little writing desk standing against the far wall, opened her diary and thumbed through a few pages, murmuring to herself about various events marked on the pages. She looked at Jennifer over her shoulder '…shall we say next Thursday at two pm? Can you make that?'

Jennifer realised that this was her cue to leave, but already she couldn't wait for the next time they would meet. She knew that whatever was in her diary would wait or have to be rearranged.

'Yes… next Thursday… absolutely.'

They moved into the hallway, and Christina took both Jennifer's hands in her own. 'Well take care then, Jennifer.'

'Yes… yes I will. See you next week. Thank you so much!'

The next few days seemed to pass really slowly, as is often the case when one is waiting for something important. Jennifer was certain that Christina would have answers to the questions and anxieties that seemed to pervade her whole existence: questions she couldn't properly form, anxieties she couldn't clearly define. She wanted to be rid of the feelings of hurt and rejection. So much of her behaviour, her reaction to those around her and her outlook on life seemed to be governed by these emotions. They were like a huge heavy collar around her neck, dragging her earthwards and sapping her of energy. She needed to be free of this burden. The only times the burden completely evaporated and she felt truly happy was during her dreams, with *him*.

Jennifer felt a stab of guilt. She hadn't told Christina everything. Almost everything, but not quite. She reasoned with herself that there had been no need to mention the sleeping tablets. They were inconsequential. They only helped her to sleep; the dreams would have come whether she got to sleep naturally or with a bit of help – wouldn't they? On the other hand, she argued with herself, if they were inconsequential why not mention them? Perhaps she felt a little reckless for trusting a drug she knew nothing about, for taking something into her body that had once caused her to remain unconscious for a whole twenty-four hours. Perhaps, too, she was afraid of being told to stop taking the tablets immediately. She believed that they were in some way her link with *him* and she couldn't bear to risk that link being severed. However, she decided not to use the tablets while she was undergoing the hypnotherapy treatment and hoped that her increasingly frequent use of them over the past couple of months wouldn't be discovered by Christina.

The first session passed without incident. To begin with Jennifer was concerned that after all she would not be able to be entranced. However Christina explained to her that the only people who can't be hypnotised are those who don't want to be, as hypnosis is merely a state of heightened relaxation and altered awareness. She explained that when a person is relaxed in this way it is possible to make contact with their unconscious mind, which is the root of emotion and therefore highly influential in a person's behaviour. Jennifer asked how hypnosis could work for her, and was told that by contacting her unconscious mind the power therein could be employed to support beneficial changes. They would need to explore her subconscious. When she expressed concern about someone being able to control her mind, Christina patiently explained that it wasn't like that at all, that Jennifer would be aware of everything that was said and that in fact her awareness would be enhanced but her body would feel very relaxed, almost as if she were drifting off to sleep. Once Jennifer realised that she would be in control at all times she felt comfortable with the process, and Christina placed her under hypnosis.

Christina first explored Jennifer's childhood and teenage years, looking for signs, incidents or behaviour that might now be shaping her strong feelings of rejection and anguish. She also explored people and events in Jennifer's life that could perhaps be linked to this eighteenth-century character who appeared so frequently and influentially in her dreams. She had done her own research and had located the man, although she could not find much of significance written about him except the recorded dates of his birth and death. Christina was extremely careful not to ask leading questions and to avoid using any wording that might be suggestive or manipulate a desired response. She discovered nothing substantive in their first two sessions.

At the beginning of their third session she decided to try an alternative approach. 'Jennifer, dear, I'd like to try a different method of therapy, with your permission of course. I believe we need to reach deep under the surface of your present life to understand your current anxieties. I'd like to use regression therapy.'

Jennifer stared at Christina blankly for a moment, blinking as a shaft of warm afternoon sunlight, suddenly liberated from behind a downy slow-moving cloud, fell across her face. Her gaze followed its beam across her lap and onto the carpet a little way across the room. She watched the dust motes flicker as they floated around in the light. She remembered the first time she had seen such a beam through a large keyhole in the front door of her grandparents' cottage. She had been only three or four, and had thought that these tiny creatures were travelling purposefully in through the hole on their way to somewhere important. She had stopped and looked at the shaft of light thoughtfully for a while before stepping forward and slowly stretching out her open hand and then clutching the air in front of her. She had been surprised to feel no resistance and had opened her hand to see what she had caught, only to find nothing there. After that she had swung her hand repeatedly through the beam to see if she could grab it or disrupt it and to watch the motes swirling around in the currents of disturbed air. As she sat there in Christina's comfortable saggy old armchair remembering a rather engaging moment in her early childhood, Jennifer slowly realised what Christina had proposed. That she, Jennifer, had a whole life previous to her childhood – perhaps several past lives – and that they could, if they wanted to, open the door to this forgotten world and walk right through.

'I know it's a lot to take in, ' Christina was explaining earnestly, 'but I'm asking you to try to be open-minded. You need to understand what it is that we would be doing. It's not for the faint-hearted. You would be travelling into the depths of your psychological composition. We need to talk about this. I cannot go ahead without your permission, and I can't accept that unless I'm sure you appreciate the consequences.'

Jennifer began to feel a mixture of excitement and trepidation punctuated by scepticism. She was more than curious to find out whether she had indeed lived a past life, if that was possible and wasn't all a lot of nonsense and merely her imagination inventing things. She wasn't particularly religious, and she was open to the idea of reincarnation. But she had significant reservations too.

'It's a bit frightening, Christina, ... I mean... what if you discover something... terrible? What if I did something awful to someone, or had something awful done to me? Once I know something... I can never *unknow* it, can I?'

'That's true, ' replied Christina, nodding her head slowly. 'There are things we may discover that may not be pleasant; conversely, there are things that may bring you joy. Most importantly of all there is something to be discovered that I believe will liberate you from your present emotional difficulties and in doing so should bring you great relief. I believe you *can* cope with the knowledge, or I wouldn't even have conceived of discussing this with you. But it's entirely your decision. I'm not going to try to influence you to go ahead if you don't feel comfortable with it.' She placed her hands in her lap and smiled comfortingly at Jennifer.

Jennifer gave a little sigh of indecision and turned her head to stare out of the window, gathering her thoughts and trying to put them in some kind of order that made sense to her. As she did so a loose curl brushed the eyelashes of her left eye. She caught it and pushed it back into the ribbon that gathered her mahogany mane at the nape of her slender neck; the *black* ribbon, the one she had found between the cushions of the sofa... *the one he had given to her.* At once an intense yearning washed through her, consuming her thoughts and making her body ache with it. She *craved* him, desired him, wished for his arms around her. So strong was her feeling of need that she found that she was hugging herself involuntarily.

Christina witnessed all of this in Jennifer's eyes and in her body language, yet she sat perfectly still waiting for Jennifer to come to her own conclusion.

Jennifer's mind was made up. 'I'll do it, ' she said assuredly. 'I need to know.'

Christina started as usual with the autogenic technique. Slowly she asked Jennifer to focus on each part of her body, starting with her feet and moving slowly upwards, relaxing each area and enabling her mind to concentrate on one small thing at a time. When the time came she began moving Jennifer back in time, further than they had gone before — back to beyond her birth.

'How are you feeling?'

'I'm floating, peaceful, *joyous*. I feel incredible… *blissful.*'

'What can you see?'

'Wonderful colours… colour everywhere… it's beautiful! The light is so bright, it's everywhere, reflecting, refracting…' Jennifer's face reflected contentment.

'What are you sensing?'

A pause. '… Knowledge.'

'What kind of knowledge?'

'I've been… reviewing… my… experiences.' Jennifer seemed to be struggling for the right words.

'Why?'

'Progression.'

'Are you alone?'

'No… my Guide is with me.'

'How do you feel about this knowledge?'

A long pause. '… I'm not ready to go back yet.'

'To go back where?'

'To earth. I like it here.'

'What are you feeling now?'

'I feel... *whole.*'

It was Christina's turn to pause. 'Shift back to your previous life on earth; go back to a happy time in your childhood.' Then, after a few seconds she asked, 'Where are you?'

'I'm in a field, ' Jennifer replied, with a little smile on her face. Her voice had changed, was somehow softer and had a slight Yorkshire tinge about it.

'How old are you?'

'I am four.' Jennifer stated proudly. 'It was my birthday two days ago!'

'What is happening?'

'A boy is chasing me. He's chasing me with a lamb's tail in his hand!'

'What are you feeling?'

'I'm laughing! I like him... he makes me laugh.'

'What does he look like?'

'He has dark hair and blue eyes.'

'What is he wearing?'

'His britches are torn and he has lost the buckle from one of his shoes!'

Christina moved Jennifer forward step by step, trying to uncover any significant events and discover clues to when this life had taken place. It seemed that this past-life childhood had been a relatively happy one apart from the mention of a stillborn sister. Although this event was described with sadness, Christina detected an undertone of practicality and acceptance.

It was later in that session that she made the discovery.

'What is happening now?'

'It is a bright moonlit night and I am waiting in the shadow of the stable wall.'

'Is there anyone with you?'

'No, I'm alone. I must not be seen. The stable lads are abed.'

'Who are you waiting for?'

'I am waiting for him! He asked me earlier today if we could meet... he said there was something he needed to talk to me about. Shhh – he is come.'

'What is happening now?'

'He is whispering to me.'

'What is he saying?'

'He is saying *Emily, I have known you since we were but four or five, some fifteen years. How I used to tease you! And how you continue to tease me, at every opportunity!* I smile and look down at my shoes. Then he says, *But we are not children now.* No, I say, we are not. My heart is beating so loud and fast I am sure it will escape my body and float into the night for all to see... for him to see. I had this *feeling* in my belly when he started whispering to me and its flooding my whole body... like... a thousand butterflies, all fluttering around inside me and in my head. I... feel... *faint* with it. I have to put one hand against the stable wall to steady myself.'

'What then?'

'Then he whispers, slowly, *Sweet Emily*, he seems to be trying to find the right words, *my heart just **sings** whenever I see you. There is nothing for it, I had to tell you.* Now the words are tumbling out of him. *I want to call you my sweetheart, I want to kiss your wonderful, beautiful lips! I need to hold you!* He catches hold of my free hand and holds it to his lips. *Will you let me kiss you, dear Emily?* I cannot speak. The feeling rushing through my body brings water to my eyes and is rising into my throat and choking me. I lift up my face to his and he kisses me. Oh Lord, how sweet and gentle is his kiss! Not like those bold kisses from Sid Giles or Fred Butler, all breathy and urgent and tasting of beer. His tenderness overwhelms me! I am overcome with it. I am engulfed by him. And I know that from this night on my heart is his and his mine and this is how it will be.'

An exquisite mix of wonderment and tenderness showed on Jennifer's face and a tear escaped her eye and rolled down her cheek, but she was not aware of it.

'What is his name?' asked Christina quietly.

'Will... my own sweet Will, ' replied Jennifer.

September 1762

It was baking day and Martha Cumley was overseeing the pastry cook. All manner of pies were waiting to be slid into the oven and breads of various sorts and sizes were cooling on the rack over the large oak table in the centre of the kitchen. The pastry cook was busy making horns to be filled for dinner. His sharp features gathered around two furrows between his eyebrows in deep concentration. Martha wiped the sweat off her brow with a corner of her apron and continued kneading dough.

It was hot in the kitchen. The fire was blazing and the two bread ovens had been steaming for hours. The room was filled with the rich aroma of freshly-baked bread mixed with the pungent smell of rosemary from the rosemary loaves and the sweet fragrance of the baked peaches that filled half a dozen tarts set to cool on the window sill.

As she pummelled and shaped the dough with her large, plump practiced hands Martha thought of what Rachel had told her. Obviously she had dismissed it at once so as not to give any quarter to Rachel, who was as likely to hang herself with it, in addition to the damage she could do to others. But she was worried. She knew Emily to be a quiet, sensible girl, not given to flights of fancy, a calm practical girl who knew the significant value of her position among the higher servants and her place in society's hierarchy. But she was also a young woman of nineteen years and doubtless had emotions and passions hidden under her calm exterior. Didn't every young woman?

If there was some truth in what Rachel had said, Emily was undoubtedly playing a dangerous game. The other option, that Master William was taking advantage of his position — after all he was doubtless possessed of similar passions and wants — was not one that Martha would easily accept. She had known William all his life. Granted, he had a wicked sense of humour, but he was not malicious. She smiled to herself as she remembered the time he had stolen into the kitchen larder unnoticed and swapped an apple and pear pie for a salmon and anchovy one, much to the subsequent consternation of his father who was sitting next to the Bishop of York at dinner when the sweets were served. The delight on William's face at the Bishop's first bite was scarcely disguised; however it remained unnoticed except by Harry Atkins, one of the table stewards situated close to William's position at table. The event had been duly reported to the house steward. The next time William came to Mrs Cumley after supper asking for a bite from the pantry to take to his room to quell his late-night hunger, she had given him a sour gherkin wrapped in a roll of pastry when he was expecting sweet strawberry. The next time she saw him she had looked directly at him searching his features for a response. He had briefly nodded and grinned respectfully.

No, he was not capable of malice, and she was sure he would not press any girl into meeting his needs by means of his position or false declarations. No – she was sure of that. She shook her head as she gathered three thin strips of rolled dough together, plaited them and joined them to the top of a long uncooked loaf. A quick brush of beaten egg on top and it was ready to be baked. As she signalled to the kitchen maid to remove the loaf to the oven, Martha Cumley decided that the liaison that Rachel had spoken of with a distinct undertone of malice barely disguised as concern for the wellbeing of Emily's soul – *Hmph! T' cheek of t' lass* – must indeed be true. If this was the case, she reasoned, they must be willing partners in crime. This being true, Emily was in serious danger of losing all she held dear. If it was discovered, Lady Charlotte would probably have no option but to remove Emily to another position where she could not tempt her son. No doubt her ladyship had grand plans for William in the direction of marriage. This would likely mean a move away from Fernleigh Hall for Emily, and no doubt to a less exalted position. Worse still, if Emily became with child she would be dismissed at once and the shame she would bring on her family could cause them to cast her out – although Martha thought this unlikely – or at least force them to keep her hidden and have to support both her and the bairn, for who would take on a fallen woman with a child?

What to do? As the last of the pinched, shaped, rolled and rounded doughs went into the oven she decided that practicality was her only option. She must speak to Emily, and soon, before it was too late.

William and his father had set off just after dawn accompanied by Antony, his father's man, Mr Bottesford, a couple of stewards and a stablehand. To William's surprise they rode first to the village of Brockby, where they called upon Daniel Popple. William's heart started to beat in an uneven guilty rhythm as they were shown into a sizeable parlour by the housemaid. He was not kept in suspense for long, however, as Daniel Popple appeared to greet them and shook him warmly by the hand.

'Please M'Lord, Master William, Mr Bottesford.' He motioned to a large oak settle furnished with a crimson velvet cushion and a couple of chairs, similarly dressed, positioned around a long oak table. The day still had a chill about it and moisture persistently hung in the early morning air, but a bright grey light found its way through the wooden latticed window, illuminating the room with the hope of a late summer's day.

The door to the corridor from whence they had entered the room lay open and William could hear busy sounds intermingled with the occasional soft lilt of a woman's voice, snatches of a gentle tune. He recognised it as one he had heard Emily sing to herself occasionally as she went about her work. William smiled inwardly. The happy sounds had given him a warm glow in his belly. He glanced at his father and for a brief moment saw a look on his weathered face that he did not recognise. There was a warmth about his father's eyes, but the muscles in his face had drawn his features into something that resembled regret – no, maybe that was too strong – wistfulness perhaps. The look vanished as quickly as it had appeared. Perhaps his father had recognised Emily's tune too, he mused.

Presently a housemaid served them with steaming hot chocolate accompanied by muffins laced with melted butter and topped with bacon. The girl was a pretty young thing with long red hair and a pale complexion. Her eyes reminded William of Emily's eyes, wide and green and as deep as a well. Then the realisation came to him that of course she wasn't a housemaid – this would be one of Emily's younger sisters. It was a good four or five years since William had seen any of her siblings. As he ate his delicious smoked bacon he calculated that this girl must have been only six or seven the last time he saw her. He tried to decide on her name – was this Georgina or Prudence? Emily did speak of her family, but had done so less in recent months. Was this deliberate, he wondered? She would miss them so very much. His thoughts spawned another; he had been in love with Emily for a very long time – forever, it seemed. In fact, thinking back to their childhood years he could not remember a time when he had not been in love with her.

William was roused from his thoughts.

'Do you not think so, William?' his father was saying. They were talking business and he hurriedly had to catch up with the conversation.

'I, er... I do apologise, I was lost for a moment, ' he said, struggling for a suitable excuse, 'contemplating the wonderful taste of this bacon, ' he finished lamely. He looked at Daniel Popple then beamed at Georgina or Prudence. She looked delighted and her ivory cheeks and slender neck flushed slightly.

'Father lets me in charge of smokin', ' she said proudly.

'Well you've certainly done a good job, ' William responded kindly.

The girl beamed again and then remembered her duty as her father gave her an almost imperceptible nod.

'Would tha be wanting ought else?' she enquired politely.

'That'll be fine just now. Go on t' thy mother.' The look of pride was clear in her father's features.

Mr Popple resumed the conversation that had been interrupted by William's praise of the bacon.

'As I were saying M'Lord, Herefords 'ud be worth considerin'. They be right beautiful beasts an' a good mature 'un 'ud grow to over three thousand pounds in weight. My cousin farms down near Leominster and swears by t' beasts. He's been running a herd for Lord Watts nigh on four years.'

Lord Fernleigh nodded towards Daniel. 'I thank you for your good opinion. It is much valued, ' he said smiling. Then, turning to

Mr Bottesford: 'Mr Bottesford, I think we'd better send word out that Lord Fernleigh will be interested in Herefords. Good quality beasts, mind, ' he added playfully. He knew he could trust Bottesford implicitly in all estate matters, including the choice of cattle breed to increase and enhance his stock; however, Bottesford was such a serious man who never missed an opportunity to reinforce his good name through the delivery of his expert opinion that Thomas couldn't resist playing with him occasionally.

Mr Bottesford nodded and had to agree that this was a good choice, adding that Mr Popple had reinforced his expert judgment in the matter.

The conversation turned to the arable planting schemes for the winter and spring months to come. Although Daniel Popple was a tenant farmer he managed some five hundred and fifty acres, by far the largest tenanted acreage of all Lord Fernleigh's agricultural land. He was highly knowledgeable in agricultural land practices, and although Thomas Fernleigh was by no means uneducated in these matters and would also rely upon the expertise of Mr Bottesford he sought Daniel Popple's opinion whenever he felt a particular need to do so, usually when making advancements or major changes to his breeding stock or considering the value or risk of planting new crops. Mr Bottesford was reliable but his conservative nature held him to conventional schemes, whereas Daniel Popple seemed to have a sixth sense about what would do well and was not afraid to take a risk or two. His risks were weighed and recalculated and usually paid off. There had been some lively discussion on the matter of enclosing and reallocating parcels of land in order to profit more effectively from new methods of mixed farming. Daniel and Thomas saw eye to eye with regard to potentially disadvantaging the poorer folk, who relied heavily upon the common land to graze their animals, and the smaller tenant farmers whose acreage was too small for them to take proper advantage of the new agricultural methods. Contrary to Bottesford's advice, Thomas had done what he could for these families against the tide of rising rent prices that seemed to be flooding the majority of England, his neighbour's estates included, partly due to the continually-increasing land

taxes. He had encouraged some of his tenant farmers to form a coop-
erative to work a consolidated area of land more effectively. It was not
easy; many of his tenants had been farming the same land for many
generations and were extremely loath to alter their ways. But Thomas
did his best to assist the folk on his lands to adapt to the changing
times, recognising that, like Canute, he could not hold back the tide
of agricultural progress. He was aware that some small freeholders
had been forced to sell out due to the impossibility of competing with
the new methods of their wealthier neighbours, but could not do anything for those for whom he was not responsible.

They discussed the quantities and varieties of seed – wheat and
barley, clover and lucerne, cabbage and kale for the vegetable garden
– to be purchased in Northallerton. Daniel Popple was requested to
give his opinion on crop rotations and his plans for increasing yields of
crops and animal stocks.

William joined the discussion when he could and listened intently
where he could not offer an educated opinion. He had some agricultural knowledge, but his expertise in these matters was akin to nurs-
ery level compared to the experience of the other three men around
the table. He was eager to learn; he might have to run the estate some
day. Although his father was keen for him to enter politics, a good
number of his father's political acquaintances were also experienced
gentlemen farmers. It paid to know a thing or two and not to leave
everything in the hands of an estate manager. After all, agriculture
was a major part of the business of their estate and lent a solid founda-
tion to their merchant ventures at home and abroad – which could be
a little more uncertain, particularly his father's current trade in the
Caribbean, not least due to the war against the French.

There was so much to be discussed that William wondered why
his father had not called for Mr Popple to attend him in his office.
Perhaps, he guessed, they would visit other tenant farmers on their
way to Northallerton and this was conveniently en route. He hoped
that during these few days he would have a chance to speak with his
father alone, man to man. The thought started his heart beating wildly again and waves of panic swept through him. He was afraid, but he

knew he had to do it. He looked at Emily's father, who was sketching a plan of clover planting for subsequent cattle and sheep grazing in a leather-bound ledger. *This man will be my father-in-law.* His stomach turned over with trepidation and the enormity of what he was soon to propose to his father.

As their discussion drew to a close they arranged to meet Daniel Popple at the cattle market in Northallerton the day after next. Popple was to assist in selecting the best-quality Herefords. He also had business of his own to conduct there. He was to be paid handsomely for his troubles with two bull calves of his choosing. As they entered the hall and turned to go, William caught his father staring through the green door at the end of the corridor into the kitchen. Emily's mother Mary appeared for a brief moment, smiled at Thomas and inclined her head in the minutest of nods before disappearing again behind the oak door. The same strange look appeared once more on Thomas' face, but for the briefest of moments. However, afterwards William could not have sworn that he had seen anything different at all in his father's countenance.

Thomas decided to call upon five other tenant farmers that day. These were purely courtesy calls born of his desire to see his tenants prospering for himself and their contentment at making a good living on his lands. He usually paid a visit to every one of his tenants on a yearly basis – or did he mean to cover his tracks? He convinced himself that it was for the former reason, though if truth be told it was a mix of the two. As they picked their way up the narrow winding track behind the village, climbing the forested ridge before they entered the flourishing mixed woodland, Thomas pulled up his grey stallion, patted him on the neck and looked back down to the little group of cottages. Daniel Popple's homestead stood out as the largest, the others being mainly occupied by farm workers of various sorts and craftsmen: a farrier, a baker, several woodsmen and a dressmaker. There was also a small inn. The thatched roofs glistened in the gathering sunshine as heavy dew droplets reflected the strengthening rays. It was a pretty sight.

Thomas, a self-disciplined and principled man, allowed himself to consider the recurring image in his mind for the briefest of moments before firmly shutting it back in the place where he kept it, locking it up and pocketing the key. Time to focus on the business ahead. He turned his mount sharply and followed the others up the track and over the ridge.

That day they visited the Halts, the Browns, the Cutters, the Higginses and the Silsons. William counted seventeen children of various ages and stages of politeness, the youngest being only three weeks old and the eldest, the twin Silson boys, who he guessed were about fifteen, strapping lads and capable, he thought, of serious mischief. At the assorted households they were given slices of port and pear pie, strawberry tart, three different kinds of cider – only one of decent quality, the other two making William's eyes water – spiced sausage in pastry and pieces of boiled fruit cake.

By three o'clock in the afternoon the ensemble were full to bursting, however their duties had been duly carried out and they were now heading for Northallerton. After a couple more hours of riding they put in at Thirsk for the night. They took rooms at the King's Arms, the larger of the two establishments that offered accommodation. William hoped that this evening would bring an opportunity to speak privately with his father.

By five thirty William, Thomas, Antony and Bottesford were settled in the tavern enjoying a large pitcher of red wine and tucking into a rather fine oyster pie. By eight o'clock, another pitcher of wine and a middling bottle of port later, William had grown rather tired of Bottesford's self-congratulatory false modesty and his thoughts had turned again to how on earth he could approach his father about Emily. He was finding the room increasingly stuffy. Smoke from the fire and countless tobacco pipes and the sweat of travellers who had been on the road for longer than himself mingled with the heavy perfume that hung in the air, seemingly originating from a small group of older ladies sitting in the far corner, doubtless en route from somewhere and breaking their journey here. They were accompanied by such a dandy of a man wearing two beauty spots, one a crescent just under his right eye and the other a small star on his right cheek, that William couldn't be sure that the perfume wasn't coming from him.

The oyster pie lay heavy in his stomach. He suddenly felt queasy. He excused himself and exited into the fresh evening air. The daylight had begun to fade and there was a strong breeze that carried with it the warm smell of newly-cut hay. William took a few deep breaths and started across the square. He meant to work out exactly what to say to his father before returning to the inn to deliver his news. His stomach turned over at the thought of what he might have to do if his father did not agree to his proposal, which was highly likely. Perhaps he should wait until tomorrow, until their business at the cattle market and seed merchant's was concluded? This might afford him an opportunity to ride back on his own if the situation became difficult. However the alcohol in his bloodstream had given him courage, and William knew he needed to talk about this as soon as possible. His stomach gave another lurch and suddenly turned over violently. He just managed to stumble into a side street before he retched violently. The force with which he spewed took him by surprise. Luckily the trajectory was such that he missed his boots. After what seemed an interminable period of retching he stayed in the alley for some considerable time, his legs trembling beneath him and sweat pouring off his brow.

This is the result of a bad oyster; damn that bloody pie, he thought.

When at last he had regained his composure he wiped his mouth on his handkerchief and set off back to the inn. The evening sky had darkened somewhat and a half moon had usurped the sun. The wind had picked up and William was glad of its cooling properties on his face and neck.

By the time he reached the inn almost an hour had passed since his departure. He found Bottesford in conversation with a seed merchant of his acquaintance. His father had evidently gone to his room. William trod the creaking wooden stairs to the chambers slowly, each one with trepidation. His mind, like his body, had become fatigued and muddled. He had no idea how to start – he supposed he should just come right out with it and accept the consequences. He knocked on the door to his father's room.

Antony opened the door, took one look at William's grey complexion and went in search of a jug of wine.

'Father, I must speak with you, ' he stumbled into the room and over the words.

Thomas looked up from the desk at which he was studying a sheaf of papers.

'What is it, my boy?' he asked, his features displaying an intense curiosity as he looked William up and down. Clearly the boy had been in some trouble judging by his dishevelled appearance. He motioned to William to take one of the two wooden chairs by the small fireplace.

'No thank you, father; I prefer to stand, ' William responded, rather formally and nervously, Thomas thought.

Suddenly William's knees gave way and he lurched across the room and sunk onto a chair.

'Whatever is the matter with you?' Thomas said concernedly, 'You look awful!'

'Bad oyster.' William spluttered.

'Oh. Bad luck. Well, you did have two generous helpings.' Thomas smiled and his eyes twinkled. But seeing the look of distress on William's face he thought better of jesting further and instead crossed the room and patted his son on the shoulder.

'Antony will be back soon with some wine, ' he said kindly as he seated himself upon the chair opposite his tousled son.

Although the evening was not cold, a small fire had been laid in readiness should it be required and Thomas took a small tinderbox from his coat pocket, extracted the firesteel and wrapped it around his fingers then bent towards the fireplace and struck a flint against it, throwing sparks at the wood shavings placed under the kindling. The fire soon crackled into life and gave the room a warm, cosy glow.

'Father, I... there is a woman... for whom I care very much.'

The words followed an audible deep breath and were somewhat projected at Thomas, almost launched at him.

Thomas gave an almost imperceptible sigh. He had thought as much. He had noticed that occasionally William had had a particular faraway look in his eyes in recent months. In fact Charlotte had been watching her son for signs of interest in Miss Susan Snaith ever since their last summer ball, when she and William had danced a number of dances together. Charlotte had spoken about it with him. He motioned for his son to continue.

'She is... that is to say... I... we... have an understanding.'

Thomas raised his eyebrows but nodded, 'Go on, ' he prompted gently.

'She is very gifted and beautiful and...'

'Is she accomplished?' Thomas interrupted.

William was encouraged and his words came more confidently. 'Yes, yes – she has many talents and opinions and is interested in the works of Galileo and Keplar, Newton, Voltaire, Hume... many great thinkers. She reads the Encyclopédie, Father!'

'Indeed!'

'Well, that is to say, I read it – translate it – for her, but she is very... interested!'

An opinionated but talented young woman – this sounded to Thomas very much like Miss Snaith, although he was surprised at her lack of French. Thomas was cautiously pleased; an alliance with the Snaiths would be advantageous indeed, and was certainly what his wife was hoping for, but for his part he hoped that William would first take up study at one of the Oxford colleges and go into politics. He was still young and had yet to prove himself. Marriage would have to wait a few years. There was time enough for both of them. He was just about to respond to this effect when there was a knock at the door. It was Antony with the wine.

Thomas thanked him and dismissed him for the rest of the evening. He poured two large glasses of wine from the jug and gave one to William, who took several large mouthfuls. Thomas smiled encouragingly.

'It would be a most propitious match. From what I have seen she could be a handful, I warn you, my boy. But an alliance with the Snaiths can only be of benefit to both families. However, you know I have long spoken of you studying at Oxford and entering political circles. There will be plenty of time for marriage; I'm sure Miss Susan will wait a while and...'

'No, no!' William burst out, his eyes wide, his features aghast. 'Not Miss Susan – I'm not talking about her!'

'Well then, who *are* you speaking of?' enquired Thomas a little frustratedly.

Just at that moment there was a knock upon the door.

'Come, ' Thomas responded distractedly.

It was a wiry young maid. 'Please sir, there is a gentleman downstairs who says you are expecting him. A Mr Sanderson, sir.'

'Yes, yes, ' Thomas waved her away impatiently. 'Please show him up.'

He turned to William. 'The tanner, ' he said. 'I arranged to meet with him. We shall have to continue our discourse another time. But please think upon what I have said about your studies. It is high time I made enquiries. I have a number of acquaintances who were at Magdalen, Lincoln and Jesus, though I should think there are a number of colleges that would suit you very well.'

William's frustration was rising rapidly.

'*But sir,* ' he tried one more time, but was again interrupted by a knock at the door, signifying the entrance of the tanner.

'Get some rest, my boy; we have a long day ahead. We'll talk again.' Thomas said, reassuringly patting William on the back.

William made to leave the room. He recognised the tone of his father's voice. It was kind and gentle but firm, conveying to him that their conversation was at an end and would not be resumed tonight. He knew better than to try to continue.

William went to his room, resigned to the fact that this attempt had been a complete disaster. Events had conspired against him this day. He must carefully work out what he meant to say and come right out and say it. There was no other way. There would be little chance tomorrow; he would have to wait until they were back at Fernleigh Hall. He could not risk being overheard should he try to talk to his father on the journey home. His father's assumption had left him highly frustrated and even more depressed. Not only would he be betraying him by breaking all the rules of acceptable social etiquette by taking a wife from the servant classes, he would also disappoint him in terms of his chosen occupation. He himself had no aspirations towards politics; matters of the estate and his father's merchant trade business were far more interesting to him.

William looked around for something to hit to vent his feelings. There was nothing that might not be broken except the hard and rather fusty mattress of his bed. He punched this several times until he fell upon it, exhausted from his earlier retching episode. This and the amount of wine and port he had consumed at least made sleep possible, and he slept until dawn.

Mr Arbuth looked like a rat, or so it seemed to Rachel. His features were sharp: he had a long pointed nose and beady eyes and the faintest of whiskers grew above his upper lip, neither growing properly nor needing removal. If he'd had a long scaly tail tucked into his breeches it would have been entirely appropriate. Like a rat, or indeed the rat that her imagination conjured up, Mr Arbuth was also a wily character whose sharp eyes were everywhere. There was not much that you could get past him.

Having already tried her immediate superior, Mrs Cumley, Rachel had been in two minds about whether to approach the house steward. She could have approached the clerk of the kitchen or indeed Mrs Preedy, the housekeeper, assistant to Mr Arbuth. However, Mrs Cumley and Mr Baker, the clerk, were as thick as thieves and she didn't trust Mrs Preedy. She was in a position of some authority, overseeing all the female staff below her, but the position of lady's maid was superior to housekeeper and Rachel thought that if Mrs Preedy had designs on a rise in status, as she herself had, this might influence her response to the news about Emily, and not necessarily in a way that favoured Rachel.

So Rachel had elected to speak to someone in authority who was in a position to act upon her information and who, she thought, would see things as she did. Mr Arbuth liked everything to be in its rightful and proper place. He was a man of principal, a strict Presbyterian who kept order in the ranks of his staff. He had a sharp disposition to match his sharp features and not many dared to cross him. Although she feared his reaction somewhat, Rachel had decided that this was her only option and plucked up the courage to speak to him. Once this was resolved in her mind she had to wait for some days to find him alone.

Mr Arbuth was busy inspecting the silver cutlery when Rachel appeared and sidled up to him in a most disconcerting manner. The girl was behaving a bit strangely, he thought. Every time he had looked at her in the last few days she had seemed to be watching him but persisted in looking away quickly when his eyes caught hers. She most definitely wanted something; the little minx was up to something, no doubt about that. Well, he was too busy to be bothered by the likes of her – best get her to come out with it, then he could deal with whatever it was and get on with the many tasks he had to undertake this morning.

As Rachel looked at him her eyes darkened, whether with excitement or fear he could not tell. His eyes narrowed as she started to speak and this had the effect of making her nervous.

'Please, Mr Arbuth. Ah mean, if it please thee, ah mean t' say ah've need t' talk t' thee...' Rachel faltered and stopped.

Mr Arbuth raised his eyebrows slightly. 'Well, don't just stand there girl, spit it out, ' he retorted impatiently.

'Well... ah hope tha doesn't mind me talkin' to thee like... it's just... ah know tha'll understand...' Rachel grappled for the right words, trying for empathy, her hands clasped tightly together. 'Ah'm concerned for t' wellbein' of a... friend, ' she said slowly.

Mr Arbuth lowered his eyebrows into a deep frown and the rest of his features adopted an apposite expression. He couldn't imagine Rachel being concerned for anyone's wellbeing except her own.

'Yes, yes, ' he returned shortly 'what is it? What are you trying to say, lass?'

'Emily's soul is bound for *hell,* ' she whispered. Rachel lent as close to the house steward as propriety would allow. 'She 'as captivated Master William an' is *lyin'* with him. I hear 'em... at night... through the wall, ' she added.

Mr Arbuth was completely taken aback at Rachel's words and had to fight to remain outwardly composed. He shook his head slowly, a look of complete incredulity on his face.

'What?!'

Rachel continued, obviously gaining a little confidence now that she had his ear.

'Master William an' Emily, ' she reported slowly, 'lyin' together, in 'er room, like'.

Percival Arbuth had to think quickly. Rachel was either telling the truth or she wasn't; there were no half measures with Rachel, of that he was certain. She was a hardworking lass but he felt he could never completely trust her. However, she hadn't misbehaved or stolen anything, as far as he was aware anyway. She seemed to be quite ambitious for a girl of her age. Her position as cook serving under the chief cook was a recent rise in status for her, having been the pastry cook for two years and before that, working in the laundry. The reward for this recent ascension, besides being taught a broad range of skills by Mrs Cumley, was a move of sleeping quarters to a room of her own. He recalled that this room was next to Emily's room at the end of a corridor on the third floor of the west wing.

If Rachel was making this story up, thought Percival, the only purpose would be to discredit Emily. Why? Perhaps Rachel had designs on Emily's position as lady's maid. Surely not! Did she really think ...? Percival Arbuth shook his head again in disbelief. He looked at Rachel. She perceived this as a sign to continue.

'God's own truth, ' she stated boldly.

'Leave God out of this, ' Arbuth replied flatly, 'I am concerned to know if *you* are telling me the truth.'

Rachel raised her eyebrows and nodded her head towards him in an exaggerated manner.

'Yes! Ah'm speakin' truth, ah swear...'

Percival Arbuth raised his hand to silence her and she shut her mouth at once and stared impatiently at him. He had to decide what to do, and quickly. He knew Emily to be a kind and gentle creature and he hoped, Lord he really did hope, that she wasn't being taken advantage of by Master William. His feelings towards Emily were rather ambivalent. Whilst he knew her to be kind and just and principled, if the latter could be applied to a woman, he felt more than awkward in her presence. Not surprisingly, since it was she who had been hanging around the stable late one night some two years ago and had interrupted a most unfortunate scene. A sudden image of flaxen hair and high round white buttocks burst into his consciousness and he hastily pushed it away, flushing inwardly. It had been his only indiscretion, his single concession to his true feelings, the most private of his thoughts, his deeply hidden lust. Feeling the boy's soft flesh under his hands, parting that flesh... the control and power... was almost more than he could bear. Theirs was an exquisite liaison, although sadly short-lived. He'd had to pay the boy off, of course, and make sure he left the county. But Emily... Emily had lowered her eyes and backed away at once, whispering *I shall not tell a soul* as she left the stable. She had been true to her word and he was now uncomfortably in her debt, though she had never spoken of it.

Percival knew that now Emily needed protection, either from a wicked untruth or from herself. In either case, the stakes were high. Once a rumour started, whether it was true or not, she was in danger of losing her position. If indeed it was true, what if she became with child? The consequences were unthinkable for a sweet girl like her. He had to silence this girl Rachel and ensure that Emily was protected.

'Rachel, ' he said seriously at length, 'who else knows of this?'

'No-one, Mr Arbuth, except Mrs Cumley.' Rachel responded quickly and not a little excitedly. Here was someone who would listen to her, who had the power to get her what she wanted.

'Mrs Cumley knows?' Mr Arbuth retorted quizzically.

Rachel lowered her eyes. 'Yes. Ah tried to tell 'er... but she wouldn't believe me.'

'And what did she say to you?'

'She told me if ah told anyone else she'd speak t' Mr Fry and ah'd be punished!' the girl blurted out. 'But ah thought tha'd wish t' know' she added meekly, 'bein' as tha'rt... close t' God like...' She paused, trying to gauge Mr Arbuth's reaction; however, he kept his face expressionless. 'Ah reckoned if anyone could save 'er soul tha could.'

'Indeed, ' he returned thoughtfully. 'Well you'd better leave this delicate matter in my hands. I will deal with this. You are *not* to breathe a word to *anyone*, do you hear?' he said sternly.

Rachel was enjoying herself now. Mr Arbuth seemed to be taking her seriously and he hadn't dismissed her at once as Mrs Cumley had done. She fancied that Mr Arbuth was probably on the verge of taking immediate action. She was picturing him taking her hand in his and thanking her, saying that he was in her debt for bringing this to his attention and that he'd do something about it at once. Perhaps one last push just to make sure.

'Master William 'ould never take advantage of 'is position. Ah'm sure of it, ' she declared. 'Like as not, she's captivated 'im.' She lowered her voice to a whisper: 'Wouldn't be surprised if she'd put a spell on 'im, ' she breathed, her voice low and spiteful, 'an' she's t' one takin' advantage.'

Rachel knew she'd gone too far as soon as the words left her mouth.

'*What!*' Percival roared, his face turning puce. 'Are you accusing Emily of witchcraft?! That's a mighty serious accusation to make and God *will punish* you for it if you are speaking untruths!'

For the second time Arbuth struggled to bring his emotions under control. Damn this girl, he would strangle her if he could. He took hold of her shoulders and shook her so hard that her cap came loose.

'You watch what you are saying, my girl, if you value your position in this household!'

He checked himself, regaining his composure, and continued quickly but with a measured degree of menace. 'If I hear you so much as *think* on this again, let alone breathe a word of this witchcraft non-sense to anyone, you'll be out of here quicker than you can speak the word. Do you hear me?!'

Rachel had raised one hand to her throat in shock and the other was busy trying to straighten her cap. She had the frightened look of a cornered deer looking down the barrel of a rifle. She blinked at him.

'Do you hear me, girl!?' he repeated.

'I... er... I... yes... yes, ' she uttered.

'Good girl, ' he acknowledged. His manner had grown calm again. 'Now go back to your duties and we'll say no more of this. You will leave the matter with me or it will be your soul as goes to hell, ' he added for effect.

Rachel nodded quickly and mumbled 'Yes Mr Arbuth, ' turned and ran down the corridor away from him, clutching her stray cap.

It was a quarter past eight, and the servants who were not en-gaged in serving brandy and cigars or waiting on the ladies were sitting together in the servants' hall completing their evening meal. They ate well, usually finishing off the dishes that had been pre-pared and served to the Fernleighs and their guests, sometimes bulked with bread or a stew made from the scrag ends and carcasses that had been boiled to make stock. Today they had dined particu-larly well on broiled breast of veal, calf's-head pie, scotch oysters, a few fried perch with melted butter and parsley and a pot of stewed peas with bacon and cabbage. They had just finished some egg and apple pudding and slices of codling pie. Martha and Daisy had been dispatched to the scullery to wash the remaining dishes. Mrs Preedy and Rachel were sitting at the other end of the long table and Rachel was receiving some instructions. Mr Arbuth and Mr Baker were engaged in a quiet conversation seated in armchairs next to the win-dow at the far end of the hall, and others were talking amongst themselves at the table.

Martha Cumley leaned towards Emily, motioning that she wished to speak with her. From her body language Emily supposed it was a private matter, so also lent forward a little.

'Miss Emily, ' she spoke in a low tone, 'I hope tha will not think me impolite. I need t' speak with thee, and 'tis a matter of great importance an' one that'll benefit thee if tha'll listen t' me.'

Emily raised her eyebrows and became immediately worried. Had she done something wrong? If she had though, it wouldn't be Mrs Cumley who would be talking to her about it. Why was the cook about to be impolite? Mrs Cumley was one of the kindest, most gentle people she knew and not given to impoliteness.

Martha picked up on Emily's reaction.

''Tis no point in worrying, ' she whispered earnestly 'but neither is 't a matter t' shrink from.' Her tone was firm but gentle. 'Tha'll need t' take some action.'

Emily's guilty conscience got the better of her and her stomach gave a lurch. She clasped her hands together quickly to stop them shaking.

'I'm sure... I don't know...' she stumbled. Mrs Cumley cut her off gently by putting her hand under Emily's elbow.

'C'mon, Miss Emily, let's take the air for a few moments. 'Tis a right nice evening.'

Emily nodded, rose from the table and followed Mrs Cumley's large frame through the passageway, past the kitchen and out into the walled kitchen garden where they could not be seen or overheard.

She knew that Mrs Cumley was about to confront her about Will. What else could it be that demanded such secrecy? How on earth had she found out? They had been so very careful. Oh Lord, how should she deal with this? Should she deny the accusation? Be affronted, demand evidence? No, she decided, that would not do, no point in asking a person to produce evidence – that was only drawing more attention to the matter. What then? What would Will do?

She could pull rank and refuse to speak on the matter. However, for all that Martha Cumley was below her in servant status she made up for it in her unspoken role as a mother figure. Ever since Emily had come to Fernleigh Hall Mrs Cumley had fostered and looked out for her. At first when she was lonely and frightened without her mother, and later when she was unsure of a task or the correct way to behave, when she was improving her reading or lacked company, Martha Cumley had always been there, dependable, reliable, a constant in her life since she was thirteen. A mother-figure – no, more than that, a second mother. Emily had surpassed Mrs Cumley in terms of education and had risen above her rank, but in terms of worldly experience she knew nothing. Mrs Cumley was as sage as an owl with respect to *life*. This would be like confessing to her own mother, something she knew she would have to face up to sooner or later.

They reached the far wall of the kitchen garden and Mrs Cumley turned to face her. Her face had reddened with the effort of walking and her breath was a little short. She put one hand on her ample bosom and motioned to Emily to sit beside her on a low wooden bench surrounded by the boughs of an espaliered apple tree until she caught her breath.

Emily knew there was no option but to be honest and that this was expected of her. She took a deep breath as Mrs Cumley finally spoke.

'Miss Emily. There's no other way of saying this, so ah'll come right out wi't and ah'd be grateful if tha'd hear me out. Ah knows about thee and Master William. Lord knows 'tis none of my business, but it were noticed and reported t' me.'

Emily couldn't help but give a little involuntary cry and her hand flew to her mouth. Mrs Cumley laid a hand on her arm in comfort.

'Now don't fret thasen, lass, I reckon situation's under control as far as that's concerned. No other folk need know. What ah'm worrying about is thee. Tha's been like a daughter t' me these past few years an' I don't want t' see any 'arm come t' thee. So ah'm goin' t' ask you an honest question an' tha'll tell me truth… are you bein' careful like… y'know … t' stop yerself gettin' w' child?'

Emily blushed scarlet and her skin prickled with the heat of it. She had never discussed such a thing with anyone except Will, and that was only in the most intimate of moments. She looked down at her feet. She had questions spinning around in her head, but they had been temporarily paralysed by this last from Martha Cumley.

'Come now, lass, tha'll come t' realise that us women folk 'ave t' mention this sort o' thing from time t' time' Mrs Cumley said gently. ''Tis vital we protect oursen as best we can, an' 'specially in thy position.'

Emily continued to stare at her shoes.

'He... Will... Master William, I mean... sometimes uses something, ' Emily whispered. 'He calls it... his, um... his riding coat, ' she finished in a flurry of embarrassment, the words sticking in her throat, almost choking her.

'Y' say sometimes? Not always?'

'Well... yes... sometimes.'

'Does he sometimes pull away, y' know... before he spends himself?'

Another wave of horrific embarrassment crashed over her. There was silence for a few moments before Emily could finally gather the courage to look at Mrs Cumley.

'Yes. He is... very... considerate... you know, ' she whispered meekly, her cheeks flushed and burning.

'Good, ' Martha said matter-of-factly. She let out a deep sigh as if she'd been holding her breath.

'Look Miss Emily, tha can't be too careful when it comes t' this sort o' thing. If you were t' go an' get wi' child that'd be thy life over as tha knows it. Tha understands that, don't thee?'

Emily hung her head and tears welled up in her eyes.

'I understand Mrs Cumley, I do, really. It's just... I can't stop. He loves me and... I love him. And... I don't know what to do!' She burst into tears and sobbed as if her life depended on it. It was a relief to admit to it, and the relief, finally given form, gushed out like milk from a spilt pail until it was spent.

They sat together for a while, the silence between them punctuated by Emily's sobs.

'There there lass, ' Martha patted her back as one who comforts a child. 'Ah've no doubt of Master William's affections for thee or yours for 'im. 'Tis a muddle of a situation an' no doubt. But tha don't want t' go makin' it worse. If tha's going t' go on lyin' with 'im tha needs t' take a bit more into thy control so t' speak.'

Emily nodded and dried her eyes with her pocket handkerchief.

'My advice is t' use bit o' sponge soaked in vinegar, inside, before tha lie w' 'im.'

Emily couldn't believe how understanding of her situation Mrs Cumley had been and, as usual, she had come up with practical advice. She nodded again in acknowledgement of the advice. She was still in the same predicament, but at least she was able to take some action, however small, to improve her fate. For the time being at least she could concentrate on that.

'Thank you, ' she said. It was heartfelt.

It was very late when the figure of a woman wearing a shawl over her head slipped out of the kitchen passage and into the beetle-black night. She trod carefully towards the eastern stable block, making sure she wasn't seen. Moments after her arrival a flicker of candlelight appeared at the window of the furthest room above the stalls. The horses moved uneasily at the intrusion but soon settled at a few quiet words from above. In the dim light three figures could just be made out. Then the light faded as the candle was withdrawn into the room, and nothing was visible from without.

A half hour or so before dawn, Rachel reappeared and headed quickly back to the main house.

My those twins wor an 'andful, and them barely seventeen! But I know how t' control them— ah'm clever ah am. Ah've got them eatin' outta mi palm. Three pairs of eyes is better than one. We'll bring thee down, missy, an' no mistake. Tha'll not be only one who can wait on 'er ladyship, oh no. We'll find an opportunity, an' if we don't, we'll make one.

Late September

Christina Peters put another applewood log in the wood burner and closed the door. The wood was well seasoned and was soon burning spiritedly, casting a cosy flickering yellow glow around the living room. The warm firelight boosted the meagre illumination from a small table lamp almost buried amongst the piles of books on a table in the far corner next to a set of battered oak bookshelves. Christina returned to her reading, glancing at her watch as she crossed the room. As so often happened, she had become engrossed in her research; the whole afternoon had gone by and the day had slipped into early evening. The days were growing shorter and dusk had already laid its thin grey mantle across the sky. As she sat back down at the table she glanced out of the window across her patio to the vegetable patch and made a mental note that the weeds between the cabbages and cauliflower plants needed hoeing. She took a sip of tea from a delicate white and rose china cup and returned her mind to the task in hand and the notebook in which she had been furiously scribbling.

She had been investigating Jennifer's dreams and possible links between her past and present lives, exploring the possibility that there could be an entity attached to Jennifer which was communicating with her, influencing her thoughts and invading her dreams, an attached earthbound soul, a desquamate spirit, a being that had not returned to the light after death but instead had been drawn to a living human being or perhaps even a series of human beings, one after another, searching for something.

Christina had wanted to try to differentiate between the possible past life experience that Jennifer seemed to have discovered and the chance that the spirit she was talking to was not a past being at all but an attached entity. To do this, at their last session she had carefully explored the time just after the death of the past incarnation that Jennifer had described. At first the being did not describe being drawn towards the light. It was confused and upset, floating in a grey place, wanting to return to Earth. But on moving the questions forward in time Christina discovered that after a period of wandering the spirit had eventually progressed towards the light. There had been no sign of this spirit joining a living person who already had a rightful spirit at home in their body; no other consciousness was involved. This convinced Christina that the experiences that Jennifer described were indeed from a past life and were not those of a usurper who was influencing her.

Having established this to her satisfaction, Christina had now turned her attention to another line of investigation in relation to

Jennifer's dreams; that of astral projection. It was commonly accepted by those in her profession that the subconscious mind contains the spirit, or astral body. She had spoken with many people who had experienced astral travel, which they had achieved through deep meditation. She herself had practiced this many times to encourage her spirit to temporarily leave her physical body and move within the astral plane or spirit world for a while before returning to her body. She was able to communicate with her Guide more clearly when she consciously enabled her spirit to travel. At these times she always woke with a falling sensation, an experience shared by numerous others, although many people did not remember their dreams afterwards as she did. She had also experienced lucid dreaming in which she was able to intentionally direct her dreams. Of course, this was just another form of achieving astral projection. This soul travel had helped her in the past to locate several missing people who wanted to be found. Christine didn't believe that Jennifer was experiencing true lucid dreaming, as a high degree of lucidity while dreaming is extremely difficult to accomplish and requires a good deal of practice. It was more likely that Jennifer's soul, her spiritual energy, was travelling spontaneously while Jennifer was asleep. But the vividness with which Jennifer remembered her dreams was unusual. Christine would need to explore this further with her. Was she able to control events in these dreams, or did they just happen to her? Jennifer certainly believed the dreams to be real as she was experiencing them, as if she were in the physical world. However, Christina believed this to be a sign of normal dreaming rather than astral travel. But what of William, this character from Jennifer's past life, the object of intense desire in her current dreams? That he had existed was not in doubt; they were sure they knew who he was. But why were Jennifer's thoughts so influenced by him? Could this be due to a connection between her past and current lives, a 'miswiring'? Past memories invading her consciousness and mixing with her current thoughts. The level of influence was unusual, to say the least. Jennifer had become obsessed by it.

Christina had asked her whether she practiced meditation and the answer had been negative. She made a note to explore this with

Jennifer too. Astral travel is commonly associated with near-death experiences, surgical operations and drug experiences, as well as with meditation. Or maybe her client was just a deep sleeper and active dreamer? Even so, this didn't explain why this particular character repeatedly came to influence Jennifer's subconscious.

Christina sighed and put down her pen. Her tea had gone cold. She was getting hungry and would need to make some supper before too long. She ran her fingers through her hair and stared through the glass door of the wood burner. The fire crackled and burned away merrily without a care, its fingers caressing the applewood, drawing its energy, further fuelled from below by the red-hot glowing embers.

It was obvious that William Fernleigh had been highly influential in a past life and that Jennifer's earlier self had been in love with him, and he with her. Christina decided that there could perhaps be two explanations. One possibility was that Jennifer's subconscious was somehow mixing events, thoughts and emotions experienced in her past life with current thoughts and memories, in which case she was partially reliving a past life, being influenced by feelings that weren't hers but belonged to another who no longer existed, was long since dead. A degree of influence from a past life was not in fact uncommon, but this was a dangerous place to be, particularly since it was colouring so much of Jennifer's present thoughts and decisions, actions and emotions, taking over and slowly engulfing her.

Christina would have to act soon to help Jennifer put things back in their rightful place, to provide explanations and reintroduce logic.

But what of the other possibility, that Jennifer *was* in fact experiencing soul travel, that her spirit *was* seeking the astral plane, and that the reason for this was to communicate with another spirit, a *particular* spirit – William's soul? Two souls that were meant to be together, *had* been together in a past life or lives and which were not yet together in this life. Perhaps the bond between these two souls was so strong, the need to communicate so urgent, that they had both found a way to leave their earthly bodies and meet in another dimension. It was as if Jennifer's spirit had persuaded her earthly body to let go without being conscious that it was happening. If this was happening,

Jennifer's awareness could be heightened so that she would be able to remember the experiences clearly afterwards. The fact that she always awoke after these experiences and didn't immediately re-enter sleep or dreams was more consistent with a spiritual travel experience than a dream.

But if this was what was happening, it would imply that the other soul — William's soul — was also earthbound. If so, where on earth was he?

Seven

*W*illiam was back from Northallerton, and Emily was desperate to speak with him. All day her stomach had been twisted and her throat choked with anxiety. Indeed, she had vomited that morning. Every time her mistress summoned her waves of fear washed over her and left her trembling as she tried to carry out her duties with as calm a countenance as she could manage. She couldn't be sure whether William had spoken to his father, or indeed whether her mistress had been informed. Each time she entered Charlotte's chamber or sitting room she felt certain that this would be the moment that her betrayal was uncovered and she herself destroyed in the process.

She had not had sight of William or Lord Fernleigh all day, and continued to imagine the worst. By half past three in the afternoon she had still not managed to eat anything, and was starting to feel a little faint.

She was helping Charlotte into an evening gown in readiness for her imminent departure to Brandsby with Lord Fernleigh to dine with Colonel Huntsford, a neighbouring landowner. Emily's shaking hands had already betrayed her; she had dropped first an ivory-backed comb and then Charlotte's favourite perfume bottle. Luckily for her the bottle had simply bounced on the thick Persian rug and come to no harm.

'My dear girl, whatever is the matter with you this day? Are you quite well?' Charlotte spoke concernedly.

'I'm so sorry, m'lady. I feel… quite strange, I do confess.'

Emily's knees gave way and she sank to the floor. Charlotte hurried to the bell cord and summoned assistance.

'Bring me some smelling salts. Quickly!' she barked at a slightly startled underfootman.

The salts duly arrived and were waved under Emily's nose, shaking her senses into action again.

'I'm fine…please, ' Emily mumbled to a gathering ensemble. 'I…it's just…a lack of sustenance. I have not eaten today. I am well enough, really.' She was not convincing.

'Silly girl.' Charlotte shook her head, 'You must go and lie down. No, ' she continued as Emily put a hand up to protest, 'I insist upon it. Mrs Preedy, would you arrange for Emily to be brought some soup in her room.' She turned again to Emily, who was being helped to her feet by Mrs Preedy and the footman. 'Now go and rest yourself – I have no more need of your services today. If you are not quite well in the morning we shall summon Doctor Porter.'

Charlotte watched briefly as Emily was escorted out of the room before picking up her coin purse and turning to leave herself. *It was probably nothing*, she thought, but something nagged at her. Emily had been out of sorts all day, which was unusual for her. She shrugged. Everyone had bad days occasionally, she supposed. All the same, she decided she would order a close eye to be kept on her maid over the next days. She made a mental note to speak with Mrs Preedy on the morrow. As for now, she was late and Lord Fernleigh would be waiting.

With a gentle hand under her arm, the footman accompanied Emily down the corridor towards the door to the back stairs, while Mrs Preedy went to order soup from the kitchen. Cleverly disguised amongst the surrounding oak panels, but for the handle the entrance to the upper floors was all but invisible. As they neared the door, as fate would have it William appeared from the grand staircase at the far end of the landing. He quickened his pace as he caught sight of Emily about to disappear.

As he reached them he inclined his head with the minutest of movements in an unspoken question. Emily responded quickly with a slight raising of her eyes towards the floor above and was gone.

William waited for the footman to descend the back stairs again and continue on to the ground floor. These steps were not carpeted, however because the doors to the first-floor corridor were thick and heavy in order to muffle sound he had to open the door just a little to allow the footsteps to be heard. He pretended to examine a buckle on his shoe while waiting, in case someone should come along.

As soon as the coast was clear he entered the back staircase cautiously, closing the door quietly behind him, then bounded up the wooden steps two at a time before warily entering the landing above. At a little after four o'clock in the afternoon, the floor was deserted. He quickly reached Emily's room and slipped inside.

She was sitting on her bed, leaning her back against the wall. She looked pale and tired, but her eyes lit up when she saw him.

'Sweetheart!' he rushed over to her and took her hands in his. 'My love, you are unwell. What is...'

'No time!' Emily interrupted him. 'Quickly, tell me, does he know? Does your father know?' There was urgency and a little panic in her voice.

William shook his head. 'Not yet. I tried, unsuccessfully. But to-morrow or the day after I will tell...'

'You must go!' Emily interrupted again. 'Be careful. I think we are being watched.' The words tumbled out of her, each chasing the last in her hurry for him to be gone. 'Stables, tonight, eleven! Now please go!' She kissed his hand and waved him away.

Although he was loath to leave her, her anxiety infected him and spurred him into action again. He left quickly the way that he had come, and just made it down the back stairs to the first floor as the large figure of Mrs Cumley began to ascend, carrying a tray on which was placed a bowl of steaming rabbit broth and a small warm rosemary loaf.

Emily felt considerably better once she had eaten some of the soup and bread and made herself calm down a little. It had been a relief to see Will and actually more of a relief to know that he had not yet informed Lord Fernleigh of their liaison. She knew that this reprieve would be short-lived, and that they would have to face the consequences sooner or later if they were to remain together. The alternative was unthinkable. However, for now, for tonight, she must concentrate on keeping their understanding a secret, away from prying eyes or ears that could do them untold harm.

Emily forced herself to breathe deeply and calmly, to focus on the warm feeling in her stomach afforded by the tasty hot broth and the pungent, comforting smell of the rosemary. Given this rare opportunity of being allowed to rest in her room in the afternoon, she planned to try to sleep a while and later to slip out under the night's black mantle to meet William by the stable block. She was not worried about sleeping too long; many of the other servants whose chambers were on that landing were not quiet about making for their beds and Rachel, who resided in the next room, was one of the least considerate. Emily knew that she would wake at least by ten o'clock, if not before then. She undressed to her shift, keeping her woollen stockings on, and crawled under the covers, pulling the cotton sheet around her head and temporarily shutting out reality. It was a while before she was able to sleep, but her body and mind were so exhausted by the stress of the day that eventually she fell into a fitful slumber.

Sure enough, she awoke upon hearing the slam of the door to the next room. It was nearly October and the nights were drawing in. The night was clear and the heavens were punctuated with glittering points of silver light. Emily was allowed a small fire in her room, which had kindly been lit some hours ago upon her retirement to her chamber earlier that afternoon and was now reduced to a few faintly glowing fragments. She took a spill from the mantelpiece and held it to the dying embers in the grate and then to her candle. Once the flickering yellow candlelight had superseded the diffuse light of the waning moon, she drew her curtains and prepared to meet her lover. She dressed quickly, choosing her warmest petticoat and a plain woollen gown. She wrapped a black velvet cloak around her hips and loosely tied it, hiding the bulge under her skirt. If anyone saw her she would say she was on her way to the kitchen to ask for some supper, as she had missed it. From the kitchen she could steal out of the passage that led to the kitchen garden.

Emily slipped out of her room and made for the back stairs. She carried her shoes, for fear of being heard, but her woollen-stockinged feet slipped several times on the well-trodden smooth wooden staircase and she had to slow her pace and proceed with care. She succeeded in gaining entrance to the kitchen passage and passing the kitchen, though she twice had to flatten herself against a doorway in the shadows to avoid discovery. The door to the kitchen was half-open and a warm glow emerged, illuminating the entrance to the servants' hall across the passage. Most of the servants were abed, although from the noises coming from the kitchen one or two were still finishing their duties. Having made it past the kitchen, Emily ran to the heavy oak door leading to the garden. Luckily it had not yet been locked and barred for the night, although it soon would be. The shutting-in had already begun. She would not be able to re-enter the house through any of the ground-floor doors. She hoped that William would have a plan as far as this was concerned.

As Emily stepped out into the night a chill in the air set her to shivering and she hurriedly found a place out of the moonlight against the near wall of the garden to extract her cloak. She threw it around herself and fastened it quickly. Her hair was loose and her curls flowed around her shoulders, their copper strands catching the silvery light. She quickly pulled the hood over her head, put her shoes on and made for the stable block, keeping to the shadows.

There was a faint light coming from the farthest room above the stalls on the eastern side. Emily made for the west wall and headed around the back of the stone building. As she did so a hand shot out of the darkness and grabbed her right arm, pulling her forcefully towards the wall. Simultaneously another hand was clapped over her mouth before she could cry out. Then she was spun around to face her assailant, the hand still across her mouth.

Relief quickly replaced fear as she saw it was Will, although her heart, now racing wildly, took some minutes to recover. Anger flared within her. As soon as he had freed her mouth she gasped and drummed her fists against his chest; a momentary reaction, the release of her fear and indignation at being assaulted.

Temporarily shocked by her response, William let go of Emily but immediately put a finger to his lips.

'Shhh!' he whispered. 'Quickly, follow me.'

He chuckled to himself as he hurried from the protective shadow of the stable wall, skirted a small paddock and started towards a patch of woodland beyond. He had hold of Emily's hand and she hurried behind him, finding it hard to keep to his pace and having to add small steps to match his stride. He was still quietly smiling to himself at her fiery nature when they reached his horse, which was tethered amongst the beeches and oaks and hidden behind a tangled mass of bramble. The chestnut mare whinnied softly as they reached her, and William gently stroked her head before turning to Emily.

'My! You are a fiery one!' His eyes twinkled.

Emily's free hand was on her chest as she stood still to catch her breath. She pulled her other hand from his.

'What do you mean by assailing me! You nearly frightened the life out of me. Was that really necessary? My heart is still racing with the shock of it!'

William was still grinning, 'I am truly sorry, my love. But a desperate situation calls for desperate measures. I could not take the risk of us being overheard.' With the last of these words, his face changed, adopting a more sombre expression. He was not smiling now. 'When I reached the stables to wait for you I heard muffled footsteps and rustlings that did not sound like the four-footed variety. It is nigh impossible to take a horse from here without it being noticed, but I felt there was something more than good stewardship at risk here. If my presence was noticed, why did not one of the stable boys or old

Robert Butler step forward to challenge me? I might have been anyone. It would be a pretty serious lapse of duty to allow a horse to be
stolen from right under their noses.'

'Do you think someone was watching you? That someone knows
it was you outside by the wall, and did not acknowledge you?' Her
voice was full of incredulity. A familiar knot was forming in Emily's
stomach again.

William shook his head. 'I cannot say. All the same, I slipped into
Redwing's stall and muffled her hooves with pieces of sacking before
leading her out.'

'Did not the others make a fuss?'

'I'm well known to them. They behaved with impeccable manners.' William smiled again gently. 'Now come, let us ride up to the
ridge and there we can make our camp and discuss our tactics.'

'You make it sound as though we are going into battle, ' Emily
said in low tones.

'I believe that in a way we are, ' he retorted seriously.

Emily shivered under her warm cloak. They mounted and rode
towards the middle of the forested ridge north of Brockby, taking
care to avoid the village.

As they set off, two pairs of eyes followed their progress along the
edge of the wood until they rounded the hill, at which one pair of eyes
and its shadowy coexisting body disappeared within the stables, soon
followed by the other onlooker.

William was aiming for his favourite place just over the sum-
mit at the western end of the ridge. The moon was still throwing its
bright light benevolently towards them, scattering radiance amongst
the trees like broadcasted seeds. The white trunks of the occasional
birches shone like silvery beacons, marking the way. A thin carpet of
leaves lay on the ground already, its red and yellow hues, now grey in
the moonlight, heralding the oncoming autumn.

Redwing conveyed them almost to the top of the ridge, whereupon they dismounted and walked in single file along a narrow rabbit
track.

Emily knew the way; they had been here before a number of times. She never failed to appreciate the beauty of this place and loved it almost as much as William did, she thought.

At length they found the lone rowan tree and settled in the hollow under its golden-leaved and orange-berried branches. William unpacked the bundle that his mount was carrying and laid a deerskin beneath them against the cold. They sat down close together and he wrapped his arm around Emily and drew her in. They could just make out the dark shapes of newly-ploughed fields between the pastures on the wide plain below them.

'I shall miss all this, ' he sighed, then checked himself and gave Emily a hug, '...although it is nothing to your beauty, and I shall not be parted from that, ' he continued, to reassure her.

Emily shivered again. She felt not a little strange. What was about to happen, what they were about to do, did not seem real. It were as though her present world was some dreamlike state, a half-reality, akin to looking at this scene before them in the half-light, colours fading to greys, shapes misplaced and becoming difficult to discern. But Will's strong arm around her shoulders, warm and steady, reminded her that above all else he was her world. He would protect her and keep her safe; he would be her guide and provider; he would keep her warm at night and laugh with her in the day. There were many things she would miss. Her family was very dear to her. Fernleigh Hall and Brockby, where she had grown up, were all she knew. Indeed, she had never been further afield than York. But her great fear of losing all she knew was tinged with a hint of excitement. After all, she was going to marry the man she loved and live all the rest of her life with him!

She squeezed his hand and kissed it and he smiled reassuringly at her. He turned and rummaged in the bundle, bringing out a small silver flask.

'Here, have a sip of brandy, for you look cold.'

He threw a large woollen blanket around their shoulders and they cocooned themselves in it like a giant chrysalis.

The brandy felt warm in Emily's throat and the warmth quickly spread downwards and into her stomach, settling its contractions and soothing the butterflies that seemed to have taken residence there these past weeks. She relaxed and started to feel a little hungry.

William had anticipated her, or perhaps it was that he himself had a mighty appetite that never seemed to be satisfied. He handed her a slice of potted venison and a cracknel from a small linen-wrapped parcel.

Emily laughed. 'Thank you, sweet Will. You think of everything to ensure my comfort! I must admit that I was feeling a little hungry.'

'Procured from the kitchen, ' he said happily as he tucked into his potted meat. 'I cannot possibly break a habit soundly formed from a very early age, else Mrs Cumley would be most disappointed in me! I can only apologise that the biscuit doesn't come accompanied by chocolate.'

As they ate they told each other of the events of the past few days. Emily did not mention the exact nature of her discourse with Mrs Cumley, for it was certainly not appropriate, and William did not disclose the part of his conversation with his father that pertained to Miss Susan Snaith, for he did not wish to upset Emily. Otherwise their interchange of information was as full as it was honest.

They came to the conclusion that whoever had informed Mrs Cumley of their liaison was unlikely to have kept this information to themselves; however, whoever was watching them now must have something to gain by not making the information public. Not yet, anyway. This was indeed a dangerous situation, and they must act soon to bring this state of affairs under their control. They tried to make a mental list of people who could have seen or heard them together or who might have something to gain from the knowledge. They decided that it was unlikely to be any of William's siblings or extended family. For one, what would any of them gain by knowing this or indeed by making it public? It was, unfortunately, not that uncommon for a man of power to take advantage of a girl in a more vulnerable position, although this was not condoned in any sense by those of William's society and was certainly not the behaviour of a gentleman. And in any case, how did Mrs Cumley come to hear of it? No, the person, or indeed persons, had to be of the servant class to have something to gain by the knowledge, and this malice would likely be directed toward Emily, they thought.

'I do not like to think of anyone wanting to cause me harm, ' Emily said, her brow furrowed as she contemplated the matter. 'And I cannot think ill of anyone, for no-one has been unkind to me or upset with me. And I cannot think that I have caused upset to any person. Indeed it grieves me to think that this may be the case and I do not even know of it, ' she continued, her voice infused with a mix of confusion, incredulity and sadness.

William sympathised with her and gave her a squeeze. He replied gently, 'Sweetheart, if all the world were full of people of sweet, gentle and kind spirit such as you it would be a wondrous place indeed.' He sighed. 'Unfortunately the world is a mix of good and bad; indeed one person may be a mix of good and bad. We none of us know what is in the hearts of all of those around us.'

'I know you are right, ' replied Emily, her mouth turned down, 'but it seems mean-spirited to sit here and conjure up in our minds a list of those we would regard with suspicion.'

'Be that as it may, and it does you credit to think so highly of your fellow man – or woman – there is no escaping the fact that someone has betrayed you and stands to gain from it, or thinks they do. What we need to do is concentrate on those who have been in a position to see or hear something, as I'm sure the list of those who think they have something to gain could be a long one.'

It was Emily's turn to sigh downheartedly. 'Well, you were watched tonight, or you thought you were. We have met at the stables before, or at least in close proximity to them. Perhaps we have been noticed there.' Emily counted on the fingers of her left hand: 'There are at least four men who work with the horses, and three of those have rooms above the stalls, not including Mr Drew.'

'Old Robert Butler would never betray me, ' William said confidently.

'Well then, three men, ' returned Emily a little impatiently.

'Agreed. Three men. The Cooper twins and Ian Drew.'

'But I cannot see what any of them would have to gain!' Emily said, frustration rising. 'Ian Drew is a good man with a kind wife and young family to support, and he does not live above the stables. I am not particularly familiar with those Cooper lads – Stephen and Brian, isn't it?'

'Humour me, ' replied William patiently. 'Is there anyone else you can think of? We have passed a number of nights together in my chambers and I have visited your chamber a couple of times. Perhaps someone saw one of us entering or exiting the other's room?'

'It is possible, I suppose. But we have been so very careful and *quiet*.' Emily thought hard. 'And it is not uncommon for me to be seen on the second floor landing.'

'Your room is situated at the west end of the third floor, front corridor, ' William calculated. Emily nodded. 'And there is a large window to that corridor on the west side.' Emily nodded again. 'So your room is only bordered on the east side, ' William continued, '– who resides in that room?'

'Rachel Cutter, the Cutter's eldest daughter. She works in the kitchen,' Emily replied, her voice slowing, 'as cook...for...Mrs Cumley.'

They discussed Rachel's relatively recent rise to the status of cook and her concurrent move to a room of her own next to Emily's chamber. Emily admitted that she had heard Rachel complain once or twice about her paucity of petticoats, but she thought her a hardworking and pleasant girl.

'Well then, ' William stated matter-of-factly, 'that's it. Perhaps she's ambitious. Perhaps she is jealous of your position.' They were not questions.

After some thought, Emily had to reluctantly agree. There seemed to be few other options, although she was saddened to think that Rachel could wish her harm. However, it did not explain why Will had thought he was being watched at the stables. Who had Rachel been talking to, if indeed it was her, and why?

Now that they had reached some sort of conclusion about who the culprit might be they still had to decide what to do next, and when.

It was growing colder as a breeze had begun to blow over the ridge towards them from the north-east.

'Come, let me show you something.'

William took Emily's hand and helped her to her feet. He stowed the blanket and deerskin back in his saddle bag and, taking his mount's reins in his left hand and Emily's hand in his right, he led the two of them cautiously down a narrow track to their right. The track followed the line of the ridge for a short distance before curving downward to the left towards a small copse of trees and along by a stone wall. The wall led them to a tiny stone building with one small window and a narrow door facing west.

When they reached the building William gave the wooden door a sharp shove and it begrudgingly allowed them in, two of its swollen panels scraping across the stone floor as it opened. He motioned for Emily to go inside whilst he tethered Redwing behind the wall under a rough lean-to attached to the back of the hut. There was an old bucket under the lean-to, and William filled it from a tiny rainwater-filled pool which had been dug into the hillside a little way beyond the building. He topped up the small stone trough at the edge of the lean-to for the horse and carried the remaining water inside along with his saddle bag.

A little moss, some dry kindling and a few hawthorn logs lay patiently to one side of the fireplace. William retrieved his tinder-box from the saddlebag and soon had a fire crackling into life. Emily filled the smaller of two battered old pans with water and set it over the fire, whilst William rummaged in his bag for the candle he had brought. Once found, he lit it and set it on a low shelf over a rough wooden truckle bed in the corner. It hadn't been slept on for some time. There was a half-used hay bale in the other corner of the room, and he spread the soft strands generously over the bed, keeping some back for Redwing.

'Who stays here?' asked Emily, as she helped William to spread the deerskin out over the hay.

'The shepherds use it in the spring and summer months, ' William replied, using some hay to plug a gap at the base of the door where one of the wooden panels had split. 'There, that should stop the draft. We can be as cosy in here as kittens at their mother's belly now.'

The fire was roaring through the kindling and licking at the logs, throwing out a good deal of heat. Its light threw shapes against the walls, and the yellow glow from the candle softly flickered. There was no sound save the crackle of wood and the slow rise of bubbles from the heating water.

They lay on the truckle bed and pulled William's woollen blanket over themselves. Emily lay on her back with her head against her lover's shoulder.

'The sheep are brought down to the valley pasture in the autumn and winter months, so this shepherds' hut is rarely used at this time of year. It's quite cosy, is it not?'

William kissed Emily gently on the mouth. She turned her face to his and responded, a long, lingering, loving kiss. They held each other for a while, each savouring the warmth, the smell and the closeness of the other.

Eventually the water in the pan suspended above the fire began to boil.

'Would you like a hot drink, sweetheart? I brought a little coffee.'

'Mmm, ' Emily murmured softly.

William took this to mean yes, and carefully extracted his arm from underneath her shoulder. She sighed and rolled over as he rose and went to the fire. By the time he had found a cup, stoked the fire with another couple of logs, made some coffee and returned to her, Emily was fast asleep.

William smiled to himself. By her own account she'd had a rough day, and now it was very late. He looked at his pocket watch. It was gone half past one. They had so few hours together before the dawn. He wanted to wake her, to kiss her and feel her kissing him back, to run his hands over her and explore her secret places, to feel her flesh give under his; to make her his. He knelt beside the bed and looked at her beautiful face as she slept. With her dark eyelashes, the delicate arch of her brow, her sweet little nose and full pink lips she was like a little china doll, like his sister Amelia's favourite with its delicate white rounded cheeks coloured with just a hint of rose and its long curly red hair. William could not bear to wake her. Instead, with one finger he gently moved a stray curl from her forehead, kissed the place where it had lain and carefully climbed in beside her under the blanket. She murmured and moved a little as he did so and he gathered her to him as if their lives depended on it, protecting her against all the world, feeling that he could never let her go.

Deep in the night Emily awoke, momentarily wondering where she was. Then she remembered and smiled a knowing smile. William was not beside her but at the small window with his back to her, leaning on the thick stone sill and staring out into the night. The fire still burned brightly and the room was warm, but Emily sensed that she had been sleeping for some hours. Will must have fed it more logs, she thought. She wanted him back beside her.

'Cannot you sleep?' she asked gently.

William turned to look at her and smiled tenderly, but his face held more than the smile and there was concern in his eyes.

'We must leave soon, ' he responded. 'I don't mean here, this cottage; I mean Fernleigh Hall...England. It is time... indeed it is overdue. We have to leave before the winter comes.'

Emily nodded. 'Yes, ' she concurred soberly, 'it is time.'

'I will speak to my uncle again and ask him to arrange passage to France. In the meantime you and I must travel north, to Scotland.'

Emily raised her eyebrows. North was opposite to the direction she thought they should be going in if they were to join a ship heading for France.

William saw the confusion in her face and set her straight, 'I mean to marry you. To make an honest woman of you. Remember? You did say yes, ' he winked. 'We need to cross the border into Scotland, for in Gretna Green we can be married with no questions asked.'

'Gretna Green sounds a wonderful place, ' Emily said happily, sitting up and leaning against the rough stone wall.

'I have heard that it is quite the place for eloping couples, ' William retorted. There was the slightest hint of regret in his voice.

'How far is Scotland from here, Will?'

'I understand that the border is some one hundred and twenty miles from Yorkshire. I expect the journey will take some three or four days. We need to travel to Richmond and pick up the stage from there. The results of my enquiries indicate that we shall need to change coaches several times; however, that is probably no bad thing if we were to be followed.'

'Followed!' Emily gasped and her hands went to her mouth. 'I had not thought... Oh Will...if we were to be caught...I cannot bear to think of what the consequences might be...what if...'

'Sweetheart, do not be alarmed' William interrupted quickly, crossing the floor to sit beside her. 'I *will not* let anyone take you from me. Besides, we have planned that by the time we leave, my parents and yours will know of our intention to marry. Recollect that we are hoping to do this *with* their consent, although I think it would be unwise to mention our plans in any detail.'

His words were meant as comfort, to allay her fears. However, they neither satisfied her concerns nor stemmed the rising feelings of worry in his heart and mind. He realised that they had to ensure that the timing of his confession and declaration to his father, and indeed her father, was absolutely right, else this could spark severe consequences for them both. The campaign had to be perfectly planned and executed or it would fail.

William had not slept yet this night but had lain awake, the comforting weight of Emily in the crook of his arm, her head against his shoulder. He had been turning plans over in his head, looking at them from different angles, trying to see the flaws and to solve the potential problems. He had of course considered the option of not telling his father anything at all, of disappearing into the night then writing to his family to tell them of the circumstances once safely in France. But his family, his mother in particular, would be sick with worry, and no doubt Emily's family would suffer the same. He had come to the conclusion that he could not treat them so cruelly, and he knew that Emily would not wish this for her kin either. So that was not an option. He was under no illusions now that his news would be highly unwelcome. His father had made it plain that he intended a career in law or politics for his only son, and a marriage to someone that William absolutely did not love; indeed he would go as far as to say that he despised her shrill voice and affected mannerisms. He had no idea how to convince his father to agree to him marrying Emily except by divulging his deepest feelings and begging him to understand – or if not to understand, to allow him the freedom to make his own choices as a man for the sake of their paternal-filial bond, which had hitherto been a strong one. If this went badly, however, it would subsequently be nigh on impossible to make their escape; they were both likely to be sent away, and he feared that Emily's whereabouts would be kept from him, thus making her rediscovery highly improbable.

No: it was all about timing, and he had, of necessity, formed a plan. The Fernleigh autumn ball was in two weeks. It was always a magnificent event, usually requiring weeks of preparation culminating in much frantic activity above and below stairs. That would be the time, the day, that he would unleash the news. Of course he did not wish to ruin the occasion for his mother, and he was fairly sure his father would feel the same. This just might give him the option of testing the waters with his father whilst the whole household, including his mother, was busy with last-minute preparations. If the worst happened they might have a chance of slipping away during the festivities. It was a risk: if this plan backfired and Thomas told Charlotte then and there, William was sure that all hell would break loose and his mother would have her ball ruined, and in a very public manner.

As William crossed the room to comfort her, Emily could see the slender outline of his fine body beneath his loose shirt where the firelight softly glowed through the thin white cotton fabric. She wanted him badly. She wanted to hold him and him to hold her, to surround her, to envelope her, to protect her. She felt as though they were on the edge of a precipice and about to fall over the edge, and she was terrified. She knew deep inside that he alone could save her, but she needed to feel the solidity of him to make it real. She wanted to feel his strong arms about her; to hold him to her and lay her hands flat on the broad muscles of his shoulders, to trace the curve of his back down to his buttocks; to hold those soft, downy fleshy orbs in her hands, pulling him towards her. She longed to kiss his chest where his hard muscles played host to the collection of dark curly hairs nestling there; to follow the narrow line of soft darkness downwards to where it flourished once again, gently cradling him. She ached to feel him harden in her hand; to take him in her mouth and feel his smooth soft skin on the tip of her tongue; to feel him deep inside her. All this in a moment.

Sweetheart, do not be alarmed...I will not let anyone take you from me...

As he reached her she threw out her arms and took hold of him. He did the same, and for some moments they sat there together as one, rocking gently to and fro, he whispering comforting words into the nape of her neck. Presently he brought his face around to hers, and the desire hitherto held back by exhaustion and consideration, by fear and love, surged forth in a torrent that burst its banks, over-whelming them both. Desperately discarding garments, their bod-ies melded into one, lips on lips, tongue on tongue, hands on skin, muscle, smoothness, moistness; cupping, pressing and grasping flesh; hands stroking hair; tongues tasting nipples, fingers exploring, prob-ing, parting; flesh against flesh, hair against hair, deepness, warm-ness, slipperiness, throbbing, quivering. They were one; one body and one spirit, and as he exploded into her and she received him they sealed their fate. Two became one, never to be parted.

They awoke as the birds celebrated the dawn and hurriedly dressed, she throwing their belongings into the bag while he saddled Redwing. It was Sunday, and a rare day off for her. After fulfilling some preliminary duties for her mistress she was to accompany her mother and father to church and spend the rest of the day with them.

Their plan was to ride to the copse beyond the small paddock next to the stables. From there they would go their separate ways back to the house. He would feign an early morning ride in the meadows and she, if questioned, would pretend to an early walk in the kitchen garden to clear a headache.

Luckily the dawn was a dry one, clear although cold. It was one of those September mornings when the last vestiges of summer mix with the promise of a fine autumn. A delicate mist rose slowly and the strengthening sun began to bleach the sky. A myriad of tiny spider's webs became visible. Many nestled amongst the foliage in splendid isolation, while hundreds more grouped themselves variously into tiny hamlets and villages in the low pasture. In the longer grass this accommodation was at various levels, while the tops of dry thistles and grasses hosted lookouts with a splendid aspect over the rest. The dew-laden webs shone in the rising sun like quicksilver as they caught the early morning light. Positioned beautifully between a dried ear of volunteer wheat, a proud thistle and a young hawthorn stem was the king of all spiders' webs. The palace – the castle – spanning perhaps a foot, was entirely round and perfectly formed, shining in the haze, a large black spider crouched at its centre ready to pounce.

They rode at first in silence, savouring the beauty and peaceful-ness of the morning, each reluctant to break the magical spell of the past night that had bound them inexorably together. At length, as they descended through the oaks, birches, beeches and pines, William be-gan to speak to Emily of his plan. By the time they had reached the copse, beyond which was the paddock, their strategy was agreed and honed as finely as a carpenter's chisel.

As they said their goodbyes in the half-light afforded by the dense canopy and prepared to set off in different directions towards the house and the stables, Emily and William both sensed that something had changed between them. A deepening of their relationship, of their commitment to one another. There was no going back.

Emily made a detour so that she could approach the house from the kitchen garden. She hurried along looking this way and that, mak-ing sure that she was alone and trying not to act suspiciously. She was nearly there when she suddenly felt nauseous and had to halt. She retched a few times and began to feel a little better. This was the third time in the last week. She attributed it to worry and a lack of sleep, wiped her mouth with her sleeve and hurried on. Reaching the kitchen garden, she darted inside its walls. She breathed a huge sigh, almost as if she had been holding her breath for the past fifteen minutes and could at last allow herself to take a breath, and picked a few leaves of feverfew and a sprig of mint to support her chosen excuse should she be seen. As she rounded the wall leading to the kitchen passage the large figure of Martha Cumley loomed in the doorway, and she was looking out for something. As soon as she spied Emily one large hand went to her bosom and the other beckoned wildly.

'There y' are, Miss Emily! Ah've been awaiting thee! An' about time too, if tha doesn't mind me saying,' she hissed in a loud whisper.

As Emily reached her she grabbed her arm uncharacteristically and pulled her in through the heavy oak doorway. Emily opened her mouth to explain, but before she could utter a word, Mrs Cumley cut her off.

'No time fer explanations, Miss Emily. Get in 'ere quickly. Come on!'

Emily's heart began to race as she followed Martha's plump frame along the stone-flagged passage and into a large larder off the kitchen. Once safely enclosed by large jars of bottled provisions and with the door firmly shut, Martha turned to her.

'Oh Miss Emily, there's been a terrible to do and tha needs t' do *exactly* as ah say, an' be mighty quick about it!'

⟡

October

Since her incredible discovery that she seemed to have lived a past life some two centuries ago as someone called Emily who was in love with a young gentleman called William, Jennifer had undergone two more hypnotherapy sessions. Far from being trepidatious, she was now filled with an intense curiosity and a strong desire to uncover more about her past life and her relationship with this man who had appeared so regularly in her drug-induced dreams, in which he courted her, made love to her, comforted her and banished her feelings of rejection when she was with him.

Jennifer had made this decision when she had been at the IMAX cinema with Sarah, watching the flight through the Grand Canyon, and now she was following it through. She had to understand why this character was so prominent in her mind during her sleeping hours; why she had become so obsessed with something her mind had seemed to conjure up; why and how her thoughts had been invaded by an actual person, long since dead, without ever having read or heard about him or seen his image; why she could always conjure him up when she took her natural remedy for sleeplessness and how she would ever be able to control this obsession while also ridding herself of her still-painful lingering feelings for Jim in her waking hours.

Jennifer had begun to feel that this was the one thing she could no longer talk to Sarah about. Sarah was a scientist and practical-minded. She analysed and questioned. She brought logic into every aspect of her life. Not that all scientists necessarily did this, Jennifer supposed, but Sarah believed there was a logical explanation for everything, whether or not science had so far discovered it. Jennifer knew that Sarah's explanation for all of this was that she had seen an image of William Fernleigh somewhere before without consciously registering it, and her desire to be loved and not to feel rejected had manifested itself in a few passionate dreams. Sarah did not approve at all; in fact she strongly disapproved of Jennifer taking sleeping tablets of un-known provenance. Of course this was eminently sensible – Jennifer knew that – but she had increasingly found that when these feelings visited her, desire overcame her, overwhelmed her, pulled at her mind and her heart, infused her thoughts, occupied her body and usurped her sense and logic. She could not banish it if she wanted to – and she did not want to.

Sarah would not have approved of the hypnotherapy, let alone the regression therapy.

Her approach to solving problems in life was self-sufficiency, strong willpower and an unswerving belief in oneself. It worked for her. She had urged Jennifer to focus on the present, to try to enjoy her work and home life, her lovely cottage and garden and of course Smokey, and to get out more, join a club or an evening class and meet some new people.

Jennifer had preferred to wrap herself up, removing herself from people when she wasn't at work, shrinking from the world. Consequently her work had become an increasing effort. She had begun to turn in upon herself and had actually been almost content to do so, perversely enjoying the reclusive life-style. Had it not been for her raging emotions perhaps she could have managed, in a self-centred sort of way; however, this wasn't to be.

Now she had begun to discover some sort of explanation for why this particular character had become so prominent in her thoughts and imaginings. Jennifer assumed that her use of the sleeping pills had allowed her to reach a deeper state of consciousness in her sleep, perhaps similar to the level of consciousness she was able to reach under hypnosis. Although she hadn't discussed the tablets with Christina – a little voice in her head had warned her against this – they had talked about the possibility that Jennifer was somehow mixing past and present lives at some level in her subconscious, her imagination drawing upon and being supplemented by recollections of past-life experiences that were not normally accessible. This did seem to make some sense to Jennifer, to offer some elucidation; for example, some of the dreams were set in exotic locations that she could easily imagine but could not possibly be past-life memories; a seventeenth-century Yorkshire lass would never have dreamed of such places.

Christina wanted to put this situation right: to help Jennifer to control her emotions, to banish rejection and the past, however long ago, and to start to live firmly in the present again.

In the last two sessions they had found out a little more about Emily and the nature of her relationship with William. Through Jennifer's regressions into this past life they had also discovered a little more about William and his family. They knew, for example, that Emily had worked in some capacity for the mistress of the house, who was also William's mother. Christina had wanted to explore whether Emily had experienced any feelings of rejection, but had uncovered nothing of that nature. Jennifer's desire to learn more of Emily and William and to discover their fate had grown stronger. However, Christina had been reluctant to explore any further than the nature of the couple's feelings and who they were. Jennifer badly wanted to complete the story, but Christina firmly insisted that this was not a wise course of action; they had discovered what they needed to from the point of view of Jennifer's treatment and should concentrate on helping her to live a happy and fulfilled life now, in the present. Christina reminded Jennifer that she had agreed to help her to overcome her depression, and that was what she was going to do.

Jennifer had come to greatly respect Christina's judgement, and so agreed to try to concentrate on the here and now. It was true: she had begun to feel more accepting about being parted from Jim. However, human nature, being what it is, seeks to replace what is lost and to redress the balance, however misplaced this may be. The focus of Jennifer's emotions for the past couple of years had been Jim's rejection of her. As these feelings slowly retreated, instead of being replaced by positive thoughts, a desire to get on with her life and to seek out new opportunities and challenges, the growing hole was being filled with an increasing fixation on her past life – a new tide of obsession with a focus on not just two years ago but two *centuries* ago.

In their most recent session Christina had told Jennifer that Jim had not been her soulmate. 'Your soulmate is to come, ' she had said.

As Jennifer sat at her rustic kitchen table that bright October Saturday morning, she knew she had some decisions to make. She poured herself a second cup of her favourite Guatemalan coffee from the large cafetière wrapped with a warmer decorated with ginger and black cats. Smokey purred contentedly on her mistress's lap as Jennifer generously spread pieces of warm bread, just retrieved from the bread-maker, with lashings of butter. The butter melted into the soft springy bread and the fusion of that delicious combination and the coffee permeated the air, filling the kitchen with bliss.

Low-angled sunlight dodged the still-green, slowly-swaying branches of the ancient oak at the end of the garden to stream into the kitchen, stippling its smooth-hewn relative with moving flecks of gold. Jennifer watched the sunlight dance on the table and reflected on Christina's words. *Your soulmate is to come; he's out there somewhere, and fate will bring you together. Relax and let Jim go. He was not intended for you.* Christina had considered that events in Jennifer's past life had influenced her behaviour in her recent relationships, given her an immense need for a soulmate, coloured her life with Jim and made her too needy. *Jim was not your soulmate. Relax and let fate take its course. Enjoy life, live for the moment. Have fun. Don't try to force things. Don't concentrate on the past or the invasive dreams of your sleeping hours. Let go of the feelings of rejection, let go of the doubts,* Christina had instructed. *Don't be drawn by the past or worry about what may come. Concentrate on the present, and the future will take care of itself.*

Jennifer took another bite of the warm bread and Smokey jumped off her lap and launched herself at a sparkle of sunlight on the sandstone flags. Jennifer laughed to see her front paws dart out, first one and then the other, patting the dappled floor, trying in vain to catch something of no substance. An impossible task. Was that what she was trying to do herself? Was it all in her head? Was she trying to accord tangibility to something that did not exist, was merely the overactive imagining of a depressed mind?

She pushed away her plate and rested her elbows on the table and her head in her hands, chin and cheeks cupped comfortingly, to better concentrate. She knew she had to resolve something before she could move on. Christina was disinclined to further pursue the regression therapy, whereas she desperately wanted – no, *needed* – to know more about William and Emily; about who she had been. Was there something that Christina was keeping back? Perhaps; perhaps not. Maybe it was simply that Christina was certain. She had unearthed enough to make her diagnosis and impart her expert council.

Whatever it was, Jennifer felt that it was vital that she discovered more before she could put this behind her and move on with her life. There was of course one thing she could do that might lend substance to the notions emerging from her subconscious mind. She could search parish and county records, registers of birth, death and marriage. If she found William, this of course being a relatively easy task on account of his lineage and status, perhaps this would lead her to Emily.

That morning the decision was made and an immediate course of action clarified. Jennifer rose quickly from the table, the feet of her chair scraping on the tiles. There was no time like the present: she would start today. A surprising thrill swept through her body and she smiled a gleeful smile to herself. For the first time in months she felt that she was actually in control. She would determine who she had been, come to terms with it and close the chapter.

That was her intention.

⌒

October 1762

$\mathcal{M}$artha and Emily were in the preserves larder, amongst row upon row, shelf upon shelf of corked and wax-sealed earthenware jars of all shapes and sizes, packed full to bursting with the recent harvest. Gooseberries in honey syrup; shining blackcurrants, their skins softened by being plunged into boiling water and soaked in sugar water; deep red strawberries delicately placed and covered with good French brandy and spices; plump purple plums with cinnamon and ginger; spiced oranges; pears in cider; damsons in brandy; peaches in redcurrant syrup, all diligently processed, pickled and preserved for the coming autumn and winter months when fresh fruit would not be available but the demand for puddings and pies, pastries and sweetmeats would continue unabated.

As she stood shivering in that cold room, lit by one small north-facing window deep-set into the thick outer wall, Emily briefly scanned the carefully-written labels and an image raced through her head of the wonderful colours of the contents of their associated jars. She had had plenty of practice bottling and pickling and making all kinds of jams, jellies and preserves, first with her mother from an early age and then under the supervision of Mrs Cumley when she had first come to Fernleigh Hall.

On the opposite side of the store were the jars of pickle and bottled sauces. Bottles of black butter vinegar, browning, fish sauce, liver ketchup, mushroom ketchup and tomato sauce stood proudly next to a collection of pickled vegetables – beetroot with ginger and pepper; Bengal chutney; lemon quarters in vinegar with mace; mustard seed and garlic; pickled mushrooms; onions in brine; prunes with cinnamon in wine vinegar; samphire with ginger; marrow with raisins and nasturtium buds with horseradish – a mouth-watering array to satisfy even the most ardent lover of pickles and the most extreme tastes. There were a few particular spaces on these crowded shelves that had been left for crops still to be harvested. Walnuts, cabbage and cauliflower would join the ensemble, similarly boiled, salted, spiced and infused in wine or vinegar in the months to come.

Emily shivered again.

If one had time to carefully read all the labels tied upon the neat rows of glazed containers, all proudly placed, ordered, counted and accounted for, the whole mouth-watering effect would be appreciated indeed. However, for the occupants of the cool store room that morning the nature of their surroundings was of the very least concern, save that they were hidden behind a locked door.

Martha Cumley was assisting Emily with removing her cloak and crumpled woollen gown, the hems of which were dew-soaked and mud-stained, the moisture having crept upwards unevenly, belying her pretence of a short walk around the vegetable garden to get some fresh air. They were frantically removing her outer garments down to her shift and replacing them with a bedgown that Martha had hidden behind a large box of recently-harvested cobnuts on one of the bottom shelves. As they did so, Martha was rapidly informing Emily in breathless whispers of the past night's events.

'Ah couldn't believe m' ears when Mrs Preedy called me to 'er room an' told me!' Mrs Cumley's plump red face could hardly believe what her lips were uttering. 'Rachel! Ah mean, of all t' things t' lass could've done.' For a moment her breathy tones trailed off.

Emily was alarmed, not only by Mrs Cumley's countenance but also from being bustled into the preserves larder and having the door locked behind them.

'Dear Mrs Cumley, please tell me plainly what this is about! What has Rachel done? Has she told anyone about me?'

Martha Cumley held up one hand, gesturing Emily to stop.

'Now don't fret, lass, ' she croaked in her calmest whisper, the words still tumbling out. 'Tha just needs t' get back t' tha room as quick as tha can. Ah know tha's been out all night, but tha certainly don't want other folks knowin' or even suspectin'. So 'elp me with this 'ere bedgown.'

Emily was frightened. What on earth had happened to create such a fluster in Mrs Cumley, whose manner was normally so calm and considered? She was usually a rock, but this morning she was like a handful of shifting sand. And how on earth did the cook know that she'd had been out all night? And if she was aware of this, who else might know of it?

Martha was rummaging around behind the cobnut box once more and came up, red-faced, with a woollen shawl which she proceeded to place around Emily's shoulders against the chill.

'Mrs Cumley, please!' I shall go back to my room directly when you tell me what has happened!'

Mrs Cumley took a deep breath to steady herself and slowly let it out through pursed lips, preparing herself to utter the next words. She took another breath and began more slowly, still whispering hoarsely.

'Rachel Cutter 'as been caught abed wi' t' Cooper twins!'

Emily's mouth dropped open.

'Both of them!' continued Mrs Cumley, 'at t' same time!' as if to emphasise the point. 'And that's not all. She's been dismissed. First thing this morning!'

Emily frowned and began to shake her head in disbelief.

'How...I mean who...who found her? When did...'

'She wor seen toin' an' froin' between house and t' stables, ' Martha interrupted, leaning forward closer to Emily, her flushed cheeks inches from Emily's nose, perspiration in her hairline, 'when she'd no business there. An' all odd times of day an' night, so I wor told. So she wor watched an' him that wor doin' the watchin', he caught her...in...well...in the most of compromisin' position, so t' speak.'

'Oh Lord!' spluttered Emily, shocked yet still partly in disbelief. 'Who?'

'Never tha mind who. It don't matter who.' Mrs Cumley returned impatiently. 'I don't rightly know, any road, ' she continued, waving the question away. 'Important thing is, tha mustn't attract any suspicion, or tha'll find thaself goin t' way of Rachel, an' no mistake!'

Martha straightened up and put her hands to her face, slowly shaking her frilled white-capped head. 'Lord, if tha's been seen...I don't know what we'll do.' She began to mumble, almost talking to herself. 'We'll 'ave to do summat.'

Emily's face had turned the colour of Mrs Cumley's cap for the second time this morning. Realisation hit her. Mrs Cumley had seen her come back. Who else had been watching? This morning? The night before? For a few more seconds she continued to stare at her ally before panic goaded her into action. She hurriedly put her wet shoes back on her near-frozen feet and bent down to fasten the buckles, instructions now ensuing in a torrent from the large frame behind her, bombarding her ears.

'Get back t' tha room an' don't be seen. If tha meets anyone, tha'll be able to tell them tha's just been t' kitchen, as tha weren't well last night an' missed supper. Or tell them tha's been out into kitchen garden t' get some fresh air. Don't worry about these clothes, ah'll get them back t' tha room. And don't tha be goin' off again neither. Ah'm sorry, Miss Emily, ah know it's not my place to be giving instructions, but tha can't take any more risks.'

As Emily stood up, wrapping the shawl around her shoulders, ready to make a dash to her room, she caught Mrs Cumley's hand and gave it a quick squeeze. 'Thank you!' she managed to utter, the tiredness and concern in the muscles of her face thinly veiled with a worried smile.

As Martha unlocked the larder door with a large key from the ring she carried in her pocket, she returned the smile with an equal amount of worry.

'Go on...before folks start t' get about. Ah'll see thee later.'

Emily started back across the warm kitchen and out into the corridor. She walked quickly past the doors to the buttery and the pantry and the locked door to the wine cellar. After crossing the entrance to the passage that led to the dairy she allowed herself to breathe a little. When folk were up and about it was the dairy that was usually first occupied. Suddenly she heard footsteps at the end of the airy passage and the clatter of pails mixed with a peal of laughter. She ran the last twenty feet or so to the back staircase, not minding the clatter of her heels on the stone flags.

Once on the staircase, Emily proceeded with more caution as it was narrow and there was nowhere to hide if she did meet someone – it would look exceptionally odd if she were to be seen trying to run up the steps – but also because she had begun to feel a little light-headed and her whole body seemed to be trembling. Perhaps it was due to the fact that she'd managed hardly any sleep, or that she had not eaten a proper meal since the rabbit broth yesterday, or because of the anxiety she was hosting. Perhaps it was simply because she felt chilled and had vomited this morning. Whatever the reason, Emily trod carefully, although determinedly. She had passed the door to the first-floor laundry and was halfway up the next spiralling flight towards the garret rooms when a pair of stout shoes and check cotton skirts came into view, quickly followed by the daunting frame of Mrs Preedy.

Mrs Preedy was unused to seeing servants in their night attire anywhere but on the garret floor; that is to say she did not encourage such practice, except in an emergency of course. Therefore she raised her eyebrows in surprise and stood firmly looking down at Emily waiting for an explanation.

Emily's heart was pounding like hooves on dry earth.

'Good morning, Mrs Preedy, ' she managed, fairly steadily, somehow filtering the beat in her chest so that her voice did not reflect it. 'I've been to the kitchen for a hot drink and some bread. I, um... I missed supper last night...and I needed a few breaths of fresh air, ' she added.

Mrs Preedy's eyebrows, now far from being surprised, pulled her face into a frown.

'I hope that you are not in the habit of going about in your bed-gown, Miss Popple. Are you quite well?' Her voice was firm and clipped but polite. 'You look pale, if I may say so.'

'I'm quite well, thank you, Mrs Preedy' Emily returned, ignoring the former comment. 'I ought to be getting back to my room. My lady will be wanting to dress for church before too long.'

'Indeed, ' accorded the housekeeper, the frown still present on her mannish features. 'Well, go on with you.'

She stepped aside to let Emily pass, making a mental note to keep a close eye on the girl, especially considering what she had heard this morning about that shameful Cutter lass. There was something about Emily's countenance that did not sit well this morning, and her breath was most unpleasant. Perhaps she would have a word with Mrs Cumley – the cook seemed to have Emily's confidence. She continued down and headed for the kitchen.

Once safely in her room, Emily collapsed on her bed. She was tired and cold, and it was as much as she could do to stop herself from easing her trembling body beneath the covers and going to sleep. As she lay there with her eyes closed for a few minutes she reminded herself that she had only to endure the next couple of hours and then she would be free to join her family in church and spend the remainder of the day with them, for she had leave to visit them today. She was really looking forward to seeing them all, especially her mother. An image of her mother's Sunday lunch floated into her head. There would probably be a chicken or two, or maybe a nice plump duck and some of her mother's tasty fried parsnips and perhaps her favourite white pot to finish.

Usually these were comforting thoughts; however, today as Emily's thoughts turned to food her stomach gave a lurch and she felt queasy once more. The sudden movement caused by the action of swinging her legs off the bed and kneeling on the floor to retrieve her chamber pot triggered the inevitable reaction, and she spewed for the second time that morning.

She felt a little better after this. As she washed her face and hands and dressed for church, Emily's thoughts turned to Rachel. She hated to think ill of anyone, and Mrs Cumley's revelation had been a terrible shock; however, she deduced that if Rachel had been in league with the Cooper twins it was almost certainly they who had been spying on Will at the stables, and the chances were that they had seen her meet him there. Coupled with their suspicion that Rachel might have seen or heard them in her room, the conclusion that she would almost certainly have drawn would be undeniable.

A wave of fear flooded Emily's senses. She sat on her bed once again, resting her head in her hands, elbows on her knees, staring at the floorboards and trying to calm herself down to consider what to do. Rachel was dismissed; she knew that much. Would she go quietly, or would she expose her? She supposed that Rachel had nothing to lose now, however what would she gain? Slander against her would also be slander against Master William, their lord's only son and heir, held in high esteem not only by his family but also by the staff. He had only to deny the story, if indeed such a charge would be taken that far. No; Emily was confident on that score. Any road, accusations of any kind might be taken as sour grapes now that Rachel had been dismissed. But what of Stephen and Brian Cooper? If they were kept on, which Emily was almost certain they would be, she and Will would most certainly have them to contend with. If they corroborated Rachel's allegation Emily could still be in trouble. She would need to have a refutation ready.

She sighed, took another deep breath and forced herself to get up from the bed. She had things to do before her ladyship rose and needed her; the repairs to her coral and ivory damask contouche needed to be finished and she would need to force herself to eat something. But first she had to get rid of the nasty contents of her chamber pot.

Her mouth tasted foul, so she rinsed it out with a little of the water left in her wash jug and spat into her pot, trying not to get too close. She cleaned her teeth with a clean rag and rinsed again with a little of the mint and vinegar mixture in the small earthenware pot on her table. It was nearly empty. She would have to mix some more.

Since it was Sunday, of her three best gowns she chose the light turquoise taffeta, woven with tiny blue and white flowers along pale blue vertical stripes and edged with a small amount of lace. A recent donation from William's sister Mary, the dress had hardly been worn. On seeing her acquaintance Constance Billington at one of Mrs Tintern's afternoon soirées clothed in the same material, albeit in a different design, Mary, and indeed Constance, had experienced the most acute embarrassment and Mary had immediately vowed never to wear the gown again and left the tea partly shortly after, feigning a headache. She had passed the gown straight to Emily. They were of a similar size, and all Emily needed to do was to take in the material a little at the waist. Turquoise was her favourite colour and complemented her complexion and the rich red hues of her hair. She was lucky indeed to have such a choice of garments; of course it reflected well upon her ladyship to have a well-dressed maid, however she seemed to have been particularly fortunate with regard to the contributions to this cause from Will's sisters.

Having washed and dressed and with her hair neatly done and under her cap, Emily started to feel better and even a little hungry, and set off downstairs.

Pot emptied into the cesspit and having breakfasted on a little bread and honey, she settled down to her mending in her ladyship's dressing room, awaiting the tinkle of the silver bell from Charlotte's bedchamber signifying that she was needed. She sat by the window where the light was better. The weave of tiny birds was complicated, and she was trying to repair a tear in the skirt. As she concentrated on the entry and exit points of the needle each side of the fabric there was the faintest of knocks at the door to the corridor. Sighing, she rose and answered it. To her surprise it was Martha Cumley, who asked in whispers if she might come in if her ladyship was not yet risen. Emily glanced behind her at Charlotte's bedchamber door, knowing that it would remain shut until she was summoned. She ushered the flushed and flustered cook into the dressing room, whereupon she sat herself upon the nearest thing to hand, her ample frame filling a delicate fret-backed Chinese chair. Emily waited impatiently for Mrs Cumley to recover her breath. Indeed, so out of breath was she that it seemed as though she had been taking the stairs two at a time, which would have been nigh on impossible, of course.

Martha fanned her throat with her hand and tried to take some deep gulps of air as her eyes darted around the room taking in the splendour of its recent refurbishment. Her presence on this floor was uncommon and was usually limited to the drawing room, where her ladyship customarily discussed the menus with her. Of course she knew of her lady's passion for drawing and that she had designed the upholstery herself to compliment the Chinese wallpaper, but she was unprepared for the exquisite effect. On the walls were figures on pretty bridges and in little boats, ladies sitting having tea in beautiful ironwork structures with oddly-shaped roofs, strange brightly-coloured birds perched on pink and white cherry trees, all intertwined with a delicate weave of intricate flowers and vines. Indian chintz framed the windows and a number of porcelain vases and figures in the Chinese style graced the tables. It really was splendid and quite took her breath away, just as she was regaining it.

'Mrs Cumley! Make haste and impart what you have to. Her ladyship will be risen before too long.'

Emily's insistent whispers intruded on Martha's momentary fantasies of far-away exotic places.

'Apologies, Miss Popple...Emily.' Martha shook her head slightly as if to bring herself back to reality from somewhere and jiggle her thoughts into some kind of order. 'Ah came t' tell thee summat and t' ask thee summat.'

'Indeed. Please go on.'

Emily, who was already concerned again, felt little pockets of fear take flight within her belly.

'Summat of a delicate nature, ' Mrs Cumley continued, reaching out and patting Emily's arm, signalling that she might want to sit down.

However, Emily quickly crossed the room to Charlotte's bureau, opened one of the small side drawers and slid her slender fingers underneath to its contents, coming out with a small brown key.

Shutting the drawer, she moved to the wall furthest from Charlotte's bedchamber.

'I think we'd best go in here, ' she motioned to her ally.

Emily located a small keyhole in the belly of one of the birds on the wall and opened a panel door leading to Charlotte's closet room. Martha hurriedly followed her inside and found herself in a small room beautifully decorated in oriental lacquer and shell-work. Chelsea-ware figurines were displayed in two alcoves. For all its formal display of craftwork, the room was more comfortably furnished than the dressing room from whence they had come. A chaise longue occupied the far wall and two comfortable chairs sat easily on either side of the tall window next to Charlotte's tambour. A small selection of books lay on an inlaid rosewood table adjacent to the chaise longue.

Emily smiled at the astonished look on Mrs Cumley's face as she admired the clever patterns of expensive swirling shells.

'Her ladyship uses this room for quiet contemplation, ' she remarked. 'She once told me that her rooms were *My Lord's concession to the Palladian*!'

The cook looked at her quizzically.

'She prefers the beauty of nature to straight lines, ' Emily explained simply.

'Ah, ' Martha nodded briefly. How far this girl had come!

'Now we are hidden and quiet. But we do not have much time.'

'Aye, ' accorded Martha sitting on the edge of one of the window chairs and leaning forwards. 'Ah'll say m' piece an' ah don't want thee t' think me prying', and ah'll thank thee for bein' honest wi' me.'

Martha's tone commanded the deference due to age over status. Emily nervously took the other chair.

'Mrs Preedy came t' see me this morning, having encountered thee on stairs.' A deep breath and wave of hand in Emily's general direction. 'She wor extremely concerned, y'know, and ah think not a little suspicious. Ah told 'er tha'd been down t' get some fresh air and a little summat t' eat was all.'

'What did she say? Did she believe you?'

'She seemed to. Tha' knows that hussy Rachel went an' accused you of layin' with Master William, as we suspected she might.'

Emily's heart pounded against her ribs and she fought a rising wave of panic. Her hand went to her cheek. Mrs Cumley patted her knee through the copious folds of her skirt and smiled kindly.

'There lass, don't be frettin' yerself. Ah informed Mrs Preedy in no uncertain terms that t' Cutter girl was talking stuff an' nonsense. I told 'er that Rachel'd tried t' tell me a similar story an' ah'd dismissed it at once an' told her if she went round telling stories like that she'd be certain t' lose 'er position, so she would.'

Emily let out the breath she'd been holding. 'Did she believe you?' she repeated worriedly.

Mrs Cumley patted her comfortingly again. '*An*' ah told 'er that it was my opinion that Rachel Cutter was just trying t' elevate 'erself at t' expense of others.' Martha inclined her head towards Emily, raising her eyebrows and nodding several times as she spoke. 'She probably 'ad 'er eye on tha position. Ah don't like t' speak ill of anyone an' thee an' me know there was truth in what she said, but that girl was a trouble-maker an' no mistake.' She looked to the domed shell-work ceiling and put a hand to her bosom. 'Lord fergive me fer lyin', but it were the girl's own sinful behaviour as got her dismissed, ' she added as justification.

Emily looked down at the floor a little ashamedly.

'Now then, lass, ' Mrs Cumley continued, firmly but gently. 'Ah wor watching thee come back over t' field this dawn, an' ah saw thee spewing and smelt it on thy breath, so 'ah did. Mrs Preedy 'as a point – tha looks out o' sorts. Tha fainted yesterday an' all. How many times 'as this 'appened?'

Emily conceded that she had not been feeling altogether well for a number of days and that she had vomited again a little while earlier. Although she couldn't possibly confess all that was on her mind, all that was happening and was about to happen, she felt comforted by divulging certain of her anxieties. This woman was the closest friend she had, next to her mother.

'When did tha last 'ave thy courses?'

Emily was taken aback by Mrs Cumley's intimate question. 'I... er...' she screwed up her face, shaking her head slightly, trying to remember.

Concern was written over Martha's face. 'Well canst tha recall which month, like? Where were thee — were thee in York, or 'ere? What wor thee doing?' she prompted.

Emily stared out of the window, reasoning it in her head for a few moments. 'I don't rightly know, ' she confessed at length, 'but I think it is some weeks. Maybe six, eight weeks ago.'

The kindly lines on Martha's ruddy face were transformed into anxious furrows as she reacted with apprehension and shook her head at the girl's innocence.

'Has tha mother never talked with thee about such things?'

Unease infected Martha's body and she clasped and unclasped her hands over and over again, considering the awful but highly likely truth. Her trepidation, so immediately apparent, alarmed Emily instantaneously. Although she was naïve in the ways of nature she was by no means a fool. Her hands flew to her mouth; shock spread itself over her face and rippled through her body. She spoke through her shaking fingers as if filtering the words would somehow lessen their meaning, their consequence.

'You mean... I... am with child?' she uttered through her anguish. 'We... at home... I mean my ma... We never spoke of such things. She... she gave me rags and told me to use them. And then I came here... to work here and... we never spoke of what *happens*. I used vinegar and a sponge, just like you told me.'

Emily's voice was reduced to a bewildered whisper and the tears which had begun to form deep within her many weeks since, fuelled by a torrent of emotions, now flooded onto her cheeks and dropped into her lap as she bowed her head and wept.

'Come 'ere, lass, ' Martha spoke gently.

Emily went to kneel at her feet like a child, resting her head on Martha's knees, and the cook stroked her head. It was a futile gesture of comfort, designed only to afford some small measure of consolation at that instant. However, Martha's simple action also spoke volumes to Emily. It at once acknowledged the situation and all its consequences; it was neither judgemental nor encouraging but proffered support and wisdom; it said *I will stand by you, I will counsel you.*

After some time she turned her tear-stained face upwards to look at the compassionate face smiling down at her.

'I know what to do, ' she affirmed quietly.

Martha nodded briefly and solemnly. However, while she was considering which abortifacient herb or combination of herbs might work best and the possible risks to Emily's health, Emily was playing out a conversation with Will in her mind, deciding how she should tell him that she was going to have his baby. She judged that Mrs Cumley would help them and decided to divulge their plans.

They both spoke at the same moment.

'I am going...'

'I know someone who...'

They both smiled weakly at this.

'Thee first, ' Martha prompted.

Before Emily could speak again the tinkling sound of a little bell trickled ethereally through the shells arranged in eddies on the walls surrounding them. Emily rose to her feet with a start, quickly wiping her eyes and cheeks with the backs of her hands and then with her apron. Without saying another word, she opened the door to the dressing room and both women hurried through it. They glanced quickly at one another before Mrs Cumley quietly opened the door to the corridor, scanning to the left and right to ensure that the coast was clear. Moments later she had disappeared, and Emily went to her mistress.

Having joined her family in church, Emily was feeling wretched. She tried for a cheerful smile at the minister, a kind word to old Mrs Cobbage, to sing loudly the resonant hymns celebrating Christ and renouncing sin, to laugh affectionately with her mother. Still she was wretched. How could she be otherwise? She was a liar and a sinner, and would betray them all. Only one thing had saved her from breaking, helping her to maintain her steadfastness – a look from her lover, the most fleeting of glances. His eyes had sought hers as the Fernleigh family had stepped in through their entrance to take up their ancestral pew. The look had said, *You're mine. We're one, you and I. Soon we'll be together, never to be separated.*

Emily clung desperately to her resolve during the service, gripping her prayer book as if her life depended on it, digging her nails into the binding as if trying to draw redemption from the pages, subconsciously willing salvation to seep out though the well-worn cover and through her fingertips into her body and soul.

Indeed, her tenacity lasted a good few hours that afternoon before she succumbed to the crushing weight of guilt that pressed in upon her from all sides until she could hardly breathe with it.

At the dinner table they dined on roasted pork and anchovy sauce with apple dumplings, stewed spinach, fried parsnips and baked onions. The pork was especially good as it was fresh, and the crisp salted skin coupled with its delicious hot smoky fat made everyone smile and remark how good it was and what a fine meal their mother had made. Daniel had patted the seat to the right of him and bade his *little E* to sit there to be close to him. Emily allowed herself an inward smile as she recalled a time in her childhood sitting on her father's knee, gripping a quill awkwardly and trying to copy his writing. He had spelled out her name in large script, and was explaining that all names began with a large uppercase letter. Hers was a big E. Then he gave her a squeeze and told her that she would always be his *little E*, his dear little Emily. This became her nickname.

Emily pushed her predicament to the back of her mind as she talked with her father about the harvest, and with her young brother Toby about how he was such a help to his mother in the kitchen garden and how his riding was coming on. She laughed with her sisters Georgina and Prudence as they recounted a comical episode in which one of the local farm boys who had arranged to meet with Georgina had tried to steal a kiss from behind, but had found his ardour quite misplaced and not a little diminished when he discovered that the cheek on which he had boldly placed his pursed lips belonged to Prudence, donned in her sister's dress and best bonnet! The whole family laughed heartily at this, and her mother shook her head, saying 'You girls, quite t' boldest in t' county I should imagine! At least you know your own minds!' as the tears of laughter were rolling down her cheeks.

'Aye and ah'm glad they do, ' her father echoed. 'They'll not end up with dimwits for 'usbands nor finish up down-trodden, that's fer sure. Our girls 'ave got some spirit! Just like their mother.'

He threw Mary a wide grin and she returned a knowing smile, quickly bidding Prudence and Georgina to side the plates.

Emily tried to avoid her mother's eye but inadvertently caught her gaze once or twice. She had an unsettling knack of seeing through a person to what was beneath the skin and could usually read Emily's countenance like the pages of the family Bible. Emily was torn between wanting to fling herself into her mother's comforting arms and tell her everything and keeping this particular book firmly shut for the moment, as she had been instructed by Will.

She had correctly guessed the pudding. Her mother had made white pot as it was Emily's favourite.

'Ah've made this 'un a little different.' Mary winked at Toby as she brought out the steaming dish. 'Toby 'elped me; didn't thee, lad?'

Toby looked proud and tapped his nose with a forefinger.

'Secret, ' he grinned.

'Well, they'll know reet enough when they taste it, won't they, little man?'

Toby beamed. 'Guess!' he shouted.

'Bread, ' Emily responded quickly.

'It's always got bread in it!' he returned.

'Currants, ' pronounced Prudence.

Toby looked at his mother for confirmation. She nodded almost imperceptibly.

'Yes! What else?' he cried, looking pleased with himself.

'Eggs?' guessed Georgina.

'Ah cracked four eggs and ah didn't get any shell in t' bowl, ' responded Toby proudly.

'Shall we give them a taste, Toby?'

He nodded as Mary dished up the pudding with a little cream off the top of the milk in a large earthenware jug.

'Hmm, ' declared Daniel, keeping the game going. 'Whatever can it be, lad? Tis very tasty, that's fer sure. Tasty an' sweet. Like as not contains sugar.'

Toby looked at his mother again.

'It always 'as sugar in it, doesn't it. A white pot's not a white pot without sugar. Now come on all o' you, eat up or it'll grow cold, ' she smiled.

'I can taste something beginning with P, ' said Emily slowly, the intonation in her voice rising.

'Pears!' exclaimed Georgina.

'Yeahhh!' answered Toby, 'I climbed t' tree and picked 'em all by ma'sen!' his little hands in the air simulating how high he'd had to reach.

'My, you are a clever little lad!' Emily laughed. 'Mmm, this is truly delicious.'

'Ah'm not little, ' he frowned. 'Ah'm big now, nearly six.'

'Big lad, then, ' Emily accorded, furrowing her forehead and nodding toward his little face in agreement.

'Aye, an' tha'll soon be big enough t' help tha Da with ploughin' and threshin', 'stead of doin' women's work in t' kitchen, ' Daniel said quietly with a wink, looking at Mary.

'Plenty o' time for that, ' she answered as she ruffled her son's hair. 'Tha's goin' t' make yer father proud, aren't tha, little man?'

'He already does, ' Daniel affirmed contentedly.

Later, as she helped her sisters wash and dry the pots, Emily's thoughts were of Toby and the joy he had brought to their family. Having had two miscarriages after giving birth to Prudence, her mother had borne a son; however, he had lived only three days. A weak chest was what the physician had pronounced. It wasn't unusual, of course, but it had hit her parents very hard. When Toby had come along they had been overjoyed and the much-missed mantle of happiness had once more fallen over the Popple family.

Emily experienced a sudden lurch of her stomach. And now she was going to have to leave them all. To go away to a foreign country, to who knows what, and she might never see them again. She might never see her little brother grow into a man. She might never again hear her father call her his *little E*, or share a confidence with her sisters, or feel the comfort of her mother's arms. It was unbearable!

Something inside her cracked.

She flung the pot that she was drying into its place on the wooden rack over the sink and rushed out of the kitchen door into the vegetable garden. Wringing her hands in her apron she paced about, staring down at the maturing cabbages and cauliflowers, trying to keep her composure. The winter vegetables, their darkening green leaves curled protectively around their hearts, stared back at her unpityingly.

Emily brushed her hands over her skirt, smoothing it down under her protective apron, trying to smooth her nerves a little in the process. A warm breeze fluttered around her cheek, carrying on it the vestiges of the low afternoon sun which was slowly dipping in the blushing sky. As she ran her right hand across the fabric that fell over her thigh Emily felt something small and hard caught in the layers of material between hand and limb. Her pocket was fastened to a ribbon around her waist. She reached into it through the outer layer of her skirt to retrieve the ring. The precious band was captive in her pocket, firmly tied to a second ribbon which hung from the first. She moved it back and forth betwixt her thumb and forefinger, feeling its solidity, sensing its significance, picturing its two companions. William similarly kept his loop about his person and the third, designed to be held by a chosen witness until the time of the marriage, was for now safely locked in Emily's box under her bed. The three bands would cleverly fit together on the day of their marriage to form one complete ring, denoting their joining, signifying their bond, their love.

Suddenly Emily knew what she had to do; she must give her conscience a voice.

Mary rose from the wooden bench outside the front door. She and Daniel had been enjoying a cup of cider in the late afternoon sun as the girls washed the pots and tidied the kitchen. Prudence had alerted them to the fact that something was up with Emily, who had gone rushing outside without having finished her task. Mary bade the girls take Toby and occupy themselves in the orchard. She knew that there was something different today about her eldest daughter – she'd known all day. She believed that if it was something Emily wanted to share with her, she would. Mary didn't believe in prying. She understood the worth of privacy, for private thoughts were a form of independence – a rare thing for a woman, especially one of their class, she reasoned. Emily was living independently from her family and had an occupation for which she was paid a respectable wage. Of course she was reliant on her occupation for her living, and thus tied to it, but who in their circle was not in such a situation? The important thing was that Emily had a small degree of self-rule – on her scarce days off she could do as she pleased – in theory, any road. Mary was pleased with the way things had turned out for Emily. That was not to say that she didn't miss her daughter; it had been a struggle when she'd first left to work at Fernleigh Hall, particularly with children of seven and nine and a babe in arms. They hadn't simply missed Emily for the contribution she'd made to their daily workload: they'd missed her lightness of spirit, her bobbing red curls, her adventurous nature with recipes – Mary smiled; there had been a few disasters, but mostly successes – and for her generosity, her gentle disposition and her laughter.

Of course she wasn't lost to them. Not by any means – just a little further away. She was in the best place; Mary was sure of that. Emily had been given opportunities that she and Daniel could never have provided. They did their very best to afford some learning to their children, to teach them to read and write and add up numbers, to instil in them the value of these things, besides the skills they needed to work the land, tend the animals and make a living out of the farm. They weren't ignorant of the pleasure that reading a book could bring, the wonder of being able to make a story come alive by understanding printed words on a page; indeed the girls each had a diary in which they were encouraged to write, under strict instructions to fill every corner, every space, every inch of precious paper.

What they wrote in their diaries was, of course, entirely up to them, and they each learned to respect the others' privacy. There was that word again – privacy: confidentiality, independence.

As she stepped into the kitchen garden Mary reflected on the choice that she and Daniel had made for their eldest daughter. It was undoubtedly the right one, notwithstanding the circumstances. And Emily had made an unqualified success of the opportunity, rising as she had from her position in the kitchen to lady's maid –almost a companion by all accounts. She was born to it. The phrase that had abruptly formed in Mary's mind, uninvited and unwelcome, brought with it a sudden flare of emotion, sweet and bitter, triggered by un-desirable recollections that knew better than to seek the light of day. She pushed them firmly away, back into the dark place where she kept them locked and guarded.

She arranged a smile on her face and touched Emily lightly on her arm. 'There, lass, ' she offered gently.

Emily spun around. Georgina and Prudence abruptly reappeared and Mary sent them off to the orchard again.

'Mother, I have something I must tell you.'

Desolation had etched itself into Emily's pretty features, worry pulled at the corners of her mouth and her eyes had at last been al-lowed to lose the sparkle that she'd tried so hard to keep within them during the preceding hours. Emily had succumbed.

Mary gave her arm a gentle squeeze. 'I know tha does, ' softly, reassuringly. 'Come sit with me.'

She motioned to a small wooden archway to their left past the re-mains of Daniel's experimental crop of potatoes. A vigorous rambling rose scrambled and twisted over the arch and along the fences to the left and right. Denuded of flower heads now, the dark green glossy leaves were all that remained of its early summer splendour when the boundary between garden and pasture was radiant with delicate pale pink blooms and an exquisite fragrance shimmered in the early morning sun.

They sat on a small bench on the other side of the arch looking west over the backs of a group of munching ewes and into the setting sun. This little area, no more than an alcove in the structure of the fence, was Daniel's concession to Mary, a departure from the serious business of growing what they needed to live on; a flower garden, Mary's garden where she could nurture a bloom for the simple sake of its beauty. It was Mary's special place. Roses were her favourite flowers and she'd planted one every time she'd known herself to be with child.

Tending them, the very fact of giving them water when they were thirsty, preventing grass and weeds from choking their developing stems, removing the greenflies from their buds, was for Mary symbolic of nurturing herself through her pregnancy, conjuring hope and good fortune as if this should be some reward for the care she took over the flowers, willing the pregnancy and birth to be successful. There were more rosebushes than children.

They sat side by side in silence for a while as Mary waited patiently for her daughter to find the words she so clearly needed to speak. At length Emily turned to her and took her hand, turning it over so that her palm was upwards. Mary looked at her hand, and then at Emily. Then, as fate would have it, several things happened at once.

Emily pressed something hard into her mother's palm and closed her fingers around it as she started to say 'I am to be m...' Concurrently there was a piercing shriek from the direction of the orchard and Prudence came running towards them screaming ''E can't breathe, 'e *can't breathe!*' Simultaneously there came a shout from Daniel, over in the yard, that the Yorkshire sow had escaped.

Mary rapidly shoved the object that had been placed in her hand into her pocket. It being a Sunday, there were no other folks on the farm to give a hand. 'Go help tha Da!' she shouted to Emily as she jumped up and started running in the direction of the orchard, Prudence racing ahead of her back to the large pear tree where she had left poor Toby with his sister.

When they got to him Toby was lying on his back on the ground underneath the tree, fighting for breath. Georgina was in floods of tears and completely at a loss for what to do.

''E can't breathe!'

Mary quickly knelt beside her little boy and raised his head onto her lap, stroking his hair. 'What happened?'

A gabbled response. ''E fell. 'E wor showin' me how 'e'd picked t' fruit for t' pudding. A branch broke. 'E fell right onto 'is back!'

Mary had thought as much. She rolled Toby over onto his side, one hand under his little cheek and encouraged him to try to breathe more slowly.

'Tha's had t' wind knocked out of thee is all, ' she said, as calmly and reassuringly as she could. 'It'll come back. Don't fret thyself, just try t' breathe normally. Tha'll be alright…tha'll be alright.'

She stroked her precious son's cheek and his hair, willing him to calm himself and start to breathe normally again. Within a few minutes Toby had regained his breath and had begun to cry. Mary gathered him in her arms and rocked him gently, bidding the girls to go help their father with the pig.

'Go on now. 'E's fine now.'

Reluctantly they did as they were told and joined their father and Emily, who had a board out and were trying to corner the huge spirited sow and channel her back to her pen, Emily trying to keep her dress clean. But having made a bid for freedom the lively animal was not giving up that easily. It eventually took all four of them and an assortment of bits of wood, straw bales and an old gate to persuade her back to the cott. It took them a while, much to the obvious delight of their two dogs, who had been rushing around barking excitedly during the whole episode.

Eventually the family gathered around the kitchen table for a drink of cider and a piece of parkin and then it was time for Emily to return to Fernleigh Hall, as the nights were drawing in and darkness would soon be falling around them.

Emily rode back with her father on his stout piebald. The evening was growing cold and the breeze, which earlier in the day had been gentle and welcome, had begun to gather itself for a storm, joining forces with neighbouring atmospheric eddies, curling around the trees of Fernleigh Wood, flushing out the multi-coloured dead leaves and those that hung weakly from their branches and sending the squirrels to their drays.

They spoke of this and that, their easy chatter inconsequential. Emily loved her father dearly but could not speak to him about the trouble that clawed at her heart. That would be her mother's unenviable task. She would need to find another time to talk with her mother, and quickly, for the Fernleigh autumn ball was only days away. At least her mother had the ring. Surely that, the symbol of what was to pass, would at least indicate the significance of what Emily had been trying to impart. She would need to find a time to slip away again in the next day or so. It would be difficult; preparations for the ball were already well underway and all hands were needed. However, Emily was now as certain as night becomes day that her conscience must be satisfied; that she could not live with herself if she did not relate her circumstances to her family, share her thoughts, her concerns and her feelings with them and tell them how much she cared for them.

She would have to find a way, and with great haste.

It was not until much later that evening that Mary had a moment to herself. Sitting in her shift at her mirror she was brushing hair and reflecting on the day whilst Daniel was busy locking up the house and settling the dogs at their respective sentry points by the front and back doors. Mary reached for her pocket, hung with her other garments over a chair in the corner of the room, and took out the object. She gasped as she touched it and again as she beheld its magnificence in the candlelight. She knew its worth at once. This was a fine ring, a ring of quality and no mistake. Not only that, it was one part of a betrothal ring! She was at once filled with apprehension. How could Emily, her daughter, come to possess such a thing? How was it that she and Daniel did not know about a possible engagement? Who would bestow upon her daughter such a present as this? There seemed to be an inscription but as the ring was incomplete she could not read the engraved words. Incomprehension quickly turned to anxiety, and anxiety in its turn to fear. Then, as she continued to stare at the ring, she feared the worst.

Her hands shook as she carefully wrapped it in her kerchief and placed it back in the pocket. She would need to speak with Emily before it was too late. Before the unthinkable... Mary shook her head. No! She would not, *could* not, think of *that*. She must see her daughter without delay. See her and get the truth from her... or the consequences could be unimaginable!

Eight

*J*ennifer had returned to Fernleigh Hall to investigate William Fernleigh, who, on the face of it, was simply a handsome man in a beautiful painting by Reynolds. In essence this was all she had to go on. She had begun with the date cited on the accompanying brass plate: '*Thought to have been painted 1762.*' How old had he been when this likeness was fashioned? Jennifer thought he looked like a young man in his twenties rather than his 'teens, but it was notoriously difficult to tell from a painting. His stature was proud, though he did not look haughty. The slight crinkles around his bright blue eyes hinted of merriment. *Those wonderful blue eyes!*

She tore herself away from his image. She needed to find out more about the painting. She had asked the volunteer posted in the long gallery, in which the painting hung, whether any more was known about it. The white-haired lady had simply repeated what was written in the brochure; that the portrait had recently been found under floorboards in a bedroom during some renovation work. Jennifer had probed further and the kindly pensioner had sought the knowledge of one her co-volunteers, a heavily-corduroyed gentleman who had been able to add a little to their meagre pool of knowledge. It seemed that on discovering the canvas the present Fernleigh family had employed a local historian to search through the surviving family papers for some information about this hitherto unknown person. So far the volunteer warden was not aware that any significant discovery had been made. On further questioning he revealed that the historian, a Doctor Finch, was based at York University.

Just as Jennifer was thanking him and his female associate and turning to leave, his brown ridged-cotton-sleeved arm stretched out towards her.

'Wait, there was something…'

'Yes?' she responded excitedly.

'Something odd that I overheard Finch say the other day when I was collecting my badge from the estate office.'

'Something odd? What sort of thing?' Jennifer prompted eagerly.

'I think he might have found some kind of family tree or some documentation of that kind. But…' the man pushed his glasses up to the bridge of his nose from whence they had slipped and put one finger to his lips, tapping gently, trying to recall, 'there was something missing from it.'

'Missing?'

'Yes… a name I think. It sounded as though a name had been scribbled out or removed or something. Well, at least that's what it sounded like.'

'Oh!' remarked Jennifer, raising her eyebrows. She nodded. 'That does sound a bit odd.'

'Well I hope that's of some help, ' responded the bespectacled man.

'Yes, yes… thank you. Goodbye.'

Jennifer's mind was full of jumbled thoughts swirling around like clothes in a half-empty tumble drier. She had called in at the estate office on her way home to enquire where she might be able to locate a Doctor Finch who, she understood, was working on some estate business, and had been told that he worked in an office situated above the stable block on Tuesdays and Thursdays and otherwise lectured at York University.

'He doesn't like to be disturbed, dear, ' a sharp-featured middle-aged woman interjected patronisingly.

She reminded Jennifer of the officious receptionist at her local doctors' surgery, superciliously protective of the medics, assuming their mantle. Jennifer didn't have a ready reply so she said nothing. It was clear that access to the academic was likely to be somewhat difficult whilst he was working on estate business. She would try the university.

She located him through the website. He was a senior lecturer in the department of History and Antiquities. A good-looking bearded man who appeared to be in his forties smiled at her from the staff profile. His clear-cut features had a conviviality about them that was inviting and most attractive, which somehow gave Jennifer the confidence to pick up the phone and try his number.

She tried three times from her office on Monday. Each time, the phone rang and rang with no answer machine or voicemail service. She tried the general university switchboard and was put through to the departmental secretary, who guessed that Dr Finch was probably lecturing or in meetings and advised her to try sending him an email. Jennifer wasn't sure exactly what to say, so she simply wrote that she understood him to be researching William Fernleigh and that she had an interest in this character and wondered if they could meet.

On Tuesday, Jennifer received a holding response – a 'thank you for your enquiry…' polite and non-committal communication that stated that he was presently occupied and unavailable for a meeting, but that if she wanted to send him her telephone number he would try to call her in a few weeks. Jennifer couldn't wait a few weeks; she felt as though she couldn't even wait a few days. She sat at her desk staring out of the second-storey window at the bustle of High Petergate below. What would York have been like in the eighteenth century? Noisy, dirty, exciting, elegant, colourful – dangerous, even? Certainly the magnificent Minster, which was only a stone's throw from her office, had not altered much in centuries, and the maze of narrow streets to the south were hemmed in by the ancient city walls to the north and north-east and the river Ouse to the south-west. So she guessed that their layout had probably not changed much in hundreds of years. Crammed full of history, York was brimming with notable buildings and structures: the medieval guildhalls, fifteenth-century churches, the Shambles' butchers' row mentioned in the Doomsday Book, evidence of a Viking settlement, fragments of the original Roman walls, Tudor inns and many fine and elegant Georgian houses. In 1762, when Joshua Reynolds stood in front of William Fernleigh and first dipped his sable bristles into swirls of pigment and linseed oil — cobalt blue, vermilion, Paris green, yellow ochre, burnt amber, sienna — the streets and passageways, snickelways and ginnels of York would have wound between the countless unchanged buildings that she could look upon today. William Fernleigh and perhaps even Emily could easily have walked these streets. Discovering more about William might lead her to Emily. There was still so much Jennifer didn't know about her; in fact she hardly knew anything at all. She was not exactly an alter ego but a former self, it seemed.

Jennifer glanced at her watch. Twelve forty-five. She wasn't getting much done here; she was unable to concentrate, restless. She would have a break and get out of the office for half an hour or so. Perhaps she could return a little more productive.

Although the weather was fairly bright and dry, a few ominous grey clouds hung against the pallid backdrop, threatening rain. Jennifer grabbed her bag and coat and exited her office, walking past the Minster into Low Petergate and turning right into Swinegate. One of her favourite colourful cafés nestled on the corner of Swinegate and Grape Lane amongst clothes boutiques, glass and china emporiums, bistros, beauty salons and restaurants.

Jennifer swung open the door of El Piano, chose a table in the window and ordered spinach quiche, ensalada Granada and a jug of fresh coffee. As she poured the steaming liquid through a metal strainer into her mug, catching the deliciously pungent coffee grains, strains of Spanish guitar in the background reaching her ears, she started to feel luxuriously relaxed. Tucking into the wonderful warm quiche as the caffeine did its work, she determined to find a way of meeting up with this Dr Finch. She decided to text Jane. Although she worked in a different department, she might know the man, or at any rate have a better idea of how to catch his attention.

Three days later she was heading across the expansive campus of York University. The Vanbrugh College building was on the northern side of a large lake which lay among the 1960s buildings at the heart of the campus. The Vanbrugh Piazza seemed to float on the shimmering water as Jennifer crossed the concrete lakeside area and headed up a wide set of steps towards the History department. A combination of friendly persuasion by Jane and further emails to Doctor Finch explaining that she thought she might have some information on William Fernleigh that would be of interest to him had done the trick; it had achieved a meeting at any rate.

Now that she was here, she felt nervous. What did she actually have? She couldn't possibly tell him the truth – that she believed that in a former incarnation she had been a girl called Emily who was having a clandestine relationship with William Fernleigh, son of Lord Fernleigh of Fernleigh Manor – the same distinguished family that was employing him to look into their family history. It sounded ludicrous. She'd look like a complete lunatic and he'd show her the door within seconds. No; Jennifer decided to keep her council as far as her source was concerned but to offer him all the information she had which she had gleaned from her sessions with Christina and her recent frenzied online searches of parish records.

She'd first been able to locate a baptism that had taken place in Brockby in the county of Yorkshire (North Riding) in 1741. The records of births in the parish records dated back only to 1761, so she had searched the baptism records, the oldest of which dated as far back as 1538. She'd set a timeline of 1730 to 1755, and there he was! A William Thomas Joseph Fernleigh, baptised on the 12th of July, 1741.

The record details read: '*William Thomas Joseph son of Thomas and Charlotte Fernleigh of Brockton 12 July 1741. Record source: North Yorkshire baptisms.*'

So now she had an age to accompany the face in the portrait. Depending on when in 1762 the painting had been completed, William would have been twenty-one or twenty-two. Jennifer had smiled to herself at this discovery. The young man in the painting looked wiser than his years, she mused. Certainly older than the average modern twenty-one year old.

She then had gone in search of Emily. She had reasoned that there was a good chance that the girl was born or baptised in the same parish as William if she had ended up working at Fernleigh Hall. This wasn't a given, of course, but it was the only position that she could start from. Jennifer discovered that she could search on the basis of a first name alone, which was just as well as that was all she had to go on. She searched the parish records for Emily and set the year of birth or baptism to 1741 plus or minus ten years to throw the net wide. She decided to just search the North Riding rather than specifying a place name, to avoid narrowing the search too much. She pressed the Search button and held her breath while the computer chugged through the records. Three entries came up: an Emily Peacock baptised in 1742 in Skewsby, an Emily Baker baptised in 1736, and an Emily Popple baptised in 1743. The entries for Baker and Popple did not have place names associated with them. Jennifer was able to view a scan of the original record for Popple, but there was an ink mark on the page over the place name. All she could deduce was that it seemed to end with a Y. As for the Baker record, there was no original document available and no place name stated on the transcribed record.

Jennifer pondered the girls' ages. The Popple and Peacock girls would have been nineteen and twenty in 1762, which was around the same age as William Fernleigh. The Baker girl would have been twenty-six, assuming of course that the children were baptised in the year of their birth. A little too old, perhaps? Possibly – but she couldn't be ruled out on that basis alone.

Jennifer investigated the location of the parish of Skewsby and discovered that in fact it bordered the parish of Brockby. Consequently there were three possible Emilys, and she would need to do a little more digging.

So she started with the Baker record. The father's name was recorded as John. Perhaps if she could find a John Baker in Brockby it might provide more of a connection. She reasoned that although people obviously did move around in those days, a smaller number were mobile compared to the modern day and many did not move far from where they were born. She knew that this was a fairly big assumption, but she had nothing else to go on. Jennifer decided to start with the parish baptism records again, reasoning that the girl's father might have been upwards of eighteen when he'd had his daughter, so she set the upper limit of her search at 1718 and plumped for a midrange of 1798 with a twenty-year span on either side.

Records for two John Bakers appeared, one born in 1696 in Haughton and the other born in 1688 in Springton. Neither of these parishes was anywhere near Brockby. After some cogitation, Jennifer decided to rule out Emily Baker on the basis of age and location. She was now left with two girls, one of whom lived – at least at the time she was baptised – in the parish neighbouring Brockby and a second who also seemed to be the right age but who could have lived anywhere in North Yorkshire.

She took the same approach as before: the father's name was recorded as Daniel, so she searched for a Daniel Popple baptised in Yorkshire's North Riding between 1685 and 1725. As she waited for the search to be completed the phone rang, and she went to answer it: a cold-caller wanting to sell home insurance to her. She dealt with the disrupting disembodied voice quickly and hurried back to her PC. There, waiting for her, was a single record: a Daniel Popple, baptised in 1718. She scanned the record line. There was no place of birth; however, there was an associated image to view. Jennifer tapped the top of her pen impatiently on her lower lip as she waited for the file to open. When it did, it was difficult to read. She enlarged the image and scanned the names in the middle column for a Popple.

There it was… '19 April 1718, Daniel son Adam & Georgina Popple' and in the left column the parish name was given as 'Brockby.'

Jennifer felt a thrill run through her body and she clenched her hands to her chest and raised her shoulders with glee, grinning excitedly to herself. She had found two possible Emilys of the right age, one in Brockby and the other in a nearby parish. If nothing else, there was at least a chance that the character in her head, the girl conjured up under hypnosis, released from her inner consciousness – the lass so clearly in love with William Fernleigh, as he was with her, by her own account – could *actually* be a real person. A person of nineteen or twenty years by 1762, residing in Brockby, the parish where William Fernleigh also lived; the William of Fernleigh Hall who had been captured in 1762 in a beautiful painting by Joshua Reynolds. It was incredible!

But now, as Jennifer walked down the long brown and cream corridor of the York University History department looking at the plaques on the heavy wooden doors for the sign with 'Dr Finch' written on it, she was less sure of herself. *Too late to turn back now though,* she thought as she arrived at his door. She knocked tentatively and a voice from within shouted 'Come in!'

The room was quite spacious, with row upon row of bookshelves on the walls to her right and left. Facing her was a large metal-framed window, and in front of that a man in jeans and jumper sat with his back to her at a massive old veneered desk piled with books and papers, staring at his PC screen.

She turned to shut the door behind her as he swung around in his slightly tatty chair and said, 'No, don't close it – I prefer it open.'

He motioned for her to take a seat and she did so, perching on a fold-up wooden chair by a small low table next to the right hand bookcase.

'Hello, Doctor Finch, I'm Jennifer Langley. Thank you for sparing the time to meet me today.'

He took her extended hand and shook it firmly. 'Hi, Jennifer. Call me Andy. What can I do for you?' His warm, friendly voice matched his smile.

Jennifer crossed her legs, placed her hands in her lap and tried to look confident. 'Well... I thought that maybe we could help one another.'

'Ah, I see. Well OK – fire away, then.' He sat casually with one leg across the other, ankle on knee.

'I understand you're researching William Fernleigh, the man depicted in that recently-discovered painting by Reynolds.'

'Uh-huh... yes?' He waited for her to continue.

'Well... I'm not sure what your remit is, but I gather that not much was known about him at the time of the discovery and I may have some information about him that could be of interest.'

'I see. Yes, you said in your email that you had something for me. Please... go on.'

He smiled encouragingly and the creases around his eyes deepened as they must have done countless times before. Many smiles had graced that friendly face.

Jennifer took a deep breath. 'I think William was having a clandestine relationship with a girl called Emily. A girl that worked for William's mother as a lady's maid.'

'I see.' Andy Finch responded with evident interest. He unhooked his left leg from the other and leaned forward, resting his forearms on his thighs and tapping the ends of his fingers together. 'And what evidence do you have for this relationship? What do you know about William Fernleigh?'

The crunch.

'I... er... I have a source who knows the girl... I mean, knows of the girl, Emily.'

It was the truth.

'Do you mean family?'

'Not exactly.'

'Well, you'll have to give me something to go on. Who's this source? What do they know?'

'I believe that William and this girl Emily were in love and that they planned to marry. But that it was all a secret, as his family wouldn't have approved. Look – I have some documents from the Brockby Parish register.' Jennifer pulled out copies of the records she had uncovered and explained what she knew so far.

Andy Finch listened patiently and then let her down gently. 'Look, this is all very interesting, Jennifer, but I don't see any documentary evidence here that links Emily Popple or Emily Peacock to William Fernleigh. Nothing to throw any light on William, I'm afraid.' He was clearly rather disappointed.

'Well... but... if William was having an affair that his parents disapproved of, then perhaps there's a reason why his name might have been removed from... family documents or something?' Jennifer reasoned, clutching at a tenuous possible connection.

'What makes you say that his name was removed from anything?'

Finch rose and crossed the office to a tray on which stood an old stainless steel kettle and an assortment of chipped mugs. He shook the kettle, confirming that it had water in it, switched it on and loaded two cups with heaped spoonfuls of coffee. 'Coffee?'

Jennifer would have preferred tea at that particular moment; her mouth was dry and tea was more thirst-quenching than coffee, but he had already filled the mugs so she just nodded. While he made the coffee she explained that she had been given that impression by one of the volunteers when she had visited Fernleigh Hall. He nodded and lowered his eyebrows into a frown, handing her a mug and placing a half-full pint of milk on the table beside her.

'Ah, the bloody grapevine again, ' he retorted disconsolately, 'people love to get hold of a snippet of information, take it out of context and broadcast it to all and sundry. That's how history has been misinterpreted so often. Look, between you and me – and don't repeat this, as I haven't finished my investigations yet – there is something odd about the Fernleigh family records around the year that the painting was done. I haven't actually found William in any of the family papers yet, which is odd, although we obviously know he existed. I have the dates of his birth and death and we know what he looked like. But in any case...'

'His death?!' Jennifer interrupted volubly.

'Sorry?'

'His death. You said you know when he died?'

'Of course.'

He looked at her questioningly, surprised that she should not know this simple fact when she had taken the trouble to find his baptism and the records of the Emilys.

She had not thought of looking in the Deaths and Burials records. She shook her head as if to shake out her stupidity. And then another thought occurred to her.

'When did he die?' she whispered.

Her skin had gone cold and her palms were damp.

'November 1762, the year of the painting, ' he responded factually.

Jennifer tried desperately to maintain her composure by making a show of adding milk to her coffee and stirring it. Suddenly all she could think about was Emily. Poor, unfortunate, ill-fated Emily. To have fallen so deeply in love with this man and to have her love returned in equal measure, to be courted and promised marriage, to have carried on their love affair in secret against the odds, against the will of his family, her employer, and then to have her lover taken away from her, her chance for a happy life with him so utterly denied. Jennifer identified completely with Emily's loss. Indeed she felt it so keenly that it felt as if a part of her had just been dealt this cruel blow. It was a shock! Tears began to well up in her eyes and she cupped her mug of coffee with both hands and put her face to it, trying to disguise her sorrow.

'Jennifer? Miss Langley? Are you alright?'

Doctor Finch was looking at her with a worried expression on his face. She looked at him but couldn't say anything. He swivelled his chair around and fumbled in a drawer of his desk which emitted the sound of crinkling paper.

'Here, ' he said smiling, 'have a biscuit. I always feel much better after a Hobnob.'

He winked at her, and just at that moment a little black nose popped up from the other side of his desk followed by a furry black snout, two brown eyes and two pointed furry ears, their tips just folded over.

'Ah, thought you might wake up at the sound of biscuits! Here, Scruffy – come and meet Miss Langley.'

The untidy little black dog came wiggling around the desk, his tail wagging his whole body, in search of the Hobnobs, nose twitching, testing the air.

'Jennifer, meet Scruffy. Scruffy, meet Jennifer.'

Scruffy came to sit in front of Jennifer and stared at her, tail wagging. His sweet little expectant face was enough to warm any heart. She sniffed and smiled at him.

'Can I give him a biscuit?' she asked at length.

'It's what he's waiting for, ' Finch returned encouragingly.

'Hello there, Scruffy. Aren't you lovely! Would you like a biscuit? You would! OK then, here you are.'

'Don't forget to have one yourself, or he'll eat the lot. He's normally at home with my wife, but she's away so he's a scholar of the university today. He's pretty good – he hasn't eaten any students yet, although I live in hope!'

Jennifer gave a little laugh and stroked the top of Scruffy's head. His fur was soft and warm and she wanted to cuddle him, to bury her head in his thick downy coat.

'Look, Miss Langley, Jennifer, ' Finch spoke quietly, 'I'm not sure what your involvement is in this Fernleigh family, but you seemed pretty upset just now. You said that I could help you, that we might be able to help each other. What is it that you think I can do for you?'

Jennifer sighed. She might as well tell him the truth. He seemed a level-headed, kindly sort of man. At least if he didn't believe her, which was highly likely, he wasn't likely to run her out of his office and call security. She told him the bare bones of the situation; that she had been undergoing a course of hypnotherapy and had been regressed as part of the treatment, and this had led them to discovering Emily. She also told him that she had seen William's face before she had first laid eyes on the painting. Jennifer didn't elaborate on this part of the story but left it to Doctor Finch to draw his own conclusions. As she tried to impart at least a scrap of normality in the account the last thing Jennifer mentioned was that Jane had recommended the hypnotherapist, who was famous for helping with police investigations. She figured that if Finch knew Jane, who was a pretty commonsensical person, perhaps that would confer some sense of rationalism onto herself.

Again, Andy Finch listened good-naturedly. He didn't interrupt with questions or interject comments. When Jennifer had finished talking he continued to sit and cogitate, staring at the floor. Some moments later he took a deep breath through his nose and ran his hands through his shoulder-length wavy brown hair. Then he looked at her.

'I don't doubt you, Jennifer.' He spoke slowly, choosing his words carefully. 'I don't doubt that the events you have spoken about actually happened. I have some difficulty with the interpretation of a past life. However... I have an open mind. Those who know me will assure you of that. If what you say has some truth, then we ought to be able, at the very least, to identify the Emily you speak of through records of payments made to the Fernleigh staff. Certainly those records exist; I have seen them myself in Charlotte Fernleigh's household accounts. Another line of enquiry we should follow concerns the possible marriage of William and Emily. I uncovered William's gravestone in a corner of the Fernleigh family cemetery; there is no other name on it but his. However, that's not conclusive regarding a possible clandestine marriage or a marriage that was not accepted by the Fernleigh family.'

Jennifer felt incredibly relieved that she had not been dismissed out of hand. She also felt greatly pleased by Andy Finch's use of 'we'. *He's willing to work with me,* she thought, *and he doesn't think I'm crazy.* It was so wonderful to be able to share her eagerness for finding out the truth with someone with an equal interest and keenness in that direction.

He gave her the task of investigating the records for a possible marriage while he continued his search of the Fernleigh family documents and they agreed to keep in touch by email and meet again when one of them had found something.

'Thank you so much, ' Jennifer said as they shook hands in the doorway of his office, Scruffy looking on from under the desk, 'for not dismissing me out of hand. It means a lot.'

She drove back to her office, her mind a jumble of transitory thoughts and emotions. She sifted them and held on to one or two, playing them over in her mind. Andy Finch had given her some pointers regarding useful genealogy websites and approaches. There was another way, of course: she could go back to Christina and try to persuade her to perform some further regression to see if they could establish whether Emily and William did marry and what had happened to them. This was risky, of course. She knew that. Regression opened up another world, a world with its own memories and emotions. She'd been trying to rid herself of the crippling feelings of rejection that had stifled her so; should she really risk experiencing grief as well and God knows what besides? Wasn't this the very thing that Christina had warned her against? Jennifer pushed her sensible self to one side. They could take it one small step at a time, surely? A marriage would be a happy event. It would be heart-warming to know that they had at least been able to experience that. She didn't have to go any further.

She was kidding herself, of course, and deep down she knew that. But such was her passion for discovering more about the life of her past self, she couldn't possibly just leave it at this. She *had* to know more.

When she got back to her office she picked up the phone and dialled Christina's number. To her huge disappointment the response was only an answerphone message. Judging by the number of beeps, quite a few messages had been recorded already. Jennifer hoped that Christina was not away, rather that she was simply popular.

She drove to Christina's house that evening and found no-one at home. The curtains in the front rooms were half-closed, that curious combination often utilised by people who want to give an ambiguous impression to the outside world when they are not in residence. This was not a good sign.

Jennifer called at the adjoining cottage. A harassed-looking young woman answered, holding a baby in her arms. The distant sound of children squabbling reached Jennifer's ears. The woman confirmed that Mrs Peters was indeed away and that she was watering her neighbour's plants. It transpired that Christina had been called away on an urgent family matter and might not be back for a while.

Disconsolate, Jennifer headed home. She would search the records, of course. But there was so much more waiting to be discovered, and Christina held the key. *Unless...*

Her thoughts turned to the sleeping tablets. She had been trying to cease taking them while her sessions with Christina were on-going. She felt a stab of guilt. She had transgressed a few times, although she'd only taken half the normal dose. It wasn't that she couldn't stop, she'd told herself firmly, but simply that they ensured a good night's sleep. Putting the final touches to the next spring collection, the myriad of deadlines with their allied pressures, had necessitated long working days. Trying to sleep with her head full of marketing figures and launch strategy had been impossible on a few occasions. It wasn't that she *needed* to enter that private evanescent world where she loved and received love – that was a bonus, she contended, though she had to admit to herself that the last time she'd used the tablets she'd woken up with an horrendous headache.

Her recent dreams had been more grounded, though. Rather than taking place in exotic or unknown locations, familiar places had featured; that old rowan tree on the ridge where she loved to sit and look over the valley towards the North York Moors, the ruined shepherd's cottage to the east of it under the lee of the ridge, and on one occasion, the old teahouse standing in the middle of the lake on the Fernleigh estate which she had once visited. There was no narrative. The reveries all shared the common theme of him and her simply being together, loving each other. And sex: the most magnificent, breathtaking, astonishing sex. Each time as the ephemeral vision was beginning to fade, he would whisper to her, *Soon, my love, soon we will be together again.*

Jennifer reached her cottage, parked the car, went in and put the kettle on while she fed Smoky. She made herself a quick supper of a cheese and tomato omelette with a thick chunk of poppyseed bread and butter and a steaming mug of hot chocolate.

The thought, once conceived and born, refused to go away. What if she could hypnotise herself? Regress herself? Was it possible to obtain a state of relaxation with the aid of her tablets that would allow her to prime her subconscious with a specific question? In short, could she engineer her dream to deliver an answer, direct her mind to go back to a particular point in time? She'd have to make sure that she was sufficiently relaxed to allow her subconscious to release its secrets. That could result in her being asleep for a good many hours.

She decided that she'd better wait for the weekend. In the meantime she could do some research on the Internet.

Smokey came in to sit on the sofa beside her as she finished her dinner and thumbed through the post that had been delivered that morning. Among the bills and unsolicited advertisements there was a note from a pest-treatment company informing her that their survey-or would be calling on Friday morning. *Damn.* She'd forgotten about that. One of the old beams in her living room had a cluster of tiny holes in it and she'd arranged for an expert to come out and take a look. She rose and went to the spare room where she kept her PC. She checked her diary – the morning was free. Good; she would work at home.

Jennifer had a full day of meetings the following day, so planned to start her online investigations on Friday evening. Friday morning dawned wet and windy, and she made and lit a fire in the living room. The surveyor arrived as arranged and began his examination of the offending holes while Jennifer worked upstairs. Later, in the living room, he explained to her that the beam needed to be treated but did not need to be replaced. There was some damage in a localised area which was easily and safely treatable with a water-based product which would also treat the fungal decay that he had found in part of the beam.

As he prodded the beam the man explained to Jennifer that the fungal decay was evident in a series of squarish lines on the surface of the timber where the rotted wood had split, indicating exposure to damp conditions at one time or another. Jennifer was relieved to learn that this was not serious, and they arranged for the treatment to be carried out.

On returning to the living room she watched Smoky darting about, patting something, first with one paw and then the other, then pouncing on it, catching it between her paws and rolling onto her back in frenzied delight before flicking it up into the air and starting the process again. Not wanting to spoil her fun, Jennifer left her to it and went to make a cup of tea. Having grown bored of the game, Smoky eventually followed, meowing for attention.

It was later that day that Jennifer noticed what looked like large crumbs on the living room carpet. Bending to sweep them up, she discovered that they were in fact fragments of wood. She discovered what it was that Smoky had been playing with – a small cube of wood no longer than the first joint of her finger. It must have become loose and fallen after the surveyor had prodded the beam.

Jennifer stood up on tiptoes and examined the rafter. She quickly discovered a small cavity, its opening shaped exactly like the piece of wood she held in her hand. However, there was something else. The hole appeared to be deeper than it was wide and there seemed to be a tiny recess behind the spot from where the wooden plug had come. Jennifer was sure she could see something in there. She grabbed a torch from the cupboard below the stairs and a chair from the dining room. Placing the chair beneath the hole, she climbed up and shone the beam of light into the hollow. Something glimmered in its white shaft. Jennifer poked her forefinger into the void as far as it would go, but could not reach the place that sparkled when she moved the light over it. She retrieved a screwdriver from the small set of tools she kept in the kitchen cupboard and tried again. This time she was able to reach the place and dislodge something. Gingerly, she moved it towards her from behind with the tip of the screwdriver, encouraging it with little sideways movements when the object became stuck on the rough inner surface of the beam. As she brought it nearer she saw that it was a small piece of paper folded a number of times around a hard object, a small section of which was visible and shone a bright gold.

Jennifer was finally able to get hold of the object with her fingers. She extracted it, jumped off the chair and sat down on the sofa with it in her lap. Her heart thumping, she carefully began to unfold the old paper, which was yellowed and mottled with age. Hands shaking, she opened out the last folds to reveal a strikingly beautiful gold ring.

Sheer astonishment impeded both movement and thought for a few moments. Then, cautiously, she reached down and stroked the surface of the ring delicately with one finger, as if it were hot, as if touching it would make it disappear. Finally she picked it up and turned it between her fingers. The gold surface caught and reflected the shaft of late afternoon light falling through the sash window, sending flashes around the room. It was exquisite. A small perfectly-formed heart sat prominently on the loop, overlapping its width on either side. Jennifer could make out some engraving on the outer surface, but was unable to determine what it was. There didn't seem to be a recognisable pattern to it, and the lines did not appear to form letters. Also, the girth of the loop did not appear to be completely smooth but was sharply ridged in places, which seemed a little unusual.

She carefully placed the ring on the coffee table in front of her and turned her attention to the piece of paper. It was good-quality parchment, by the look and feel of it. The only writing on the page consisted of three letters and a date:

D F B 1762

The bottom edge was a little jagged as if it had been carefully torn off. But at the top of the page there was a crest. A lion upon a shield. The image looked familiar. *Could it be...?*

Jennifer's heart beat wildly in her chest as she ran upstairs to her desk drawer. After a few moments of rummaging around she pulled out a leaflet with information on opening times and events at Fernleigh Hall. And there it was... the Fernleigh coat of arms. A lustrous red lion in front of a white shield.

Jennifer's legs gave way and she sat down on the floor suddenly, feeling lightheaded. She put her hand to her mouth and stared at the crest, trying to absorb the significance of her discovery.

Oh my God!

A ring, of some value by the look of it, carefully wrapped in parchment bearing the Fernleigh coat of arms, secreted away and undisturbed for scores of years inside a beam in her cottage! A cottage that would originally have belonged to the family estate, that would have housed estate workers, perhaps tenant farmers. What might a farmer be doing with a ring that had obvious connections to the Fernleigh family? Was it stolen? What did the letters DFB mean?

Jennifer needed a drink. She returned downstairs and poured herself a large glass of Lagavulin. She sat back on the sofa, turning the glass in her hands, staring at the ring. At length she decided that it was unlikely to be stolen. Why steal a ring and not benefit from it? Why hide it away with clear evidence of a connection to its likely source?

Slowly, Jennifer began to realise that there could be another connection. A correlation so incredible that she hardly dared think it. She needed to get hold of Andy Finch, and fast.

It was Saturday, and they had arranged to meet in Café Concerto at three o'clock. The lively eatery was just down the street from her office, which was handy because York was busy and parking spaces were scarce. She parked in her small office car park and went to meet Doctor Finch. The popular cafe was also busy, but she found him in a corner at the far end. He had some papers with him. As she brought her coffee to the table he looked up and gave her a big grin.

'C'mon, sit down. Let's see it!'

Jennifer took out a matchbox which now held the ring, carefully wrapped in the refolded parchment. Andy opened it slowly, as she had done, savouring the moment of discovery. When at last the ring was laid bare on its wrapping, he whistled through his teeth.

'Jeez!'

He turned it back and forth, examining its form and markings. He ran a finger around the inside of the hoop, then took a small magnifying lens from his jacket pocket and scrutinised it more closely.

'Well, bugger me!' he uttered, completely absorbed.

'It's beautiful, isn't it?' Jennifer laughed, proud to have made the discovery.

'It's a little more than beautiful, ' he articulated. 'Jennifer, have you any idea what this is?'

'Well…' she answered slowly, 'it's obviously a valuable ring, presumably once belonging to a member of the Fernleigh family. Though why it should end up hidden in my cottage…'

'Miss Langley, ' he declared with mock seriousness, 'I believe what you have here is more than just a ring. I will need to get this verified, but I think this is one shank of a gimmel ring!'

'A what?'

'A *gimmel* ring, ' he repeated. 'It's a ring with two or three hoops that fit together to form one complete ring. The name gimmel comes from the Latin *gemellus*, meaning twin. The shanks should interlock, and each is sculptured so that when they're joined together a design emerges.'

Jennifer's mouth fell open slightly and her eyes widened as he continued.

'Sometimes they're referred to as joint rings. There are quite a few references in the literature – Shakespeare, Dryden, for example. A common design incorporated clasped hands and sometimes a heart.'

'But what were they used for?' Jennifer looked puzzled.

'They were commonly used as betrothal rings. The idea was that the betrothed couple would each wear one loop and then join the loops together to form one complete wedding ring. When there was a third loop this could be given to a witness to the betrothed, someone who was entrusted to keep their part of the ring until the wedding day. Do you see what this means?!' Andy returned excitedly.

Jennifer considered for a brief moment, trying to take it all in, then the full significance dawned upon her. 'So there's got to be another ring somewhere! One like this. Its twin. God! Do you think that this could have anything to do with Emily and William? I mean… look at the date on that parchment – 1762. Though I can't think what the initials DFB could stand for.'

'Hold on… there's more!' Andy pronounced, tapping the sheaf of papers on the table next to his coffee cup. 'I haven't been idle either, you know.'

He shot a wide smile in her direction and sifted through the copied documents.

'Here we are. I checked the household accounts from the 1750s to the 1770s, and guess what I found? Here's an example.'

Jennifer could hardly contain herself. Andy swivelled the piece of paper around and pushed it towards her across the table. She scanned the tiny neat handwriting. It appeared to be an extract from an accounts book. At the top of the page was written:

'*C.F.F. Accompts ~ March 7 to May 30, 1762.*'

On the left side were listed items paid for, and on the right were the amounts paid in three columns for pounds, shillings and pence. The payments were made under various headings. Under the category '*Children*' were listed payments to a French master, a music master, a writing master and a dancing master. Jennifer chuckled at the latter entry. It read:

'*Pd to Mr Martin for dancing instruction vis-à-vis Mary, Anne, Rebecca & Elizabeth. £12.10s.6d*'

And underneath:

'(*Little improvement. Reconsider*).'

Another entry detailed:

'*Allowances: Catherine, Charlotte, Amelia £188*'

Underneath this was the heading:

'*Clothes and Personal Items*'

There appeared all manner of entries here relating to the purchase of made-up apparel and material furnishings including payments to a mercer, a mantua maker, milliners, haberdashers, a hosier, a maker of stays, a weaver and a cobbler. There were also entries for china of various sorts and a hairbrush.

Under the '*House Accompts*' category there was a single entry:

'*Pd to Mrs Preedy vis-à-vis house book £29.18s.4d.*'

Jennifer looked up at Andy for an explanation.

'These are Charlotte Fernleigh's accounts, ' he enlightened, 'I found separate account books kept by the housekeeper for food and linen, etcetera, and the wine purchases are recorded in Lord Fernleigh's accounts – Thomas Fernleigh, that is. In large households such as theirs it would have been usual for the housekeeper to look after the accounts for provisions, most probably overseen by Lady Fernleigh. Look further down, ' he prompted eagerly.

Jennifer nodded and continued her examination of the document. The final category on the page was entitled '*Servants Wages.*' Positions and names were recorded and the list appeared to consist of females in order of rank.

Next to the entry '*Housekeeper*' was recorded '*Constance Preedy.*' And there, underneath the first entry, it read:

'Lady's maid ~ Emily Popple £18.17s.8d.'

Jennifer clasped her hands to her mouth. Excitement swirled through her body and the hairs on her arms and on the back of her neck stood up, as if electrified.

'Emily Popple.' She said the name to feel how it felt in her mouth. It felt comfortable, familiar.

Andy Finch was looking at her, wearing an expression of cautious satisfaction. He scratched his short, slightly greying beard, then signified with one finger.

'Step one – we can link the Emily Popple, baptised in Brockby in 1743, with the position of lady's maid. Actually the accounts, which are surprisingly complete, show her first appearing in the servant's category as a kitchen maid. That was in 1756. She would have been about thirteen then. It looks as though she worked her way up through the ranks, as her name appears against entries for under housemaid and upper housemaid at various times. She must have impressed the house steward or the Fernleigh family because she was first recorded as a lady's maid in the second half of 1760, when she would have been only seventeen. That's unusual for a girl of her background.'

He took a sip from his cup and found it was empty. 'Would you like another cup?'

'Mmm, yes please, ' she replied, quickly downing the remains of the first cup, which had gone cold in the bottom. She replaced the ring and paper in its matchbox, put it back in her handbag and continued to study the accounts while he was ordering. She noticed that all the servants appeared to be female. That was odd; no male servants. Her mind returned to Emily Popple. It was so strange to think that the name documented there in black and white represented a real person with an occupation, a family, hopes, fears – and possibly a forbidden lover.

Now that she was looking at actual records, Jennifer felt rather ambiguous about a possible past life. Part of her felt it to be absolutely true, without question. Yet she couldn't seem to comprehend how on earth she, a living person, flesh and blood, sitting here at this café table drinking coffee, could possibly have lived another life all those years ago; been born, lived and died in another century.

She rested her head in her hands for a moment. God, she had so many questions! And anyway, they hadn't proved any connection between Emily Popple and William Fernleigh. It was as Andy Finch had said; this was only step one.

He returned to the table with the coffees and two large slices of banoffee cheesecake.

'My favourite, ' he grinned sheepishly. 'Couldn't resist! Anyway, I think we should allow ourselves a celebratory cake-eating ceremony.'

Jennifer laughed and shook her head. 'You know, ' she retorted, feeding a large forkful of creamy banana toffee and biscuit into her mouth, 'I have countless questions, but you've found a way to shut me up, at least temporarily! Mmm, this is lovely, by the way!'

They each appreciated the cheesecake for a moment or two.

'Scruffy would have enjoyed this, I bet, ' she said between mouthfuls.

'Oh yes, but too rich for him. He's enjoying the other of his favourite pastimes at the moment, which is much more healthy. My wife has taken him for a long walk with one of her friends. So, ' he finished the last mouthful and wiped his mouth with a serviette, 'all the more for me!'

'Sorry to drag you away from your family at a weekend, ' Jennifer apologised.

'Not a problem. I was excited to see your find. Anyway, I also have something more for you.'

He gathered up the copies of Charlotte Fernleigh's accounts pages, paperclipped them together and replaced them in an old battered brown briefcase, pulling out another sheaf.

'Step two, ' he declared.

Jennifer leaned across the table towards him in eager anticipation.

'Now for Thomas Fernleigh's estate accounts, ' he pronounced. 'One or two of the books for the period I've been researching are missing, but we've still got a pretty solid picture. I can't show you everything – actually I shouldn't be sharing any of this stuff, as obviously it belongs to the Fernleigh family – but in confidence I can share this with you. It looks like you may have a bone fide vested interest.' He inclined his head towards her and raised his eyebrows as he spoke the last words.

Jennifer waited nervously for what he was about to impart.

'Can you tell me, does your cottage have a name?' he asked.

Jennifer frowned. 'Yes. Why?'

'What is it?'

'Primrose Cottage.'

He banged one hand loudly on the table in triumph. '*Yes!*'

Jennifer stared at him. The couple on the next table looked over.

'You're not going to believe this! I almost don't believe it myself. But here it is, in black and white. Well, in quill and ink.'

Again, he placed a scanned copy of an account document in front of her.

'Look at the entry about three quarters of the way down.'

Jennifer scanned the page then began trying to decipher the handwriting. It was as small as Lady Fernleigh's script but less neat, and there were ink spots disguising some of the words.

'It's pretty messy handwriting,' she remarked. 'Thomas Fernleigh isn't as neat as his wife.'

'Oh, that's not Thomas' writing, it's his steward, his agent. A man called Bottesford. He would have run the estate, overseen by Lord Fernleigh. Thomas ran his own accounts. Bottesford and all the male staff are detailed in those accounts.' He leant over the table and peered at the document upside down, screwing up his eyes, trying to spot the relevant text. Having found it, he pointed to the line in question.

'There.'

Jennifer read the entry.

'*Primrofe Cott.*'

Her heart jumped into her mouth. She looked along the line.

'*Popple.*'

Her stomach turned over and she felt a rush of adrenaline which left her feeling a little shaky. She sat back in her chair and took some deep breaths. The records indicated that a rent was being paid by the Popple family to the Fernleigh estate for Primrose Cottage. They already knew that Emily Popple had been baptised in Brockby. That there may have been another Primrose Cottage in Brockby belonging to the Fernleigh estate was too much of a coincidence.

She was living in the cottage once occupied by Emily Popple.

Andy Finch was beaming at her. 'As I said, there are a couple of gaps, but the records of rents paid for the tied cottages is fairly comprehensive. Of course, they weren't known as tied cottages in those days. There is something rather odd, though.'

'Odd?'

'Yes, the amounts are recorded on pretty much a monthly basis; that is until November 1762. At that point the entries for Primrose Cottage and Popple are still present in the accounts but with zero pounds, shillings and pence written against them. I checked the records for a few more years and they remain consistently recorded like that. I'll do some more cross-checking. We'll also need to try and figure out what those initials stand for.'

Jennifer heard the words being spoken to her, but couldn't quite take it all in. She was still reeling from the revelation that she and Emily Popple had another, more tangible connection.

'The ring!' she gasped.

She took the matchbox out of her pocket and unwrapped the ring again. It glinted in the yellow glow of the café wall lights.

'We're one step closer, ' she whispered.

'Yes. A step closer, ' he accorded.

⟨━━⟩

October 24ᵗʰ 1762

Preparations for the Fernleigh autumn ball were becoming increasingly frenzied. The butler and the clerk of the kitchen had been having words about provisions, in particular the shortfall in olives. Mr Cowper, who was of course responsible for the distribution of wine and plate and would be present when the dishes were presented that evening, was furious at his perceived incompetence of Mr Fry's abilities to ensure a ready supply.

'You won't be the person to be held to account when the olives run out!' he hissed through gritted teeth.

Mr Fry was blaming the chief cook for not making her instructions clearer but she was having none of it, and Mr Cowper was defending her and pulling rank. In the end Mrs Cumley shooed them both away, hands flapping.

'Ah've one 'undred an' one things t' do! We'll just 'ave t' make do, is all. Ah've no time t' argue an' yer both in m' way.'

The household was a tumult of activity. Chambermaids were preparing the remaining unoccupied guestrooms. The groom of chambers was busy moving furniture with two of the under footmen. The under butler was polishing candlesticks and complaining that he'd not had much assistance from Mr Cowper so far this morning. Mr Cowper and Mr Fry had put aside their differences for the time being, and were now occupied in the wine cellar. Mrs Cumley was conducting the cook, the pastry cook and an army of kitchen maids and footmen were scurrying from one part of the house to the other delivering messages between family members and instructions to staff, ushering in guests and satisfying the demands of visitors. It was all hands to the deck, with only a few hours to go before the ball.

Having dressed Lady Fernleigh and ensured that all was in order in her dressing room, that the garments she would wear that evening were ready, that she had the necessary items for the Pompadour hairstyle that she would create later on and that the caskets and boxes of her ladyship's toilet set were necessarily primed, Emily decided to try to slip out. She had to get to see her mother somehow. There had been precious little time over the last couple of days as she had been sent to check over and procure a crimson contouche that had been made up for Charlotte by a seamstress in York. Charlotte had been indisposed and so could not go herself, and she did not trust anyone other than Emily to see that the gown was finished properly. Emily was under strict instructions to ensure that it was absolutely as designed and not to leave until she could bring it back with her — and of course it had to be ready before the day of the ball.

Now was Emily's only chance. Later, when the ball was in full swing, she and Will would meet at the stables and make their escape. If she was to see her mother it had to be now, and she did not have much time. She slipped down the back staircase. The downstairs corridors were crawling with staff rushing here and there, carrying things to and fro like ants, each too busy to stop and talk with her or even to notice her. As long as she did not encounter Mrs Preedy...

Emily made it to the door at the end of the kitchen corridor. She avoided the kitchen garden, where vegetables and herbs were being busily harvested to service the activities in the kitchen. Instead, she turned right and headed through the orchard, skirting the left-hand hedge until she found a gap large enough to squeeze through. Then she turned for Brockby and began the three-mile walk home.

William was reading the London Evening Post in the library, trying to keep his mind off what he was about to do and what he would say to his father later. He had been going over matters again and again in his head and he felt emotionally and mentally exhausted. The reports from the war on the continent and in the West Indies and the Americas were variably encouraging and discouraging. In one report, letters from Cleves advised that *orders were received there from the court of France, to provide winter quarters in that country for 24, 000 men; by which it was thought that peace between England and France was not at a great distance...* Part of a letter originally published in the Amsterdam Gazette described an express from the Duke of Bedford revealing that the Marquis de Grimaldi, the Spanish Ambassador at the French court, had dispatched a courier to Madrid the moment he had heard of the taking of Havana, asking for fresh instructions on how to behave in the negotiation of peace between the French and English courts. Various reports were published concerning the Duke of Bedford's expected arrival in Paris from Fontainbleau on October the fifteenth; having been assured of the King of Spain's consent to the peace, he was *just going to sign the preliminaries, when news came of the surrender of the*

Havana. The negotiation hath since taken another turn, and the public don't know the state of it at the present. Similarly, *The conferences with the Duke of Bedford are still continued; but we do not find that the negotiation advances; It should seem that the obstacles to it increase.*

So it seemed that England's position regarding France had not particularly improved and he was about to cross the sea and make his home on that foreign soil, facing whatever dangers lay in store. Not only that, but he was taking the person he loved most in the world with him, risking her life too. But there were others he loved. Here. His sisters, his mother and his father.

He ran his fingers through his hair and sighed deeply. There was no turning back. There was no other course of action to be taken. He would have to hope that his family would eventually forgive him.

William threw down the paper, rose and poured himself a glass of whisky from an engraved globe decanter on a nearby table. He paced back and forth for a few minutes, turning the glass in his hands, watching the amber liquid coat the inside of the tumbler. Then he took a large sip of the fiery liquor and another as, deep in contemplation, he walked up and down alongside shelf upon shelf of books, running his hand over their spines, enjoying their musty, leathery smell.

He had spoken with his uncle again, who had confirmed the date that the captain of their ship to France was aiming to set sail from Liverpool. The 6th of November. They had thirteen days. It would take two or three days to reach the Scottish border and another two or three days thenceforth to Liverpool, if luck was on their side. They would not travel via Paris and Orleans, as originally planned. The timing would be right to join the Brigantine in Liverpool. William did not know exactly how long the crossing would take. They would first sail to Dublin, then south into the Celtic Sea and thence into the Bay of Biscay to La Rochelle. He had been informed by his uncle that it was 130 miles or so from there to Limoges. A voyage in four parts, on which he was about to embark this night. And between the first part of the journey and the second, his beloved betrothed would become his wife.

Uncle John had been most supportive and exceedingly helpful on his account. William was relieved to have an ally, and one with all the right connections, it seemed. His uncle had secured a place on the ship and arranged the letting of Monsieur Beauenne's cottage.

John had assured William that he would write a letter of introduction to Monsieur and Madame Beauenne to inform them of the imminent arrival of his nephew and 'wife'. He had assured William that they were most discreet. Uncle John had even promised to try and smooth matters over with William's father in William's absence. Of course John did not know the full extent of William's plan as far as the marriage was concerned: William had remained cautious about that.

William had inherited 10, 000 pounds on his twenty-first birthday. Two days ago he had withdrawn the majority of this princely sum and arranged a second account at the only other bank in York. By the time the news reached his father, as no doubt it would, he would be miles away and would have access to the money. He had purchased a modest amount of gold from a bank that did not have a longstanding allegiance to his father, which he planned to use as surety during the first few months until he could set up an arrangement with an agent in France. He felt guilty about this, as about everything else, but it could not be helped.

He had packed two leather saddlebags with a few clothes, money, his dagger and some provisions for the journey. In a third he had placed a deerskin, a woollen rug, a tinderbox and his silver hunting flask in case they were forced to sleep rough, although he hoped that this would not be necessary. A fourth bag was left empty for Emily's possessions. The bags were hidden in the woodland north of the paddock, half-buried and covered well with branches and fallen leaves. He planned to reach the stables before Emily. The stable lads would be a problem, but he had thought of a way to deal with them. In any case there would be much coming and going with visiting grooms looking after their charges and horses and carriages everywhere. Besides, he would be armed with bottles of rum, which the servants would no doubt enjoy to the full. It should not be too difficult to slip away with two horses. Everything was set. He now had to face his father, and he had to get the timing right.

Mary saddled up the dun mare. Daniel was inspecting the wheat and barley crops, Georgina and Prudence were busy pickling walnuts and Toby was with his father. She told the girls that she had an errand to run and would be back presently. With the ring safely tucked into her pocket, she mounted and began making her way towards Fernleigh Hall. Once out of the village, she turned off the track and headed south-east across the pastureland. This was the quickest way. Mary steeled herself to pass close to Fernleigh woods. She could not bear to go anywhere near that place, even now, so many years since. But she gritted her teeth in absolute determination and repeated to herself, *This is the quickest way.*

As she passed the hedgerow where she had been picking blackberries all those years ago she fought with the memory that tried to seep into her consciousness like a stain, slowly poisoning her from the inside. Her skin turned cold and images appeared before her eyes unwanted and uninvited.

With a massive effort she pushed them away, banished them and forbade them to return. She focused her thoughts on Emily and pulled her cloak a little tighter around her against the grey drizzle. The wind was getting up. Sullen clouds scudded across the sky malevolently. Another storm was on the way, likely in more ways than one. She lowered her head and urged the mare into a canter.

Emily had no sooner reached the road west of the house and was about to turn north-west across the fields when the sound of hooves and wheels on grit came up fast behind her. She swung around, and the hood of her mantlet was blown off in the strengthening wind as she turned her head. The frill of her cap flapped around her face as she struggled to retrieve and replace the covering over her head.

It was old Robert Butler. He pulled the dog cart up beside her and leaned forward to steady the bay in the harness. He tipped his hat.

'Owist? Wheer's ta bahn, lass?'

'How do, Mr Butler. I'm on my way to Brockby to see my mother.'

'Ahm off theer m'self 'as it 'appens, Miss Emily. Me un Tinker 'ere'll give thee a lift.'

The old groom started to climb down to help her up, but Emily put a hand on his arm.

'Don't worry, Mr Butler. I can manage, thank you.'

She lifted her skirt and pulled herself onto the back of the two-seater cart so that they sat back to back, for there was no room beside him. She turned her head a little.

'Where are you off to, Mr Butler?' she asked in a raised voice to combat the effects of the wind.

'T' farrier's, ' he responded in an equally loud tone. 'She needs new shoes. Reckon ah'll get mi'sen a bevy an' a bit o' black dag whilst ah'm waitin' like.'

'That sounds like a good idea on a day like this!' she laughed.

Tell t' truth, ah'm glad t' escape all t' bletherin'. Too many folks around t' day fer my likin', ' he shouted.

'Indeed, ' she accorded.

The wind whipped around their heads and carried their words into the hedgerows beside them. Presently they gave up trying to communicate until they reached Brockby. The farrier was on the near side of the village. Emily said that she would walk from there, thanked Robert Butler and headed up the road and over the green, where a group of goats were grazing.

The old man watched her go and wondered to himself. He hoped that she could take care of herself. There were folks none too kind around; that lovely lass needed to be careful.

Emily picked her way through the goats and made her way to the farm, only to be told that her mother was out on an errand and her sisters were unsure when she'd be back. They bade her stay and have a bite to eat with them, but she replied that she had little time and should return to the Hall, as her ladyship would be in need of her soon enough. She made light of it, pretending that she herself had been on an errand and had called by perchance to see them.

It nearly broke her heart.

As they said their goodbyes, Emily hugged each of her sisters tightly. She squeezed their hands and bade them convey her love to their Ma and Pa.

'And tell nipper to be good, ' she smiled; inside, she felt as if she was dying.

'We're allus tellin' t' lad t' behave, aren't we?' affirmed Prudence, looking at Georgina.

'Aye, so we are, ' Georgina concorded. 'Take care yusen.' She kissed Emily on her cheek.

'Bye sister, see thee again soon.' Another hug from Prudence.

Emily could stand it no more. She turned away quickly and walked out into the bitter air. Tears stung her eyes as she faced into the worsening weather and began the walk back to Fernleigh Hall. Rain and tears intermingled and fell soundlessly over her cold cheeks. She was utterly wretched. She felt as though the rain were washing through her, dissolving her very soul. All she wanted to do at that moment was to turn around and run back home – back into the safe, warm loving arms of her family.

William entered his father's study. Thomas was sitting at his bureau with a glass of red wine in one hand and a book in the other. He looked up, smiled at his son and nodded.

'Having a few quiet moments to myself amidst the clamour, ' he admitted. 'Come and join me.'

He poured William a glass and William took it readily. Thomas resumed his position in the walnut armchair, however William remained standing.

'Will you not sit, man?' Thomas enquired.

'I prefer to stand, Sir.' William was shaking. He downed the wine and poured himself another glass. 'I have something I must tell you, Father.'

Thomas looked concerned. 'What is it, my boy? What ails you? Are you feeling unwell?'

William emptied his glass a second time and placed it on a table.

'Sir, please hear me out. I have tried to tell you several times, and each time I have failed miserably.'

Thomas frowned and leaned forward.

'I am betrothed. That is... I am to be married.' William paced the floor in front of his father's desk. 'I am in love with Emily Popple. Indeed, I have loved her for most of my life. In truth, I cannot remember a time when I did not love her!'

'WHAT!'

Thomas stood up abruptly, sending his chair clattering onto its back and his wine spilling over the papers on his desk.

'Father, PLEASE. Let me speak! I wish to take Emily Popple as my wife. She is a good, honest, intelligent person, ' William pleaded. 'She is held in high esteem, not least by Mama, and...'

'ENOUGH!' roared his father. His face was white with rage and his eyes full of anger.

William stepped back. It was as if his father's fury had taken physical form, amassed its forces and hit him squarely in the chest, knocking the wind out of him. He had expected an argument, but was unprepared for the vehemence of his father's response.

'I will *not* hear you speak of marriage and Emily Popple in the same sentence! You are the son of a lord of the realm and she is a servant. It is preposterous! Unthinkable!'

William sat down and put his head in his hands. Then, looking up at his father with tears in his eyes, he said quietly 'Have you never loved someone more than your life? I cannot live without her, Father.'

'You speak to me of love?' Thomas replied angrily. 'You think I haven't loved? You think I haven't known what it is to give your heart and soul to another, to adore someone with such a passion that you'd die for her, to want to live all your days with her and never to be parted?! Oh, I can assure you I know love. But you and I were born privileged. And with privilege comes duty!' He banged his fist on the desk. 'Duty to your family, duty to the Fernleigh name, to the household, the estate, these lands and the families we employ and support. What do you think would happen if we all turned our backs on duty, eh? If we all rebelled and did as we pleased? Chaos, lawlessness, anarchism, revolution – that's what!'

William was taken aback by the implication that his father had loved a woman other than his mother; by his father's use of the word 'but'. He let that thought pass for the moment and focused on his obligations.

'Father, I understand my responsibilities and accountability, ' he retorted forcefully.

He rose and began pacing again, staring at the floor, chopping the air in front of him with every sentence.

'I do not intend to evade my obligations. And I love my family and do not wish any harmful consequence to arise as a result of my actions. I do not intend to fail you, or to abandon the estate, or to neglect any part of my duty.' He turned and looked at his father and took a deep breath. 'If I were to take Emily away, far away, and bring her back as my wife… Educated, refined, in every other sense of the word, a lady… What harm could it do?'

He raised his shoulders and turned his hands palm upwards, imploring his father to be moderate, to act with compassion.

Thomas's hands were shaking and beads of sweat had appeared on his brow. Suddenly there was a look in his eyes that William did not recognise and could not quite identify. A mixture of horror and revulsion, almost terror.

'Have you bedded her?'

'Sir?'

'Answer me! Have you *bedded* the girl?!'

The instant the question was asked William knew that there was danger in the response. His intuitions, his instincts, his senses, were all crying out for him to be careful. It was enough warning.

'No, Sir, I have not, ' he lied, with as much conviction as he could muster.

William could see relief in his father's eyes as Thomas recovered his chair and slumped back into it. William waited for the pronouncement. There was nothing else that he could say. He knew his father too well. He must await the verdict.

Thomas stared at his son, almost not seeing him. He was enraged that his son had forced him to face a situation that was, but an hour ago, unthinkable. He tried hard to control his rage so that he could think clearly, so that he could capture the thoughts and images whirling around in his head and arrange them into some kind of order that made sense. It was quite clear that William must be sent away for a while and that a new position would need to be found for the girl. He had made a promise to Daniel and Mary Popple many years ago that he would ensure her safety, and had guaranteed that she would be well cared for. He was not about to renege on a promise. He was also determined that Charlotte would not know of this until after the ball. He would absolutely not have her upset on this day of all days. She had been planning and looking forward to this celebration for weeks. Thomas was convinced that his dear wife would take this very badly. Her hopes for William lay in the direction of Mistress Snaith – and to be deceived by her own maid, a maid that she liked very well and had a high opinion of, well... He would have to handle Charlotte very carefully.

Thomas focused his eyes upon his son, who was sitting in front of him, hands clasped tightly together, eyes pleading. *Damn the boy!* He was so like Thomas himself had been at his age. Full of fervour, with a lust for life, eagerness to please those around him whom he loved and capable of loving with unbelievable passion. But unlike his son, Thomas had known where his responsibilities lay and in the end had chosen obligation over adoration, trustworthiness over tenderness, duty over devotion.

It was now paramount that William and Emily were kept away from each other. Their liaison had already gone too far. Thomas shuddered involuntarily. He rose and faced his son.

'Listen carefully to me, and do not counter. You are my son and heir and you *will* obey me.'

Of necessity, his tone was quiet but menacing.

'You are not to speak to Emily Popple again or have any manner of contact with her. You are to leave this room and ready yourself to leave Fernleigh Hall at dawn tomorrow morning. You will travel to

Oxford, where you will engage yourself in the study of law, and you will remain at Oxford until your studies are complete. You will speak of this to no-one, least of all your mother. Do you hear me, Sir?'

Thomas determinedly held his composure as his son crumpled before him. Then, shakily, William arose, turned his eyes from his father's face and walked slowly to the door. As William turned the handle he paused momentarily, then opened the door and went quietly out.

Mary arrived in the kitchen garden as the rain started to fall steadily, whisked sideways by the wind. She located the large heavy door to the kitchen passage, tied her mare to a nearby fence and cautiously stepped inside. Someone pushed past her from behind, carrying a basket of mushrooms.

'S'cuse me, ma'am, ' Mary heard as the woman scurried down the corridor and into the kitchen. Mary followed her and stood in the corridor by the opening to the kitchen, looking into the room and trying to locate someone she knew.

All manner of food was being prepared for the feast that evening and two large food presses were already groaning with finished dishes. Potted venison and trout, oysters, loaves and curried eggs competed for space with whole fish in pastry, marinating calves' tongues and a thatched-house pie. Burnt almonds and candied apricots sat side by side with lemon pralines and marzipan fruit. A magnificent Salamangundy had been created and was waiting on a side table, and a whole hog was roasting over the fire. An assortment of fowl were being variously stuffed and rolled and there was a selection of pies and pastries in diverse states of readiness. Sauces and gravies simmered on the stove whilst a large caldron of onion soup bubbled away beside them.

Gazing on the ensemble, Mary felt hungry in spite of the deep anxiety within. She spotted Mrs Cumley's large frame at the far end of the kitchen preparing perch, caught the attention of a nearby kitchen maid and asked her to convey a message to her. Some moments later Martha Cumley came, somewhat breathless and red-faced, out into the passageway. She motioned to Mary to follow her into the servant's hall where they might have some quiet.

Mary wasted no time. 'Mrs Cumley, Martha, I need t' speak with Emily. 'Tis urgent. I must see 'er, ' she stated urgently, laying a hand on the cook's plump arm.

'Why Mrs Popple! Whatever is t' matter? Is someone unwell?' Mrs Cumley took one look at Mary's exasperated expression and dishevelled appearance and changed her mind. She put one hand up, palm outward towards Mary.

'No, don't trouble y'sen for a reply. I'll get t' lass brought down... wait a moment, ' and she hurried out.

She appeared again a minute or so later with a small glass of brandy which she handed to Mary, bidding her take a seat by the fire. Mary was grateful for the warming effect of the liquor and the heat of the fire. She was starting to feel a little chilled as the rain had thoroughly soaked through her clothes.

Ah've sent a girl t' look for 'er, ' Mrs Cumley smiled reassuringly. 'She'll no doubt be down before too long. Ah told girl t' say it was urgent like.' She patted Mary on the arm. 'Is there ought I can do for thee?'

Mary smiled. 'Yer a kind woman, Mrs Cumley. Ah'm grateful for thee askin'. There's nowt tha can do. Ah just need t' speak with Emily. There's summat ah need t' know from 'er is all. How're tha keeping? Ah can see tha's mighty busy t' day.'

It took all of Mary's effort to maintain a pleasant chatter whilst waiting for Emily. Eventually the flushed kitchen maid appeared.

'She's nowhere t' be found. I looked everywhere, I did!' she blurted out worriedly. 'She weren't with 'er ladyship, an' no-one's seen 'er this past hour or two!'

Mary's eyes darted around the room worriedly as if her daughter could be hiding somewhere there. Then she looked anxiously at Martha.

'Don't fret thasen, Jane, ' the cook said to the maid. 'Thank thee, lass. She'll turn up. Go an' finish those king cakes.'

Martha turned to Mary. 'Emily's most probably out on an errand or summat, ' she said calmly. ''Tis chaos 'ere and no mistake. Ah'll make sure she gets t' message as 'er mother needs t' speak with 'er. Perhaps she'll be able t' get away in a day or so, ' she smiled hearteningly.

Mary bit her lip so hard that she drew blood and turned to leave the room, then changed her mind and swung around.

'If ah can't see Emily ah I need t' speak with 'is lordship' she said steadfastly.

Martha was taken aback. ''Is lordship'll be mighty busy, what wi' folks arrivin' for t' ball and such.'

Mary's features set themselves into a look of dogged determination, reflecting the way she felt inside. The little seed of dread that she had kept hidden away inside, put away in the dark and mostly forgotten, had started to germinate the moment her eyes had met the ring. It had grown and grown and had started to take hold of her, twisting its tendrils of trepidation around her insides and pressing on her chest, weighing her down with fear. There was nothing else for it. She could not risk waiting any longer for Emily's confirmation. She knew in her heart of hearts who must have given her daughter that ring. It was no use pretending: the time for caution had passed. This was the time for action. She had to speak with Thomas Fernleigh.

'Ah can't help that, ' she answered firmly.

Martha sighed. 'Ah'll get one of t' footman to give 'is lordship a message. Tha'll 'ave t' hope that 'e'll see thee.'

'Oh, 'e'll see me, ' Mary returned determinedly.

Fifteen minutes later she was standing in Thomas's study in front of his desk. He was standing by one of the windows looking out at the foul weather, his back to her, tumbler of whisky in hand. In the circumstances he'd offered her one too but she had refused. With difficulty, he turned to face her again.

'The ring – can I see it?'

She nodded, took it from her pocket and placed it on the desk, where it sparkled in the glancing firelight. He walked over to the desk, looked at it and shook his head sadly.

'William came to see me this afternoon, only an hour before you arrived. He informed me... of his... feelings for Emily.' Thomas avoided Mary's eyes, instead focusing on the ring before him.

Mary let out a cry and put a hand to her face. Thomas rushed to her side and with a hand under her arm, guided her to a chair.

'Dear lady, ' Thomas said, as calmly as he could manage, though his features belied his acute concern, 'please do not be concerned. All is in hand. I am sending William away tomorrow and have absolutely forbidden him to have anything more to do with your daughter.' He chose his words carefully.

'But... Emily... what of Emily?!' Mary cried, fighting hard to control her emotions and losing.

Thomas bit his lip and put both hands on his desk, palm down, to stop them shaking. This was going to be hard. He took a deep breath.

'There is a... that is to say... my wife has... a distant cousin, who... resides in Devon. I have determined that Emily will go there... I know that you will appreciate that this is the only way. William will not know of her whereabouts.'

Mary gasped. No!' she cried. 'Devon is... so far away! Is there no other way t'...?'

'It is for the best' Thomas interrupted gently, 'you must see that.'

Mary gave a low wail, covered her face with her hands and wept. The burgeoning apprehension had turned to agony and guilt. Why could she have not foreseen this? Why could he have not prevented it? He had promised that Emily would be taken care of. He had broken his promise and that son of his had.... No, she would not think of it – *could* not think it!

Thomas started towards her but thought better of it. He proffered his handkerchief and at length she took it begrudgingly and dabbed her eyes.

'You said that she would be cared for in your service, ' she whispered eventually.

Thomas thought for a moment before responding gently. 'And she has been. Perhaps too well.'

Mary looked up at him sharply.

'Mar... Mrs Popple. She is greatly valued in this household. I would go so far as to say she is loved. She has been afforded liberties and privileges perhaps beyond her station. And we have treated William to a great deal of freedom... and of course trust.' He shrugged slightly and shook his head sadly. 'I believe our overindulgence on both counts may be partly to blame.'

Mary returned his apologetic, tortured expression with one of bitterness and reproach. Bitterness towards the man in front of her for not keeping better control of events under his roof; reproach at herself for failing to notice a change within her daughter; bitterness at Master William for his ungentlemanly behaviour; and reproach at her daughter for... for what? For falling in love? No, for failing to confide in her mother, who would have understood but who would have counselled her and taken action to prevent events from ever reaching this dangerous stage.

She shook her head reprovingly, though she dared not go too far with his lordship. She knew that there was nothing to be done except what he proposed. Yet Devon was so far, so very far away. She voiced her opinion quietly.

Thomas had taken a seat at his desk. His heart was still beating fiercely but his hands had stopped shaking. The worst was over. They each knew what must be done.

'This has been the most terrible shock, ' he said kindly. Please do try not to be too upset, I beg you. Devon is indeed a long way from here, and that is precisely why she must go there. We both know that. However, I do not propose to remove your daughter from you without giving you some means of seeing her. You shall see her whenever you wish, and I shall arrange it. You and Mr Popple, of course.'

Mary took a deep breath to steady herself. Knowing that she would be able to see her daughter afforded such little comfort. Knowing was one thing and doing quite another. It would be difficult for her and Daniel to leave the farm for any length of time, and there were the bairns to consider. She supposed that it might be possible with the help of his family. Though it broke her heart to acknowledge it, his lordship was right: there was nothing else for it. However it would be so very hard for all of them, and most of all for Emily. It would be impossibly hard for her. She would see it as a punishment, and for what? Her crime – falling in love with the wrong person!

Mary shook her head despondently and stared at the polished floorboards through a curtain of renewed and bitter tears. It was the way of things, but that didn't mean it was right. Why did her kind always have to bear the brunt of misfortune, of the destructive wishes and wants of the aristocracy, of their bad decisions and poor management? She'd known sacrifice in her life, indeed she had. But this was different; this was not her sacrifice but the penalty to be paid by her poor, unsuspecting daughter.

At length, she reluctantly accorded. 'Ah should be grateful t' see Emily. When she's in Devon.'

Thomas smiled sympathetically and nodded. 'She shall see you before she goes.'

Mary rose to leave. 'How shall ah ever break it t' Daniel?' she faltered.

'I shall write a letter to your husband, if you like; explaining the circumstances and describing the new position. I shall make it worth her while, ' Thomas replied. Then, 'You shall have the carriage to take you home'.

'I thank thee, sir, I 'ave my mare.' She spoke flatly.

'Your mare can run behind. The weather is foul. It's the least I can do, ' Thomas affirmed.

Mary nodded and walked towards the door. 'Ah ask thee not t' make mention of t' ring. Ah'll deal with that part m'sen.' It was an instruction rather than a request.

'I blame myself, of course, ' Thomas uttered.

She turned around to look at him briefly before turning to open the door. A footman, waiting in the corridor, stepped to the side to allow her to exit and closed the door after her.

Later that day, having returned home and exchanged her wet clothes for dry ones and placed her wet things in front of the fire in the parlour, Mary stood in her chamber, ring in hand, deliberating on a safe hiding place. She could not use the bureau as both she and Daniel employed that for their letter work, and valuables were concealed in its locking drawer. The plant behind the wainscot was another shared hiding place. There was only one other place she could resort to.

She returned downstairs and sent the girls off into the barn to help their father and Toby to assist with the milking on the pretext that the light would be fading soon and she wanted them all in the warm and the doors locked against the weather as soon as possible – it was a partial truth. Once on her own, she set a chair under one of the oak beams in the parlour, took off her shoes and climbed upon it. There were a series of small cracks in the wood, no bigger than the width of a cat's whisker, where the damp had intruded at some point. With the point of a knife, Mary carefully eased a small block of the beam far enough out of its setting to be able to grasp it between forefinger and thumb. She pulled it out carefully, revealing a larger recess behind it. With the knife, she pulled a piece of paper towards her and retrieved it from the cavity. Climbing down from the chair, she crossed the wooden floor to the fireplace, opening the parchment. She read the letter, then folded the top of the paper over, made a crease and tore off the uppermost portion of the page. She hesitated for a moment, then placed the letter in the fire and watched it burn. She folded the remaining paper tightly around the ring and placed it deep inside the compartment in the beam, pushing it to the back with the butt of her knife. Then she worked quickly to replace the block of wood, which went back as tightly as before. She was closing a chapter in her daughter's life, and in her own too.

William was making polite conversation with as many guests as he could decently manage, moving amongst them, trying not to get drawn into too deep a discourse. His mind and body seemed to be floating amidst the swirling colours of silk and satin, taffeta and lace, damask and velvet as ladies and their gentleman partners performed minuets and gigues, sarabandes and gavottes. He was the perfect host. He introduced acquaintances to his unmarried sisters, busied himself fetching refreshments for the older ladies and fulfilled his dance duties. Of course he had to ask Miss Snaith to dance, but he could not be expected to dance more than two dances with her. At the onset of the contradances he was obliged to dance the Cotillon with Miss Trent, the Allemande with Miss Foster, the Anglaise de la Reine with Miss Adams, the Anglaise la Cosak with Mrs Snaith and the Rond with Miss Susan Snaith.

William conducted himself with poise and dignity. He was the very epitome of decorum and politesse, but inside he was numb, counting time until the supper break.

Supper was called at a quarter past ten, and not a moment too soon for William. He escorted his dance partner into the grand dining room and saw that she was comfortably seated as all the guests filed in and found places around the various tables, which had been laden with the feast. Amongst the hubbub and general disorder William took his chance to slip away.

He made his way to the library and retrieved a small sack containing bottles of brandy, which he had hidden inside the grandfather clock. The front entrance to the house was guarded by two footmen. William gave them each two bottles and bade them distribute the liquor amongst the coachmen and footmen waiting with their carriages in the cold.

He slipped outside and ran around to the back of the house and thence to the stables. The place was lively. The stalls were full, the coach house crammed, and the Fernleigh stable lads and visiting grooms were mostly drinking beer in one of the haylofts and had been doing so for quite a while by the sound of them. William intercepted a lad on his way back in after having a piss against the big chestnut tree behind the northern block. He gave the lad the sack with the remaining brandy in it and bade him share it among the staff with the compliments of the Fernleigh family. The young lad was surprised and delighted, and rushed off to do as he was told.

William quietly entered the tack room in the west stable wing. A lone figure presided there, sorting the tackle by candlelight, sifting through sursingle and crupper, bridal and breast collar, reins and rowlers. The man stiffened as William's left foot hit a comb that had accidentally been dropped. As old as he was, Robert Butler spun around with a whip in his right hand. William readied himself to strike, but on seeing who it was Robert's arm fell to his side. He dropped the whip and put his hand to his chest over his heart, swearing under his breath.

'Lord fergive me, Master William. Tha gave me one 'ell of a fright, so tha did!'

William made light of it. 'Apologies, Robert. I brought the men some brandy. Won't you go and join them?'

'Ah… tis very kind of thee, Sir. Ah'd rather not, if tis all t' same to thee. Ah prefer me own company these days. Not bein' mardy like.'

'That's a pity. It's good brandy, ' William encouraged.

'Ah'm better off wheer ah am. Ah mean no offence.'

William sighed. He would have to do this the hard way. He looked hard at the old man. 'I'm taking two horses, Robert. I've come for the tack.'

At that moment, Emily appeared quietly in the doorway. Robert looked from William to Emily and back again and understood. He thought for a moment and cursed again.

'Ay-up, ' he shook his head, 'We'll take t' Berlin, ' he pronounced decidedly.

Emily and William looked at one another, astonished. William spoke.

'I cannot possibly let you d…'

'Master William, ' Robert interrupted, 'ah've known thee since thee wor a small lad and tha's known me. These old eyes 'ave seen a lot o' comin' and goin' over t' years, and what they 'aven't seen isn't worth seein'. Tha thinks ah wouldn't 'elp thee on a night such as this? Ah'll take thee as far as Northallerton.'

He turned to begin gathering the necessary tackle. 'Thee'll be able t' get fresh horses or a stage from there, an' ah'll see 'em off like.'

Emily and William questioned one another silently. William shrugged. He trusted Robert and they had no time to lose. Emily nodded in William's direction, but something the old groom had said worried her.

'Who, Mr Butler? Who will you see off?'

'Them as are likely t' come after thee, lass, ' he replied factually. 'Them scallywags up there; most o' them 'll be sleeping 't off come one or two o'clock when folks leave t' do, but there's a few lads supposed t' be waiting out front with drivers. An' when they're not where they're supposed t' be, some'uns likely t' come looking for 'em in t' stables, an' they might just notice carriage missin', 'specially if Cooper lads have owt t' do wi'it.' He turned around with an armful of harness and a hunting rifle. 'Better make 'aste.'

Worry set itself on Emily's face as she saw the rifle.

'Don't worry thysen, lass. Any folks is around in a storm like this has got t' be mad. 'Tis just a precaution.'

William and Emily followed Robert into the stable, where he picked out a horse. William tied sacking around its hooves whilst Emily helped Robert to put on the bridle and harness. The Fernleigh Berlin carriage was positioned near to the door of the coach house and they had no trouble fixing the harness to the thill and leading it out. They needn't have bothered with the sacking: the rain was beating down so hard that it drowned even the noise of wheel on cobblestone. William gave Robert his cloak as additional protection against the driving downpour and told him to head northwards on the track that led past the paddocks so that they could retrieve the saddlebags.

Emily had brought with her two good dresses, a small assortment of underclothes, her comb and brush, a packet of letters and a shell that Will had given to her. She wore her loop of the gimmel ring on her left ring finger. She bundled her few possessions into the carriage and climbed in after them.

Once out of the stable yard they set off at full gallop northwards towards the ridge. The ground was soaking and the track nothing more than two mud-filled ruts, making progress difficult, and they had to slow down substantially; however, they made it to the edge of the wood. William jumped out of the carriage to search for the saddlebags whilst Robert removed the sacking from the horse's hooves. The night was as black as pitch. William cursed to himself, regretting that he had hidden his possessions so well. He'd made a mental note that they were next to a dense patch of brambles to the right of the birch tree with two branches pointing south that looked like arms, which stood just off the path leading to the top of the ridge, but it was hard to see anything. The woodland afforded little protection from the force of the storm, and what leaves were still on the trees were brown and withered and unable to stand up to the insistent rain. With every gust of wind, leaves were whipped from branches and thrown around in the air like snowflakes in a blizzard. Leaves swirled around William's face and rain stung his eyes.

Suddenly Emily and Robert were at his side, scrambling around in the undergrowth, brambles scoring skin and ripping clothes, searching for the feel of leather. Eventually William found the saddlebags and dug them out. They returned to the track and wiped their hands and the bags on a patch of long grass, trying to remove the worst of the dirt.

'We can't go over t' ridge, Master William. Berlin'll not make it in this. Track's too muddy. We'd best 'ead back along track 'til we meet with t' Brockley Road that skirts t' ridge. Then we'll 'ead north-west through Thirsk.'

William nodded grimly. 'We're in your hands, Robert.'

'Best get goin'. We've more than thirty miles t' cover wi' only one nag, an' if we stay 'ere much longer we'll get stuck.'

William dug into one of the bags and pulled out the deerskin, which he insisted Robert wrap around his shoulders, and they set off again. Once inside the carriage William and Emily packed her possessions into the empty saddlebag, the inside of which was still surprisingly dry. William opened out the woollen rug and they huddled up underneath it as best they could, William's arm around her shoulder, her head against his chest.

William stroked Emily's hair and cheek with his free hand. Her face was wet, whether with rain or tears he could not tell in the gloom of the dimly-lit carriage. But she turned her face to look up at him with such exquisite tenderness that it filled him with an almost unbearable longing and he gathered her to him and kissed her with a passion so strong he felt that it would consume them both.

The single candle, imprisoned in its brass lantern, finally gave up and spluttered out in the draft, and they held each other tightly as the carriage sped through the storm towards their destiny.

As the carriage left the stable yard all was quiet but for the incessant rain, which drowned out the raucous noise originating from the hayloft. The men were clearly enjoying their beer and brandy. With Robert gone, one lone figure remained, now hidden in a stall in the eastern stable block, looking out over the cobblestones at the disappearing carriage wheels.

Rachel hadn't heard everything that had passed between the old groom, Master William and that hussy, but she'd heard enough. She hadn't been in the least bit surprised when Emily had appeared. She had been waiting and waiting for this very moment. Those Cooper boys were useless – they were supposed to be on the lookout. She'd have to raise them. She wasn't shy about entering a hayloft full of drunken men; she gave them a mouthful for their lewd banter and grabbed the nearest Cooper boy, which happened to be Brian. She caught him by the hair, whispered to him and encouraged him to get to his feet. He grinned, first at her and then at the others, as she led him towards the ladder. The men cheered and whooped and Brian looked delighted to be singled out. Various vulgar remarks were hurled in his general direction as he disappeared from view.

Once safely away from the loft, she slowed her pace and he, stumbling to catch up, launched himself towards her, grabbing her breasts from behind. She allowed him a moment or two of fumbling to keep him wanting before turning and slapping him hard across his face. He stumbled back, surprised, hand on cheek.

'Waass that fer?'

'Tha was supposed t' be lookin' out fer Master William or Emily Popple! Tha bloody lazy doylum. Ah can 'ardly go t' house t' report on them m'self, can ah!'

'Eh?' He was trying desperately to register the meaning of her words.

'Master William an' Emily!' she repeated, frustrated. 'They've taken coach an' 'orse an' taken off t'gether! Not only that; owd Robert 'as only gone wi' 'em.'

Rachel shook Brian Cooper by the edges of his unbuttoned jacket. 'We 'ad a deal. Now it's time for thee t' fulfil thy part!'

The young stable lad stood there swaying, blurred thoughts echoing around his head, his vision going in and out of focus. Rachel became more angry, grabbed a nearby bucket that was half full of water and threw it over him. She dodged his arm as he swung towards her, fists clenched, in reaction to the soaking, then ran at him, tipping him over into a pile of hay.

'Sober up, man!'

She left him to go and get his brother. Two drunken tykes were probably better than one. Climbing the ladder again, she emerged head and shoulders into the hayloft and hollered to Stephen Cooper, beckoning him towards her.

'Bloody 'ell, he wor quick!' someone yelled, and the bawdy comments started up again.

'Ah'm next!' a dirty-looking lad announced as he knelt up and began unbuttoning his breeches.

'Sit down, man, or ah'll slap thee daft, ' Stephen uttered in a low voice as he pushed the lad backwards and headed past him to the ladder. As he climbed down he gave them a wave and grinned. 'Carry on wi'out me, lads'.

Another cheer and the men went back to the serious business of drinking.

As Stephen reached the bottom of the ladder he swung around and caught hold of Rachel's wrist, pulling her towards him. His eyes narrowed as she pulled away from him and he grabbed her around the waist and dragged her into an empty stall. She turned and let him kiss her, but as she pulled away again to tell him about the elopement, he pushed her to the floor and clasped one hand over her mouth as he positioned himself on top of her.

Rachel had to think quickly. Brian Cooper was easy to handle but his brother could be dangerous, especially when he was half sober.

She'd miscalculated. But time was moving on, and with every minute that carriage would be farther away. She lay still. She'd learned that struggling was of no use. He liked a struggle and it incited his violent nature.

'Now now, missy, ' he breathed menacingly close to her face. 'Tha'll not refuse yer favourite Cooper.'

She shook her head and he freed her mouth.

She spoke quickly. 'Ah wouldn't refuse thee, tha knows. Tha can take what tha wants, but be quick about it – Master William an' Emily eloped not fifteen minutes since in direction of Northallerton. Thee and thy brother 'ave a job t' do. We 'ad a deal.'

He raised his eyebrows, and a slow sneer came over his face. He had the upper hand.

'Fifteen minutes ago, y' say? Ah, well, a few more minutes won't make any difference then will 't? If tha does what ah say, missy, we'll be on track carryin' out t' plan in no time.'

He pulled a dagger from his belt, slid it under the laces of her stays and slit the cords. Then, ripping her shift downwards, he exposed her full breasts before pulling up her petticoat. He used each of her orifices in turn, roughly turning her this way and that like a rag doll, his movements becoming fiercer and fiercer until at last he was spent.

Inwardly Rachel was afraid and silently pleading for it to be over. Outwardly she showed no signs of her anxiety, no emotion. She gritted her teeth through the ordeal. This wasn't the first time and no doubt it would not be the last. It was a means to an end. Nothing more or less. And if the end meant getting her position back or, even better, proving her worth to the Fernleighs and becoming a lady's maid, it was a small price to pay.

Once he'd let go of her Rachel half staggered to where Brian was sitting, trying to rearrange her garments as she did so. Stephen was close behind her. He kicked his brother's leg.

'Get thysen up, brother. We've a job t' do.'

Brian headed out into the rain towards the house to fulfil his part of the plan. The soaking had sobered him up a little, and the weather did the rest. He was looking forward to getting himself in the warm for a little while. He might even get a bit of late supper.

Stephen saddled up a chestnut gelding and set off in pursuit of the carriage. He was bound to catch it, as he'd be able to make much quicker progress, especially in this storm. Indeed, the storm was a good screen and would allow him to conceal his presence from them easily. He put his head down against the wind and let the gelding have his.

Robert, William and Emily reached Northallerton just after five in the morning and put in at the Fleece Inn. The landlord was somewhat grumpy at being woken, but begrudgingly produced a pot of hot coffee and some cold mutton and pickled walnuts with a small loaf of bread. He also instructed a maid to stoke up the fire in one of the sitting rooms and set a fire in one of the upstairs chambers, and instructed his boy to see to the exhausted horse.

The three of them gathered around the burgeoning flames, trying to warm their tired bodies until their aching muscles relaxed a little. Having consumed the coffee and mutton they began to feel a little better, though they were not sated. William ordered some eggs and more coffee. Robert disappeared to make enquiries about possibilities for their onward journey, and reported back that there would be a stagecoach passing through at around ten o'clock that morning heading northwest towards Cockermouth and another arriving later that morning on its way to Newcastle. They agreed that when questioned, Robert should say that they had taken the route to the port of Newcastle in search of a passage to Holland.

William bade Emily go and rest, assuring her that he would be following in a short while. She said goodbye to Robert Butler and thanked him for his part in their absconsion, wishing him Godspeed on the journey home.

William and the old groom shared the remaining contents of William's flask by the fire and William urged him to sleep a while in their sitting room.

'I thank thee, Master William. Ah may just rest mi owd bones a little longer. Then ah'll be 'eading back.'

296

The groom winced quietly as he moved his legs to a slightly different position and settled himself in the chair.

William looked at him kindly. 'I cannot thank you enough, Robert, for your loyalty and kindness. I really don't know how we'd have managed without you.' William paused. 'It's hard to serve two masters. That moment... in the stable... there was a look in your eyes. Why did you decide to help us?'

Robert shifted in his chair again and gazed into the fire with a faraway expression. He didn't look at William but eventually he spoke softly.

'Please don't think ah'm speaking out o' turn, Master William, but ah've seen a certain look in thy eyes in recent times. Same look as ah seen in thy father's eyes many moons ago. Once, an' only once mind – an' ah 'ave t' say 'e wor mighty... well 'e wor off 'is 'ead – thy father confided in me. 'E wor reet un'appy, ' Robert shook his head sadly, 'reet un'appy. E' loved this lass y' see, loved 'er wi' all 'is heart. But 'e couldn't marry 'er; wouldn't never 'ave been allowed. Besides that he wor married t' thy mother.' The groom gave a sigh. 'Ah'll never know who she wor, an' that doesn't matter 'ere an' now, any road. But ah do know one thing... it broke 'is heart, it did, an' that's a fact. Broke all communication with 'er. Dedicated 'is life t' thy mother.' Robert lowered his head.

William felt a mixture of shock and sadness. The groom's revelation had taken him by surprise. He recalled the words that his father had spoken to him only hours before. ...*You think I haven't known what it is to give your heart and soul to another, to adore someone with such a passion that you'd die for her...* William downed the remains of his brandy and ran his hands through his hair. Resting his elbows on his thighs, he held his heavy head in his hands and stared at the floor, not seeing the worn oak floorboards beneath his boots.

'He chose duty, ' he muttered.

Robert looked at William fondly and spoke softly. 'Tha must know, Master William, in thy 'eart, thy mother an' father grew t' love one another. Tha can see as well as me, they're t' happiest pair ah ever did see, of that ah'm sure. S' don't fret thysen over an owd man's remembering. But ah'll never forget t' look in thy father's eyes that evening when 'e confided in me. That's why ah'm helping thee, Master William, though doubtless ah'll lose my position over 't. Ah couldn't bear to see thee suffer like thy father once did.'

William smiled grimly and nodded. 'Thank you Robert, for being honest with me. I will ensure that you do not suffer any consequences on my account. I will write to my father assuring him that you had no part in this; that it was I who instructed you to bring us here and not to utter a word to anyone about it.'

He put his hand in his pocket, pulled something out and pressed it into the old man's hand, covering it with his own.

'I must retire and get a few hours sleep, and I suggest you try to do the same. Farewell, Robert. I hope we shall meet again in better circumstances. Please take this – if not for yourself, for your family.'

Sadness wrote its name on Robert Butler's features as he tried to smile. He doubted very much that he would see this young man again.

'Ah'll sithee, Master William. Godspeed.'

Robert watched William leave the room, then opened his hand. Lying flat in his palm were three shining gold guineas.

Emily was asleep when William reached their bedchamber. The room had warmed up nicely and the fire threw a comforting glow around the room. William quickly undressed, set his wet clothes by the hearth and climbed into bed beside her. She stirred and murmured but did not wake. As troubled as his mind was, he was asleep within minutes.

Nine

Late October 1762

When Brian Cooper appeared, banging on the door to the kitchen passage, the house steward answered the call. He shouted to the caller to make himself known. The slow thick tones of Brian Cooper were recognisable anywhere, and he was admitted into the servants' hall and allowed a seat near the fire.

Mr Arbuth called for a glass of beer to be brought, and after a few minutes to allow the young under groom to warm himself, called the lad into his office. He could smell liquor on the man's breath and guessed there'd be trouble brewing. He shut the door against prying ears.

Brian gathered himself and determinedly set down his tankard on the steward's desk. He spoke slowly, as if repeating lines he had learned and was having trouble remembering.

'Master William 'as taken carriage... no... no... Robert Butler and Emily Popple... no.' he corrected himself, took a deep breath and started again. 'Master William an' Emily Popple 'ave made off in carriage an'... an' Robert Butler, 'e's driving it. Northallerton. Yes. Northallerton is where they're going, like.' He paused. 'We thought thee should know, ' he added concernedly, for effect.

Mr Arbuth let out a long sigh, rose from his chair and told the groom to stay where he was and on no account to move or speak to anyone else. He called Mrs Cumley into his office and instructed the other staff to carry on as they were, adding that the ravings of a drunken man were of no concern to anybody.

He and Martha Cumley stood with their backs to Brian Cooper talking in low tones. Martha fought to keep her composure as she heard the news and put a hand on the windowsill to steady herself, the other to her neck. Percival Arbuth had chosen to speak with Mrs Cumley initially as he was aware that she had also spoken with the Cutter girl. This news, if indeed it was true – and that they had yet to establish – sounded ominously as though the Cutter lass had been telling the truth. If this was the case it was a shock indeed. That a lord, or his son in this case, should bed a servant girl was hardly unusual, if a little cruel and certainly ungentlemanly; yet a liaison was one thing and elopement quite another.

The cat was out of the bag. Martha Cumley decided that she should at least confirm the liaison, but kept her counsel about Emily's condition. Percival Arbuth turned his head and his sharp eyes focused on Brian Cooper, who was humming to himself, lost in a haze again.

'There's more to this than meets the eye, ' he decided.

Martha agreed. The house steward opened the door to his office and ushered the under groom out, giving instructions to a nearby maid to fetch him some supper.

'I'll deal with this matter and you keep quiet. Do you understand?' he said in a low threatening voice as the Cooper boy left his office.

It was not a question but an order. At least Brian Cooper recognised that. Any road, he'd done what he'd been told to do and now he was looking forward to a bit of supper. He settled himself at one end of the long table and tucked into a nice piece of boiled tongue and a large piece of veal pie.

Meanwhile Martha and Percival had to decide what to do. Each had their reasons for wanting to protect Emily, yet each knew that the matter could not be contained much longer. They agreed that Rachel was involved with the Cooper twins, and that this must somehow be linked to Brian Cooper's presence at the house tonight. So what was the purpose of an under groom reporting – on the face of it – the use of a carriage by the master's son? Whether anyone else was in the carriage or not should matter not to such a person. The head groom was driving it. Both men out-ranked Brian Cooper. Brian was a nice lad: gentle and slow-spoken – he wasn't one to raise his head above the parapet. No – either his brother had put him up to it or it was the Cutter lass. Martha and Percival couldn't see what Stephen Cooper had to gain, either. It had to be Rachel. Was she hoping to regain her position? More likely she was after Emily's.

They decided that they should do nothing until the morning. When questioned, they would say that they had not believed the ramblings of a drunken lad, preferring to trust in the good nature of his lordship's son. At least this might give the couple a few hours' grace. Lord Fernleigh was sure to send men after them to bring them back.

Brian Cooper was dispatched back to the stables with a stern warning to sober up and to caution anyone else who might be in the same state to do the same, or there would be trouble for them in the morning. As he exited through the kitchen passage door, followed closely by Percival Arbuth, Brian turned for a moment.

'Oh... ah forgot t' say...', he frowned and stared into space, trying to remember what he had forgotten to tell them that he had remembered only seconds before. 'Oh aye, ' he focused briefly on the house steward's stern face, 'm' brother's gone after 'em... t' Northallerton. ''E'll track 'em down, thee'll see if 'e won't. 'E'll wait in Northallerton for reinforcements.' He nodded, pleased with himself, then muttered, 'Though knowing 'im, e'll not wait long.'

Percival Arbuth watched him swaying and staggering in the direction of the stables for a few moments before shutting the heavy door and locking and bolting it again. Having done so, he turned and leaned against it, letting out a deep breath, dismayed by the last intelligence. Stephen Cooper could be unpredictable. But surely he wouldn't harm Robert Butler, and certainly not Master William? That would be counterproductive if he was to keep his position. And if Emily Popple was in their care, she would be safe too. No; Percival decided that this was more likely a bit of bravado to ingratiate themselves with his lordship. He should stick to the plan agreed with Mrs Cumley.

Stephen Cooper had caught up with the Berlin within a couple of hours. The conditions had made the going difficult and there was no moon to guide him, but he knew his way to Northallerton and there was only one route fit for a carriage. He had kept what he judged to be a safe distance and followed them all the rest of the way. Their exhausted horse and the carriage had been accommodated at the back of the Fleece Inn. He watched and waited for the boy to feed and water the horse and disappear back into the inn, then he led his own horse into the stable, located the feed and water and saw to it himself. He rested a while until he heard people about again and, leading his horse back out of the stable, applied for something to eat at the kitchen door.

Presently he settled himself and his mount further along the main street, across the road behind a large oak on a patch of green. The gelding busied itself munching the grass. Stephen Cooper positioned himself so that he could just see the front of the Fleece Inn and waited. Dawn brought much coming and going: servants bringing their master's horses around from the stables, carts drawing up with deliveries, a packhorse owner making calls and folks going in and out. Neither Master William and Emily nor Robert Butler were anywhere to be seen.

Stephen began to feel impatient. Where were his lordship's men? Surely they should be here by now if his brother had played his part and delivered the message. Doubts flitted across his mind for a moment and then he dismissed them. Rachel would have made sure that Brian had done what he was supposed to do. Stephen smiled to himself. She was a fiery lass, that one. She wasn't going to give up easily. She thought she controlled him, but it was the other way around and he enjoyed letting her know it on a regular basis.

The gelding had strayed a little so he pulled it back, closer to him behind the tree. He took another look in the direction of the inn and recognised the old groom standing outside talking to a man in a black coat and brown breeches. They seemed to be deep in conversation for a while and then they shook hands and the stranger walked up the street and disappeared into a side alley, whilst Robert went back inside the inn. Presently a stagecoach and four horses passed him and pulled up outside the Fleece.

William and Emily appeared in the doorway followed by two servants carrying saddlebags.

Damn! Where the hell were Fernleigh's men?

Stephen jumped to his feet and gathered his horse's reins, unsure of his next move. At that moment the Berlin appeared from the yard at the back of the inn with Robert in the driver's seat. The carriage was being pulled by a black cob and the original Cleveland bay had been tied to the back of the carriage on a long rope. The old groom brought his carriage around to the back of the stagecoach, facing down the street towards Stephen. The saddlebags were loaded onto a rack on top of the stage and William and Emily climbed aboard.

Fernleigh's men were obviously not going to make it in time. Stephen had to decide what to do. He opted for recovering the Berlin; at least he could do that much and make himself look good. But first he had to find out where the stage was bound and how far William and Emily would be travelling. He tied the chestnut to a low branch and waited for the stage to leave. Shortly afterwards the Berlin passed the oak tree, heading south again. Stephen crossed the street and walked quickly to the inn. He called to one of the servants who had carried William's bags and asked him where the stage was bound. Once he had his answer he bought some beer to fill his canteen and proceeded back to his mount.

As he rounded the tree and took hold of its reins, something hard struck him on the back of his head and he fell to the ground in pain, clutching his skull. The pain seared through his head from where the blow had been struck to his forehead and behind his eyes, making him sick and dizzy. He couldn't focus his eyes; the world seemed to be spinning and growing dark. The last blurred image he had was of a man leaning over him, dressed in brown and black.

The Fernleigh house was in an uproar. In his dressing room, on hearing the news from Percival Arbuth of his son's disappearance with his wife's lady's maid, Thomas had turned puce, the skin at his temples throbbing and his mouth twitching in a most peculiar manner until at length he could begin to shape it around vowels and consonants – which in point of fact he could barely control. Eventually, and in deadly earnest, he began a campaign of damage limitation and attempted recovery of the dreadful situation. Speaking slowly, and indeed, as it seemed to his house steward, most strangely as if through clenched teeth, Thomas managed to recover himself sufficiently to issue a very deliberate set of instructions.

The steward was to instruct the few staff who knew what had happened not to utter a single word about it to anyone on pain of dismissal, and they were to be sure that he would carry out his threat. The house was full of guests and their staff, and on no account was this to be made known to anyone, with the exception of Thomas's three sons-in-law, who were to be informed discreetly and were to meet him in his study within the hour. Thomas himself would break the news to her ladyship. Their house guests were to be informed that she was unwell and had taken to her chamber. Thomas instructed Percival Arbuth to consult with Mrs Preedy and appoint a suitable temporary replacement lady's maid for his wife until they could find a more permanent resolution. Mrs Preedy and the other staff were to be told that Emily had been taken ill and fetched home to her mother, where she was not to be disturbed. If anyone asked after William, he had been called to London on urgent business.

Arbuth dismissed, Thomas poured himself a large whisky and drew himself together to face his wife. He was kind and considerate according to his sensibilities, but also resolute with regard to the proper course of action.

No-one was allowed to disturb Lady Fernleigh that day with the exception of Mrs Cumley, who had been instructed by the house steward to take her ladyship some broth. However, if the staff had been allowed access to their mistress they would have seen the most terrible sight: disappointment and betrayal, heartache and dismay, incomprehension and bewilderment; and sobbing quietly into a goose-feather pillow to avoid being heard.

Percy Foster, James Napier and Bertram Chatham slipped away from the house guests and saddled up. It appeared that some of the stable lads were a little the worse for wear; there was much groaning and clutching of heads, and some, it was said, had not surfaced at all that morning. There would be consequences, that much was obvious. However, the three men were highly focused on their immediate task: to seek out Robert Butler and his charges, the runaway pair, and to apprehend them and return them to the hunting lodge at Fernleigh Hall in the most discreet manner. From there they were to be dispatched without delay to their separate fates; William to Oxford and Emily to Charlotte's cousin in Devon.

Thomas' three sons-in-law set off with grim determination in the direction of Northallerton. The ground was sodden after the night's storm; however, being skilled horseman and following Colonel Napier's expert military judgement they chose the fastest route across country, avoiding both the major areas of low-lying land, which had become exceedingly boggy, and the potholed roads, which were nothing if not treacherous for a horse's delicate fetlocks, and in any case did not afford a direct route to their target.

The bright cold air stung their faces like lemon juice on cracked lips as they galloped across arable and pasture, over ridge and through dale. Three miles or so from Northallerton the men skirted west to come upon the Thirsk road, which ran south from Northallerton. This was likely to be the route that the carriage had taken. A mile and a half south of the market town they came upon the missing Berlin with old Robert Butler in the driver's seat, a black cob pulling it at a walking pace towards them and a tired-looking bay walking behind.

The three men quickly surrounded the party. The air was thick with horse and man sweat. Their beasts' flanks were flecked with foam and their sides rose and fell deeply as they began to recover their breath. They snorted at the carriage and blew towards the horses attached to it, gauging whether friend or foe. Percy seized the bridle of the cob as James came alongside the carriage and mounted the driver's seat. He made to knock the groom to the ground, but the old man put up no fight. His face was tired; his worn skin hung loosely over his cheek bones and the rims of his eyes were a reddish hue. Indeed, to their surprise it looked as if the old man had been crying.

The groom handed the reins to his subjugator, doffed his hat and greeted each of his pursuers briefly but courteously.

'Colonel Napier, Mr Foster, Mr Chatham.'

Bertram Chatham was checking inside the carriage and, finding it empty, informed the others.

'Where is Master William? What have you done with him?' Napier barked, his perspiration-laden face inches from Butler's.

The groom sounded remorseful and downhearted. 'Please, Colonel Napier, ah wor only followin' orders, so ah wor. Ah truly am sorry like, t' go agin Lord Fernleigh. That is t' say agin what ah suspect Lord Fernleigh'd wish. 'Course isn't ma business what 'is Lordship wishes and what 'e don't.'

Robert was carefully playing for time, at once attempting to placate the obvious anger of the three hunters whilst doing his best to delay their progress. If they did not believe him and took it upon themselves to conduct their own investigations they might well discover that a stage bound for Cockermouth had left Northallerton only a little over two hours ago, and indeed that the stage for Newcastle had departed not an hour ago. Whichever they chose to pursue there was a fair chance that they would catch up with it, given fresh horses, which they would no doubt be able to procure with ease. If they chose to chase the Newcastle coach they would of course discover before many hours had passed that Master William and his fiancée were not aboard; however at least if they decided to head north towards Newcastle it would delay their progress in any other direction for some further critical hours. Of course, who was to say that these loyal servants of his lordship, his dutiful kin, would not split up and pursue a number of courses or indeed engage more men to assist in their quest?

'I tell you, man! My patience is expended and you too are expendable in this matter! You will tell us where it is that Master William is gone or by God, man, you will feel the sting of my whip!'

Percy Foster's enraged and menacing tones broke through the veil of thought into Robert Butler's consciousness. The earl was not to be put off any longer. Following his orders, the old man compliantly confessed that Master William had informed him that he and Miss Popple were headed for Holland and meant to sail from the port of Newcastle. On further questioning he added that he did not know whether they had taken a stage or employed the services of a private carriage and driver. All he knew was that they had departed before him and he had not seen them since his eyes had closed in front of the fire at the Fleece Inn, where he had sat with a belly full of eggs and his wet clothes steaming as they dried over his aching old bones.

Colonel Napier gave the old man back the reins, removed himself from the driver's seat of the Berlin and remounted his horse. He was anxious to continue the pursuit and it was obvious that they could glean nothing further from the old groom. He had been acquainted with the man for some years and he knew him to be a loyal sort. His father-in-law had certainly spoken well of him. There was nothing more to be done here.

'Get you home, man, and do not breathe a word of what has passed to anyone. Do you understand? *No-one.* You have been on an errand for Lord Fernleigh, nothing more.'

Napier's piercing eyes sternly fixed on Robert Butler, conveying a message of warning. *Do as I say, and you will not take the blame in this matter. Disobey, and you'll rue it for the rest of your life.* It was a look that had served him well in his command of regiments, often in difficult and dangerous situations. His men had obeyed and respected him.

Robert Butler was not about to cross him. Indeed, he'd done all he could. The matter was out of his control.

'Aye, Sir. I thank thee, Sir.' Robert bowed his head.

Foster let go of the cob's bridle and the Berlin continued slowly on its way home. Foster, Napier and Chatham proceeded into Northallerton and headed immediately for the Fleece Inn. They entered the hostelry in a most portentous and ominous manner, commanding instantaneous attention from the frightened barmaid, who rushed at once to fetch the landlord. Within moments a stocky, slightly dishevelled man entered the bar, wiping his hands on a grubby cloth; but he was not to be intimidated. He informed Colonel Napier that he was not acquainted with anyone bearing the name of Fernleigh.

That much was true, William had not used his real name, and had chosen the Fleece Inn principally because when visiting Northallerton for the cattle markets, he and his father lodged at the Crown, which was situated at the other end of the main street.

The landlord was questioned further, the three men giving detailed descriptions of the man and woman they sought.

'Oh, aye, ' mumbled the barman at length, scratching his beard. 'Tha means Mr Rawson an' 'is wife. Weren't 'ere fer long. Woke me up, they did! All t' same, reet polite like. Y' mean Rawson weren't 'is real name? Cheeky bugger!'

'Where are they? Which chamber are they in?' Foster demanded, impatience pulling at his features.

'They're not 'ere, ' replied the Barman shortly, disliking being addressed in such a manner.

'Well, where the bloody hell did they go, you insolent man?' Foster continued, pointing his riding crop into the landlord's face, its tip inches from his nose.

Bertram Chatham interposed. Placing a hand on the crop and lowering it, he stepped in front of Foster and spoke calmly.

'My dear man, we have come a long way in search of Mr Fernleigh and he is most urgently sought. If he and the... er... lady have departed your premises, did they happen to mention where they were bound?'

The barman stuck his hands in the pockets of his crumpled coat and looked at the three gentlemen in front of him. His fingers closed upon something hard and round in his right pocket.

'Newcastle wor mentioned'. He spoke sullenly. 'An' if tha wants t' know, ' he addressed Chatham, 'stage fer Newcastle left 'ere an 'our or so since. If tha hurries, thee'll m'be catch 'em up by nightfall. Them stages can make a bit o' progress these days.' He added the last for effect.

Napier and Foster were already halfway to the door. Chatham thanked the landlord and asked where they could find fresh horses.

'Out t' back. M' boy'll see to ye.'

As they left the room the landlord turned his back on them and smiled. 'That's what tha gets fer showin' no respect, ' he muttered to himself. 'Any road, them other folks wor respectful despite their standing, an' they paid well.'

He hadn't exactly lied. Newcastle was indeed mentioned, but not in the context he'd just implied.

The three men led their horses around the side of the inn to the stables at the back. Napier spoke to the stable boy, negotiating fresh mounts and making arrangements to recover their own in due course. As they were talking, Chatham noticed a man lying in an empty stall, seemingly unconscious. The man's face looked familiar, but he couldn't quite place him. He stepped closer to examine his face. Recollection came upon him slowly, revealing snippets of blurred images, nothing quite in focus. For some reason he thought he'd seen this man that morning at his father-in-law's stables – but that couldn't be right, could it? He looked up at the stable lad, who gave him a wide grin.

'Insensible 'e is. Too much of the old…' He made a sign with his hand of a beaker being turned upwards towards his mouth. 'Out cold. Sleep it off's t' best thing fer 'im.'

At length, furnished with fresh horses, Napier, Foster and Chatham set off after the Newcastle stage, leaving Stephen Cooper to come to his senses in his own time.

A chambermaid awoke William and Emily at around nine. They rose, dressed in fresh clothes, breakfasted and were ready to leave by ten o'clock. They took the stagecoach bound for Cockermouth and Workington as far as Brough, some forty miles to the north-west, travelling between the wild moorlands of County Durham and Cumbria to the north and the wilderness of the Yorkshire Dales to the south. The day was fresh and bright and nothing remained in the air of the previous night's storm. A steady breeze blew from the south-west, which had the effect of drying the rain-soaked ground so that by the middle of the afternoon their passage along the roads became a little easier. The stage made stops at Richmond, Barnard Castle and Appleby to change horses before reaching Brough just after five o'clock that evening.

There were still a couple hours of daylight left, and William was keen to make further progress. He managed to rent two horses and paid an ostler to accompany them for the next part of their journey and then return the animals. They pushed on to Penrith, reaching the town just after eight o'clock exhausted and aching in every joint. They took a room at the Dockray Inn, where William ordered supper to be brought to their room and made enquiries about onward travel. It was some twenty miles to Carlisle, and a further ten miles or so to the Scottish border. He determined that they should make it to Carlisle by around two o'clock on the Lancaster–Carlisle stage. From there he planned to acquire horses or a carriage for the remaining journey. He did not wish to waste time on another overnight stop.

Their room was warm and cosy with a fire burning merrily in the grate. Heavy red velvet curtains arrested the cold beyond the casement window and the chamber was prettily furnished with a mahogany desk-cum-dressing table, a mahogany table with two chairs to match situated beside the window, and an armchair on either side of the fire. In the centre of one wall there stood a comfortable carved oak four-poster bed, and there was a washstand in one corner next to a small oak wardrobe.

Emily was busy hanging up their crumpled clothes – those that were reasonably clean. She left the doors to the wardrobe open to give the musty material some warm air. She would need help to wash her woollen gown and Will's brown breeches and twill coat. She had tried brushing them firmly, but the mud stains had refused to budge. She was on her way out of their room in search of a sink when a maid appeared, bringing wine. The maid looked surprised when Emily enquired where she could wash the clothes, and promptly removed them downstairs to be attended to by the laundry maid. Emily had to remind herself that she must play the part of the gentlewoman, and scolded herself for making such an error. They could not afford to arouse suspicion.

She'd no sooner taken a seat by the fireside when William appeared. As he strode across the room she gazed at him. Illuminated by the radiance of the blaze and the glimmer of the candles on the mantelpiece and table, he had a glow about him, a warmth that seemed not just a reflection of his cosy surroundings but perhaps a manifestation of his happiness at the two of them being together, alone; the beginning of many such times.

Emily's intuition was seldom wrong. He hung his jacket on a chair and held out his arms to her, grasped hers and pulled her out of the chair towards him. Then, clasping her around the waist, he swung her off her feet in a circle. She laughed and held onto him. They kissed, a long, slow exquisite kiss that seemed to melt her mind and her heart, sending waves of excitement through her flesh, making her fingertips tingle and her knees weak. He slipped a hand beneath the silk covering her breast, cupping her in his fingers. She emitted a groan as her body cried out for his.

There was a knock at the door. Giddily, Emily steadied herself on the edge of the bed whilst William went to answer it. It was the maid with their veal pie supper. William bade her place the tray on the table, gave her a coin and locked the door behind her against the world.

He was full of intent as he returned to Emily. He picked her up and deposited her in the middle of the bed then leaned over and kissed her, this time with urgency, and she responded equally. William slid a hand beneath her skirts and stroked the inside of her leg, moving his fingers upwards with small strokes. She closed her eyes and gave herself to the delicious sensations beginning deep inside. He reached the place where she joined but did not linger there, instead tantalisingly brushing one finger directly over her before moving his hand down to stroke the other leg. She gave a small cry and arched her hips towards him. He smiled. He was going to take his time; to savour the soft flesh of her thighs, the sensitive places behind her knees, the curve of her breasts, the fullness of her nipples, the smell of her, the taste of her.

He leaned back on his haunches and took one of her legs in his hands, raising it above the embroidered bedspread and resting her foot on his thigh. Slowly he removed her garter and rolled down her stocking, kissing the flesh beneath as he did so, before removing the other stocking in the same way. Pulling her from the bed towards him, he kissed her on the mouth whilst slipping one hand behind her back and pulling loose the laces that held her robe tight. Slipping her robe off her shoulders and over her arms revealed the swell of her breasts. He laid her back down, unlaced her stays and pulled them apart, stroking her stomach and breasts beneath the thin cotton shift. It was like unwrapping a present; a beautiful, soft, warm, delicious present. With each layer removed his anticipation grew, and hers too. She felt uncovered, exposed, vulnerable – and she delighted in it.

He made her stand and take off her shift, revealing her perfect nakedness. Her soft red curls fell around her ivory shoulders, glinting in the firelight, accentuating the beauty of her face, the slant of her green eyes. He sat for a moment, lost in the wondrous sight before him. Then he pulled off his shirt and slid off his breeches and stood in erect splendour before her.

'Till death us do part, ' he said quietly.

She nodded. 'Till death us do part, ' she whispered.

She folded her arms around his neck as he lifted her once more onto the bed. He spread her legs and put his face to her, tasting, probing with his tongue and then his fingers, kissing the delicate skin on her stomach and nipples and finally covering her mouth with his own as he entered her. Their bodies dissolved into each other as they were joined. She moaned as he drove himself deep inside her, cupping her buttocks, pulling her towards him. With each slow rhythmic thrust their exhilaration mounted and mounted until the final moments of ecstasy.

They lay, quiet in the afterglow, bodies entwined. At length, Emily pulled away from William slightly and turned to look at him.

'I have something to tell you.' She spoke quietly.

He kissed her forehead contentedly. 'What is it, my love?'

'I am with child.'

It took a few moments for the news to sink into his consciousness, for his mind to sift and register it. Then he was filled with the most indescribable elation.

'Oh, Emily, my sweet Emily! 'Tis wonderful news!' He gathered her to him and hugged her tightly as if he could never let her go. 'We are to have a child!' he murmured, as he rocked her to and fro. 'I cannot believe it... we are to have a child!'

She closed her eyes and smiled, and was full of contentment.

William and Emily reached Carlisle at around two-thirty the next day. The journey had been uneventful. The day had started with a white bright sky, however they had come into persistent drizzle soon after leaving Penrith. They rested and ate at the Rose and Crown. As the weather was inclement William decided to hire a small carriage and driver to take them on to Gretna Green, and bade the landlord to make enquiries. The next stagecoach travelling in that direction, en route to Glasgow, was not until the day after next.

By four o'clock they were on their way to the Scottish border with a little over ten miles to their final destination. They eventually arrived at Gretna Green as dusk settled its mantle over the small collection of whitewashed cottages. The mist had begun to seep through the village, curling its fingers around the houses, bleeding dampness into every nook and cranny. A church spire shot heavenwards as if trying to escape the earthly clutches of the fog.

They put in at the Queen's Head and, for the sake of decency, obtained two rooms. The inn was small but comfortable, and the chambermaid soon had fires going in their chambers. Whilst they waited for their supper William made discreet enquiries of the landlord, who beamed at him and informed him in a friendly, booming voice that there was no need for discretion this side of the border. All the same, William advised caution and wished for the ceremony to be performed as soon as it was possible to do so. It transpired that they had a choice of venues including a blacksmith's and another hostelry. Since a private dining room could be reserved for the purpose of marriage ceremonies at the Queens Head and because William did not think that Emily would want to be married in a blacksmith's shop, he decided upon their present accommodation.

The landlord, whose name was Kerr, seemed to be able to arrange everything. He explained that he would obtain the services of a Mr George Gordon, an old soldier who had a licence from the government to perform such ceremonies.

'He'll do well for ye,' Kerr affirmed. 'Ye'll need two witnesses. I can arrange a couple o' local laddies, or there's a bonny couple staying if ye'd like an introduction.' Kerr pointed out a respectably-dressed young couple dining in the tap room. William took up the offer of an introduction, but said that he first needed to go and make himself respectable after the day's travelling.

Emily had had the same thought, and was washing her face and hands when William knocked at the door. He told her of the arrangements made and she beamed at him, agreeing that they should speak to the couple Kerr had mentioned.

They took their supper downstairs in the tap room also. The white chicken broth soup with poached eggs was extremely tasty, and the dressed beef steaks and stuffed cabbage were delicious. They washed the excellent fare down with a respectable bottle of Burgundy and ordered French pancakes. At the port stage, Kerr made the introductions and they invited the young couple to join them.

It transpired that Mr and Mrs Kirkpatrick resided in Edinburgh and were en route from Carlisle, where they had been visiting Mr Kirkpatrick's aunt. Mr Kirkpatrick owned a successful printing business and gave William his card. They were recently married themselves, and were only too happy to act as witnesses for William and Emily. They discreetly refrained from enquiring after William's circumstances, discerning from his manner that he was likely a gentleman of high status. William had given Kerr, and thus Mr and Mrs Kirkpatrick, his real name, considering that this would be required in any case for the marriage to be legal. They had used a variety of false names on the journey in order to throw any would-be pursuers off the scent. Emily had preferred Mr and Mrs Hewitt to both Agar and

Rawson, but she couldn't wait to take William's name and had felt a little uncomfortable using fictitious names.

Kerr came to their table and confirmed that all was set for half past the hour of ten the following morning. They spent a pleasant evening conversing with the Kirkpatrick's and retired to their separate chambers respectably early.

Emily was awoken by the sound of knocking at her chamber door. She rubbed her eyes and rolled over to peek out between the red moreen curtains that clothed her bed, shielding her from drafts and cloaking her in privacy. The room was dark, though a gap in the matching moreen window hangings revealed that the dawn was just upon them. The knock came again. Emily sighed and reluctantly climbed out of the warm bed to answer it. She wanted to stay beneath the covers for just a few minutes more, relishing their kindly comfort. She opened the door to a chambermaid who had come to stoke the fire and deliver a surprise. Two more maids appeared, carrying a tin bath which they set in front of the fire. They disappeared and came back with large jugs of hot water with which they proceeded to fill the vessel, and one of them opened the window curtains just a little to let in the daylight. Seeing the look of surprise and delight on Emily's face, one of the girls remarked that they were following instructions from Mr Fernleigh, who had requested that his betrothed be allowed the luxury of a long soak on the morning of her wedding.

Emily was over the moon! This was indeed a treat! She couldn't wait for the bath to be filled. Once it was ready she removed her shift and stepped into it slowly, savouring the warmth between her toes, over her ankles and around her lower legs. She gently lowered her aching body below the steaming water. Her muscles seem to melt in the soothing liquid washing over them. The water was as hot as she could bear and she delighted in the rare sensation. Sinking further, she laid her head back into the water and luxuriated in the feel of the wet heat on her scalp and the sight of her curls emanating out across the surface of the water around her shoulders. She closed her eyes and sighed deeply in absolute contentment.

The maid had left a small bar of rose-petal soap for her to use, and after a little while Emily washed the dust and dirt from her hair and body and felt reborn. Relishing the remaining time until the water would become tepid, Emily lay back and gazed in delight at her wedding gown, which she had hung to air outside the wardrobe from the top of its door. She had insisted that she didn't need a new gown — she had her two best gowns with her, although admittedly they were rather crumpled and not a little dusty — but William had been equally insistent. He'd wanted her to feel cosseted, and he'd wanted her to have something new, something that only she would wear, unsullied by a previous owner.

They had had little time for the pursuit of such a thing. However, a couple of hours in Penrith had produced unexpectedly successful results. The light blue open-fronted mantua was beautifully complemented by a petticoat of shimmering ivory. The beautiful moiré silk caught the light and sent it in all directions so that the gown flickered and sparkled. Set in the window for display purposes, the gown was already made up and needed only a few alterations, which the seamstress had obligingly carried out within the hour. Emily had also chosen a new shift with Brussels lace around the cuffs and neckline which would be visible and complement her new gown perfectly.

It was time to leave the relaxing comfort of the bath and begin to experience the rising excitement of the events to come. Emily had almost not let herself believe that this day would ever arrive, and consequently had enjoyed the hope of it for what seemed like a very long time. To put away the hope in order to actually experience the event itself was in fact quite difficult and left her feeling a little vulnerable. However, as she stepped out of the water and began to dry herself in front of the fire; as the rising sun burned through the suspended mists of the previous night, sending them vanishing into the blue sky above; as she stroked the delicate lace and shimmering silk of her wedding gown with her fingertips; as the sunlight began to stream in through the gap in the curtains, bringing with it the promise of great things in this new day; as she combed her long hair and the strands began to separate and curl as they dried before the flames; and as she thought of Will and the life they were about to start together, Emily's hope turned at last to excitement, and the excitement mounted and grew and filled her heart until she felt she would burst with it.

They met in the private room downstairs. The friendly chambermaid had helped Emily into her gown and fixed her hair so that some of her curls were caught up together and others allowed the freedom to tumble down her back. As she entered the room, William, beautifully clothed in a new bright white cotton shirt, a silver-embroidered silk waistcoat and midnight-blue velvet coat and breeches, stepped forward to take her hand and kiss it as he bowed slightly before her. To her left stood Mr and Mrs Kirkpatrick smiling at her and in front of her was a gentleman in a red military dress uniform and jackboots, who also bowed to her and flamboyantly waved his large cocked hat.

'Emily, my dearest, let me present Mr George Gordon. He is to conduct our ceremony,' William explained.

'Mistress Popple,' the striking character nodded and smiled. 'Enchanted to meet you,' he said in a loud, forthright manner.

Emily curtsied a little nervously. 'Very good to meet you, Mr Gordon.'

As they moved towards a small table placed by the lead latticed window, William whispered to her, 'You look absolutely, stunningly beautiful!'

She gave him the most gorgeous smile; a smile which illuminated the room and filled him with love.

They clasped hands and Mr Gordon read from the Book of Common Prayer the Form of Solemnisation of Matrimony. Without a congregation present and due to the particular circumstances, Mr Gordon seemed to take leave to alter the familiar words somewhat. Emily had attended quite a number of marriage ceremonies for folk in the Brockby community and the service was generally familiar to her. But it mattered not; they were certainly not taking their matrimony lightly or wantonly, though no doubt some could accuse them of acting unadvisedly. They were most definitely entering into that holy state reverently and soberly, and above all discreetly, Emily reflected.

Mr Gordon read on. *'Firstly, it was ordained for the procreation of children, to be brought up in the fear and nurture of the Lord, and to the praise of his holy Name. Secondly, it was ordained for a remedy against sin, and to avoid fornication; that such persons as have not the gift of common continency might marry, and keep themselves undefiled members of Christ's body. Thirdly, it was ordained for the mutual society, help, and comfort, that the one ought to have of the other...'*

As Emily listened to the words being uttered by the formidable figure in red before them she wondered whether God might approve of this marriage. They had rather anticipated the first and second reasons for matrimony, having neither avoided fornication nor waited to engage in the procreation of children. However, Will's intention had always been to marry her, and she consoled herself with the thought that it was better to marry a little late than not at all. Surely God would approve of that?

'... any man can shew any just cause, why they may not lawfully be joined together, let him now speak, or else hereafter for ever hold his peace.'

Silence. Emily's heart involuntarily began to thump in her breast. After a few moments, Mr Gordon continued, looking first at William and then at her. *'I require and charge you both, as ye will answer at the dreadful day of judgement when the secrets of all hearts shall be disclosed, that if either of you know any impediment, why ye may not be lawfully joined together in Matrimony, ye do now confess it. For ye be well assured, that so many as are coupled together otherwise than God's Word doth allow are not joined together by God; neither is their matrimony lawful.'*

Mr Gordon paused again, playing his part with relish. William squeezed Emily's hand reassuringly whilst looking their licensee straight in the eye with a sober expression. Eventually Mr Gordon continued. *'Wilt thou have this woman to thy wedded wife,'* he smiled at William then, *'to live together after God's ordnance in the holy estate of matrimony? Wilt thou love her, comfort her...'*

Emily felt a thrill run through her body as William looked at her with exquisite tenderness and at last spoke: *'I will'*. Then it was her turn to make her vow to him. As she listened to the words being spoken, each took its rightful place in her heart in an orderly and proper fashion, slowly forming the oath by which she would live her life from this moment onwards; the promise to obey and serve him, to love and honour him, to care for him and to be faithful to him all the rest of her days.

'*... keep thee only unto him, so long as ye both shall live?*'

'*I will,* ' she declared with her heart and soul.

Subsequently they pledged their fidelity to one another. It was the first time that Emily had actually heard William's full name – William Thomas Joseph Fernleigh. It had a fitting ring to it, she thought. William spoke confidently and with conviction, holding her right hand in his as he spoke the promise '*... take thee to my wedded wife... Till death us do part, according to God's holy ordnance; and thereto I plight thee my troth.*'

Emily fought hard to hold back the emotion which threatened to turn to tears as she spoke. '*I, Emily Mary Popple, take thee, William Thomas Joseph Fernleigh, to my wedded husband...*' Her voice broke slightly. A polite cough came from somewhere to her left and she briefly glanced in its direction. Mrs Kirkpatrick, wearing a perceptive look of understanding and encouragement, gave an almost imperceptible nod. It was enough to give Emily the strength to find her voice. '*... to have and to hold, from this day forward, for better, for worse, for richer, for poorer, in sickness and in health...*' she continued, gaining confidence with every word, whilst William squeezed her hand tightly until she had finished her promise.

They smiled tenderly at one another, still holding hands, and Mr Gordon prompted William for the ring. William removed his band from the ring finger on his left hand and signalled to Emily to do the same. Both hoops were laid on the table in front of them, and William waited for Emily to provide the third. A flush of remembrance came over her as she realised that she did not have it in her possession. The glance she threw William was a mixture of concern and apology.

'My mother!' she whispered.

William understood. 'No matter, ' he returned her whisper kindly, 'they will all three be joined ultimately.'

His words comforted and reassured Emily. The implication that their marriage would, sooner or later, be witnessed by her mother, that she would see her family again and that she and her husband would face them together as one brought joy to her heart.

William joined the two hoops together and placed the circlet on the ring finger of Emily's left-hand. *'With this ring I thee wed, with my body I thee worship, and with all my worldly goods I thee endow. In the name of the Father and of the Son and of the Holy Ghost. Amen.'*

The booming voice of George Gordon came again. *'Those whom God hath joined together, let no man put asunder.'*

He smiled, evidently pleased with his performance. William was about to speak, but the ex-soldier held up his hands, signifying that he had not yet finished. He drew himself up to his full imposing height.

'For as much as William and Emily have consented together in holy wedlock, and have witnessed the same before God and this company', here he looked at Mr and Mrs Kirkpatrick, *'and thereto have given and pledged their troth either to other, and have declared the same by giving and receiving of a ring, and by joining of hands; I pronounce that they be man and wife together.'*

On hearing the last of these words William turned and stepped towards Emily, and taking her face in his hands, kissed her with a passion so great that it almost knocked her off her feet.

'Bravo!' Mr Kirkpatrick declared.

'I take it you don't wish me to read the psalm or the sermon, ' remarked Mr Gordon in a somewhat relieved tone.

William looked questioningly at Emily and she shook her head. They were truly man and wife! It was enough. William evidently felt the same and grinned at her. He turned to their self-appointed 'priest'.

'The parish register, Mr Gordon, as we agreed.'

'Aye, of course.'

The register was duly produced and William watched as the entry was written. He had furnished George Gordon with the particulars before the ceremony, and although it was unusual to remove the register from its residence in the church he had insisted to Kerr the previous evening that he wanted to witness the marriage being recorded, not wishing to trust it to anyone to record at a later date.

That done, William bade Mr Gordon stay and take some refreshments with them, which the man was only too pleased to do. Judging by his ruddy appearance, this was a regular perk of his well-chosen latter occupation.

The small party dined on delicious rolled partridge and roast lamb, followed by apple fritters with lashings of brandy cream. They celebrated with a claret and brandy punch. The Kirkpatricks were excellent company, and it transpired that they too had been married in Gretna Green not six months before. The particulars were not discussed, of course, but William and Emily discerned a distinct sense of fellowship that comes from a common understanding or a sharing of circumstance.

Later in the day William and Emily took some air. The day was bright, if a little cold, and they walked slowly through the village to the church. Emily took her husband's arm for the first time and the pride that filled her heart was manifest in the delight on her face. William could not keep the happiness he felt from pulling his mouth into a grin, and his eyes twinkled with it. Thus the love-struck couple floated down the main street.

They each said a prayer in the empty church before returning to their hostelry and retiring to their chamber. Their lovemaking was slow and deliberate, gentle and tender, each savouring the comforting sensation of unhurriedness. The minutes, hours, days and years now belonged to them and they could see their time together stretching into the far distance. It was a wonderful feeling.

The firelight flickered in Thomas' study, sending shapes around the cabinets and bookcases and over the Moorfields carpet, conferring a comforting glow on several of the depicted ancestors who stared down from the walls. No such comfort was felt by Thomas. The heat from the fire would neither warm his heart nor console his soul. He had of course quizzed Robert Butler on his return and was assured that the old man had simply been following orders. There was a deep remorsefulness about him, and Thomas cursed his son for putting the loyal groom in such a position.

What in God's holy name was his son thinking! Travelling to Holland! Although he prayed that his sons-in-law would apprehend the pair before it was too late, he feared the worst and had to do his duty. He sat down at his desk to write the most difficult letter of his life.

Daniel Popple was relaxing by the fire smoking his pipe when the banging at the door came. The dogs sprang up, barking. He instructed them to be quiet as he asked who was there. Once the messenger had declared himself and been allowed entry, he delivered the letter and waited for a reply. The dogs continued to growl quietly.

Daniel read the contents stone-faced, his features impenetrable, belying the torment of shock and emotion he began to feel inside.

'No response, thankin' thee, ' he nodded to the messenger, who promptly left.

Mary popped her head around the door from the kitchen, where she was putting away the last of the pots and plates. Daniel bade her come and sit with him by the fire and gave her the letter to read. Her stomach churned as she read the words, one hand over her mouth. At length she folded the parchment and stared into the fire.

'It is too late, ' she uttered in a small disconsolate voice.

Daniel's mind was racing. As he went over the written words in his head and thought on the situation he experienced rage, then hope, then rage and hope again in turn. Rage at the Fernleighs: they had promised to look after his daughter. Rage at William: he had trusted and liked Master Fernleigh. Rage at his daughter for not telling them. But didn't the letters say that Lord Fernleigh was doing everything possible to locate the couple and bring them back? That Thomas Fernleigh vouched for his son's intentions towards their daughter and for Emily's safety? Knowing Lord Fernleigh as he did, Daniel had no doubt that Thomas would relentlessly pursue all courses of action open to him until he had achieved his aim. And William – he was an honest, straightforward and kind man. They'd known him from a child. Surely he would not take advantage of a vulnerable young woman? *Woman*. The word sounded strange and false. She was not yet one and twenty. How could she know her own mind?

Mary was weeping into her hands and rocking back and forth in her chair. Daniel went to her, putting an arm around her shoulders and laying his head against hers. She turned to him, and flinging her arms about him, sobbed into his shoulder. He stroked her hair.

'Mary... Mary my love... *listen* to me. William's a good man. "E'll not use our Emily an' 'e'll see she comes t' no harm besides. They're misguided, but they must love one another... or they wouldn't 'ave run off t'gether. Console thyself with that.'

Mary shook her head but did not raise it.

'Too late, ' she repeated, and continued sobbing and mumbling to herself into the seam of his jacket.

Daniel pulled her in front of him. The emotions within were still raging, but he had to be strong for the sake of his wife. Concern knitted his brow but strength and compassion chose the words he spoke. He looked at her with gentle eyes and held her by the shoulders with powerful hands.

'Listen t' me. We must believe in 'er, our precious daughter. She'd not lie to us. She's most probably trying t' find t' right words. We 'ave t' believe in Master William an' all. We've known 'im all 'is life – 'e's not t' sort t' go takin' advantage, an' thee can see devotion to 'is family in 'is eyes.'

Aye, 'e'll not 'ave done this lightly, he thought.

He continued: 'Ten t' one they'll be back before tha knows it. An' Lord Fernleigh – 'e's not t' one t' be giving up neither. At this very moment there'll be folks out there looking fer our Emily, thee can be sure o' that, oh aye.'

Daniel wiped Mary's tears from her cheeks with his thumbs and held her unhappy face in his hands.

'C'mon, my love, ' he encouraged, 'it'll be all reet.'

But Mary was inconsolable. She had known that whatever happened she would lose her daughter... but this! This was the stuff of nightmares! This was her worst fear taken shape, formed into reality – unthinkable reality. She was shaking and beginning to feel nauseous. God was punishing her, punishing them all! She rose and rushed to the sink in the kitchen and vomited.

Daniel put his head in his hands and stared into the flames. A piece of wood cracked and spat out an ember onto the hearth. 'At least Emily has chosen well, ' he muttered. That was the irony.

'That is precisely the tragedy, ' uttered Mary, wiping her mouth on her apron, 'that has led to this catastrophe.'

Late October

The wind whipped around the sandstone cottage. Swirls of rust, sunshine yellow and faded green eddied over the lawn past the windows. As the wind hit the glass, begging to be let in, Jennifer was sitting at her desk with a steaming mug of hot chocolate, staring out from the warmth of her office at the low afternoon sunlight reflecting off the branches of the oak tree. As she lifted the mug to her mouth the aroma of chocolate and Grand Marnier filled her nostrils; a perfect drink for a cold autumn afternoon.

She was searching for marriage records and wasn't having much luck. She'd searched for the names Popple and Fernleigh in the parish records of marriages in the Brockby area and come up with nothing. She supposed that this would have been too good to be true – it was unlikely that a forbidden love affair would lead to a marriage recorded in the very parish in which the lovers resided. However, she'd had to start somewhere. She had tried widening the search to the North Riding, removing the date of birth cited for the name Fernleigh and allowing for variants of the name. She had chosen the year of marriage as 1762; the default variation about this date was plus or minus five years, but according to what had so far been discovered it had to be 1762 or nothing. However, this time she accepted the default. She pressed the Search button again. This time she was excited to see that two records came up bearing the name Fernleigh, both in Brockby. Scanning the lines of each record she saw that there had been two marriages, one in 1758 and one in 1759, the first for a Charlotte Fernleigh and the second for an Amelia Fernleigh. Could these women be part of William's family, his sisters perhaps? She examined the accompanying records and sure enough, the father in each case was cited as Thomas Fernleigh. Charlotte Elizabeth Fernleigh had married a Colonel James Napier and Amelia Fanny Fernleigh had married a Bertram Chatham, whose occupation was stated as 'gentleman'.

So it appeared that William had had two sisters who had married in the parish; however, there were no records for William. Jennifer sighed and buried her hands in Smokey's fur. The cat had come to sit on her lap, sharing her warmth, in turn imparting heat to Jennifer's legs. She could feel the vibrations of Smokey's purr as she stroked her silky back and thought about what she should do next. If they had married and it hadn't been in Yorkshire, where would they have gone? To London perhaps? If they were after anonymity they could certainly find it amongst a crowd. It was worth a try. She tried various combinations of locations and dates but again came up with nothing.

At length she decided to email Andy Finch. She figured that if he was working he'd pick up the email and she wouldn't be disturbing him, and if he wasn't working he'd answer it on Monday and she'd have to wait.

How goes it with you? Searched marriages in Yorkshire and London — came up with two that look like William's sisters, but nothing for William. Suppose they eloped? They could have gone anywhere!

She went to make another mug of creamy hot chocolate and to raid the biscuit tin. The low afternoon sun had been replaced by purple-grey clouds, and large spots of rain started to appear on the kitchen window. She decided to light the fire in the living room. She was glad that she'd swept out the hearth and made a fire up that morning before going shopping; it would save her having to go out into the cold to the wood store now. As she held a match to the tightly rolled ball of newspaper stuffed underneath the kindling and coals, Jennifer felt a deep sense of disappointment. She so wanted William and Emily to have married, to have fulfilled their dream, to have been able to formalise their vows to each other despite the odds stacked against them; to show the world that love can win out in the end.

She returned to the kitchen. Reaching up into a cupboard for the bottle of Grand Marnier she unscrewed its cap and poured a generous slug into her mug. *Huh*; she shrugged her shoulders; it was ironic that here she was, free to love, craving love after a failed relationship, and her alter ego in 1762 experiencing the most loving of relationships which, however, was totally forbidden. She returned upstairs to her study, scooped Smokey up from her chair and sat down on her warm seat, placing the cat back on her lap. There was an unread email in her inbox. It was from Andy.

Spent two days last week sorting through three boxes of documents from one of the attics — only another 13 to go! Many family diaries and letters here, but so far none of William's. I agree, they could have gone anywhere, but without their parent's consent, they may have found it difficult to get married in a regular church. After 1753 English law forbade irregular marriages, hence the documented elopements to Gretna Green, where a couple's own consent to marriage before witnesses was legal. You might try the Scottish records, after all Gretna is only just over the border and probably only a few days ride from North Yorkshire.

A thrill ran through Jennifer's body. As was becoming customary Andy Finch had managed to give her a boost, to provide a glimmer of hope, something else to try, another lead. She had to register with the Scottish records provider, *Scotland's People*, but once that was done she was able to access the Old Parish Registers for 1553-1854, which seemed to be the appropriate database for the type of record she was looking for and the relevant time period. From the list of Old Parish Registers within the county of Dumfries, *number 827* listed marriage records for Graitney (or Gretna) between 1732 and 1819. She decided to throw the net wide to start with, choosing William Fernleigh, including all variants thereof, and not specifying the spouse's name. She plumped for records in Gretna between 1755 and 1762 and waited...

One record appeared!

Jennifer's stomach turned over and a wave of adrenaline caused her to feel a little lightheaded. She positioned her mouse over the record and clicked. A scanned page appeared. At the top in the middle was the number *76*, in brackets and underlined, and at the top of a hand-written column on the left-hand side the date *1762* was written. There seemed to be a series of dates, the month followed by the year, and under each was a series of records, with eleven or twelve on the page.

The first record read: '*George Collier and Mary MacRobert were married regularly. January 10th.*' And in the left-hand column by the entry was written '*Collier*' and underneath '*MacRobert.*'

All the entries were recorded slightly differently. Jennifer scanned down the left-hand column to find Fernleigh. There it was, near the bottom of the page, and underneath was written *Popple*. Jennifer's heart was in her mouth and her right hand was shaking as she placed it on the page and followed the script of the entry with her forefinger: *William Thomas Joseph Fernleigh, Gentleman, Yorkshire, and Miss Emily Mary Popple, daughter of Daniel Popple, Brockby. October 27th.*

She'd found it! William and Emily had actually married! Jennifer laughed out loud and placed her hands on her head, leaning back and swivelling in her chair. Smokey dug her claws into Jennifer's thighs and hung on. Jennifer didn't care; she punched the air and continued swivelling. *Yes! They'd done it!*

Smokey jumped off Jennifer's lap, deciding that this was the safer option. Jennifer jumped out of her chair and did a victory dance around the office with both arms in the air. She was elated! She had to let Andy know.

Got it! They did it! When can we meet?

She attached the record to the email, pressed Send and went downstairs to pour herself a celebratory glass of wine.

Andy Finch took the lid off the seventh box of documents. Another jumble of letters, papers, notebooks and diaries. Whoever had boxed the remains of the Fernleigh family's personal documents had not been particularly interested in their contents. When he had taken on this task he had been advised that the documents in these boxes had originally been housed in three large trunks that were discovered in one of the attics during repairs to the roof. The trunks had shown signs of having been affected by damp and the contents of the attic had had to be removed in order for the roof to be repaired. The documents were transferred in evident haste to the stationery boxes that Andy was now sifting through. It seemed that they had not been ordered, rather, bundled in. At least they were preserved in a dry environment now, in the back room of the estate office.

Andy was systematically working to record and file the documents by their respective authors, by subject matter and by date, while also looking for any information on William Fernleigh. He had discovered some notebooks belonging to Thomas Fernleigh; however, so far the man seemed to have limited his scribing to events and matters pertaining to the management of the estate and his various businesses in agriculture, seed oil and textiles. The nearest he came to recording personal events was to mention the occasional birthday or dinner party of particular noteworthiness. Andy felt that he might have much better luck if he could find more of Charlotte Fernleigh's diaries. She was a much more effusive writer than her husband; he had discovered a diary of hers from 1750 in which she mentioned eight children, one of which, Elizabeth, was only a year old and the eldest was a daughter named Catherine who at the time was nineteen. There were numerous mentions of William, aged eight or nine, but nothing unusual; nothing that would give any clue to future possible events. However, so far he had not uncovered any other writings of Charlotte's – diaries, letters or otherwise.

As he began to search carefully through the next lot of musty pages, Andy sighed and scratched his chin through his beard. If anyone thought that research was glamorous they could think again. Most of it was hard graft, meticulous sifting, methodical searching though endless documents, albeit infinitely interesting and delightfully time-consuming. On numerous occasions he'd had to stop himself veering off-track down fascinating side routes to follow particular exchanges of gossip in a series of letters, or a trading of recipes with comments on how the dishes turned out, advice on particular breeds of horse and cattle or getting a prize-winning pig to mate, children's birthday presents, educational successes and disasters, refurbishments, wall hangings, artefacts, fashion, music and theatre, opinions on politics that would be regarded as outspoken if uttered in company, candid opinions on social acquaintances and frank opinions about others' opinions. It was endlessly fascinating.

A small brown leather-bound journal caught his eye and he lifted it from beneath a stack of parchment. It was dated 1762 and had belonged to a John Fernleigh. Andy consulted the printed family tree pinned to the corkboard on the wall beside him. The only John he could find that fitted the date was Thomas' only brother – so this must be his.

He started to read. The narrative was infinitely more descriptive than that in Thomas' diary. After an absorbing hour or so Andy felt that he had the measure of John Fernleigh, and he didn't like the vision that was becoming apparent. It was clear that there was certainly no love lost between John and his brother Thomas, and John's opinions were at the very best blunt and at worst distasteful in the extreme. However, Andy had gained a small but exciting breakthrough; there was an entry in August of that year which referred to a *'confession of circumstance'* by his nephew, William. The narrative around this entry seemed to indicate that John had gained not inconsiderable pleasure from this discussion with his nephew. Andy hurriedly began looking for other entries that might pertain to this discussion. Slowly he began to piece together a scenario in which William's uncle appeared to be encouraging William's elopement. France was mentioned, although no further details, dates or places were recorded. Andy began to feel uncomfortable and a sense of unease slowly crept through him as he deciphered line after line of the small untidy script. The more he read, the more apprehensive he became. Given the nature of the relationship between William's father and his uncle, the support and encouragement that John Fernleigh appeared to be giving his nephew seemed both out of character and not a little suspicious. A curious entry on October the 18th raised the hairs on the back of Andy's neck; *'Paid to B Faulks, Liverpool, sum of 20 guineas for services to be performed before November sixth, in return for GR.'*

Twenty guineas was a large sum of money. What was John Fernleigh paying twenty guineas for? What 'services' for such a sum would be discreetly mentioned in a personal diary, the implication being that the transaction may not have been recorded in official account books? Andy made a mental note to try and cross-check this if he could.

He ran his hands through his hair, sat back in his chair and stretched his neck and back, arms above his head. Then he got up and paced across the room to stretch his legs; he'd been sitting too long, bent over the manuscripts. He glanced out of the window over a pasture, enclosed by iron rail fencing on which a flock of sheep grazed contentedly, a scene which in all probability had remained unchanged for hundreds of years. The hexagonal art deco wall clock above the fireplace indicated that it was nearly noon, and he felt hungry. He returned to his desk and rummaged around in his battered brown briefcase, eventually pulling out a plastic sandwich box. As he retrieved a thick-cut ham and mustard sandwich a head popped around the door and asked if he wanted a cup of tea. He nodded gratefully and returned his attention to the diary in front of him. He carefully scanned the entries between August and the 18th of October again, looking for any references to GR. Who was GR? John Fernleigh had generally been most frank in his testimonial. Why was this entry so coy? There were no other references to the mysterious GR, but an entry on the 14th of September described how John had the opportunity to '…*set matters right.*' Another, later that month, commented: '*My boy should come into what is rightfully his as he will make better use of it.*'

Andy started to document the sets of entries that he believed were related, in chronological order. He really had something here. This was the first indication of anything out of the ordinary happening in the Fernleigh household. However, if the journal implied that all was not as it should have been, the entry for the twenty-fifth of October was startling in its implication of foul play:

'*W and his whore disappeared into the night like ravens in a storm. How delightfully sordid! Let the course of events run smooth as honey from a jar and taste as sweet. Liverpool beckons.*'

There! That was the link. It was evident, then, that B Faulks, GR, Liverpool, the services to be carried out for 20 guineas and William's elopement were all somehow connected. What was in Liverpool?

Andy wrote each of these words on a piece of scrap paper and stared at them for a while, his elbows on the desk, supporting his chin with one hand which stroked his beard absentmindedly while the fingers of the other hand tapped the dented old bureau obliviously. Slowly he began to understand. He began to form an electrifying but shockingly dreadful scenario in his mind.

But he didn't have proof – he needed some kind of proof. And he needed to check the deeds to the estate. And a trip to Liverpool might be in order. His mind was now racing, throwing thoughts about and catching them, hints and notions, fragments of ideas, sifting together and falling into place like flour shaken through a sieve. He had to find some hard evidence and he now knew what to look for. It might be like hunting for a needle in a haystack, but he had to start somewhere – and he knew exactly who to start with.

He jumped up, thrusting his chair backwards, at the same time catching his jeans on an oblique splinter of wood jutting out from the leg of the bureau. As he made quickly for the coat stand by the door he put his hand down to the place where his leg was smarting and felt a rip in the material. Damn. Another pair of trousers consigned to dog-walking. Perhaps he could patch it and no-one would notice – except his wife, of course. She'd say '*Get yourself another pair, you earn enough*', but he never seemed to have time to shop for clothes and, to be fair, he wasn't really interested. There were far more exciting things to be done!

He grabbed his jacket and scarf and headed out of the estate office, across the cobbled courtyard of the stable block and towards the kitchen entrance to the main house where the staff entered and exited. He went in search of the curator and found her in the long gallery talking to a group of Japanese tourists.

Andy waited impatiently for her to finish, shifting from one foot to the other like an edgy schoolchild. Eventually she finished her spiel and sent the group on their way into the next room to meet one of her colleagues. Andy almost bounded across the polished wooden floor and stood in front of her, blocking her way as she turned to walk towards the music room.

He spoke excitedly, 'Janet! I'm glad I caught you; there's something I need your help with.'

'Oh, hello Andy, ' she replied, looking at her watch, 'I was just about to take my lunch break. Do you fancy a cuppa?'

'If we can find what I'm looking for, it'll be worth far more than a cuppa!'

He looked at her pleadingly, aiming for the endearing, if rather sycophantic, *little boy lost* look, then changed it to *eager enthusiast*.

'If I know you, this'll not be straightforward, and before I know it half my afternoon will have gone. You're supposed to be doing this research, not me.' She smiled with mock seriousness.

She was cracking. He linked her right arm in his left and ushered her towards the end of the long gallery towards the main staircase.

'Ah, but you do it so well. You said it yourself; time spent with me just flies by. Most enjoyable... and productive of course! You know, I'm really onto something now and you just might be able to help me find the missing piece of this puzzle – well, one of the missing pieces at any rate.'

She nodded resignedly and raised her eyebrows at him. 'Okay, how can I help this time?'

'Great! Let's start with John Fernleigh's personal belongings.'

'Well... there are the artefacts that he brought back from his Grand Tour; fragments of Pompeii mosaic, some nice pottery, souvenir sculpture, that sort of thing. Then there are some rather nice examples of the vedutisti: Pannini, Piranesi, Canaletto. John Fernleigh actually introduced Antonio Zucchi to his brother Thomas Fernleigh. Zucchi and his wife Angelica Kauffman spent some time here. The ceiling vesicas in the large dining room were painted by her.'

Andy raised his eyebrows.

'I know, I was surprised too, given that John had a reputation for being rather boorish. But I understand that he liked to show off, like many others of his time, I suspect, and what better way of showing your wealth and influence than filling your rooms with art, books, sculpture and cultural items for all to see?'

'Ah, but they weren't his rooms, were they? I know we're looking for his possessions, and I know you have many of them here, but I'm not actually that clear on why they're in *this* house. This wasn't John Fernleigh's main residence, was it?'

'Actually he and his wife moved here when his son inherited the Fernleigh estate, although John only outlived his brother by a few years. I'm sure you know that Thomas and Charlotte only had daughters – apart from William, that is.'

'Yes, yes, of course.'

It was making sense, and Janet had just confirmed what he had suspected.

'Are his souvenirs all in one place, or are they scattered around the house?'

'Some of the smaller items are displayed in cabinets in the library. The larger items are displayed in various places.'

'Can you show me the cabinets?'

'Sure. What is it you're looking for?'

'I'm looking for a ring – well, part of a ring actually.'

'I don't recall a ring, but we can have a look.'

The cabinets contained small artefacts collected not just by John on his Grand Tour but also by several other members of the Fernleigh family: jewellery, decorative glass and enamel objects, relics of archaeological significance and several small sketches. But the ring that Andy Finch was looking for was not among them.

'Is there anything else here that John Fernleigh might have treasured, more like... personal to him?'

'Yes, actually there is. There's a cabinet containing his hunting gear and various associated memorabilia. But there's no jewellery at all in that one.'

Andy stared at her for a moment, lost in his thoughts. That was it! If it was going to be anywhere it would have to be there amongst the hunting trophies. But it wouldn't have been on show. No, this would have been a prize of the utmost private nature. Excitement surfaced and bubbled over.

'Where is it, the hunting stuff? Can you show me? Quickly!'

'It's in the games room where the card tables are, next to the pipe collection.'

She turned to lead the way but Andy was already ahead of her and disappearing into the corridor.

'C'mon, Janet! No time to lose!'

When she caught up with him he was staring through the glass. Amongst the items were a beautiful carved antler powder measure, a bone-and-metal game hook, two bone-handled belt knives, a couple of straps, a belt and a leather knife sheath. But it was the brown calf-skin hunting pouch that particularly caught his attention.

He looked up at her with an odd expression as she approached.

'Can we get the glass off? I need to have a good look at that hunting pouch.'

'Well, we're not supposed to touch the items. But I could get you a pair of gloves if you like.'

'No need. I have some here, ' he said matter-of-factly.

He pulled a pair of leather driving gloves out of his jacket pocket and proceeded to put them on, wiping the fingertips vigorously on his jeans.

'C'mon, Janet, let's get the glass off!'

She sighed. He was incorrigible. All the same, she produced a set of small keys on a ring from inside her skirt pocket and proceeded to unlock the cabinet. 'I really shouldn't be doing this.'

His heart was beating wildly as Andy reached inside and carefully lifted the leather pouch, cradling it in both hands. He took it to a walnut desk beside one of the windows. What if he was wrong? Or what if he was right, but the ring wasn't here? It could be anywhere! And it could be nowhere. Well, if that was the case he'd just have to think again. He was going on a hunch, and his hunches had paid off before. He just had a feeling about this; John Fernleigh's diary entries, the nasty kind of man that he was, the fact that his son had indeed inherited the estate just as John had wished, the gimmel ring. GR. ... *services to be performed... in return for GR.*

'This is definitely his? John Fernleigh's?'

'Yes, absolutely — well, as sure as we can be. It bears his initials, see there, sewn into the leather. And it was kept and passed down along with some other of his possessions. Please just wait a minute. I'm going to get you a proper pair of gloves.'

Andy certainly couldn't wait, but he almost couldn't open the pouch either; he wanted to delay the moment, to prolong the excitement or defer the disappointment. He gently stroked the brown leather, pursed his lips and carefully lifted up the front flap. Inside was the main pouch, and there was a smaller pouch directly under the front flap. The small and main pouches appeared to be empty; however at the back of the main pouch was another flap of soft calfskin. Holding his breath, Andy lifted back the soft leather fold. On a small cylindrical lace of leather fixed to the very back of the hunting pouch, hitherto hidden from view, were strung a number of small trophies; a boar's tooth mounted in silver, the tip of a stag's antler, a dried hare's paw and what looked like a fox claw. He was crestfallen. As interesting as these items were, they were not what he was looking for, what he had hoped to find. If his theory was true it should be *here*. He replaced the calfskin tab, but as he did so he felt something hard between his thumb and forefinger. Peering closer he discovered that the leather fold was actually made of two thin pieces cleverly sewn together with minute stitches. As Andy took out his penknife, chose the smallest blade and carefully cut the stitching, he experienced only a moment of guilt. And there, hidden in the flap covering the little personal hunting mementos, was a small gold ring. It was exquisite. It was the same size and the same shining colour as the ring that Jennifer had discovered; however, unlike that loop there was no heart set upon the circle. Instead there was something else that he could not quite make out. He took the magnifying glass that he used for reading tiny script from his pocket and looked at the ring more closely. The loop carried a single, tiny delicately and perfectly fashioned cupped hand.

'You fucking bastard, ' Andy uttered through his teeth. He turned to the curator, who had just returned with a pair of white cotton gloves, and pointed to the ring. 'I don't suppose I can borrow this? No, I didn't think so.'

As Janet, flustered, began to find her voice, 'But how did...? I've never seen...', he slid the ring back into its hiding place, closed up the hunting pouch and carried it back to the cabinet, then lowered the glass.

He hit the air with his palm of his hand in a virtual stop sign. 'Lock this back up, ' he instructed forcefully. 'Don't let anybody near it. Don't tell anyone about it. I'm onto something. Give me a couple of weeks. Oh, and sorry about the stitching – I take full responsibility.'

He didn't wait for Janet to reply but left her standing open-mouthed as he whisked out of the room and was gone.

He walked out of the building and made his way back to the estate office as quickly as he could. It was all beginning to add up, and he'd have to let Jennifer know. She'd have to bring her ring to Fernleigh Hall, though he had known immediately when he saw the ring in the hunting pouch that he'd already seen its twin. He'd still need to try to find some kind of documentary proof to support his theory, at least of William's intentions subsequent to his marriage to Emily. And there were still a number of unanswered questions... actually quite a lot, now he thought about it. He might have answered the *why*, but not the *who,* the *how* and the *where*, although Liverpool might be a clue to the latter. What did the initials DFB stand for, and how did they relate to the rings? And what of Emily?

He'd have to choose the right words to tell Jennifer, of that he was certain. The other thing that he was now sure of, although further corroboration or substantiation would be required, was that William had been murdered.

❧

October 31ˢᵗ

*J*ennifer was pacing agitatedly back and forth across the carpet of her study. She was markedly distressed and had to decide what to do.

She had tried ringing Christina Peters again, but with no success. Evidently Christina's family crisis was a serious and lengthy one.

Whatever the reason, Jennifer's confidant was not at home, her answer machine was full and there was no knowing when she might return. At that point Jennifer had started to weigh up her options.

Last night Andy Finch had phoned with news of the gimmel ring and his sobering theories about William's fate. They were to meet in a few days' time. The news had upset her and she was shocked by just how much she had been moved. She tried to reason with herself; after all, both Emily and William had been dead for well over two hundred years. But the connection she now felt with Emily had gone deep within her and manifested in ways she could not have imagined. She felt a strong emotional bond with William, or at least with the character who constantly appeared in her drug-induced dreams; the character who loved and cherished her, made passionate love to her, made her feel wanted, valued and protected and always left her with the promise that they would be together again soon. She had fallen in love with this character, this vision, this ghost. She had fallen in love with a man *who had lived more than 200 years ago*, a man that her alter ego, Emily, had passionately loved. The past and present seemed to have merged. Was she experiencing her own feelings towards William, or those of Emily?

Jennifer had been carrying out some research about the village and life in the eighteenth century. She wanted to get an idea of what Emily's life might have been like, how she had grown up, what her responsibilities would have been, her pastimes, what difficulties would she have faced and what celebrations would she have enjoyed. She had come to know Emily, to experience her excitement, understand her anxieties, empathise with her choices, suffer her sorrows and sense her joys. In short, Jennifer had come to care for her.

Through all of this, there was one thing that she had been avoiding. It stood to reason that if she could locate the record of Emily's birth she should also be able to find a record of her death. She hadn't wanted to know. She had wanted to discover Emily's life piece by piece, to follow her chronologically as if through the pages of a book or in a film. She wanted to experience her burgeoning and maturing relationship with William Fernleigh year by year. But the knowledge of William's death had thrown a dark mantle over everything. To Jennifer, it seemed imperative now that she should discover something of Emily's life as William's wife, as they were not destined to spend myriad years together as a young newly-married couple would expect to do. Added to this was the expectation that, although it might have been terrible, she may be able to discover something of William's death which would help Andy Finch in his research for evidence of the vile event, if indeed it was as Andy believed.

Earlier that day she had received a phone call from Sarah. She and her new man, Benjamin, were spending a long weekend in the Dales and wanted to come and stay on Monday night on their way back home. Jennifer hadn't met Benjamin yet, but of course she'd heard a lot about him. Sarah and Ben had been seeing each other for a couple of months. Sarah had wanted the relationship to mature a little before introducing him to anyone, and he had felt the same. But evidently they had been getting on fantastically well and were very happy in each other's company.

Jennifer hadn't seen Sarah for a while, and her friend's call had grounded her somewhat. The reality of her existence came to bear every Monday to Friday when she went to work, but her time at home had been so wrapped up with the Fernleighs and another existence which had become a reality for her that she felt she was living in two worlds – and she knew which she preferred to be in right now.

Sarah's voice on the phone had jerked her from one reality into the other. She knew that in the end she would have to finish this business – to discover the truth, draw a line underneath it, leave it behind her and get on with living the rest of her life. Sarah somehow seemed to be connected with that. Sarah's logical and level-headed approach, her rational and reasonable attitude, sometimes made Jennifer's feelings and beliefs seem outlandish, fantastical and completely unbelievable. Sarah's presence had the effect of making Jennifer question herself. She loved her friend dearly and looked forward to seeing her, but the fact that she was coming on Monday night seemed to inject urgency into matters, and she was caught up in it.

Earlier that day, while out shopping, she had ventured by the little shop where she had obtained her sleeping tablets; the tablets that had sparked off the ingress to her other world, the catalysts of visions, the facilitators of dreams. However, the purveyor of natural remedies was gone – she was nowhere to be seen and had left no forwarding address. Jennifer was shocked, crestfallen. This was a situation she had never imagined or even considered. Dazed and upset, she had stood staring at the empty little shop, trying to take in the enormity of what this meant to her. No chance, then, to prolong her encounters, to continue to seek these spirits. No more private reveries. Without the tablets the only way to reach her other self was through Christina, and the hypnotherapist had made it clear that she did not think further regressions would be helpful to Jennifer's state of mind. When the tablets were gone, they were gone… and that was it. The discovery was devastating.

There were three and a half tablets left.

Over the last few weeks Jennifer had been experimenting with different doses, trying to achieve a deep sleep and a connection with Emily with as low a dose as possible. Two tablets was the minimum she needed to experience a dream involving William, but this dose did not give her access to her past life. Two and a half tablets seemed to stimulate her memory such that it facilitated regression. The doses that she had taken in recent weeks had left her immensely drowsy afterwards and with a severe headache.

Of course she knew she shouldn't do it. The sensible side of her conscience, if indeed there was any sense involved at all, *screamed* at her not to do it. But what choice did she have? Time was running out and the tablets were running out. In her mind there was absolutely no other way.

She went downstairs, fed Smokey and gave her two extra portions in case she was asleep for longer than she meant to be. She picked her precious cat up and gave her a big hug.

'See you in a few hours, my lovely, ' she murmured to the purring creature.

Jennifer heard Smokey disappearing through her cat flap for a tea-time stroll as she settled herself under the duvet. The metal-grey sky was slowly turning crow-black as Jennifer turned on the table lamp beside her and picked up her glass of water. Only three and a half tablets left. If she took two and a half, that would leave her with only one. One was not enough to do anything with. So why waste it? If she used it now it might just help to prolong the regression, giving her more time to discover what had happened, more time to live in Emily's world for the very last time.

She knew it was reckless, but continued anyway. Having swallowed the tablets, she settled down to re-read the documents she was holding, to focus her mind on the events which she hoped would lead her to the place in Emily's life where she needed to be. The marriage record and the other, the one she had discovered only that morning. The one that had finally precipitated her decision.

Within minutes she was asleep.

Ten

They basked in their shared privacy, unfettered by duty, un-encumbered by the expectations of others. Solely William and Emily, in glorious, united solitude. They ate, drank, slept and made love in the seclusion of their room. They talked and laughed and shared confidences and swapped stories about their childhood. They made wonderful love, passionate love, tender love. It was breath-taking, delicious, exquisite! They luxuriated in the blissful state of new marriage.

For Emily, it was still incredible that she could spend every waking and sleeping moment with the man she loved passionately and without question; the magnificent, glorious man with whom she would spend the rest of her life. For William, it was incredible that this delightful, exquisite creature was now his wife. It was more than he could ever have hoped for or dreamed of. He loved her fiercely and would protect her until his dying day.

After thirty-six hours they emerged, as if from hibernation. They blinked and rubbed their eyes and set forth into their new life to-gether, into the sunshine of their existence.

Liverpool beckoned. They were about to embark on another ad-venture, the next stage of their voyage into uncharted reality. They were brimming with excitement now that this was finally upon them.

William engaged the services of a driver with a coach and four so that they could travel in privacy. In bright sunshine on a crisp and frosty morning they set off from Gretna in the direction of Penrith, thence to proceed to Liverpool. The air was still and cold with the promise of warmth to come from the autumn sun. The frost had been hard and had spread its icy tendrils over every blade of grass, every leaf, every stone, cloaking everything with intricate white crystals which, now slowly melting, refracted the watery sunlight. A myriad of colours hung in droplets from the branches of trees, glistened in globules of melt-water trapped in the pasture and shone from tiny beads caught in countless spiders webs. Yellows, oranges, blood red, pink, greens, blues and violet; Emily could see almost every colour of the rainbow twinkling around her as she made her way from the warmth of the inn to the draughty carriage.

They had prepared well for the journey: they were dressed in their warmest clothes and carried plenty of provisions, including a flask of whisky tucked into one of William's saddlebags. William had purchased a couple of deerskins and, sitting on one for extra comfort and wrapping the other around them, they settled in for a long ride.

After four hours or so, having stopped once to change the horses, they reached Penrith and took a meal at the Dockray Inn, taking the chance to warm their feet by the fire and to let their driver do the same. Emily was feeling slightly queasy and uncomfortable, and was glad of the rest. She took some brandy to calm her stomach and hoped that it would give her some relief from the ache in her belly and her lower back that had come on in the last hour or so. It was not surprising: the road was little more than a dirt track in places, and there were plenty of potholes. It was a miracle that the horses didn't break their fetlocks.

Travelling long distances didn't really agree with Emily; she had suffered similar aches and an inconsistent bowel on the journey to Gretna. She supposed it was to be expected, given the amount of shaking around that her body had endured in the carriage. She hoped that a trip to the privy would sort the matter out and set off in search of one. She was directed to an earth closet enclosed in a small wooden lean-to situated behind the stables at the back of the inn. As she gathered up her skirts to squat in the dirt, Emily noticed a few small spots of dried blood on the shift underneath her petticoat. She hadn't had her courses for some while and understood that this was|because she was now with child, so she looked to see if she had somehow injured herself, but could find nothing. She shrugged to herself – *no matter.* She should be getting back to William as they would be setting off again before too long. They faced another four or five hours' journey if they were to make it to Kirby Kendal that evening.

They made good progress for the first hour or so. The fresh Holsteiners had brought new vigour and the road seemed to have improved in places. As they made their way south, the late October sun rose in the pale sky and the air became a little warmer. Of necessity, progress became slower as they climbed towards Shap Fells and the southerly breeze gathered pace somewhat.

Emily's back and stomach were still aching, despite the brandy and the fireside rest. Instinctively she was cradling her belly in crossed arms, leaning into William and trying to brace herself with her feet against the jolts and trembles of the carriage and the shudders and grumbles of the wheels as they turned fiercely against earth and stone. She had tried to half-lie with her back against William and her feet upon the seat, but there was only enough room for the two of them side by side and precious little space for her legs on the seat as well; indeed this position had seemed to make her backache worse. William was growing concerned, and was doing his best to hold her in a way that steadied her from the movements of the carriage.

They stopped at the Greyhound Coaching Inn on the main street in Shap for another change of horses; these Cleveland Bays would see them through to Kirby Kendal, their driver assured them. William purchased some more brandy, and Emily took the opportunity of resting by another warm fireside. The atmosphere was welcoming and they ordered some brown onion soup for themselves and the driver. The hot soup was tasty and Emily felt it warm her from the inside. She relaxed for a short while; however, the stubborn aches refused to leave and relieving herself made no difference. The brandy, though, was making her feel a little sleepy. If she could just sleep for a couple of hours the pain might go away.

William read Emily's discomfort in the lines of her face and had a word with the innkeeper. Apparently there was a well-regarded physician in Kirby Kendal, but since that was twenty miles away this was no use to them at the present time. However, the ostler's mother-in-law knew something about herbs and might be able to help. She was duly summoned and took Emily into a quiet back parlour to question her in private.

Emily stared at the lines on the elderly woman's weathered face as she answered her questions, and thought how wise she appeared to be. Seemingly uneducated, Mrs Postle, a bony woman with smiling eyes, seemed to be asking perceptive questions with respect to Emily's condition, all the time nodding knowingly at the answers given.

'I'm with child, ' Emily whispered to her anxiously. 'Are these pains anything to do with my bairn?'

'Now don't you go worrying yourself, ' the dark-haired head shook reassuringly and a wizened hand patted Emily's. 'I can give you something to stop the bleeding and dull the pain. With a bit of rest you'll be as right as rain in a couple of days, you'll see. Now let me see... corn poppy for the pain – that'll help you to sleep, too, ' she nodded at Emily, 'and willow bark. Yarrow root to stop the bleeding, and lady's mantle if I've got it...'

She rummaged around in a large battered leather bag pulling out little glass jars, each wrapped in snippets of frayed material and containing numerous coloured powders and crushed leaves, adding various quantities of the selected herbs into a teacup.

'Hmm, now let me see – have I got some mallow for your digestion? Perhaps a pinch of columbine and a little betony.'

Having found what she needed, Mrs Postle added some hot water to the teacup from a kettle hanging over the fire and stirred the mixture vigorously with a small teaspoon for a minute or two.

'There you go, lass. Drink that – all of it, mind.'

Emily took a sip of the warm liquid and shuddered. It tasted bitter, but she determinedly managed all of it in a few gulps. She thanked the woman wholeheartedly and gave her a shilling.

They set off again, following the winding road over the fells across the top end of Borrowdale.

William wrapped the two deerskins around Emily and she settled into his shoulder and managed to sleep a little. They reached Kirby Kendal after nightfall. Their driver took them to the County Inn where they took two rooms, one for him and one for themselves. The inn was relatively clean and pleasant enough; most of all it was warm, and there was a hog sizzling and crackling on the roasting spit, affording plenty of hot succulent meat which was served in a rich gravy.

Emily's body was aching all over and she did not feel hungry, however she knew that she needed to eat something to feed her strength. William ordered a fire to be lit in their room and the sheets on their bed to be warmed, and sent a boy to locate the doctor. Emily and William sat at the fireside in the parlour and she managed a very little meat and gravy and a small glass of wine.

Presently William helped Emily to bed, freeing her hair of its pins and helping her to undress to her shift before returning to the parlour to wait for the doctor. He had been shocked and alarmed by the size of the blood stain on her shift. In God's name, where was the physician?

William drummed his fingers on the table impatiently. He knew little of medical matters and even less about childbirth, however, he'd seen enough cows calving to know that what was happening to his darling Emily was not supposed to happen at this stage, and it pained and worried him greatly to see her in any kind of distress. He had been concerned since she had complained of an ache in her belly, but the shock of seeing the white cotton turned red heightened his concern a hundredfold. He feared for her. She appeared to be losing a lot of blood, and that concoction that the old lady in Shap had given her had done little to stem the flow, it seemed.

For the first time in his life William felt utterly helpless, unable to do anything except call on others for help. This vulnerability and anxiousness made him angry. He downed his wine, scraped back his chair and was just about to call for another boy to send after the first when the latter burst in through the door, briefly scanned the room and hurried over to him.

'What news? Where is the physician? Why have you not brought him with you?' William shook the boy by his shoulders unappreciatively.

The young boy spewed out his message with great haste, his words tumbling over one another.

'Sir, it is bad news! Mr Goodall is taken ill with a bad fever and is being nursed in his bed by his sister, who forbade me to see him and told me on no account to bother her with questions. She told me he is in and out of consciousness and she is mighty worried. She has sent for a friend of theirs, who is also a physician, but he is journeying from London and will not be here until at least the day after tomorrow, probably the next day.'

The boy waited for an answer nervously. Although he was only the bearer of this bad news and not the cause of it, he could see that his words had a grave effect on this man by the way his mouth and jaw were set, his cheeks sucked in, his eyes narrowed as if in pain.

'Perhaps... when this other doctor gets here... he will be able to treat your wife?' he offered helpfully.

William lowered his head, 'I fear it may be too late by then, ' he said quietly.

He ran his hands over his head and face, trying to think quickly. His stomach was churning and a wave of panic had come over him. The young boy stood silent at his side.

It seemed they had but a single option. They must press on towards Liverpool and hope that there was a reputable physician in Lancaster or Preston. It was clear that Emily needed rest and that the travelling was doing her no good; however, it was too much of a risk to stay here another few days awaiting a doctor. She needed the attention of a good physician urgently before she became any weaker. He would have to let her rest a while, but William feared the passing of too much time. He could send a rider to find a doctor, but it would probably be quicker if they at least made it to Lancaster. Nevertheless, he could send a rider ahead.

The nights were becoming longer, impinging on the daylight, suspending the break of day. William did not want to wait for the dawn before setting off. This was as far as their current coachman was taking them. He was at this moment arranging their onward travel. If they were to travel in the dark they would need a guard, and this would also need to be arranged. William instructed the boy to go in search of their coachman with this message. They would leave at around five the next morning. He obtained a bottle of brandy from the barmaid and ascended the creaking stairs to check on Emily.

Emily was lying on her side with her knees drawn up to her breast. This was the most comfortable position that she could attain – anything else seemed to accentuate the hollow ache in her belly. Long fingers of pain stretched themselves throughout her back and stomach, probing and exploring, seeking their victims, clawing and scraping, gripping parts of her body and squeezing so that pain flooded out and swamped her consciousness. She had changed her shift and placed a cotton petticoat between her legs. She was still slowly bleeding, but this simple act had made her feel a little cleaner at least. She was frightened and anguished; she had never experienced pain like this, and the amount of blood that she was losing alarmed her. This was not like her usual courses – it was countless times worse. Something was wrong, and she knew that it was something to do with the child inside her. She was really fearful now, not only for the child but also for her own wellbeing. When she was a child she'd once seen a pregnant sheep die, before the end of its term; before it had been able to give birth. Her father had tried to save the lamb, but when they had cut the sheep open they had found that it was dead.

Was that what was happening to her? Had the child inside her died? The child that she and William had made, conceived out of the deepest love that two people could possibly have for one another? Was she going to bleed to death? Perhaps this was a punishment for their sin, for all the times they had lain together out of wedlock. Could God really be so cruel as to allow them to fall in love with one another under circumstances that had prevented their marrying, and now punish them when they had joined together, properly, with prayers and dedication to Him and with His blessing?

If the child inside her had died, how would it be removed without the sacrifice of her life? If it was alive it wasn't ready to be born; she knew that much. She knew because she had seen her mother with child and giving birth to her baby brother after nine months. But she had also seen her mother lose a child after carrying it for two months – and live. She wasn't sure how long she had been with child, but she reckoned that she hadn't had her courses for some months, perhaps four or five.

As she lay cocooned in the warm bed, clasping her knees to her, curled around her pain, Emily thought of her mother and longed for the reassuring comfort of her voice, the touch of her hand stroking her hair and her cheek, the sound of her wise words born of many years of experience of life and passed down to her through past generations of mothers. Her ma would know what to do.

Suddenly Emily knew what she had to do. She needed her mother more than at any other time in her life. Indeed, she felt as though her life might actually depend upon it.

When William entered the room, carrying a flask of brandy, she looked up at him and tried to smile, but the pain in her heart and her belly was evident upon her face.

'I'm so sorry, ' she whispered, shaking her head slightly. 'So sorry.'

William put down the flask and immediately rushed to her side.

'My love, my love, ' he said gently, 'you have nothing to be sorry about... nothing! Please, do not worry yourself. I have all the arrangements in hand. We will get you to a physician as soon as possible.'

He took her outstretched hand, the hand that she had allowed freedom from the warmth of the covers so that it could join with his and bring her consolation. Tenderly stroking her soft skin, he smiled at her, a smile that smoothed all the creases of concern from his face, removing them to a place where he could express them in private; a smile that lit up his beautiful blue eyes and made them sparkle like stars on a clear night in an indigo sky; a smile that was full of kindness and love and exquisite with devotion; a smile that freed her heart from its pain. Emily smiled back at him weakly, but her own smile faded when she comprehended his words.

'Is there no physician here?'

'There is, but he has been taken seriously unwell and is indisposed.' William made light of it. 'However there is bound to be a good physician in Lancaster, and if not there, we will try Preston. I am sure that there will be a doctor in Lancaster, perhaps more than one... it is after all a much bigger place than this. I will send a rider ahead and we will leave before dawn, when you have had the chance to rest for a few hours.'

The anxious knot in Emily's stomach reappeared as quickly as it had diminished.

William rose from his knees by the bedside and moved to the little table on which he had placed the flask of brandy, pouring some for Emily and some for himself into two small glasses set out on a tray.

'Drink this and I'll pour you another. It will help the pain and allow you to sleep.'

He lifted her head from the pillow, supporting her so that she could drink from the glass. She was glad of it and felt its warmth as the fiery amber liquid made its way down her gullet and into her stomach. Emily nodded at her husband, signalling that he should refill her glass. As he was doing so, she made an attempt to sit up slightly but a sharp pain in her belly made her collapse back down again.

'I need my mother, ' she stated simply. 'She will know what to do.'

William stared at her for a moment, comprehending the implication of her words.

'But... your mother is not a doctor, ' he said gently. 'You need a physician.'

Emily spoke assuredly. 'I know, but she has had children and she has lost children and she has survived. She will know what to do. And there is also a good physician nearby, ' she added 'the one that attends to the needs of your family, and mine when we cannot do without him. I *need* to see my mother.'

William responded tenderly but firmly, trying to weigh up the risks of remaining on course and attempting to locate a reputable physician en route against a longer journey and the sure knowledge of a reliable doctor at the end of it. There was so much at stake. It was an almost impossible decision. 'We will seek a physician in Lancaster. It is not so far.'

Emily was silent for a few moments. Then she gripped his hand hard as she spoke.

'William... I beg you... *Take me to my mother and Doctor North.*'

Emily imparted the last in a manner that was not to be argued with and William could not deny her, though his heart sank at her words. Nevertheless the decision was made; they would return to her parents. Lord only grant they receive a better reception there than they would at Fernleigh Hall – and he was intending to stay away from that place. William judged that it would be difficult, though not impossible, to secrete themselves somewhere in the vicinity of Emily's parents without it becoming known in the wider community. In any case, they had to take that chance.

William nodded his acquiescence at Emily and kissed her hand.

'It is a long journey' he said simply. 'It will take ten or twelve hours. Can you manage it?'

'I *will* manage it' Emily responded with as much conviction as she could manage, though her voice was weak. 'However, I'd rather we left sooner than later'.

There was a deeper meaning in her words than was conveyed by the simple stating of them. Not for the first time, William felt a wave of panic rise up through his body to his gullet, nearly choking him. He swallowed hard.

'I will make the necessary arrangements. Take some more brandy and try to get some sleep. We will leave in a few hours.'

November 1ˢᵗ 1762

They set off just after five in the morning. William had instructed that twenty sacks be filled with straw and laid on the floor of the carriage, piled one upon the other until they reached the height of the seats, with a further layer laid over the seats and right across the interior of the carriage. Upon this was placed one of the deerskins, the whole arrangement forming a wide soft place to rest. It was highly irregular, however William did not care. Carriages were exceedingly uncomfortable, and he wanted his dear Emily to travel the rest of the journey in as much comfort and warmth as possible. Once she was loosely dressed in her warmest clothes, he carried her in his arms from their bedchamber to the carriage and placed her on the makeshift bed, covering her with a woollen blanket and the second deerskin.

The guard sat up front with the coachman and William climbed in beside his beloved wife. He lay down beside her and cradled her in his arms. They lay, mostly in silence, through the hours of darkness before the sun rose weakly in the grey cloud-ridden sky. They made slow progress in the dark with just two dim lanterns to light the way, but at least they were on the road and heading in the right direction, and they were able to speed up a little as it grew light.

At Sedburgh they took on some provisions – bread and cold beef and some more brandy. Emily was too weak to be moved, but managed a little of the warm chicken broth that William brought out to her. She had started to experience acute pains, and with more regularity than previously. The straw buffered the jolts and bumps of the carriage wheels on the rough road beneath and the deerskins kept her warm. She lay on her side, alternating from one side to the other but always cradled in William's arms.

By the time they reached Hawes she had started to suffer a fever. William smoothed the hair from her face. He had obtained a cold wet cloth from the inn where they had changed horses, and gently pressed this to her forehead and delicate pale cheeks. He could do nothing else except comfort her. He held her in his arms, speaking to her of their future plans, of all the things they would do when they reached France, of the sunshine-filled days they would spend together, of long evenings to be enjoyed sitting around a cosy fire, of balls and banquets, of quiet walks in the countryside, of children and family. She would smile and squeeze his hand and ask him to paint another picture for her, another scene in their future life together, and another, and another.

At Leybourn they put in briefly at the Mason's Arms. As was customary, the guard had signalled their arrival as they approached and a fresh team of horses was being assembled. William disembarked and entered the inn to obtain food and a hot drink for them all and to seek out a rider that he could send ahead with a message. As he was talking to the landlord a young man in his twenties with dark hair entered the bar from a back entrance. He looked familiar, and William recognised him as one of the ostlers from the King's Arms in Thirsk. The man clearly recognised William, as he came straight up to him and said good day. It turned out that he had been delivering a horse and was about to make his way back home. William knew him to be a trustworthy sort and so asked him if he might undertake an errand. The man said he was only too pleased to be of assistance, confirming, upon William's insistence on total confidentiality, that he was indeed dependable, upon his honour and the honour of his family.

William obtained paper and quill from the landlord and wrote a short message to Daniel and Mary Popple. On another piece of paper he wrote the name of the doctor who resided in Brockby and where he could be found. He gave the ostler a handsome five shillings, promising another five when he had completed his task. He was to deliver the note, then find the doctor and bring him to Daniel's farm and wait for William there, and on no account was he to announce William's forthcoming arrival to anyone else, particularly to anyone at Fernleigh Hall. William wished him Godspeed. Shortly afterwards, having partaken of a good mutton stew, they set off in the direction of home.

Emily was unable to eat anything, but took a little brandy. She was very weak now, and could barely lift her head from her straw pillow. She was at least warm inside the cocoon of deerskins, whilst outside the grey sky grew purple with storm clouds and large drops of rain began to tap upon the carriage roof. The wind grew restless and eddied around stands of trees, flicking branches in sudden gusts and playing amongst piles of shed leaves, tossing and spinning them, laughing at their hapless fate.

Throughout the journey Emily held on to William and he to her. They spoke to each other quietly and intermittently between Emily's bouts of heightened pain and the flushes of fever that swept through her body.

'If I die, you must know this, Will, ' she whispered, turning to him with tearstained cheeks: 'You have made me happier than I could have ever thought possible. I am...'

'Shh, my love. Do not speak of death, but think only of life. You have a life to live, with me, and we are *going* to live it!'

He looked down at her, her head cradled in his lap, her beautiful sunny red curls radiating out over the straw-filled sacking, and he stroked her hair. This small, vulnerable, exquisite creature was his world. He could not bear to think of existing without her – he absolutely would not conceive of it.

Her voice was weak, but insistent. She squeezed his thigh where her right hand lay upon it.

'No... I must say this, you must hear me out. Then I promise I will talk no more of dying.' She waited for him to respond, but he stayed silent. 'I love you, William Fernleigh. I think I have always loved you. Indeed, I think I was born to love you. And that you love me back and married me, *dedicated your life to me*, despite our different circumstances, seems in itself a small miracle. I am the luckiest woman alive. I have your child inside me and both of us know that there is something wrong. I want our child to live and I want to live – however, if that does not come to pass, if God decides to take me, you must know that you changed my world and that I am blissfully happy. I have felt elated whenever you were near me. The time we have spent together has been joyous and wonderful and absolutely irreplaceable. And whatever happens we will always have the memories of those times in our heads and in our hearts.'

A single tear ran down her cheek, but she kept it hidden from him, her hair partly obscuring her face. She gently stroked his thigh where her other cheek rested.

He could not speak, but looked away, into the distance through the dark of the carriage window. He looked, but did not see. She knew that he was weeping and she lay in silence until he was ready to speak.

By the time he spoke he had gathered himself together again. He spoke tenderly, but with absolute conviction.

'Emily, my sweetheart, you are *not* going to die. You are my world. I will not let you leave it. You must have faith: your body is weak, but inside you are so strong. My love, believe this. Dr North is a good physician who has attended our family for years – and yours too, you said it yourself. And your mother is a good mother who has experienced similar difficulties. You are strong, like her – you will come through this. And one day, when we're sitting together at our hearth, old and wrinkled but very happy, we will look back upon this time as a dreadful episode, with relief in our hearts and love in our souls.'

Emily did not reply but squeezed his hand tightly. They were less than an hour from home and remained quiet for the rest of the journey save the occasional cries of pain that Emily emitted when her contractions became too much to bear.

They arrived at Primrose Cottage in a howling gale and rain that drove horizontally across the leaden sky from the north-east. The calculating wind spread its tentacles around the carriage, seeking gaps through which it could vent its fury, and slammed the door in William's face as he tried to jump out the moment the wheels came to a halt. The guardsman, dripping and shivering, jumped down and held the door open. As William emerged, Daniel appeared from around the back of the cottage leading his horse, which was fully saddled up. There was a strained look on his face and determination showed in his tired eyes. The moment he saw the carriage he ran towards them.

'William! How is she? How's mi' daughter?' he cried.

'She is weak, Sir, ' William replied quickly. 'She needs a doctor. Did my young messenger fetch Doctor North? Where is he?'

Daniel shook his head, turned it towards the cottage and bellowed 'Mary! They're 'ere!'

He turned back towards William and together they carefully lifted Emily into a position from which they could retrieve her safely, still wrapped in her deerskins.

Daniel stumbled over his words in his effort to respond to William, to alert his wife of their daughter's arrival and to assist in delivering Emily from the carriage. His heart was racing uncontrollably and there was panic in his voice.

'The boy lost 'is way a little as it grew dark, but arrived 'ere about an hour ago and delivered tha message. 'E couldn't find the good doctor at 'is 'ome... Mary!... 'E asked at several of t' cottages... *Mary!...* and was eventually told that Doctor North was visiting at Fernleigh 'all. Go ahead and lift, I 'ave 'er legs.'

'Well, where is he then! Why didn't the boy pursue Doctor North to Fernleigh!' William cried in frustration.

Together with the guardsman and coachman they succeeded in bringing Emily safely out of the carriage and, protecting her face from the stinging rain, began carrying her up the stony path towards the cottage.

''E was mindful of tha words to him Sir, ' Daniel shouted over the wind, 'that on no account should 'e alert anyone, particularly those at Fernleigh, of tha presence. 'E galloped back 'ere t' appraise me of situation as quick as 'e could and ah saddled up and was just about t' leave for Fernleigh 'all when you arrived.'

Mary appeared at the front door and ushered them into the drawing room, where a truckle bed was made up in front of the fire. She looked haggard, as if she hadn't slept for days, and worry had chiselled lines across her forehead and pulled at the skin under her eyes, which, once as bright as Emily's, were anxious and full of tears. The tears spilled over and ran down her ashen cheeks as Emily cried out in pain with another contraction as they placed her upon the bed. Mary rushed to her daughter's side, groping for her hand and smoothing the hair from her face. Beads of sweat glistened on Emily's forehead and her neck and hands were wet with perspiration. She was convulsed with fever.

'Emily! Mi' Emily! You're home now, mi darling daughter. Ah'm 'ere t' look after thee. Oh Lord, what a state thee's in. Looks like thee's having this babbie whether it's ready or no.'

Fear set Mary's body on edge and her fingers trembled as she held Emily's hand. She had to take control, or she'd be no good to her daughter. With a tremendous effort she took a deep breath, composed herself and looked up at her other two daughters, who had gathered apprehensively in the doorway. She took charge of herself and the situation.

'Georgina, take t' men's wet coats and sit 'em down in front of t' fire in t' kitchen. There's soup an' potatoes an' chicken pie. Please…' she indicated to the coachman and guardsman, 'go with mi daughter and warm thaselves by t' fire. Prudence, set t' laundry pan t' boil agen – ah filled it earlier.'

Her daughters rapidly set about their business and Daniel and William both turned to leave. Daniel placed a hand on William's arm, signalling him to wait.

'Ah'm going after Doctor North. Stay with tha wife, William, she needs thee, ' he pronounced kindly.

It was simultaneously an instruction and a declaration of acceptance, and William was gratful for it. But he knew that he was the one who must go.

'I thank you sir, but it is me who must fetch the physician from Fernleigh. It is me who should face them, and it is my responsibility. Please… stay with your daughter, she needs her mother and father at this moment.'

William ran out into the storm, without waiting for an answer. 'May I borrow your mare?' he called back as he ran down the path.

'O' course! Return quickly man!' Daniel's last words were lost to the tempest.

William rode as hard as he could through the freezing blizzard, razor-sharp sleet driving into his face so that he struggled to see. He pulled his tricorne down, bowed his head and set his eyes to a squint, staring out into the murkiness through his eyelashes. No matter – he would know the way blindfolded. His mount seemed also to know the route. With the rhythm of the mare's hooves on the mud, William repeated a mantra to himself, partly to prevent abandoned panic from engulfing him and partly because he needed to convince himself: '*She will be saved, she will be saved*'.

The front entrance of Fernleigh Hall had been locked against the dreadful night. William cantered around to the back and dismounted at the door to the kitchen passage. He slung the reins over the hook in the wall, entered the building and ran up the corridor towards the back stairs, shouting instructions in the direction of the servants' hall and kitchen as he went. His commands, to take him to the physician immediately and to make Doctor North's carriage ready, were met with astonished faces. Nevertheless, several folk suspended their duties and rapidly came to his aid.

It was Mr Arbuth who led William to the library, where his father and Doctor North were conversing over a brandy. William motioned the house steward to leave before he burst through the double doors.

The two men wheeled round to face him, surprise written on their faces, though noticeably more evident in his father's eyes.

'Good Lord! William! Where on earth...'

William briefly ignored his father. 'I am here for the good doctor!' he cried. 'Doctor North, please come with me immediately. There is someone in great danger of losing her life and we need your assistance!'

'Now just wait one minute!' His father spoke quickly and angrily. 'You disappear without so much as a by-your-leave, no letter, no indication of your whereabouts; you abduct a young maidservant...' Thomas raised his hand, palm vertical, towards his son to signal that he was not to be interrupted; '...yes, I say *abduct* – you did not seek permission from your mother to commandeer her maid, or indeed from the girl's parents, who I declare have been sick with worry. And you *expressly* defied my very specific instruction not to have anything more to do with the girl!'

Thomas was uncharacteristically beginning to throw his arms about, his rage rising with every word uttered. 'And now you suddenly turn up here, demanding the attentions of the good doctor when you have offered no explanation for...'

William's frustration and panic finally boiled over. 'Father I have no time for this! Emily is sick – she's *dying!*' he screamed at his father.

He turned to Doctor North, who was looking decidedly uncomfortable, pulling at his stock to loosen it with one hand whilst downing his brandy.

'I entreat you sir, she will die if you do not attend her. She is with child but very ill. And she has a fever and...'

'*What!*' roared his father.

Thomas was suddenly unsteady on his feet and he gripped his writing table for support. The rage of colour that had flushed his face had suddenly disappeared, had been stunned into greyness by shock. Alarm and distress traumatised the blood in the vessels beneath his skin, chasing it back into deeper veins, leaving his countenance a ghostly white.

Doctor North interjected cautiously, but firmly and calmly.

'Sirs, Sirs, please! I have no part in your quarrel and indeed no business to come between you, nor the stomach for it. However it is clear to me that there is someone in urgent need of my assistance. Therefore I should...'

'He has brought this on the girl!' Thomas interrupted shouting, pointing a finger at his son. 'He has brought this on both of them!' He bowed his head and shook it. Staring at the rug beneath his feet he uttered, 'It would be best if she were to die.'

William and Doctor North responded simultaneously.

'*Father!*'

'*Lord Fernleigh!*'

Williams mouth was open and he stared at his father with complete incomprehension. The physician looked equally shocked, but it was he who spoke first.

'Lord Fernleigh, you cannot mean what you say; I cannot believe it. You have had a shock, and it is that which is provoking these words. Please, sit down. Master William, would you be so good as to pour another brandy for your father.' He looked at William sideways and added quietly, 'I'm sure he will come to his senses in a little while.'

'Sirs, ' he continued, addressing both men again, 'I have sworn by Apollo the physician to care for the sick, whoever they may be, according to my ability and judgement. I am urgently needed elsewhere and I must take my leave of you.'

He bowed to Thomas and nodded to William, who simply said, 'The Popple place. I will follow.'

On his way down the grand staircase Doctor North encountered Charlotte, who was hurrying up the steps.

'I take my leave of you, Madam. I have urgent business to attend to. Thank you for a most wonderful dinner.' He bowed briefly and continued on his way.

'Doctor North... it is true then? William is returned?' Charlotte called after him. She was flushed with excitement and expectation.

Doctor North turned briefly to respond. 'He is, indeed he is. Although it seems perhaps not under the best of circumstances. Your husband and son are engaged in a most terrible quarrel.' The physician checked himself. 'Apologies, Madam – I speak out of turn. I meant only to warn you. Now please excuse me; I must take my leave.'

He hurried on down the staircase and out through the front door into the turbulent night, where his carriage was waiting.

Charlotte turned and hurried up the rest of the staircase. She could hear raised voices coming from the direction of the library and made her way along the corridor. When she reached the doors, she hesitated. Although she could hear the two men shouting she could not make out what they were saying. The shelves of books and the heavy oak doors muffled the sound from within, which was, in one sense, fortunate – at least they could not be overheard by the staff. However, she could hear their tones – and she had never heard Thomas's timbre so angry as this. Charlotte stood outside the library doors for some moments, vacillating, hand on doorknob, unsure whether to intrude. Then she carefully opened the door a little, the better to hear what was going on.

Inside, both men were still in a state of shock. They stood away from the door, facing one another across Thomas's secretaire.

'I cannot understand you Father – I cannot fathom what is in your head. You made clear to me your objections to my liaison with Emily and I declared to you what was in my heart. I *told* you how much I cared for her and you expected me to just simply *let her go*. I could not do it!'

'I expected you to do it because you were instructed to do it, because I had *ordered* you to do it! The expectation of complicity was

359

founded on the nature of our bond and the fact that you are heir to this estate, and all the responsibility that goes with that!'

William shook his head as if he could not believe what he was hearing and thumped the table. 'You talk of responsibility; what about my responsibility to Emily? To the girl I love, whom I have courted and made promises to! What about the responsibility to my own heart? Emily is an intelligent and gracious person who is well liked and indeed respected in this household, not least by my mother. I know full well the expectations of our society, the value conferred upon prospect, breeding and fortune. But I ask you this: is my ability to ultimately care for your estate, to do right by its tenants, to profit from its agriculture, to feed its people, to invest wisely and to preserve it for future generations, really dependent upon me marrying someone of your choice? I do not think so.'

It was Thomas's turn to thump the table, although he came back to a similar argument. 'There are reasons to which you are not privy. Indeed, I do not expect to have to inform you of my motives, to persuade you to agree with my rationale, to debate with you! You should know me well enough to know that I do not make decisions lightly or without good cause. I am your father, and I expect to be obeyed! Without question or argument!' he yelled.

'I do know you, Sir, and all my life I have respected and had faith in you. But you seem not to know *me* or respect *my* aspirations!' William countered, leaning over the table, his face, twisted with rage, inches from his father's. 'You liked Emily well enough when she was Mama's maid. Indeed, at one point I thought that Mama might confer upon Emily the honour of being her companion, so well did she esteem her. She may not be a lady by birth, but by God she is a lady by nature! She is kind, gentle, compassionate, she has good manners and is well-read, she is quick-witted and able to converse easily, with anyone, of any standing. She is clever and bright and beautiful and...'

'*And she may be your SISTER!*' Thomas roared.

William fell back in horror, his mouth open, eyes staring wildly. '*What?... No!*' He shook his head in disbelief. 'I... I do not believe it!... I *will* not believe it... It cannot be so! We are *married!*'

'Then you are dammed, ' uttered Thomas, slumping down into his chair, aghast and spent.

At that moment there was a terrible thud behind them. They turned to find Charlotte on the floor, having fainted and fallen in through the doorway.

Upon seeing his wife Thomas jumped up from his chair. His face was contorted with dismay and remorse. He closed his eyes in instant regret.

'Oh God!' He was at once filled with guilt and self-reproach, but also, in that moment, with a fierce hatred of his son, who had brought to bear the worst possible outcome, a scenario of nightmarish proportions, the very situation which he had barely been able to conceive of but would have given his soul to avoid.

Dazed by incredulity at his father's confession, the room spinning around his head, William staggered backwards then turned towards the door. He saw his mother lying on the floor but was unable to register the event or do anything about it. The words his father had spoken were unthinkable, absurd. Now, one thought and one thought only occupied his mind, driving out all other thoughts and feelings. He must return to his dear Emily, his wife by way of a marriage performed in the sight of God, *blessed by God*. His place was at her side and he needed to make haste.

As he rode hard through the gale to Primrose Cottage, William thought only of Emily. He hoped that by God's grace she was strong enough to survive this and that the physician would prove his worth. Before long he was back at the Popples' farmstead and banging on the door. Prudence opened it; she had been crying.

'Hasten, Sir! She's been askin' for thee.' She rushed past him down the front path to see to the mount.

William ran into the drawing room and straight to Emily's side. Mary and Daniel were supporting their daughter in a sitting position, whilst Doctor North was busy between her knees. She was barely conscious and almost delirious with pain and fever. William could not help the tears that rolled down his cheeks on seeing her worsened condition.

'The child is premature, ' the physician whispered, 'and in my opinion is likely dead, although if born alive I regret to say, will not survive. You must prepare yourself for this.'

William nodded his acknowledgement of the situation and looked briefly at Daniel and Mary before addressing Doctor North quietly.

'Is this the cause of Emily's fever? What of the loss of blood? She has lost so much blood, she is so weak. Good doctor, I beg you, tell us, can you save her? You *must save* her.'

Emily gave a cry and squeezed Wills hand.

'Push! Emily, one more push!' cried Mary.

'Aaaaghhhhhhhhhh!' she screamed. In a final, incredible effort of will power, expending what little strength she had left, Emily gave birth.

The baby was indeed dead. Daniel laid his daughter back upon the pillow whilst his wife cleaned and wrapped the tiny body in a cotton cloth. Daniel made to take the bundle from her, but Mary refused.

'She'll want to see him, ' she stated quietly.

William was cradling his wife's head and shoulders in his arms, dipping a cloth into a fresh bowl of cold water brought by Georgina and pressing it gently against Emily's forehead and cheeks and wiping the perspiration from her neck and hands.

'You are over the worst now, sweetheart. You gave birth to our son, and he is with God now. He was not meant for this world, but he has a place in heaven. Take consolation from that, my precious, precious love.'

He sought her right hand and gently stroked the back of it with his thumb. Emily nodded and her fingers closed softly over his, but her eyes filled with tears.

'May... I... see... him?' she whispered hoarsely, each syllable requiring an immense effort to bring forth.

Mary gave the precious bundle to William before placing another pillow under her daughter's head to raise her up a little. William pulled the cloth from the tiny baby's face and held their son in his arms for Emily to see. His little face was serene and perfectly formed.

'Daniel... Fernleigh' she breathed, smiling up at her mother and father and her husband.

It was her last breath.

The room was suddenly still. All their joy and laughter, their happiness, their hopes and dreams, had followed her to that other place. William, Daniel and Mary looked at one another in horror, unable to believe what had just passed. Doctor North retreated quietly into the back room, gathering Emily's siblings together with him and closing the door.

William's long strangled cry broke the silence.

'*NO!!!*'

He bent over Emily's limp, warm body and held her tightly to him, rocking back and forth on his knees, his sobs muffled in her beautiful red hair.

'No!... No! Don't leave me! Emily... my Emily!'

Daniel gathered Mary to him and they sat silently, trying vainly to comfort one another. After a while William fell quiet too, but remained on his knees by the fireside with his wife in his arms. He was staring past her into the room: staring, but seeing only what was in his mind. His body had ceased its rocking but his head was still making the tiniest of movements, up and down.

Slowly, very slowly, as a great rage began to build within him, William's countenance began to change. Sorrow was temporarily driven aside by wrath, distress giving way to fury, vehemence burying mourning and all saturating his body and pervading the deepest recesses of his mind. There are many sides to grief, but at this moment the ferocity of William's growing anger was not to be denied.

Suddenly he was upon his feet with Emily still in his arms. He had lifted her small, limp body within her blood-stained clothes and carried her to the door.

Daniel looked up dumbfounded, Mary's face buried in his shoulder, his hand on her head, stroking her hair.

William disappeared through the front door into the raging night, carrying his dead wife. He looked up to the heavens and the rain pelted down upon him and his soul was washed from his body and mixed with Emily's blood in the mud beneath his feet.

'We were *innocent!* How could you punish us so?!' he yelled at the unseen deity. *'Look what you have done!'*

He held Emily's slight body out in front of him. The wind tore at her hair and the rain ran in rivulets over her bloodless face.

'You allowed us to meet, yet in circumstances which were beyond our control. You allowed us to love one another, as man and woman do, with a passion so fierce that we should lie together or be forever wretched! You allowed us to *marry!*' he cried, 'and you said *nothing!* You allowed us to utter oaths, to swear to live together in your Ordinance in the holy state of matrimony. You allowed us to conceive a *child!*'

He was screaming now, his wrath matching the thunder in the crow-black skies above.

'If we did not know – we are innocent. If it is untrue – we are innocent! What sick and twisted God arc you, that you should lead us to this point and then abandon us to your anger! How could you *take* her? If our sin was so great, why did you not take *me?!*'

There was no response. No sound but the crashing together of great indistinguishable rainclouds above; of water turned to ice splintering on rock and stone as it hit the Earth from a great height; of the gale that whisked around him as William stood alone in the storm on that terrible night with Emily's corpse in his arms – all that was left of his life.

'I will *never* speak your name again. I denounce you!' he shrieked into the firmament.

William turned his back on God and took Emily's drenched body back into the cottage. Her parents, numbed by their grief, watched wordless as he placed her, dripping wet, back onto the bed in the parlour. He carefully dried her face with the corner of a sheet, smoothed back her long curls, gently kissed her forehead and pulled the sheet over her head.

He turned to look at Daniel and Mary, but could find no words. He made to leave, crossing the room to retrieve his cloak and tricorne, when Daniel came up behind him and laid a hand on his arm.

He turned to see the face of a man old beyond his years, with tears streaming down his cheeks, proffering something in his hand. It was Emily's loop of the gimmel ring.

'The lass'd want thee to 'ave it'. Daniel nodded and choked, encouraging William to take the ring.

William briefly returned the nod and gently took the ring. He kissed it before placing it in a small pocket inside his waistcoat.

'There it shall remain, close to my heart, ' he whispered hoarsely before turning to go. Then he opened the door to the cottage and disappeared into the blackness.

In the early hours of the morning Mary descended the stairs and entered the parlour to be alone with her daughter for the last time. The tiny child had been carefully wrapped and placed on Emily's body.

Together forever in death.

Mary stayed with Emily for some hours, going over matters in her mind. Could this awful tragedy have been avoided? Could she have done more? Indeed she could. She had done too little too late. When Emily had tried to speak to her in the garden that day she should have pursued the matter straight away. She tried to reason with herself: after all, she herself had miscarried, and she had also delivered a stillborn child and come through it, but she knew others who had not. However, the guilt she bore, the guilt from that brief affair, the liaison that had ended before she was married, the guilt that she had lived with since that time, had once again leaked into her consciousness from her conscience. It seeped through every vein, infused every sinew, every fibre, filled every organ and pervaded her mind, and she knew she would never be free of it.

The ignominy of not knowing which man was the father of her child had been a burden she'd had to bear, but she had done so with great resolve. The appalling comprehension that her rape may have resulted in a child was something that she'd had to live with. However, she'd not had to suffer this alone. For Daniel, who was good and kind and loving and was always there for her, shared this understanding. And the uncertainty that was conferred by the fact of their lying together made it so much easier to endure. And after all, Emily was her precious daughter, whom she loved fiercely, and not a soul could take that away from her. But the secret that was her love for Thomas Fernleigh and her lying with him had been shared with no-one. Emily could equally have been his child as his brother's or Daniel's. She would never know. And now she had lost her firstborn — her precious, precious child. There was no doubt that God was punishing her for her past sins. Indeed it was clear to Mary that it had only been a matter of time. The loss of her beloved and cherished daughter was her sentence, and she would have to suffer the guilt for that, alone, for the rest of her days. She did not know how she would bear it.

She reached for the family Bible, which stood upon a stand on a small table in the corner by the window. She opened the tattered leather cover. There inside the front cover were written in tiny script by various hands the names of all the members of the Popple family who had been born and died for over one hundred and fifty years. She scanned the page; the last name to be recorded was Toby. Before him and after the names of her three daughters was written:

Fanny Popple was Born December 19th 1754. Died December 19th 1754. Her soul is with God.

Mary's sad eyes fixed on the entry recording Emily's birth and she stroked the line of script lovingly with one finger, reaching out to her daughter through the faded black ink which had dried so long ago. She rose to fetch quill and ink and sat back at the little table with the Bible in front of her. Her right hand shook as she dipped the sharpened tip of the feather shaft into the ink pot. *I shouldn't be writing this... Emily's child should be writing this in years to come.* She took a deep breath and after the words:

Emily Mary Popple Born August 12th 1743, she slowly penned *Died November 1st 1762. Aged 19 years. May her soul be safely delivered unto heaven.*

Mary brought the tip of her quill, newly loaded with ink, down to the page below Toby's name. She glanced over her shoulder at the little bundle, the little boy conceived of love, who would never be known except for the fact of his being and his name. '*Daniel Fernleigh*': her daughter's last words. She returned her attention to the page in front of her and the entry to be written, but something made her hesitate. She knew only too well what it was, and fought with it for a few moments, but reverence and indeed fear won out. She could not risk displeasing Him after all that had happened. However, she was determined that her little grandson should not be forgotten. She thought for a moment and then rose and placed a chair in the middle of the room underneath the long oak beam where she had hidden the ring. With not a little difficulty, and more by touch than by vision – the light thrown around the room by the single candle standing on the table was meagre – she extracted the ring in its paper wrapping.

Mary unwrapped the ring and took it to the candle with the piece of parchment, which she smoothed out in front of her.

'Daniel Fernleigh, born 1762, ' she murmured.

On the parchment, underneath the Fernleigh crest, she wrote DF B 1762. Then she carefully rewrapped the third loop of the gimmel ring in the inscribed parchment and laid it to rest deep within the old oak beam that supported the Popple family home.

November

*T*he helicopter took off from Brockby's village green in a tornado of autumn leaves, fleetingly illuminated in the wavering beams of its searchlights. The team of medics on board worked seamlessly in a flurry of activity to stabilise Jennifer. Within ten minutes she was being whisked into York Hospital's intensive care unit.

As a team of doctors began their physical examination of Jennifer, Sarah was questioned about her friend's medical history; at least she was encouraged to give them any information she had about medication and any past episodes of unconsciousness. Before leaving the cottage she had grabbed the empty pill bottle that had stood on Jennifer's bedside table. This was now being analysed. Sarah had told them all she knew, which, she admitted frustratingly, wasn't much. She had then made all the necessary phone calls, and Jennifer's distraught parents had arrived from Kent within hours.

Jennifer had been diagnosed as being in a coma, as a charming neurologist with kind eyes subsequently gently explained to them. An examination of her vital signs – temperature, blood pressure, pulse, respiration pattern and so forth – had been encouraging; however, further tests were needed to determine the likely cause of this state and the severity of any potential damage to her brain. Her level of consciousness had been assessed through her response to vocal and pain stimuli and her posture suggested that her brain stem might have sustained some damage. The young consultant went on to explain that they were doing everything they could to establish the cause and status of Jennifer's condition so that they could treat her accordingly. The results of the preliminary investigations were consistent with possible drug use, although he stressed that they could not be sure at this stage and that a battery of further examinations were being performed.

As he spoke, Sarah desperately tried to absorb what he was saying but her mind kept visualising the look on Jennifer's face when they found her lying on the bed, clutching a sheaf of papers in one hand, the other to her stomach; that strange indefinable look, seemingly frozen in time, revealed when Sarah had cautiously brushed back the long mahogany curls that obscured her features.

Sarah tried to focus on what the young doctor was saying, to concentrate on his mouth forming the words. She saw the dark shadow of emerging stubble over his top lip and on his chin and cheeks, leading the eye up to his sculptured cheekbones, but she couldn't grasp his phrases. Her mind floated: *He must be at the end of a long shift*, she thought. *This can't be happening. She was fine on the phone yesterday... only yesterday.*

The neurologist excused himself and went back to his examination. The four of them – Jennifer's mother and father, Sarah and her boyfriend Ben – sat in the small, quiet, blank-walled relative's room, staring at each other for some moments, each lost in their own thoughts, until Ben helpfully offered to go and get them all something hot to drink. It was enough to pull her mind into focus and she offered to help him, feeling slightly better for doing something.

A little while later Mr Gray, the neurologist, returned to give them an update. He spoke considerately but practically. Jennifer was still unconscious but her oculocephalic reflex – the way her eyes moved when her head was rotated, he explained – indicated that her brain stem was intact. This was good news, he elucidated, because this part of the brain, adjoining the spinal cord, is responsible for connecting the motor and sensory systems in the main part of the brain to the rest of the body, regulating the central nervous system and cardiac and respiratory functions. He went on to clarify that the brain stem is also critical in maintaining consciousness and regulating the sleep cycle. That the tests they had carried out so far did not show evidence of damage to this part of the brain boded well for Jennifer's recovery. However, the smallness of her pupils indicated a possible drug overdose, and they had good reason to believe that she had taken a powerful sedative.

Everyone spoke at once. Both of Jennifer's parents hastily and vocally protested that their daughter was certainly not on drugs and had never taken drugs except those medically prescribed. Sarah disputed the implication that her best friend would deliberately take a drug overdose and insisted that Jennifer had been happy and looking forward to seeing her when they spoke less than twenty-four hours before she was found. But it was Ben who took control of the situation. Having never met Jennifer he was able to remain detached from the frustration and denial being experienced by the others.

'Hey, hey... hold on, everyone. Wait a minute. It's okay. Mr Gray isn't necessarily implying that Jennifer was on drugs or was trying to take her life, ' he said, trying for a mix of authority and compassion while desperately seeking calm. 'He's just saying that she took something which has had this effect. Is that right?' Ben turned his blonde spiky-haired head in the direction of the doctor for confirmation.

'Yes, yes, absolutely right, ' Dr Gray affirmed positively. 'There is no indication at all that Jennifer was trying to take her life.' he emphasised. 'Sarah…' his dark eyes fixed on her, 'you told us that Jennifer was having trouble sleeping and that she was taking some kind of natural remedy.' He waited for acknowledgement.

Sarah nodded tearfully. 'I told her not to trust them! I *told* her…'

Ben put her hand on her arm, squeezing it slightly, encouraging her to stay calm. She hunted around in her pocket for a tissue, found a well-used one and attempted to wipe her eyes with what was left of it.

Mr Gray reached for the box of tissues, thoughtfully but rather obviously placed on one of the glass coffee tables, and handed it to Sarah.

'What we discovered from the analysis of the residue left in that bottle of pills that you so helpfully brought with you that it was a mixture of opiate derivatives, among other compounds. Natural, yes. Legal, no. But the label, such as it was, indicated a remedy for sleeplessness. You told us that you don't know where Jennifer obtained these tablets…'

Sarah nodded again, but this time stayed silent.

'…and the source of these pills will need to be investigated in due course. But for now we need to concentrate on Jennifer and her recovery.'

He smiled kindly at the fraught faces, all fixed on him. 'I know you are all desperate to know how serious this is and Jennifer's chances of recovery. She is currently undergoing some brain scans to check for any abnormal brain functioning and we'll continue to monitor her brainwaves using an EEG. The blood work we're doing should confirm our theory about the tablets. Comas can last from several days to several weeks, so you should be prepared. Recovery will be gradual. I won't lie to you, ' he continued, 'the situation is serious; however, the early indications are that there is no serious damage to her brain from the initial trauma.'

Jennifer's parents continued to ask the consultant questions in their desperation to find something to hang onto – some small glimmer of hope, a sliver of a chance of full recovery. If she wasn't in a deep coma, did that mean she would come out of it quickly? If she came out of it quickly, would she have a better chance of full recovery? If the tests they had done so far boded well for recovery – did that mean full recovery? If she wasn't likely to recover fully, what did that mean – what damage was she likely to have suffered? She wasn't breathing when she was found – did that mean she would have suffered brain damage from oxygen starvation?

Mr Gray patiently answered every question as well as he could. The outcome depended on the cause of the coma and the location and extent of neurological damage. Recovery wasn't necessarily linked to how deep the coma was. It was hard to predict the chances of recovery, particularly at this stage. People can emerge from a coma with physical, psychological or intellectual difficulties or combinations of such problems. If this was the case these would need special attention. He stressed again that any recovery typically occurs gradually, with patients usually gaining more and more ability to respond as time goes on.

Finally he said, 'Let's just wait and see, shall we? Take each day as it comes. I *promise* you that we will do everything we can for Jennifer. I would suggest that you go home for a while and try to get some sleep. We will contact you if there's any change.'

At ten o'clock the next morning Sarah was in Jennifer's kitchen trying to force down a piece of toast. She didn't feel hungry, but she knew that her stomach would benefit from it. It was sleeting outside; tiny pieces of ice dashed against the windows, sliding down in watery trails. Jennifer's phone rang. Sarah answered it groggily. She hadn't got to bed until five a.m. and had slept only fitfully.

'That's not Jennifer!' said an unknown, smiling voice.

Sarah's stomach turned over. She may have to tell this person, whoever he was.

'Um, no, Jen is… she's not here at the moment.'

'Ah, is she going to be back soon? I have some exciting news for her!' The voice sounded enthused and eager and hadn't picked up her tone.

'Uh… mm. She's not going to be here for a while. I'm sorry, who is this calling?'

'Oh?' The voice sounded disappointed. 'She didn't say she was going away. Sorry, it's Andy, Andy Finch. Jennifer and I are working on a project together and there's an important development that I wanted to share with her. I've been trying her mobile and I've emailed her but I haven't had a response, which is unlike her. Who am I talking to, by the way?'

Sarah felt a rush of trepidation moving through her, causing her head to feel light. She sat down on the nearest chair at the kitchen table. She didn't know who to tell and who not to tell. She wasn't sure if Jennifer would want all her work colleagues to know. She'd heard her talking about one or two of the senior people that she worked with and knew she had to inform Jennifer's company, but she didn't want to go around telling just anybody. She had to find out a little more about this person first.

'Are you a work colleague of Jennifer's? I'm just about to ring her office, actually. She's… she's not very… she won't be in the office for a while.'

'No, I'm not a work colleague. I'm an historian at York University. Jennifer and I have been working together on a project for some time – nothing to do with her daytime job – and she will *definitely* want to hear the information I have for her.' The voice was getting a little impatient. 'I need to get a message to her. Can you do that for me? Why isn't she answering her mobile? She is okay, isn't she?'

Sarah rested her forehead on the fingers of one hand, elbow on the table. The pain behind her eyes was beginning to spread to the top of her head and the base of her skull. Despondently, she took a deep breath. She would have to break the news to this Andy Finch. But how do you do that? Do you try and break it gently, or do you just come out with it? *My best friend is in a coma, she might never wake up, if she wakes up she might be brain-damaged, she might die.*

She told him as gently she could. 'My name is Sarah. I'm Jennifer's best friend. I'm looking after things for her. You see, Andy – may I call you that? You see…' another deep breath, 'Jennifer is in hospital…'

'Oh no! Has she had an accident? Is she okay?' Andy interrupted.

'I'm afraid it's bad news, ' Sarah continued as calmly as she could, although her hands were shaking. Saying it out loud somehow made it even worse, forced her to face it. 'We… that is, my boyfriend and I… found Jennifer unconscious last night. She was taken to York Hospital and I'm afraid she's still unconscious. We're just about to go back in to see her and to speak to the consultant. They're doing lots of tests. I'm afraid that's all I can tell you for the moment.'

'Jesus Christ!'

'I'm… I'm sorry to have to tell you this bad news.'

There was silence on the end of the phone for a moment.

'Mr Finch? Andy? Are you still there?'

'Yeah, yeah… God, I'm so sorry. I don't know what to say – we only spoke a few days ago, she seemed absolutely fine then. Had she been attacked?'

'No, nothing of that sort.' Sarah was cautious about saying too much. 'We're waiting for some test results.'

'Is she allowed visitors? I'd like to see her.'

'I don't know. She's still unconscious. Look, we're going to the hospital now. If you give me your number I'll call you back later.'

'Okay, please do. I'd be very grateful for any news.'

Jennifer was more stable but still unconscious when they saw her. The drips and machines and wires surrounded her like a damaged, loosely-woven fishing net. Like a fish caught in the midst of it, she could have escaped – but she didn't. She just lay there, motionless, not seeing and not showing any signs of being able to hear anything.

The tests had confirmed that the sleeping tablets had been the cause of her condition, but also that there was apparently no serious damage to the brain. Mr Gray informed them that Jennifer showed good signs of stabilising and had scored fifteen on the Glasgow Coma Scale, which was the highest possible score and very good news as it indicated little or no brain injury. Doctors were continuing to monitor her brainwaves with CT scans and EEG. He was confident that there was no risk of asphyxiation as she seemed to have good control over the muscles in her face and throat and her breathing was good. His caring eyes continually scanned Jennifer's parents and Sarah as he spoke to them, gauging their reactions to what he was saying, reassuring them and giving them hope. Sarah liked him. He told it as it was, but he did it in a way that was informative and didn't insult their intelligence, and he didn't give them false hope where there was none or try to fob them off.

Sarah went to sit with Ben in one of the waiting areas and Jennifer's parents stayed with her for a while. They told her that they loved her and held her hands and stroked her hair and pleaded with her to wake up. After some hours they reluctantly left her side, reassuring her that they would be back the next day, that she should rest and prepare to wake up and that they'd always be there for her.

Sarah took unpaid leave and set up base camp in Primrose Cottage together with Jennifer's parents. All three visited Jennifer every day, sometimes in shifts and sometimes together. They sat around her bed, holding her unresponsive hands, surveying her seemingly lifeless body for any infinitesimal sign of improvement. Other visitors came and went. Everyone was encouraged to talk to her, about anything, just to talk in case she could hear something, register a voice, recognise a familiar sound. Mr Gray was frequently there and Sarah found it comforting to see him.

On the third day Andy Finch appeared at the hospital and introduced himself to Sarah and Jennifer's parents, who all went off into the centre of York for a couple of hours to give him some time alone with Jennifer. He'd spoken to Sarah over the phone and she had filled him in on the details of what had happened and the status of Jennifer's condition.

Andy pulled a chair up beside the bed and retrieved a sheaf of papers from his battered briefcase, laying them on the covers. He took Jennifer's right hand in his and squeezed it, then replaced it on top of the cover and patted it before starting to sort through the papers.

'Right then, young lady, ' he said matter-of-factly, 'there's no point in just lying there, you know! I've got some news for you that you'll want to hear. So liven up and listen! Okay? Concentrating?' He looked up from the papers, patted her hand again and continued.

'Right. Where were we? Last time I spoke to you I told you I'd found one half of the gimmel ring in John Fernleigh's hunting pouch. And I told you about the entries in John Fernleigh's diary and my theory about what might have happened to William, and that this B. Faulks person, the gimmel ring, Liverpool, the services to be carried out for twenty guineas and William's elopement were all somehow connected. If William was murdered and John Fernleigh was behind it – which makes sense seeing that his son eventually inherited the estate – we have the *why*. The name B. Faulks might be a clue to the *who*. And there were indications that the *where* could be Liverpool. So what do you think I did?'

Andy looked sadly at Jennifer's still, porcelain face, hoping that she could hear him, *willing* her to hear him, to respond, to wake up and say *I guess you went to Liverpool, then*.

He continued, in bogus bright tones. 'Yep. You guessed right. Well done. At least we had a date to go on, November the 6th 1762. Since the "services to be carried out", Andy made invisible quotation marks in the air with his index fingers, 'had to be done before this date, my guess was that William and Emily had probably planned to board a ship and set sail on November the 6th, with his uncle's help of course, the bastard. So I went to Liverpool to the Merseyside Maritime Museum and did some digging around in passenger lists in the archives. I couldn't find any passenger lists relating to that time; the embarkation lists seemed to be mainly limited to those of pilgrim ships from England to America in the early 1600s, Jacobite Rebellion prisoners aboard ships to the West Indies and America, or nineteenth-century emigration records – there were plenty of those. Ironically, debarkation passenger lists for the eighteenth century seem to be much more comprehensive, but that's no good if we don't know where they were going – and they never got there anyway. So I had to find another way of trying to trace what ships had left Liverpool around November the 6th. I found out that Liverpool's shipping was subject to a series of Acts of Parliament which required the details of vessels to be registered from about the mid-eighteenth century on-wards. So I looked through the ships' registers, which was no mean feat, I can tell you. These registers record details of vessels and their ownership. Are you with me so far?'

Andy shuffled the papers in front of him and then took Jennifer's right hand in his left and squeezed it tightly. He continued to hold her hand as he spoke, gently stroking her delicate white skin with his thumb.

'C'mon Jennifer, buck up. Show me a sign that you're keeping up. I know you can hear me.' He tutted and raised his eyebrows: 'Tch, you're like some of my students! Okay then, I'll continue, but you'd better be listening.'

'Right; so I looked through the records of vessel owners in the transaction books, but these only gave me vessel registrations and changing ownership, which didn't help much except to give me an idea of the names of some of the vessels sailing out of Liverpool. There was another register that gave details of vessels visiting the port but which weren't registered there, but that only started being recorded in 1788. So I tried a different tack: I looked in the Customs bills of entry. Records around that time are a little variable – they got much better later – but at least they covered the incoming and outgoing voy-ages of merchant ships. I thought if I was able to find one that sailed on November the 6th there was a chance that they took a few paying passengers on board as well as their cargo.'

'Not surprisingly, Customs bills of entry – do you know what those are?... No? I guess not then. Jennifer, I have to say you don't look very interested.' Andy inclined his head at her and raised his eyebrows in a mock scold. 'Where were we? Oh yeah, Customs bills of entry, in other words the incoming overseas and coastal traffic in-formation. Well I found that these were much more comprehensive than the information documented about exports. Which is a shame, since they seemed to be pretty good at recording all kinds of useful details about imports. The bills of export mostly give only summary detail, but at least these records included cargoes and destinations, and which vessels loaded in which docks, and the names of the agents responsible. But it seems that I was in luck, because I knew the date of departure so I could trace the vessels that left on that date. And what do you think I found?'

Andy stopped stroking Jennifer's hand with his thumb, instead squeezing and patting it again in turn.

'Okay, now we come to the really exciting bit! Now concentrate, Jennifer – listen and take it in. This is what we've both been working towards, one of the final pieces in the jigsaw. You excited? Me too.'

He smiled at her regretfully. *God... wake-up Jennifer! Come on! We've nearly solved the puzzle... we're so near. This is what you wanted; you need to hear this, you need to get closure.*

'I found a record of a ship called Brigantine carrying a mixed cargo bound for Dublin and then Bordeaux. And what do you think the agent's name was?'

Andy looked up from the papers now strewn over the bed and stared at Jennifer's closed eyes, *willing* her to open them.

'Yep, ' he nodded, 'a Mr Bartholomew Faulks! Jesus, Jennifer, my heart was in my mouth, I can tell you! And I got a pretty weird feeling that I'd seen the name of that ship before. So I looked back in the transaction books and I found that bastard's name... John Fernleigh. He only owned the ship! It was all beginning to come together, finally. God, I was so excited! So I examined the cargo records of the Brigantine for November the 6th 1762 and found it to be mainly rum and sugar, but also wool – *and* there were some paying passengers listed!'

Andy took a deep breath and let it go slowly. He smiled at Jennifer and nodded.

'There it was, right on the page in front of me, the name '*Fernleigh Willm.*' And written next to that was '*plus wife.*' I couldn't believe my eyes! But you know, the odd thing was that the '*plus wife*' text had been crossed out. So it seems from the records that William had boarded the ship without Emily, which I didn't understand at all. That is, until your friend Sarah showed me the papers you were clutching when they found you. Emily's burial record.'

Andy looked at Jennifer ruefully. He sighed and scratched his chin through his beard, letting go of Jennifer's hand, then stretched his arms in the air, yawning. He was getting a little stiff sitting on the hard hospital bedside chair. It was an old chair with a red plastic wipe-able seat cover that was split and frayed at the edges, the slightly grey stuffing showing through. He made to get up and caught his trousers on the edge of the split where a piece of plastic stuck out. *Damn, another hole – yet another pair of trousers consigned to dog walking!* He pulled the back of his trousers from the chair, got up and paced around a little, glancing out of the window into the car park. The sky was purple with storm clouds. *Jeez, will it ever stop raining?*

After stretching his neck a little from side to side and back and forth and yawning again, he sat back down beside Jennifer.

'Y' know, Jennifer?' he said with renewed brightness, nodding his head at her, 'you're working with a pretty clever bloke! I look forward to you telling me that one day, ' he smiled. 'Anyway, so I managed to find the customs bills of entry for the Brigantine for Dublin and I'm sorry to say that as I suspected, William's name wasn't on it. So as I see it, that leaves us with two possibilities. Either William was murdered somewhere between Liverpool and Dublin and his body thrown overboard – there was no mention of a corpse being unloaded at Dublin, and anyway in those days it was common for people to be buried at sea; a body could have hardly been left on a ship for days on end. Or... the records show that he boarded the ship, but perhaps he was killed before it set sail, in which case the captain was probably in league with the agent. However, I suspect that involving others in the plot would have been quite risky, even if you paid them well.

'Whichever way it happened, William's ring was no doubt returned to John Fernleigh, and his body was buried at Fernleigh Hall. We know that because there's a grave and a burial record. I had to think about that a while. So if it happened at sea, it must have happened fairly near the coast for his body to wash up and be identified somehow, perhaps as they set sail. They could have made it look like an accident or suicide easily enough. They could have thrown him in and then fished him out again as they set sail, leaving him behind in the charge of the ship's agent. I suspect we'll never know. What's also bothering me is that I don't know what happened to Emily, and why she was buried in Brockby only a couple of days before they were due to set sail.'

He looked at Jennifer's ingenuous face a little disapprovingly, shaking his head slightly.

'But I suspect you know what happened, don't you? I suspect that's what led you to this hospital bed, lying there all innocent, in a bloody *coma!*'

The anger inside Andy, which had been suppressed under a lid of positivity and bright determination, finally boiled over like escaping steam and bubbling liquid from a saucepan that had been abandoned on the heat for too long. He thumped the bed beside Jennifer's legs and stood up suddenly, running one hand through his hair, knocking his chair backwards to fall to the floor with a crash. He felt like kicking it, but instead picked it up slowly and tried to compose himself.

What he hadn't seen was the faintest movement in Jennifer's eye lids as the chair hit the floor.

He took a deep breath. 'There's also something else which isn't quite right... to me, anyway.' He continued to try to talk to her calmly as he sat down again. 'There would have been, ' he paused, '*no doubt* there would have been correspondence between William and his family. Yet I haven't come across any yet in all the papers I've searched through. So why is that?' Andy shook his head, screwing his face up so that his eyebrows headed towards one another.

'So I'm going to continue to dig.' He took a deep breath and straightened up in the chair. 'And you, my girl, are going to come out of this ridiculous coma! *Do you hear me!*' He glanced towards the door. 'Oh, look sharp, ' he smiled and inclined his head towards Jennifer again, 'there's a nurse coming to check up on you, so behave yourself. I'd better be going... but I'll be back – oh yes, you can be sure of that. And when I return, you'd better have opened your eyes!'

He leaned over and kissed Jennifer lightly on the forehead before exchanging pleasantries with the nurse and leaving her room.

A few more days went by. Sarah visited Jennifer every day and watched the stream of visitors that came and went. Some people talked to Jennifer, some played music to her, others sat in silence, holding her hands. Every day the neurologist came to examine her, and each time he had some kind words for Sarah.

Eventually the day came that everybody had been wishing and hoping for, praying and willing to happen – Jennifer's eyelashes fluttered and she opened her eyes, just for a second or two. Jennifer's mother was with her at the time, and it sent her running down the corridor to fetch the nurse, hands in the air waving frantically and grinning like the proverbial Cheshire cat.

The following day Jennifer's eyes stayed open a little longer and she murmured her first words. When she opened her eyes it was clear that she was confused. She didn't recognise where she was, and it seemed that she didn't recognise the faces around her. She wanted to know where her baby was. Jennifer's mother gently tried to bring Jennifer to focus on her and her husband, but Jennifer simply repeated the question Where's my baby? Where's my little babbie? When tentatively questioned about this, Jennifer replied with the tone of one who is incredulous that the question is even being asked.

'Daniel of course. Daniel Fernleigh. My little man. Where is he?' she muttered.

Eleven

William arrived in Liverpool on the evening of the 5th of November and located the ship's agent as his uncle had instructed. He was dead inside. Outside, bone and skin, but inside, nothing. A hard, dead core. He cared not whether he slept or fed. The bustling port was nothing to him; he did not register it. He saw only blackness. He spoke merely a few words to the agent, and when asked where his good lady wife was to be found, he muttered simply, 'She is dead'.

Mr Bartholomew Foulkes, a short, slightly shabby man with an ill-fitting wig, looked at him curiously and gave him instructions on where to find the ship the following morning, pointing him in the direction of an inn where he could lodge for the night.

That night, by the light of a meagre candle whose flame bent to the will of the cold draft that emanated from the small casement window, William wrote a letter to his father. He did not know what he intended to do; he cared not if he lived or died. He had no inclination to make a decision on the matter – he was simply following a set of instructions and fate would take its course. Perhaps he would throw himself overboard; if the mood should take him. Perhaps he would arrive in France and wander aimlessly until he perished one way or another. It was all the same to him. The one thing that he was certain of was that he could never return home. For that he blamed his father, and was determined that he should know this.

William dipped the tip of the quill in a small glass bottle of dark ink, tapping it briefly on the rim of the vessel. He rubbed his eyes with the thumb and forefinger of his left hand and took a deep sad breath as he placed the nib on the parchment laid out in front of him.

Father.

It is with deep sorrow that I write these words. However I must clear my conscience and you Sir shall know what suffering you have conveyed upon your son.

You taught me to behave honourably and though I strayed from the path of propriety, my intentions towards Emily were always respectable. From the very moment that love for her filled my heart, I determined that we should be married. This was not a flight of fancy, a trifle, a thing to be taken up and put down again as excitement and dullness dictate. This was not a passion that could be deflected by duty, or cast aside for conformity. If you believed that Sir, you were vastly mistaken.

You spoke of duty, of obedience, of conventionality. Those are weighty words indeed, yet they are no match for the deep passion, loyalty, devotion and commitment that filled my soul and yet reign over my heart. And Sir, do not underestimate the strength of my allegiance to my family — the deep affection in which I hold my sisters, the love I bear Mama. And you Sir, you surely must concede knowledge of the respect and esteem I have always borne you.

And yet you could not retain belief in me. You spoke of obligation as if I were an unapprised child who could not grasp the concept. You spoke of passion, but of a passion that was usurped by privilege and accompanying responsibility. Such a passion I cannot understand. Oh, but I understand now only too well the vehemence with which you delivered your verdict upon me. An intensity fuelled by the knowledge of one who knows what it is to be in such a position. One who knows and chose to turn his back on it. One who has lived with regret.

Three years separated Emily and me and a good many more, my elder sisters and she. What say you of faithfulness, of fidelity? How will you answer on the Day of Judgment?

As for me, you should know that my conscience is clear. I had a lover and wife and <u>seven</u> sisters, no more, no less. You forced me to choose between my family and the brightest light in my life. A hopeless, miserable choice. I followed the course I chose because you forced me to do so. Ultimately there was no option but to turn my back on my most precious family in order that the love which Emily and I bore one another could continue to illuminate our world. Now the light has been extinguished and I am choking on the smoke and stumbling in the darkness.

I have imparted the last of my sentiments to you. I am empty now, devoid of sensation. There is a numbness at the very core of me and I will never be rid of it. I welcome it. I embrace it, for it is a barrier against the pain, which I cannot bear.

I care not what becomes of me. You shall convey to Mama and my sisters what you will.

So that you shall know that this is truly my hand, though impossible to doubt it, I enclose my loop of the gimmel ring which I bestowed upon Emily on the occasion of our engagement. You shall find its twin in the possession of Emily's mother, who we intended should be witness to our union. The third loop, the ring which I placed upon Emily's finger upon our wedding day, I shall keep close to my heart until the day I shall die.

Your son, William.

As soon as the ink was dry, William withdrew the gimmel loop from the ring finger of his left hand and placed it in the middle of the parchment. He folded the paper carefully around it and addressed the letter to his father on the plain side. He took the candle stub from its holder and dripped a pool of wax onto the folded edges, sealing the ring inside and the document from prying eyes. Taking a small seal from his jacket pocket, he made his mark – his final mark. Like the candle, he was spent.

He finished the pitcher of indefinable red wine on the table beside him in easy gulps of necessity rather than enjoyment and rose to seek the innkeeper for more wine and to summon a messenger.

Having delivered the letter safe into the hands of a rider, William lay back upon his bed, wine glass in one hand and pitcher in the other. At some time during the night he dispensed with the glass. He did not sleep.

William rose wearily at dawn and made his way unsteadily to the harbour, where the Brigantine was tugging at its moorings. He gave his name to the captain along with a pouch of silver coins and boarded the vessel, carrying only his saddlebags. He went below and was shown to a tiny room in the aft of the vessel by a ragged boy who looked barely ten years old and had no shoes on his feet. He dropped his bags onto the small wooden bunk and went up on deck for some fresh air. The crew were busy preparing the ship for embarkation and bringing last-minute provisions on board. Mercifully, they were too busy to engage with him and he kept out of their way.

He took some deep breaths of cold salt-laden air and tasted the smell of rotting fish heads, tar and seaweed. The Brigantine swayed in the strengthening breeze and William swayed with it, though he could not be sure whether it was the undulation of the waves in the harbour or the effect of the wine that dislodged his balance.

Suddenly his feet were somehow not beneath him and his head hit the deck with a loud crack. He groaned and momentarily closed his eyes against the sharp pain that darted through his temples and filled the front of his skull. He opened his eyes again to a pair of scuffed black leather shoes, incongruously adorned with large square silver buckles. He took the hand that was proffered to him and, squinting against the bright white sky, saw that it belonged to the shabby ship's agent. He was pulled unceremoniously to his feet by Bartholomew Foulkes, whose face was wearing a strange look somewhere between a smile and a sneer.

The man lent towards him and whispered, 'With the compliments of your Uncle John.'

Before William could respond Foulkes hit him squarely in the stomach so that he doubled over in pain and struggled for breath. He sank to his knees, gasping, trying desperately to inflate his lungs with air and for an instant he struggled to think. How did this man know his uncle? What did this man have against him? Surely they'd only met for the first time the evening before? Why was he being attacked? What had any of this to do with John Fernleigh? The words resounded in his consciousness; *With the compliments of your uncle John*. Then, just as it became too late, he finally understood.

The final blow came across the back of his head. William lost consciousness until he hit the freezing water. The blood that was gushing from the gashed skin and the fissure at the bottom of his skull merged with the foul harbour water and invaded his lungs as he involuntarily tried to breathe through his open mouth.

Unable to fill his lungs with air, William felt his head instinctively tilt back and his arms bear down upon the water in an effort to raise his mouth long enough to take a breath, but he could not seem to keep his mouth from going under. Again and again he tried, but it was no use. He found that he could not call out, and somehow his limbs did not feel connected to him any longer.

His head was spinning, and for a few moments he felt strangely euphoric. Now Emily's beautiful smiling face was before him and she was beckoning him, mutely, willing him to come to her, to be with her.

William reached out to her silently. All was now black around him – all but her exquisite face. And he was moving towards her. Soon he would be with her again. It was all he ever wanted. He smiled as the last of his breath left his body.

Bartholomew Foulkes quickly wiped the butt of his pistol on a rag that he had carried in his pocket for that express purpose and concealed the weapon under his coat. He looked around him. He had carried out the deed with ingenuity, if he said so himself. The crew were all still busy with their various tasks, focused by the impending deadline of making the Brigantine ready to set sail just after the turning of the tide, when the water was at its peak in the harbour and the current would assist their passage against the prevailing south-westerly wind. Indeed the tide was already on the turn; debris bobbed around in the water, being pulled towards and off shore in turn by each ebb and flow, though hardly moving at all. Foulkes smiled to himself. It was the perfect time, and his plan had so far worked superbly. A body would float around in the harbour for a short while yet before being dragged out to the open water. He had only to complete the second half of the scheme.

Foulkes indulged himself for a moment, allowing his mind to settle on the sum of money that he would be paid. Indeed it was an extremely handsome sum, and would suit him very well. Then, with the mind-set of a colonel carrying out a meticulously-planned campaign, he chose a purposeful stride and walked towards a stack of casks that were being brought onto the ship. He took a small notebook out of his coat pocket and pretended to look at it whilst examining the casks. He dared not take too long over this task; he knew that he must make haste and leave the ship but was wary of drawing too much attention to himself, and his pretence of examining the cargo against his notes was a useful diversion. Time was pushing on, however, and he must make his way to the dockside.

On reaching the wharf, Foulkes sought one of the watermen, who were usually preparing for their daily routine at this time. He spied a group of men preparing a small boat for departure and noted the man giving orders. Again his stride was full of purpose. He walked over to the man, who was standing on the dockside coiling a skein of rope. He started to make small talk with him about the dreadful state of the harbour. He mentioned casually that it must make it difficult for the man to carry out his responsibilities effectively, given all the debris floating around, although perhaps when a ship had been lured onto rocks and smashed up by the waves the floating remains would deliver some sort of a clue to whether illegal activities had been going on. But surely that would be too late, would it not?

'Why, there is even a cask bobbing around out there now, Sir, if my eyes do not deceive me, ' he said in the tone of one who was trying to be helpful.

The waterman, a burly but fit fellow, qualities essential for doing his job well, turned his head of bleached curls to look in the direction that Foulkes was indicating with his eyes. He ignored the remarks about the state of the harbour and concentrated on the object bobbing about in the water.

'Your eyes do deceive you, Sir. If I am correct, and I mean you no insult, that is no cask.'

The waterman's well-trained eyes focused on the object and the way it moved in the water and the level at which it lay in the undulating swell. It was worthy of his investigation, and he called to his assistants.

The group of customs men rowed out to the body and pulled it alongside the boat with a boarding pike. One of them took hold of William's coat and the other his breeches, and together they hauled his body on board. The water had slowed the blood-clotting process and the gash on his skull was still bloody and highly evident. Several creatures had already settled themselves in his hair and had begun to feed. Expertly and without rocking the boat, the men turned the corpse over so that the face was staring towards them. The eyes were shut, but unusually the face had the most serene look upon it. They rowed the corpse up to the harbour wall and landed it, four men carrying it roughly up the slipway and placing it on the coarse stone flags.

Quite a crowd had gathered on the dockside at the top of the slipway. This was not an unusual occurrence; however, folk always liked a bit of gossip to start the day. Foulkes joined the crowd. The waterman asked the gathering throng if anyone knew the man.

Foulkes feigned a mixture of shock and disbelief. He frowned. 'Aye, I do, ' he said incredulously, 'I only met the man yesterday… when he came into my office asking for directions to the Brigantine. He and his wife were on the passenger list. I sent him in the direction of the Edgewater Inn where he could lay his head for the night. I forget his name, but my records will show who he is. He seemed well enough, although somewhat dispirited when I met him not twelve hours ago. I enquired after his wife, but he told me she was dead.'

The waterman nodded. 'Anybody else see him?' he enquired. 'Did he board the Brigantine?'

The little cabin boy who had shown William to his quarters had forced himself through the legs of the standing crowd, much to the annoyance of a particularly short woman who until this moment had had an uninterrupted view of the proceedings. He now found his voice.

He pointed at the Brigantine and cried 'I recognise him, Sir! I showed him onto that ship there. Only this morning, I showed him to his cabin. I don't think he had his sea legs, Sir, ' the boy continued, enjoying the attention focused upon him. 'He looked wan.'

The boy remembered the shilling that the man had given him. It was a generous reward for the small service that he had performed and he felt a little loyalty to this unhappy pale-looking stranger. 'He seemed troubled, ' he added.

Instead of the scolding he expected for giving his opinion, a silver-buckled man with an ill-fitting wig agreed with him and seemed interested in what he had to say.

'Unhappy, you say? Troubled, you say?'

The boy nodded and wiped his nose with the back of his dirty hand.

'Did this man give you any money?' said Foulkes. 'Did he pay you to say this?'

The boy thought for a moment, then shook his blonde curls in denial. He wasn't going to declare the generous sum that this strange benefactor had left him with in case he was made to give it up.

Foulkes looked at the waterman for some decisive action or declaration. The waterman was stroking his short greying beard, trying to decide what to do. The body was too large for him to take back to the customs house, as he had nowhere to put it. The storerooms were full of stolen and mislaid goods waiting to be investigated or dealt with. He was a busy man, and this corpse was an irritation to him.

A young girl stepped forward shyly. Foulkes narrowed his eyes. He recognised her as one of the barmaids from the Edgewater Inn, to which he had directed the deceased last evening. His stomach gave a small lurch. What might this young woman have to say? He must be ready with a rebuff or a response of some kind.

'This man stayed at the inn last night, ' she volunteered shyly, her breast heaving at the sudden unwanted attention focused upon her, but speaking out of duty. Foulkes noticed her timidity, which pleased him. Her inexperience would be easy to deal with. Her voice trembled, and the waterman looked at her kindly and nodded.

'Go on, ' he said encouragingly. If she had something worth saying then he'd better hear it and get this matter over with as quickly as possible.

'I took him a pitcher of wine, but he asked for no food. Later in the evening he asked for a second jug of wine and I could tell he was very unsteady on his feet. He left without a word this morning, but I could see he was intoxicated by his gait.'

'Did he have company?' the waterman asked solemnly.

She shook her head. 'Not as far as I am aware, Sir; he drank alone. When I visited his room to bring him the wine he seemed to be writing letters.'

'I boarded the Brigantine this morning, Sir, ' Foulkes interjected. 'I did not see this man. However, I was busy checking the cargo. If, as these fine folks here say, this man seemed to be intoxicated when he boarded the ship and was unsteady on his feet it would not be surprising if he were to fall overboard. Perhaps those wounds on his head are a result of his falling from a great height and hitting the rocks at the bottom of the harbour before he resurfaced. That could explain the other marks on his body perchance?' Foulkes volunteered in his most practiced, obliging voice. He employed a number of voices and mannerisms to suit the occasion in the course of his business, and was usually pleased with the results.

The waterman nodded and looked over at the Brigantine swaying gently to and fro on its moorings, eager to get away on the morning tide. The height of the main deck was likely twenty-five feet above the water. He acknowledged Foulkes' observations.

'It is possible, sir. You are indeed perceptive. There does appear to be some bruising on this body.'

The waterman arose from his kneeling position. 'Thank you, kind folks, ' he said abruptly. It was an instruction for the gathering to disperse, 'I will deal with this matter from now on.' He muttered to one of his assistants, 'All we have to do, Roger, is find a place to lay him out whilst we conclude our investigations and then hand him over to the judiciary.'

Foulkes pricked up his ears and stepped in. It was the perfect opportunity that he had hoped for.

'If I may be of any further assistance please do not hesitate to call upon me. You know where my offices are, do you not?' Tentatively, and with the perfect amount of reverence, he added, 'We do have room to lay this poor man out if you wish.'

The waterman looked at his assistants and they at one another. They did not want to have to lug this corpse any further than they had to. Their leader concurred.

'That would be most kind of you, sir. We would indeed be grateful, as we do not have a great deal of room within the customs house at the present time.' He smiled ruefully. Business was good for the smugglers, and in truth for them too.

The four men trudged the sixty yards or so to the agent's offices carrying the sodden corpse and laid it out, dripping, on a large oak table from which Foulkes had quickly gathered a number of large charts, depositing them on his desk by the window.

Foulkes, ever the helpful gentleman, furnished each man with a small tot of rum from a decanter and a number of silver-rimmed glasses standing on a silver tray on a small table in the corner. He poured one for himself and raised his glass. 'Against the cold, ' he toasted.

The men reciprocated, each downing the warming liquor in one. The waterman looked at Foulkes as he drank his. He had never really liked the agent, though he was dammed if he could tell you why. There was just something about the man that stuck in his gullet. He wasn't a true gentleman, though he had pretensions to being one. He did not dress particularly well, and often sported incongruous adornments; he worked long hours to earn his living, yet his office was furnished with extremely fine taste; the silver and cut-glass decanter set was particularly fine. The waterman had an eye for these details, having come across much finery – mostly smuggled or stolen, or both – in his occupation. Yet the agent had always been most polite towards him and never given him cause for suspicion. He shrugged his misgivings off. He'd better be about his business. He had to go and notify the judiciary, and he was already late with the day's other duties.

The watermen thanked Foulkes and left him alone with William's body.

Foulkes drew the shutters closed and bolted the door to his office. The bolt was a useful barrier between him and the outside world; he had had it fitted about eighteen months ago to prevent unexpected visitors from disturbing him at his various duties. He knew that he did not have much time; the waterman would undoubtedly be seeking the judiciary, for he did not have the ultimate authority to conclude this matter.

William's body lay on Foulkes' large oak table; one of the men had thoughtfully covered the face with a rag, no doubt fished from his pocket for it smelt as if it had lain damp for quite a while. Foulkes shivered. Today was cold and not a little dampness hung in the air. He dared not have a fire lit in his room just yet because of the presence of the body.

He had to be quick. His sharp eyes scanned rapidly over William's body for the ring that he had been instructed would be there. It clearly was not. Foulkes frowned and his mouth settled into a mean, determined pose. He set his teeth and began rummaging around inside William's outer coat, searching the pockets and the contents thereof. He found nothing of interest in the outer pockets: a handkerchief, a Fernleigh seal, two guineas, some shillings and a few pennies. He left the money where it was. He would have no need of it once he had received his fee from John Fernleigh. Better to leave the coins where they were so as not to arouse suspicion – after all William Fernleigh was a wealthy man by appearance and to all intents and purposes was setting off on a long journey; it was to be expected that he would carry a decent sum of money about his person. His hand hovered over the guineas, his long, nimble fingers closing upon one of the coins. One guinea would not be missed; its twin would remain to allay mistrust. Concern rose in him as he searched for the ring. If he did not find it and send it back to John Fernleigh he would be paid no fee. He may have killed the man, but there would be no proof that this was William Fernleigh. In fact he had risked much and had little to gain from the murder he had just committed. This man was nothing to him. He had killed men before, but he would not risk the hangman's noose for a trifle. Indeed the fee offered was a life-changing sum and he could do much with it to enhance his social position.

He would not take the coat off as it would be difficult to put back on again in a hurry, particularly as it was wet. However, Foulkes undid the waistcoat and peeled it back to reveal two inner breast pockets, one on either side. He felt first in one and then the other. In the left pocket his fingers came upon the small hard object. He smiled a slow sly smile, almost a sneer, and his thieving fingers reached inside the pocket and drew out a bright golden ring.

He walked to the window and held it up within a thread of light that penetrated the darkened room through a chink in the shutters. There were some markings on it which he could not make out; however, that was exactly as John Fernleigh had described it to him late one night in the Navigation Inn over a fine bottle of brandy and a beef and oyster pie. Foulkes placed the ring in his own breast pocket, returned to the shadowy body and quickly buttoned up its waistcoat and coat. Then he half-opened the shutters, slid the bolt on his door back and sat at his desk to write two letters.

The first was to Lord Fernleigh, informing him of the tragic death of his son with many condolences. The second, in which he enclosed the ring wrapped in a small parcel of parchment, was of course to John Fernleigh, to whom he simply wrote:

The task has been carried out according to your instruction.

Please find enclosed evidence that I speak the truth.

I remain your most humble and obliging servant.

Yours etcetera, B.F.

He folded and sealed each letter carefully, placing them in his coat pocket while he went to send for the messenger, a particular young man that he used whenever there was business of the utmost importance to attend to. The young man was in Foulkes's pay and very much in his pocket. He was reliable, not least because he was well paid when the occasion called for it and he knew that Foulkes would punish him severely if he did not carry out the tasks he was given in a satisfactory manner. The young messenger arrived and was given the letters and his instructions. He was to deliver John Fernleigh's letter first and then the second to his brother, Lord Thomas Fernleigh.

Foulkes handed the messenger a coin and looked at him sternly. 'This is for your expenses, ' he said. 'You shall be paid another on your return.'

The man looked into his palm, in which a shiny guinea lay. He gasped and smiled in amazed gratitude. It was more than he had ever been paid before. This must be a delivery of incredible importance.

'Look sharp, and on no account are you to misplace these letters or indeed to show them to *anyone*, ' Foulkes barked. 'The Fernleighs will be expecting each seal to remain as it is.'

The man nodded and protested that he had always carried out Mr Foulkes' instructions satisfactorily, had he not? He was desperate for his employer to trust him – desperate to receive the second guinea. Foulkes inclined his head at the young man. His wig was already slightly askew, and the angle of his head exaggerated the slant and had the effect of making him look quite comical. However, the messenger was not smiling. The look on Foulkes's face was deadly serious.

'And do *not*... on *any* account... deliver the wrong letter to the wrong Fernleigh, or your head will end up on my dinner plate! Do you understand what is being asked of you?' Foulkes spoke every word with menace.

The messenger nodded and muttered 'Yes sir, of course sir, ' and backed away quickly before he could be detained any further in this man's threatening presence. He knew Foulkes spoke the truth. He'd better do the job and be back with proof of the deed or he would indeed lose his head. He would guard these letters with his life, as his life depended on it. And he would ensure that they were delivered safely. He could think on the sum that he was being paid whilst he was doing it.

At a little after a quarter past ten the magistrate arrived to take a look at the corpse. Having listened to the evidence presented to him by the waterman and seen the damage to the body with his own eyes, he rapidly concluded that the cause of death was accidental, brought about by a fall from the ship's deck due to the subject being intoxicated. The magistrate was pleased: this was a simple case and he had other, more pleasurable business to attend to. He would be able to conclude his report by lunchtime, which would suit him most favourably as he had a rendezvous planned with an attractive young woman.

Foulkes arranged for William's body to be carried back to Fernleigh Hall and the matter was concluded within the day.

November 30th 1762

Sleet threw itself carelessly at the long windows of Thomas' study. Thomas was sitting at his secretaire, staring blankly through the glass panes. Though he stared, he saw nothing of the world outside him: the furious wind, the gale whipped out of nowhere, the frozen rain attacking all in its path unfeelingly, cruelly. The world was angry at the waste of human life: two innocent lives lost. God was angry and He had sent a storm to imprison Thomas in his home. The storm had raged on and off for the eighteen days since the funeral of his beloved son, matching Thomas' fury and punishing him at the same time.

As he sat there Thomas could no longer hold back the tears, which tumbled down his cheeks in a torrent. It was a release. He had tried to be strong for his family, for his dear wife, whom he loved deeply and who had lost her beloved son, and for his daughters, for whom he cared fiercely, each one experiencing the terrible loss of her only brother.

The family was in pieces. Thomas had tried to remain strong, to keep things together for the sake of everyone else. Holding the Fernleigh family together was more important to him at this time than any of his own feelings.

In the long days since the funeral the family, who had all come together to support one another in grief and in the face of their appalling loss, had gradually dispersed, Catherine and Charlotte returning to their homes with their husbands, Amelia and Bertram leaving only that morning.

On hearing of her beloved son's death from her husband, Charlotte had emitted a long strangled cry of absolute anguish and collapsed. When, later, she found herself in her bedchamber with Thomas at her side, she had dismissed him and had not spoken to him since. Her husband was to blame; her husband and only her husband. She could not bear to look upon him. She felt as though she had been cut down like a willow sapling under the heavy hand of a basket weaver; like a tree felled for a purpose no longer relevant, almost forgotten, but felled just the same. Indeed, since she had learned of Emily's possible parentage Charlotte had hardly spoken a word to anyone. She could not bear to speak – not even to her own daughters, which had caused them no end of incomprehensible pain. However their very presence reminded her that she had a family, and that one member of that family was missing and she would never be able to look upon his beautiful face again. She wanted the world to disappear; she wanted to disappear herself. The only company she allowed herself was that of loyal Mrs Preedy, and even this was limited to the fetching of broth. She could let nothing solid pass her lips.

Charlotte had been stunned like a frightened rabbit at the approach of a hungry fox, not knowing whether to stay or to run. She had remained frozen within that dreadful moment at which she had learned the truth. Upon William's disappearance after the death of his wife, anxiety had added to her pain. Her stomach was constantly churning and moved in great leaps and lurches so that she felt queasy most of the time. Her heart beat wildly in her breast, now and then to an irregular rhythm; sometimes she feared that it was missing a beat or would overexert itself and give out altogether.

She had stood side by side with her husband in the little churchyard in the village of Brockby at the funeral of poor dear Emily, the maid who had betrayed her, the girl she had allowed herself to love and who had let her down and taken away her son. She had done her duty. Her face had shown nothing of the torment within. She had looked across at the face of Mary Popple. She had not felt anger towards the woman then, but pity, for Mary had lost a child and Charlotte could imagine that anguish.

Thomas had sent a carriage to convey the Popple family to the church behind the hearse, and they themselves had followed second as a mark of respect. Whilst Charlotte hid her emotions from the world, Mary could not conceal her suffering, which showed itself in her eyes, across her forehead, in the way her mouth set itself and in the wringing of her hands.

The baby had been placed in Emily's coffin and no-one but the Popple family, the good doctor and Thomas and Charlotte knew of its existence. The child – William's son, the possible heir to the Fernleigh estate – *her grandchild*. Charlotte could not keep the thoughts from whirling around her mind. If Emily had been Daniel's daughter, or even John's, the little boy would have been the heir to the Fernleigh estate. If Emily had been Thomas' daughter... *dear God!* It was unthinkable, and she had heaved the thought from her mind at that moment.

Charlotte had stood there next to her husband at Emily's burial wearing an impenetrable mask. No-one, not even her husband, could see what was beyond it. She had even managed a nod and a sympathetic smile towards Mary.

'I am sorry for your great loss, ' Charlotte's conscience had bestowed kindly, though a smaller, meaner voice inside had whispered, *This woman is your enemy.* This woman had betrayed her; she had betrayed her own daughter.

Thus Charlotte deprived herself of her daughters' company, as her daughters reminded her of the loss of her son and she did not know how she could carry on without William. William, the sun of her days; William's smiling twinkling eyes, William's gentleness and perceptiveness; William's humour; William's logic and sentiment; William's kind words; William's plans for the estate; William's soft kiss upon her cheek; William's laughter.

Charlotte knew somewhere in the murky recesses of her mind that she would have to face the world sometime; however, she had entered a long period of mourning and it was not expected that she make calls or receive visitors for many a month. For now it was enough to stay in her room and stare out at the long winter days ahead, the chill of the icy November days reflecting the feeling in her heart.

This morning, the older girls having departed, Mary reading in her room and Anne, Rebecca and Elizabeth at their embroidery, each lost in their own thoughts of their beloved brother, Thomas had again entreated Charlotte to talk to him, to let him talk to her, but again she had refused. He would need to give her time – plenty of time. They had had a strong marriage; he hoped that it was enough. Through the long years of their marriage they had grown to love one another and had always supported each other. Of course he bitterly regretted the affair that he had started – he alone was to blame for that. But since that time he had devoted himself to his wife and his family and would do anything to keep them well and happy. He told himself that he *had* done the right thing – he had ended the affair before Mary's marriage to Daniel. He had taken the right and proper course of action, even though it had broken his heart to do so. And he *had* thought of his wife, and of the children she had already borne him. From that moment on he had been a devoted and loving husband and father. Emily was as much likely to be Daniel's child, or John's for that matter, as his, and he had protected the girl. He had given his word to Mary and he had kept it to the best of his ability. He had given his son strict instructions, and his son had disobeyed them. Thomas was a tumult of emotions and contradictions. First a burning rage and then the deepest grief. His emotional pendulum swung inexorably between the two.

This morning Thomas had finally found himself unable to hold back the barrier between the mask he portrayed and his true feelings. His emotions had burned a hole in the facade and issued forth with relief. He had shut himself in his study and given strict orders that he was not to be disturbed. Now he was weeping silently as he read and reread William's last letter to him. Thomas had been reading through all of his son's letters to him, which he kept in a small, locked walnut casket. As a boy, William had written to his father whenever he was away from him, even for only a few days. With each letter Thomas's grief grew stronger, and the tightness in his chest and the ache in his heart were unable to satisfy it.

However, as Thomas's grief grew so did his rage. Rage at being disobeyed and the consequences that had ensued. If William had not disobeyed him he would still be alive; Thomas was convinced of that. If William had not disobeyed him, his dear wife would not have had to suffer the appalling shock of learning of her husband's betrayal of her in the early years of their marriage and she would still love and trust him. If William had not disobeyed him, that sweet innocent girl might still be alive, and dear Mary and her poor husband would not have had their lives torn apart. If William had not disobeyed him, his loving daughters would not have had to suffer their mother's rejection, particularly at a time when each of them was needing to be loved and to give love, to feel useful, to dampen the burning pain that was their loss too.

William must share the burden of responsibility with his father. William must share the blame. William was to blame.

Thomas rose suddenly and, in a frenzy of rage, seized the walnut casket and threw its contents onto the fire. The flames licked their fingers greedily and curled them around the nourishing parchment, flaring a bright yellow in response. Within seconds the timeless words were reduced to ash.

Thomas immediately regretted his rash action, but there was nothing to be done. The letters were gone. Such was his anger that he even blamed his son for this. His rationality blinded, Thomas' gaze fell upon a small portrait of William which hung to the right of the fireplace. He grabbed it and looked upon the face of his son. The sculptured chin and high cheekbones, the straight nose and fine dark hair were William's, but the eyes were his. His own blue eyes, staring back at him, piercing his thoughts, laying bare his faults, revealing the wanting in his marital behaviour, exposing the failure in his fatherly responsibilities.

'Arghhh!' Thomas shivered involuntarily and cried out, dropping the likeness as if it were molten metal. The portrait fell upon the hearth and he kicked it into the rapacious blaze. He could not bear the penetrating veracity that it had seemed to convey upon him. Irrational and still incensed, he rang for Mr Arbuth and gave the startled house steward orders to collect and destroy every portrait of his son in the house.

'Begging your pardon, M'Lord, ' Mr Arbuth ventured gently, 'Do you really mean to destroy all likenesses of Master William? Your son?'

'I know who he is... was!' Thomas cried. 'Damn it man, do as I say!'

Leaning with one hand on the mantelpiece for support, he was shaking and tiny jewels of sweat on his pale forehead reflected the dancing firelight.

Mr Arbuth solemnly nodded his acknowledgment of the task, letting nothing of his extreme dismay show in his loyal face.

'Can I bring you something, M'Lord?' he asked kindly, 'some brandy perhaps? Come, rest here by the fire and allow me to pour you a glass.'

Perception being vital to his role and a much-used skill, the house steward had quickly appraised the situation. A walnut casket where his lordship kept private letters was open and empty, a small painting of William was missing from its place on the wall to the right of the fireplace, Thomas had been crying and the remains of a gold-leafed picture frame smouldered slowly amongst the logs, the canvas already consumed. His lordship had been under immense strain for many weeks and the death of his son had all but destroyed him. He looked at his master as he helped him into a chair that he had moved closer to the fireside; in his eyes there was a rage that he had not often seen and a sadness that he hoped never to see again. But there was something else – something that he did not recognise in his lordship's countenance.

Percival Arbuth crossed the study to a small mahogany table near the window on which lay a decanter and glasses, passing Thomas' secretaire as he did so. He noticed a single letter lying on the polished surface, its seal broken, and noted that the handwriting was William's. At least one letter remained, then. Internally he felt relieved; externally his expression remained professionally impassive.

The house steward poured his master a large brandy and delivered it with a kindly smile.

'Can I bring you anything else, M'Lord?'

'Thank you Arbuth, no. I wish to be left in peace, that is all.'

Thomas, slumped in his chair, spent and defeated, glanced at the house steward over the top of his brandy glass.

The pain that was conveyed with that look told Percival Arbuth all he needed to know. Sadly, his lordship would never find peace; the emotion that he had hitherto been unable to identify was guilt.

When Mrs Preedy cautiously informed Charlotte of his lordship's irrevocable instruction to Mr Arbuth she cried out in anguish, bringing her hands to her face in an attempt to hide from the inevitable turn of events.

'I am so very sorry, your Ladyship, ' Mrs Preedy said softly, her heart almost breaking for her beloved mistress, 'but Mr Arbuth thought it best that you be told… in case…' she faltered, uncertain how far she and the house steward should go in their disobedience towards his lordship, 'in case… you may wish… to… to… try to change… his lordship's mind…' Her voice trailed off and she stood in silence, waiting nervously for a response.

Eventually Charlotte removed her fingers from her tear-stained eyes, placed her hands back in her lap where they mostly languished these days and stared down at them, biting her lip, seeing nothing but her son's face before her. Challenging her husband meant allowing him access to her and she could not bear to look upon him, nor to hear his voice, nor hear her own in answer to his. Not yet – not for a long time. She was too weak for that. It was as much as she could do to rise from her bed and sit, in her bedgown and shawl, in this chair by the window looking out day after day upon a meaningless world. Yet it was utterly unbearable to think that she would never again be able to look upon a likeness of her son. Where was her husband's mind? Was he insane? How could he be so merciless? He had already deprived her of her son; was he to dispossess her of all images of him as well?

A tiny spark of defiance kindled at that moment – the merest of flickers. But it was enough. Enough to fuel a decision; enough to support an ember of strength to continue on.

She turned slightly to look at her housekeeper and that small determination showed in her eyes as plainly as if she had spoken. She bowed her head almost imperceptibly.

'Thank you, ' she responded graciously. Her voice was cracked, unused.

She held out a hand and felt the housekeeper's rough palm against hers. The human touch, the simple kindness, was almost her undoing. She swallowed, trying to maintain control and her dignity.

Mrs Preedy nodded her understanding. There was no need for words at that moment. At length she simply stated 'We'll see to it, M'Lady.'

As the housekeeper crossed the room from the window to the door she received the instruction.

'The Reynolds.'

'Yes, M'Lady. Your favourite.'

It was a quarter to three in the morning when Thomas rose wearily from the chair beside the large fireplace in his study. The last of the embers had burnt themselves out. He had long dismissed Arbuth and had given him strict instructions that he was not to be disturbed by anyone, not even his valet or the butler, Cowper. A single candle, come almost to the end of its wick, spluttered and shivered in the cold dark air, too weak to light anything but a small circle around itself.

Candlestick in hand, Thomas trod heavily over to his secretaire to close and lock it on his way out of the room. The dim flickering light picked out a single letter lying on the smooth surface. It was of course William's final letter to him, the one he had been reading hours before.

Thomas shook his head slightly and his mouth set into an ironic half-smile. *Hmmph.* Of all the letters to survive it had to be this one. Well, he finally conceded, this was probably a message from beyond the grave, one that he should heed.

He set the silver candlestick carefully on the desk and sat down, his fingers running over the folded parchment. He'd no need to read it again: he knew every word off by heart and those words would stay with him for the remainder of his days. However, just as a reminder of his past folly and as a ward against any such behaviour in the future, he would keep this letter close to him; hidden away, but near enough to be a constant warning.

He opened the wide top drawer in front of him, pulling it out toward him as far as it would come. Turning his palms upwards, his fingers reached inside the drawer to the top back corners. He felt around for some moments until his two middle fingers came upon slight grooves in the walnut. With the tips of his fingers, he pressed into the grooves. The hidden catches were released with a satisfying click. He was now able to liberate the drawer all the way from its niche. In its separated state, it could be seen that the drawer had a false back. Beyond where the drawer was supposed to end a slim covered compartment ran across its width. Thomas released the last of the secret catches underneath this compartment and its lid quietly opened.

His face held a smile as he fingered the contents. A gold and enamel ring given to him by his father bearing a miniscule portrait of his mother; a lock of Charlotte's hair held in a small glass locket; a tiny tooth from his firstborn – he remembered how Catherine had come running to him, hand over mouth, one of her front teeth hanging by a thread, and how he had skilfully removed it with one jerk and no fuss, kissing the top of her head and sending her off to the kitchen for a comforting cup of hot chocolate; a shining guinea bearing the head of King George II, one of the first minted in 1727, the first year of his reign, and bestowed upon Thomas as a child; and its successor, a guinea minted just over two years ago marking the beginning of the reign of the current monarch.

Thomas opened William's letter one last time, checking that it still held his loop of the gimmel ring. Holding the glittering hoop carefully between thumb and forefinger, he closed his eyes and kissed his son's ring before wrapping it once more inside the letter and placing it into the concealed compartment.

With the drawer and its contents safely locked away, Thomas extinguished the sputtering candle and made his way to the door of his study by the dim light of the new moon.

Like this phase of the moon, he reflected, the coming years held not only the ghosts and memories of the past, which would always, always be present, but also the promise of new opportunities – to learn from the past, to make amends, to heal the near-fatal wounds within his family, to ask for God's grace and forgiveness, and to dedicate himself to his dear wife and daughters. And he would begin this day.

⸻

December

The moment that Jennifer had uttered the words *Daniel Fernleigh*, things began to fall into place for Andy Finch. Jennifer had continued to be confused and distracted for several days, waking only momentarily and each time fretting about her baby. Then, very slowly, she had begun to focus more on the faces around her. Day by day her recognition of familiar people – her parents, Sarah and eventually Andy – grew while her confusion gradually diminished. It was a painfully slow process. However, after a few weeks she at last understood who she was, where she was, and what had happened.

Jennifer herself remembered virtually nothing of the few weeks leading up to her coma. However, her amnesia was punctuated by the occasional image that flashed before her or brought itself into sharp relief against an unfocused background of confusion. Finding the gimmel ring hidden in a hole in the oak beam in her living room was one such image. However, her memories of Emily and of William seemed to be as real as her contemporary thoughts.

Mr Gray was unworried by this. It was perfectly normal for people to suffer from amnesia about the period preceding a trauma such as this. Given what he'd been told about her regression, if these memories were real they were embedded deep within her subconscious and were not newly acquired. Amnesia usually affected a shorter period of time relating to the laying down of recent memory, he explained.

There were certainly gaps in Jennifer's understanding, and Andy Finch was the only one who could fill in those gaps. Through all her confusion, he alone could gently explain to her that the baby she spoke of was not hers, did not belong to Jennifer but to Emily Popple, her alter ego, in another life, in another time; that the memories she carried of a lover named William were also not of her present life; that she was living here, now, in the twenty-first century, but that through her remarkable experience she had played an absolutely critical role in the discovery of events in history hitherto completely unknown and unrecorded.

Jennifer's parents, Sarah, Andy and Mr Gray all worked hard with her, helping her to regain the majority of her memory and a rational perspective. She experienced a myriad of emotions while trying to disentangle the past from the present and cope with each new memory that presented itself as if for the first time. She was emotionally and physically frail. However, with the unswerving support of her family and friends and the constant assistance, expert care and encouragement of Mr Gray – Adam, as she had come to know him – Jennifer's recovery progressed and she became stronger day by day.

Daniel Fernleigh. It made sense to Andy now. A boy, born to Emily and William, the likely cause of Emily's death; a lovechild named for the grandfather and the father, conceived out of wedlock but born within a clandestine marriage – not christened, not recorded, kept a secret and forgotten in history. Ah, but the birth of this little baby *was* recorded. Emily's mother had seen to that. *D F B 1762*: Daniel Fernleigh Born 1762. The child of the marriage signified by the gimmel ring, born into the Fernleigh family as denoted by the Fernleigh coat of arms; witnessed and verified in secret by the actions of a devoted mother and grandmother.

Andy Finch was sitting at his desk in the back room of the Fernleigh estate office with a shining loop of the gimmel ring between the thumb and forefinger of each hand. He placed them carefully together, slotting one above the other, the tiny ridges of one fitting perfectly into minute depressions in the other. It was an incredible object; however, it was not complete. As the loops were brought together the exquisite hand cupped itself around one side of the heart. But there was clearly a loop missing; the loop with the missing hand.

Andy stared at the ring for some time, contemplating what to do next. The weak winter sunlight, suddenly finding a break in the clouds, shone over the wet meadow and in through the small glass panes of the estate office windows onto the intricate facets of the precious circle between his fingers, sending shards of golden light flashing around the room as he turned it.

It seemed an impossible task. The missing loop could be anywhere and nowhere. It could be lost or destroyed or passed down to some unknown person. Then there was the matter of the Reynolds, discovered under the floorboards of one of the main bedchambers. Clearly somebody had ordered the destruction of William's image, and someone had wanted to save it. Andy figured it was possible that whoever had wanted to destroy the image had also destroyed letters and documentation belonging to, or from, William. It seemed unlikely that this could be William's mother. From the way Charlotte Fernleigh had written about her son in the diary that had survived it was clear that she had been devoted to him, at least in his childhood. Could a mother really obliterate the only likeness of her son? Andy didn't think so, but then as a professional he needed to maintain a detached view. Of course the responsibility for this act need not have belonged to a contemporary of William's. However, by examining estate records and artefact logs from the 1820s Andy had established that the Reynolds had not been present at or beyond that time.

It was possible that William's uncle John or his son, who eventually inherited the estate, might have wanted to destroy William's image. However, such an act would be difficult to explain and might throw suspicion their way. No, Andy decided, there was a greater likelihood that this was carried out by somebody who had been wronged or offended by William. Given William's clandestine relationship with Lady Fernleigh's maidservant and his eventual marriage to her, the persons most likely to feel wronged would be his parents, Thomas and Charlotte. This led Andy back to Thomas Fernleigh.

He decided that he must try to find some more documentary evidence and search for the missing ring, however improbable the chance of finding it. He would start with possessions known to have belonged to Thomas, or at least present in the house around that time.

He engaged Janet's assistance once more and she, in turn, roped in a number of discreet volunteers. Every evening, as soon as the public areas of the house were closed, this small group of staff searched carefully for the ring. Although it was a long and arduous task there was a strange buzz of excitement amongst them; a hope that it would be found, a belief that the treasure they sought would be here somewhere in this massive house, and an unspoken competitiveness with regard to who might find it first.

Evening upon evening in room after room they systematically searched cupboards and cabinets, coffee tables and card tables, side tables, dressing tables, dressers and chests of drawers, desks and clock cases, consoles, sideboards, sofas and secretaires, wardrobes, workboxes and writing boxes, card boxes, trinket boxes, jewellery boxes and vanity cases, tea caddies, blanket chests and document boxes – in fact every conceivable hiding place the house possessed.

Because it was such a huge task the library was left until last. By this time the initial excitement had waned a little and nobody was particularly looking forward to sifting through the hundreds of books.

That said, and perhaps because the library was the last room left to search, everyone agreed that if a document or small object had to be concealed, the library might be one of the best places to do it. So, in the late afternoon of the 20th of December, the small group of dedicated seekers entered the library to begin their search. Six of the volunteers were assigned a bookcase each and started to carefully remove books one at a time, delicately flicking through them and examining their bindings and inner and outer covers before replacing each one and taking out the next. Meanwhile the remaining four members of staff started to examine the furniture.

While two ladies investigated a fine inlaid mahogany and rosewood multi-compartmented gaming table, Andy's attention was drawn to the polished burl walnut secretaire by the window. Standing on four delicately-carved legs with ball-in-claw feet, the desk comprised two main compartments, one on each side, each containing two shelves fronted by carved doors displaying exquisite ivory and ebony marquetry. Above these compartments, lying across the full width of the piece, was a shallow drawer with a brass handle matching the brass keyhole escutcheon and the doorknobs, and above this, the surface of the desk. Some two feet above the writing surface, set back, were two doors that opened to reveal a complex façade of drawers and pigeonholes.

Andy beckoned to Janet and they set to work removing and examining each of the small drawers. A number of the pigeonholes contained secret compartments – false backs which, upon releasing a catch, opened to reveal further cavities. All were empty. Nevertheless, Andy's sense of excitement mounted. This was exactly the sort of piece in which one might expect to find a concealed document or object. He and Janet continued their search meticulously, working their way down through the compartments from top to bottom.

On reaching the wide desk drawer their search halted temporarily as the drawer was locked. Catching up a stray lock of her dark greying hair with the fingers of her left hand and deftly fixing it behind her ear, Janet smiled at Andy, knowing that he would be impatient for the drawer to be opened.

'Can't leave keys in locks, ' she raised her eyebrows and inclined her head to one side. 'A key in a lock is like a red rag to a bull for our visitors, I'm afraid. Way too much temptation. The keys either fall out and get lost, or they get stuck, or the furniture can get damaged by being handled. You know how it is.'

Kneeling on the floor, Andy was subconsciously tapping his fingers impatiently on the sides of his thighs whilst he waited for Janet to sort through the baffling multitude of small keys on her specific system of key rings.

She chose the correct ring and tried a couple of keys to no avail; however, the third key she tried seemed to fit the tiny lock. She turned the key, pulled the handle and the drawer slid open. They both stared inside it. It was empty. The cumulative sense of disappointment of the past days circled around them as thick as a dawn mist and settled heavily upon their shoulders; Janet was about to close the drawer and begin to examine the cupboards beneath when Andy laid a hand on her arm.

'It's not deep enough, ' he said slowly, lowering his eyebrows, trying to figure it out.

'Pardon?' she replied.

'It's not deep enough, ' he repeated. 'The drawer – it doesn't go back far enough.'

Seeing the confusion on her face he got down on all fours and crawled underneath the desk, then turned to lie on his back with his arms in the air. Arms outstretched with fingers together, he measured the distance roughly from the back to the front of the secretaire, then with some difficulty wriggled out from under the desk, trying to maintain his arms in the same position, keeping the distance between them.

Janet laughed at his ridiculous pose. 'We could have measured that from the side!' she giggled, 'no need to go wriggling around on the carpet.'

He winked at her. 'Maybe I like wriggling on the carpet!' he teased.

She raised her eyes at him. 'Come on then, Dr Finch, out with it.'

He pulled the drawer out again as far as it would go. 'Janet, look… the depth of this drawer is significantly less than the depth of the whole piece. There must be a false back to it. Can you pull it right out?'

Evenly and with both hands she carefully eased the drawer out again, but could not remove it entirely.

'There seems to be something preventing it from coming away.'

Andy looked underneath, but the bottom of the desk was solid. 'Can you get your fingers in over the back of the drawer?' he asked with mounting excitement, 'Your hands are smaller than mine.'

She reached in with slender fingers, screwing up her face in concentration as she did so. 'There's no gap above the drawer. Certainly not one big enough for me to get my fingers over.'

Andy felt underneath the drawer, but its external bottom and sides were smooth. 'Try running your fingertips around the inside of the drawer', he encouraged. 'Can you feel any notches or grooves or catches?'

The warm polished walnut was smooth as silk on the tips of Janet's fingers as they worked their way over the inner surfaces of the drawer. Eventually she reached into the top back corners and came upon two small grooves into which she pressed her fingertips. On the release of the hidden catches she gasped, and her face wore the pure excitement that quivered through her body as she looked at Andy in amazement. Andy jumped up from the floor and together they carefully eased the drawer completely from its setting. Having discovered the false compartment at its back, it wasn't long before they had located the last of the secret catches underneath. The partition's cover softly opened, modestly revealing its secrets.

Given the extraordinary nature of the hidden compartment's contents, the way in which it gave up its secrets was understated, remarkably unassuming. It was like two hands, palms upward, fingers outstretched, quietly surrendering to their vanquisher. *You solved my mystery – my reward is yours.*

Janet gave another gasp and Andy stood stock still for a moment. Neither of them could believe their eyes. They exchanged a stunned glance, and Andy ran his fingers through his hair in shock. The gasp had attracted the attention of the volunteers, who quickly gathered around the drawer. One quick-thinking man took off his jumper and laid it across the gaming table so that they could lay the drawer upon this without scratching the table's beautiful polished mahogany surface. This gave them more room to examine its contents.

A stunning enamel and gold ring carrying an exquisite minute head-and-shoulders portrait of a beautiful young woman lay next to a tiny tooth that looked as if it might be a child's milk tooth. A curl of fair hair was held tight in a small gold and glass locket on a delicate chain. There were two guineas in mint condition, one bearing the head of King George II and the other that of King George III, each dated in the first year of their respective reigns.

Lastly, a small square of yellowing parchment, which looked as if it had been folded upon itself a number of times, lay in the left-hand corner of the compartment. Where the outer folds of the paper came together there were the remains of a greyish wax seal. Andy took out his pocket magnifying glass for a closer look and identified the Fernleigh coat of arms.

'May I?' He raised his eyebrows at Janet, who swallowed and nodded.

Andy pulled on the cotton gloves she presented to him. His heart was racing and his fingers trembled as he lifted the parchment carefully from its hiding place and laid it upon the table. Delicately, he unfolded the two edges, trying not to disturb what was left of the wax seal. As he handled the ancient parchment he felt something hard beneath his fingertips. His blood was pumping so hard that it resounded in his ears and he felt almost dizzy. *Could this be what we've been searching for, the final piece in the puzzle?* He almost couldn't dare to hope. Almost.

He held his breath as he undid the final fold in the paper. And there, denuded of its protection, lay a bright gold ring whose form was now familiar to him. A wide smile, starting at the corners of his mouth, quickly spread over his face and through his entire body. He picked up the ring and held it aloft.

A massive cheer went up from the gathered crowd and various cries of *Yes!* and *We did it!* were heard. Andy reached into his jacket pocket and took out a small, green, slightly battered jewellery box purloined from his wife's dressing table. He took out the other two parts of the gimmel ring, already joined together, and slotted their missing triplet into its rightful place. The newly-discovered shining loop bore the missing hand, and, now in its rightful place, the exquisite hands cupped themselves around both sides of the heart.

Not only was the heart now protected, as it should be, but the inscription instantly became legible. In tiny, precise and inconceivably beautiful script, it read:

'William & Emily ~ joined together by God ~ never shall be separated.'

It was an incredible moment, and one that Andy would never forget.

Eventually he placed the complete gimmel ring into the jewellery box and set it on the far side of the gaming table so that the others could have a closer look. He turned his attention to the parchment, which was clearly a letter.

'May I take this to the window?' he asked Janet.

She smiled gently and nodded her agreement. In the last few months she had come to know him quite well. If this was the missing piece of the story he would want a few moments of solitude to absorb its full significance. His passion for the task he'd been set by the Fernleigh family, though begun with extreme interest, had grown exponentially over the last months, particularly since Jennifer had become involved. She knew that this was not just a passion for history and mystery but something much greater. He had become emotionally involved. Whether or not the letter would answer all of their questions – indeed it was unlikely to answer *all* of the unknowns – whatever was in it was likely to affect him deeply. Janet gathered the volunteers around her to show them how the ring came apart and fitted together and to explain some more of the background to the discovery in order to deflect attention from the letter.

Andy walked slowly over to the window, carrying the parchment delicately on the upturned palms of both hands. As he did so he reflected on the events that had bought him to this moment. He placed the letter on a small semi-circular side table and sat beside it on a straight-backed satinwood chair. The low watery afternoon light was rapidly fading so, letter in hand, he moved his chair closer to the window, turning around so that his back was to the room. He was perfectly able to read the script on the parchment, but this gave him a greater degree of privacy.

Andy realised that he was delaying the moment at which he would read the contents of the letter. There was something about the anticipation of discovery that set his spine tingling. He dreaded disappointment, but surely that could not be the case today? For this letter, with its most precious possession, had been deliberately kept and hidden, secreted away from the world, for over two hundred and fifty years. That the letter was saved with the ring could be no coincidence. There had to be a relationship between the two – some significance.

He would delay no longer. Andy opened out the final two folds of the parchment and began to read.

'Father.

It is with deep sorrow that I write these words. However I must clear my conscience and you, Sir, shall know what suffering you have conveyed upon your son.'

As he read William's letter to his father, Thomas Fernleigh, Andy's eyes slowly filled with tears. William's deep love for Emily, the vehemence of his clearly carefully chosen words, the rift between father and son caused by William's relationship with Emily, the clear call to duty from Thomas, the accusations, the loss, the terrible pain were all there in black and white. The summary of a passionate young man's life, and even a suggestion of its ending:

'The third loop, the ring which I placed upon Emily's finger upon our wedding day, I shall keep close to my heart until the day I shall die.'

As Andy's eyes beheld the words at last he understood so much. He realised that it had been Emily's ring that William had had about him when he died – when he was murdered. Emily's ring that was taken from his body as a trophy, to end up in the possession of the vile, despicable John Fernleigh. Andy felt real hatred for the man, even though he'd been dead for hundreds of years, although he took some small comfort from the fact that by the time William met his death he no longer cared whether he lived or died, such were his feelings of grief and loss for his dear Emily. Perhaps it was a relief?

However, there were certain aspects of the letter that he did not comprehend. The references to William's sisters, the underlining, was curious.

'I had a lover and wife and <u>seven</u> sisters, no more, no less.'

It was apparent that Thomas had been unfaithful, to his wife and presumably to his family, or at least to those of his children who had already been born at the time.

'What say you of faithfulness, of fidelity? How will you answer on the Day of Judgment?'

However, Andy didn't understand the link between Emily and William's sisters:

'Three years separated Emily and me and a good many more, my sisters and her.'

Andy blinked away his tears, quickly wiping his eyes on his jacket cuffs lest anyone should notice, and recomposed himself. He glanced over his shoulder at Janet, who was busy with the group. However, as he got up and replaced the chair in its niche she gave him the briefest of looks. A glance that at once enquired whether he was okay, whether the letter was significant and whether it was okay for her to take a look at it. He smiled gently and nodded almost imperceptibly.

She thanked the volunteers wholeheartedly for their generous efforts to locate the ring and promised to update them once the Fernleigh family had received a full report. Contents removed for placing in the safe, the drawer was placed back into the secretaire and relocked. The group of volunteers adjourned to the local pub for a celebratory drink; although sworn to secrecy for the time being, they would whisper about it between themselves.

Once this was done, Janet and Andy removed themselves to her office so she could concentrate on the letter. Andy wandered around her office picking things up and putting them down, waiting for her to finish reading. As soon as she replaced her reading glasses on the desk in front of her he turned to her expectantly and spoke hurriedly, anxious to share his thoughts.

'I don't understand the references to William's sisters.' He was impatient for her opinion. 'And why is he talking about age? I mean, the relative ages of Emily and William and his sisters?' He frowned and shook his head. 'It's all so sad, though, isn't it?' he continued without giving Janet a chance to reply. 'They hardly had any time together as man and wife before she died and he was murdered!'

He started pacing the room, thinking aloud. 'William had a lover/wife, i.e. Emily, and *seven* sisters. He had *five* sisters older than him, ' he counted them out on the fingers of his right hand, 'Catherine, Charlotte, Amelia, Mary, Anne. And he had *two* younger sisters, Rebecca and Elizabeth. That makes seven. And he says that Emily was three years younger than he... we know that already from their birth records. So obviously William's elder sisters were quite a bit older than Emily.' He shrugged and looked at Janet. 'So what?' He held his arms out to the sides, palms turned upwards, fingers outstretched, to emphasise his incomprehension. 'What is William trying to say?'

Janet gave him a strange look. 'I think I may know, ' she said quietly.

Despite usually being caught up in his own thoughts and words, often to the exclusion of those around him, Andy knew when to stop and listen and Janet's look made him stop in his tracks. She signalled for him to set a chair down beside her and laid the letter on the desk in front of them. He began running a forefinger and thumb through his beard as she spoke, as if this helped his powers of deduction.

Janet focused hard on the script in front of her, mentally putting pieces together, trying them for fit, discarding some and retrying others. She spoke her thoughts.

'William seems to be emphasising the number of sisters that he has. *No more, no less* means exactly, exactly seven. Well, we know that he has seven sisters. Thomas is his father – why should *he* not know the number of sisters that William has? It doesn't make sense... unless you consider that there may be another sister.' She looked at her fellow problem solver, eyebrows raised.

Andy nodded slowly. 'Okay... go on, ' he responded at length, his words stretched out, head inclined, his mouth set in a way that indicated that he wasn't yet convinced but was prepared to consider all possibilities.

'Okay, hold that thought, but put it to one side for a moment. Then there is the question of Thomas's infidelity. With whom has he been unfaithful? Look, I think the clue is in this section here about the vehemence with which Thomas spoke to William about his obligations. William seems to be implying that his father was once in the same situation but *chose to turn his back on it,* and he's accusing his father of making the wrong choice, of regretting his decision.'

Andy began to see where Janet was coming from. 'Right, so if Thomas was once in a similar position, then he could have been divided by love and duty, as William was. But surely having any kind of affair must lead to a decision between love and duty, mustn't it?'

Janet persisted on her course. 'Yes, but I think when William is saying *'one who knows what it is to be in such a position'* he is likening his father's situation to his own. I take this to mean that Thomas must have had an affair with someone unequal to him in status, as Emily was to William. I mean, I could be wrong, but it seems to fit with the other pieces of this puzzle.'

'Are you saying what I think you're saying? That Thomas' affair, possibly with a maid or something, could have led to another child, a girl? Another sister?' Andy sat up straight in his chair and tapped the fingers of his right hand on the table, thinking the situation through.

Janet looked at him sadly. 'Yes, but more than that.'

'More than that, ' Andy repeated slowly, the possible awful truth beginning to dawn on him. 'The critical words are in the sentences here, aren't they?'

'I think so, ' accorded Janet.

He read the lines again, aloud. *'Three years separated Emily and me and a good many more, my sisters and her. What say you of faithfulness, of fidelity? How will you answer on the Day of Judgment? As for me, you should know that my conscience is clear. I had a lover and wife and seven sisters, no more, no less.'*

'Jeez!' Andy shook his head. 'William is linking Thomas' infidelity to a timeline, a timeline in which he was married to Charlotte and had a number of children by her. So he had his affair well into their marriage, perhaps during the whole of their marriage. I guess we'll never know. But...' he hurriedly continued, 'more importantly, is William saying what I think he's saying? That *Emily* is the lovechild? But no – he can't be saying that, because he's adamant that he has only seven sisters!'

'I think that's the implication, ' Janet responded. 'But I agree with you; William is absolutely convinced that Emily is *not* his sister. But Thomas, or someone, must have told him that she was! I suppose that may explain the forcefulness implicit in William's description of his father's verdict upon him.'

'Oh my God!'

Andy ran his hands through his hair and looked at Janet in shock. She had tears in her eyes. Her voice was barely a whisper.

'Imagine being passionately in love with someone, *marrying* some-one, and being told that you're brother and sister! It just doesn't bear thinking about.'

They sat side by side without speaking, staring down at the yellow parchment.

Eventually he heaved a great sigh. 'Have you got anything to drink in this office of yours?'

She shook her head, then remembered. 'Actually I picked up a bit of shopping at lunchtime from the estate farm shop. There's a bottle of Shiraz. In that bag, over there.'

She pointed to a hessian bag in the corner of the room. Andy went to fetch the bottle while she took two mugs out of one of her filing-cabinet drawers.

'I'm afraid it's only mugs.'

'Don't care. I'd drink out of the bottle if you weren't here!'

She laughed, wiping away an escaped tear with the back of her hand. 'Yes, I expect you would! And I expect you're the sort of man who carries a Swiss army knife.'

'Absolutely, got it in one.'

He opened the bottle and poured two generous measures. They sat for a time in silence, sipping wine from pottery mugs fashioned on the Fernleigh estate, each contemplating the shocking discovery.

'She doesn't have to have been his sister, ' Andy said at length.

Janet looked at him hopefully over the top of her mug.

He topped them both up from the bottle. 'William is convinced she isn't. Now you might think that anyone in his position would persuade themselves otherwise, but it's not possible to do that unless there's *some* doubt over it. Is there.' It was a statement rather than a question.

Janet thought for a few moments. 'You're right, ' she replied. 'You're absolutely right!' She grasped at the happier, more palatable option and her eyes reflected the relief she felt that there could possibly be another scenario.

'Well, I guess we'll never know.' He thought for a moment. 'I don't think I'll tell Jennifer about the letter – not just yet, anyway. Perhaps later, when she's stronger.'

He looked out of the window into the darkness beyond the stable block. Large snowflakes had begun to fall silently, their purity, their brilliant whiteness, illuminated by the radiance of the cosy glow from the windows. Andy turned to Janet and raised his mug.

'Let's at least celebrate their happiness, ' he smiled. 'William and Emily!'

'To William and Emily! However short-lived it was, they triumphed in love and in marriage!' toasted Janet.

Sarah walked along the hospital corridor towards Jennifer's small single room. She was so pleased that Jennifer was still allowed a space to herself. 'She needs to be quiet, not distracted or confused by the busy goings-on around her', one of the nurses had explained. Sarah reached the half-glass door and looked through it towards Jennifer's bed to check whether she was there or had gone to see the physiotherapist. Jennifer had been promised that she might soon be able to leave the hospital, but first she had to get little stronger. The aim was to have her out of hospital and back at home by Christmas, only six days away.

Jennifer was sitting on the bed, fully dressed, legs crossed casually. Her head was thrown back and she was laughing heartily. Mr Gray stood by the bed, looking down at her and grinning. Sarah recognised a sparkle in Jennifer's eyes that she had not seen for a very long time.

She smiled to herself and was at once filled with a warm glow of love for her friend and unbridled joy at her return to happiness. She backed away from the door, turned and retraced her steps. She would go back and make Jennifer's cottage the cosiest, warmest, most welcoming place on earth in readiness for her homecoming.

Jennifer sat on the bed, leaning against her pillows, listening to Adam Gray's soothing tones and watching the movement in his face and stubbled jawline as he spoke: the creases around his green eyes when he smiled or laughed at one of her remarks; his large strong hands, with their down of fine hairs which appeared to continue up his forearms, disappearing under the cuffs of his white coat; his slightly tanned skin and the little group of hairs at the very top of his chest which had shown themselves, tantalisingly, on the occasions when he had come to visit her off-duty, wearing a T-shirt.

They had been talking about her leaving the hospital and the things she needed to continue to do to maintain her excellent rate of recovery. But, as throughout her long recuperation, in between the instructions, the advice and the guidance, the seriousness of it all, he was always able to make her laugh. She realised that for the most part what she had been lacking for many, many months, years even, was laughter, one of the most critical aspects of being human, essential for a normal, happy meaningful life. And she was indeed happy — and lucky, so very lucky. Fortunate to be alive; fortunate to have her amazing, loving parents and a devoted, fabulous and oh-so-caring best friend around her; fortunate to have been able to place her tempestuous relationship with Jim in its true perspective; fortunate to have been able to explore her feelings with a kind and considerate professional and to discover her past with a fun, passionate historian who believed in her and encouraged her to believe in herself; and fortunate to have met this new, wonderful, handsome, funny, clever man, who seemed to think the same about her!

Jennifer had come to believe that her present existence was but an interval in a long journey through time. Whatever the future might hold, she had resolved to seek happiness and a peaceful continuity. In doing so she believed she could fulfil her newfound responsibility to Emily and share with her an expression of love that was once also Emily's – but for such a brief moment in time.

Adam Gray squeezed her hand. 'I shall miss your smiling face around the ward, ' he grinned. 'I shall have to visit you at home to get my fix now!'

'Any time… all the time!' she smiled. 'My saviour.'

He nodded and patted her arm. 'You're the strong one. You healed yourself – I just messed around the edges.'

'Come for Christmas, ' Jennifer said suddenly. 'That is… if you haven't… I mean… if you're not… doing anything… else?'

'I'd love to.'

Jennifer watched as he strode the short distance to the door and her eyes caught sight of something at the nape of his neck. His shoulder length hair was, as usual, tied back. But today it was not caught up with the usual rubber band but with a long, thin, black silk ribbon.

Epilogue

Seventeen months later

Sarah pushed open the heavy door and began the long walk along the magnolia and blue hospital corridor. She was so familiar with these damn passages that she could have negotiated them blindfold; the once-confusing signs that led you towards your goal and then suddenly disappeared just before you reached it, leaving you lost again, retracing your steps, trying to find that wrong turn you must have taken; the signs that took you to sets of stairs when you needed to get the wheelchair into a lift; the corridors that all looked the same until you read the names on the ward doors; the endless twists and turns; the tracking of that blue band on its off-white background like a thread of wool in a maze; the almost stifling warmth and that familiar hospital smell.

But today was different. Today her journey started on its familiar route but at some point she would make a turn in a different direction. She passed a row of empty chairs sitting side by side, backs to the wall, facing into the corridor expectantly. She took the opportunity to put down the flowers for a moment and remove her cotton jacket, tying it around her waist by the sleeves. God, it was hot in here! It was unusually warm outside for May, but at least there was a nice breeze out there. Still, she thought, shouldn't complain, lucky to have the sunshine. She ran her fingers through her spiky blond hair, settled her jacket more comfortably on her hips, picked up the flowers again and resumed her course.

Now, if she remembered correctly the turn that she needed was left just around the next corner. She reached the sign that she was looking for; yes, this was right. Now what was the name of the ward again? She fumbled in a jacket pocket somewhere near her knee and took out a small piece of crumpled paper. Ah, that was it. She reached the relevant double doors, entered and found herself opposite a sort of reception desk. No-one was staffing it, but several nurses were rushing to and fro. She'd better ask.

'Hello. Could you possibly tell me where Mrs Gray's bed is?' she asked a slightly plump woman in her mid-forties with rosy cheeks.

'Sure. She's in Ward 4, down there on the right, ' the nurse smiled.

As she walked the final steps towards the room where Jennifer was Sarah felt her heartbeat rise to the occasion. She entered Ward 4, which contained only four beds. The light-blue curtains were drawn around the bed immediately to the right so she couldn't see Jennifer straight away. Her friend was at the far end by a window, next to the drawn curtains.

She was in a bed surrounded by cards but partly obscured by the back of a tall man, who was sitting by the bedside. As she walked towards them Sarah felt a thrill run through her entire body, and the joy that she felt inside pulled her mouth into a wide grin.

She placed a hand on the man's shoulder. 'Hello, Adam, ' she whispered.

He spun around on his chair, stood up and gave her a big hug.

'Sarah! Great to see you!'

'Congratulations!' she beamed. 'So wonderful! I couldn't wait to get here.'

'She's done all the hard work, ' he grinned, inclining his head at Jennifer, who was half-lying on a stack of pillows with her eyes shut. 'She's so tired – my beautiful, clever wife!'

And there, cradled in Jennifer's arms, was a tiny newborn baby with a fine down of black hair on its little head and perfect little fingernails on the tips of its miniature curled fingers.

'I'm not asleep, you know, just resting my eyes for a moment, ' came Jennifer's relaxed, sleepy tones. She opened her eyes 'Sarah, ' she said warmly, 'so lovely to see you. Look, isn't she perfect!'

She looked down at her baby daughter with exquisite tenderness.

'This is Auntie Sarah, ' she whispered. 'Auntie Sarah saved my life… and she's going to be so important in yours.' Jennifer looked up at her friend and her happiness spilled over. 'Would you like to hold her?' she asked through her tears.

Sarah swallowed hard and nodded, holding out her arms. 'What are you going to call her?' she asked softly, rocking the little baby gently to and fro.

Jennifer and Adam looked at one another and smiled. Jennifer spoke.

'She's called Emily.'

8626989R00242

Printed in Great Britain
by Amazon.co.uk, Ltd.,
Marston Gate.